Written according to the new syllabus of **T. Y. B.Com.**
prescribed by University of Pune from June, 2010-11.
Also useful for other Universities

I0611899

Cost and Works Accounting

Overheads and Methods of Costing

[Paper II]

Prof. Suresh Bhirud
Ex-member, Board of Studies and Faculty of Commerce,
Pune University, Pune

Prof. Bhaskar Naphade
Ex-member, Board of Studies and Faculty of Commerce,
Pune University, Pune

Diamond Publications

Cost & Work Accounting
Overheads and Methods of Costing (Paper II)

Prof. Suresh Bhirud
Prof. Bhaskar Naphade

First Edition : July 2010

ISBN : 978-81-8483-308-9

Type Setting :
Diamond Publications

Cover Page :
Sham Bhalekar

Publisher :
Dattatray G. Pashte
Diamond Publications
1255, Sadashiv Peth
Lele Sankul, Nimbalkar Talim Chowk,
Pune - 30. Phone - (020) 24452387

E-mail : diamondpublications@vsnl.net
Web : www.diamondbookspune.com

Sole Distributor :
Diamond Book Depot
661, Narayan Peth
Appa Balwant Chowk, Pune - 411030

Preface

We have atmost pleasure in placing this standard text book on **'Cost and Wroks Accounting'** Paper II (Overheads and Methods of Costing) for T. Y. B.Com. students. This book is designed strictly according to new syllabus prescribed by University of Pune for T. Y. B.Com. students from June, 2010.

The highlight of this book is that, it has been written in a simple language and answers has been given below the objective questions and the practical exercises wherever possible.

We sincerely thank the senior teacher of the subject for guiding and constantly encouraging us in our efforts.

We are also thankful to Mr. Dattatray Pashte and the entire team of Diamond Publications for their earnest help in bringing out this text book with vigour and accuracy.

We hope that the students would welcome this text book and find it very useful for appearing university examination.

Prof. Suresh Bhirud
Prof. Bhaskar Naphade

Content

Chapter 1

Overheads

1.1. Meaning and Definition
1.2. Classification of Overheads
1.3. Exercises

1.1. Meaning and Definition :

Total cost is classified into direct cost and indirect cost. The total of direct material, direct labour and direct expenses is called direct cost. Total of indirect material, indirect labour and indirect expenses is called indirect cost or overheads. Overheads may be called as oncost, indirect cost, expenses supplimentary cost or non productive cost. Thus, overheads is the aggregate of indirect material, indirect labour and indirect expenses. Indirect cost or overhead cannot be allocated on cost centre or cost unit.

Some of the definitions of overheads are as under.

1) "Overhead is the aggreagate of indirect materials, indirect wages and indirect expenses."

- CIMA London.

2) "Overhead may be defined as the cost of indirect materials, indirect labour and such other expenses, including services as cannot conveniently be charged directly to specific cost unit. Alternative overheads are all expenses other than direct expenes."

- Wheldon

3) "Overhead costs are operating cost of a business enterprise which cannot be traced back directly to a particular unit of output."

- Blocker and Welther.

4) "Overheads are those costs which do not result from the existence of individual cost unit."

- Harper

Thus, overhead is the total of all indirect expenditure. Indirect cost are incurred for the benefit of number of cost centres or cost units. Indirect cost, therefore cannot be conveniently identified with a particular cost centre or cost unit but it can be apportioned to or absorbed by cost centre or cost units. In general terms, overheads comprises all expenditure incurred for or in connection with the general organisation of the whole or part of undertaking i.e. the cost of operation supplies and services used by the undertaking including the maintenance of capital assets.

Overheads can be indicated as follows

Overheads

Indirect Materials   Indirect Wages   Indirect Expenses

Factory Expenses   Administrative or office Expenses   Selling and Distribution Expenses   Research and Development Expenses

Accounting and control of overhead cost is more complex than that of other element of cost i.e. direct materials and direct labour. This is because overheads by definition are indirect costs which cannot be conveniently allocated to cost unit. Hence, many problems may arise for apportioning these indirect cost to cost units or cost centres.

1.2 Classification of overheads

Overheads can be classified according to their common characteristics. They can be classified as follows.

Classification of overheads

(1) Functional Classification
   (i) Factory Expenses
   (ii) Selling Expenses
   (iii) Distribution Expenses
(2) Elementwise classification
   (i) Indirect Material

(ii) Indirect Labour or wages

(iii) Indirect Expenses

(3) Behaviourwise Classification

(i) Fixed Expenses

(ii) Variable Expenses

(iii) Semi Variable expenses.

(4) Controllability

(i) Controllable Expenses

(ii) Uncontrollable Expenses

1) Functional Classification :

When overhead expenses are classified with reference to major activity division of concern, it is called functional classification of overhead. The main groups forming the basis of the classification are as follows -

(1) Factory Expenses / Overhead : Factory expenses are also known as production expenses, manufacturing expenses, works overhead etc. They are the indirect expenses of operating the manufacturing divisions of a conern and cover all indirect expenses incurred by the undertaking from the receipt of the order until its completion ready for despatch either to the customers or to the finished goods. It is the aggregate of factory indirect cost, indirect wages and indirect expenses. Examples of these overheads are : lubricants, consumable stores, depreciation of factory building, indirect wages, factory power and light, depreciation of plant and machinery, insurance of factory building, storekeeping expenses, repair and maintenance rent, rate of factory.

(2) Office and Administrative Overheads : These overheads are of general nature and consist of all cost incurred in the direction, control and administration of an undertaking which is not related directly to research, development, production, selling activity or function. Examples of office and administrative expenses are : general management salary, audit fee, legal charges, postage and telephone, stationery and printing, office rent and rates, office lighting and salaries of office staff.

(3) Selling Expenses : Selling overheads are those overheads which are mainly incurred for creating demand for product and for securing order. It is incurred for promoting sales and retaining customers. Examples of selling overheads are : salaries and commissions of salesmen, advertising, showroom expenses, travelling expenses, bad debts, catalogue and price list, sample and free gifts, after sales service expenses, fancy packing to attract sales etc.

(4) Distribution Expenses : Distribution expenses include all expenses incurred from the time the product is completed until it reaches its destination. It is the cost of process which begins with making packed product available for despatch and ends with making reconditioned return empty package available for reuse. In short, expenses incurred for the distribution of product to ultimate customers are called as distribution expenses. Examples of distribution expenses are : salary of godown staff, expenses of delivery van, carriage outward, warehouse expenses, special packing for bulk transport like bales, crates, chests etc, losses in warehouse stock and finished goods damaged in transit and cost of repairing and reconditioning of empties and wastage of finished goods.

(5) Research and Development Expenses : According to ICMA, "Research cost is the cost of searching for new and improved products, new application of materials or new or improved methods." It is carried out by the research staff of the organisation. Such expenses include the cost of initial experimentation, all types of tests and subsequent trial run in order to improve the result of research.

Development Expenses is the cost of process which begins with implementation of the decision to produce a new or improved product or to employ a new or improved method and ends with the commencement of formal production of that product or by that method.

2) Elementwise classification :

Under this method, the classification is done according to the nature and sources of expenditure. This method follows logically from the definition of overhead costs. On this basis expenses are classified as follows.

(a) Indirect Materials : Indirect materials have been defined as "material cost other than direct material cost." In simple words materials which cannot be identified with individual cost of a unit is called indirect material. Indirect materials cannot be allocated but they are absorbed by cost unit or cost centres. Examples of indirect materials are : consumables like cotton waste, brooms, lubricants, rays, cleaning materials, pins, nutbolts, screws, thread, tools for general use, losses, deficiencies and deterioration of stores etc.

(b) Indirect wages / Labour : Indirect wages are those which cannot be allocated but which are to the apportioned to or absorbed by cost centres or cost units. In other words, wages paid to labour which is employed other than on production constitute indirect labour cost. Examples of such labour are : charge-hands and supervisors, maintenance workers, departmental coolies, men employed in service department, material handling and internal transport, trainees and instructors. labour employed in time office and security office, holiday pay, leave pay, employe contribution to fund, wages of sweepers, idle time wages, maintenace and repair wages, foreman's pay, chowkidars pay etc.

(c) Indirect Expenses : All indirect expenses other than indirect material and indirect labour are termed as indirect expenses. These expenses cannot be directly charged to production. It is the cost of giving service to the production department. In simple words expenses which cannot be allocated but which are to be apportioned to or absorbed by cost centre or cost units are indirect expenses. For example: power, depreciation, insurance taxes, rates and rent, factory expenses, administrative expenses, selling and distribution expenses etc.

3) Behaviourwise Classification :

On the basis of behaviour overheads may be clasified into (i) fixed overheads (ii) variable overheads or semifixed or semi variable overheads.

(i) Fixed Overheads : Fixed overheads are overhead or expenses which tend to be unaffected by variations in the volume of output. Fixed overhead remain fixed in total amount for a specified period of time. Fixed overheads do not increase or decrease when the volume of production on output changes. For example, rent or insurance of building remains constant and do not change with the change in production label. But fixed overhead 'per unit' increases when the volume of production decreases and decreases when the volume of production increases. For example : if fixed overhead cost is Rs. 1,00,000 per month, per unit fixed overhead cost may be as under.

No of units produced	Fixed cost per unit
1,000	1,00,000 ÷ 1000 = 100
2,000	1,00,000 ÷ 2000 = 50
5,000	1,00,000 ÷ 5000 = 20
10,000	1,00,000 ÷ 10000 = 10

In short, when production increases, fixed cost per unit decreases as per production volume.

(ii) Variable Overheads : Variable overhead is a cost or expenses which tend to vary directly with the variations in the volume of output. In other words, when the volume of production increases, total variable overheads also increases and when the volume of production decreases, total variable overhead also increases. But the variable overhead per unit remains fixed or constant if the production is increased or decreased. Thus, variable expenses fluctuate in total amount but tend to remain constant per unit. Direct material cost, direct labour cost, direct expense, power etc. are some of the examples of variable overheads. The features of variable overhead cost are as follows.

(1) Variable overhead per unit remains constant.

(2) Total variable overheads vary in direct proportion of output.

(3) Variable overheads can be controlled by department heads.

(4) It is easy to allocate and apportion variable overhead to cost centre or department.

The nature of variable expenses can be clear from the following illustration. Suppose that per unit variable overhead is Rs. 10, the total cost will be changed as per the volume of production.

Per unit cost (Rs.)	Total output (unit)	Total variable expenses Rs.
10	10000	1,00,000
10	8000	80,000
10	12000	1,20,000
10	16000	1,60,000

(iii)Semi fixed and semi variable overheads : ICMA defines semi variable overhead as "a cost containing both fixed and variable elements, which is therefore partly affected by fluctuations in the volume of output or turnover." These overheads include partly fixed and partly variable, i.e. these are partly fixed and partly variable. A semi fixed or semi variable cost has fixed or constant element, below which it will never fall upto particular level of product. But the variable element in semivariable overhead changes as per volume of production. For example telephone expenses include a fixed portion of annual / monthly charge (minimum charge) plus variable according to calls made. Thus, total telephone expenses are semi-variable or semi fixed. Other examples of such overheads are depreciation, repairs and maintenance of building or plant, supervision, profession tax etc.

4) Controllability :

The concept of responsibility leads to the classification of overheads as controllable and uncontrollable overheads. Under this, costs are classified according to whether or not they are influenced by the action of a given member of undertaking.

(i) Controllable Overheads : Controllable overheads are generally chargeble to a budget or cost centre, which can be influenced by the action of person in whom control of centre is vested. These overheads are generally regulated at a given level at management authority. Variable overheads are generally controlled by departmental heads For example, cost of raw material may be controlled by purchasing in large quantities. But sometimes, overhead cannot be controlled by concered authorities due to variation in budgeted and actual performance. For example, excessive scrap may arise from inadequate superision or from latent defect in purchased material.

(ii) Uncontrollable Overheads : Uncontrollable overhead is an overhead which is not influenced by the action of a given member of undertaking. For example, it is very difficult to control overheads, like managerial salaries, factory rent, factory insurance etc. Generally, all fixed costs are not controllable. These overheads are beyond the control of management.

The distinction between controllable and uncontrollable overheads is very sharp and may be left to individual judgement. Some expenditure which may be uncontrollable on short term basis can be controllable an long term basis. In short, it is practically difficult to make difference in overheads as controallable and uncontrollable.

1.3 Exercises

Fill in the blanks -

(1) Overhead is the aggregate of ...., ..., ...
(2) Overhead is also termed as ......, ...
(3) Overheads partly fixed and partly variable are called as ..... overheads.
(4) The overheads controlled by management are called ....
(5) The overheads which are incurred for creating demand are called ....

Ans : (1) indirect material, indirect labour, indirect expenses (2) on cost expenses, (3) semi variable or semi fixed and semi variable (4) controllable overheads (5) selling expenses

Theoritical questions.

(1) Define overheads. State the classification of overhead.
(2) Explain the classification of overheads.
(3) Explain the meaning and classification of overheads.
(4) Write short notes on :
   (i) Functional classification of overheads.
   (ii) Elementwise classification of overheads.
   (iii) Behaviourwise classification of overheads.

Chapter 2

Accounting of Overhead (Part I)

Overhead Accounting :

Direct costs are charged directly to the cost centre or cost unit without difficulty. But this is not possible in overhead cost. Distribution of overhead costs to cost units is one of the most complex problems of cost accounting. This is because overhead costs cannot be identified with individual cost units and there are no accounting means of exact distribution. Therefore, such costs are analysed and distributed to various cost centres and cost units on arbitrary basis. For example, it is not possible to exactly calculate the amount of rent that should be charged to a particular cost unit and thus it has to be distributed on same arbitrary basis. The cost accountant is constantly searching for equitable bases to distribute overheads costs to units and divisions of business enterprises and quite often he needs to exercise his own judgement in this regard. For instance, he may apportion rent to various departments of the factory on the basis of area occupied by each and such department. Similarly, labour welfare expenses may be apportioned on the basis of number area occupied by each and such department. Similarly, labour welfare expenses may be apportioned on the basis of number of workers in each department.

The procedure of distribution of overhead costs in overhead accounting is discussed below :

Steps in Overhead Accounting :

Unlike direct materials and direct wages, overheads cannot be allocated to cost units directly. The various steps taken for distribution of overhead costs are as follows :
(1) Collection and classification of overheads.
(2) Allocation and apportionment of overheads to production departments and service departments.
(3) Re-apportionment of service department costs to production department.
(4) Absorption of overheads of each production department in cost units.

(a) Collection :

There are seven main sources of cost data relating to factory overheads. :
(1) Purchase Day Book;
(2) Invoice;
(3) Stores requisitions.
   These three are meant for collection of indirect material cost;
(4) Wages analysis book for indirect wages;
(5) Cash Book and Petty Cash Book.
(6) Nominal Ledgers.
(7) Other registers like plant and machinery.
   These four are meant for collection of indirect expenses including depreciation of plant and machinery.

(b) Classification :

(1) Plant overheads;
(2) Overheads relating to production cost centres and;
(3) Overheads relating to service cost centres.
   All the factory overheads are to be classified to suit the purpose of cost accounting. Whether itemwise. i.e. rent, insurance, depreciation etc. or functionwise. Standing order numbers are used for covering the

factory overheads. Cost account numbers are used for covering the administration, selling and distribution overheads.

(c) Allocation :

Allocation is the allotment of whole items of cost to cost units or cost centres, whether they are production cost centres or service cost centres, for example, indirect wages of production department 'A' are to be allocated to Department 'A' only. Similarly, wages of Services department 'S' are to be allocated to Department 'S' only.

(d) Apportionment :

Apportionment is the allotment of proportion of items of cost to cost centres or cost units on suitable basis after they are collected under separate standing order numbers. It may be the basis of services rendered by a particular item of expense to different departments or by survey method. Sometimes, the basis will be the 'Ability to pay method' i.e. ability of the department to bear such share of items of overheads.

(e) Absorption :

Charging overheads to individual product or job is known as absorption. Thus, purpose behind absorption is that, expenses allocated and apportioned to departments or cost centres should be absorbed in the cost of output of the given period.

Standing Order Numbers :

After overheads are classified, it is found useful to allot each group of expenses a number of symbols so that each such group is easily distinguished from others. Such number of symbols are codes for overheads and are sometimes called 'standing order numbers'. Each standing order number denotes a particular type of expenditure so that items of expenses of similar nature, as and when they are incurred are appropriately classified into one of these. A schedule or manual is maintained enlisting all standing order numbers. There cannot be a standard list of standing order number as the number and type under which overheads may be sub-grouped vary with the

(a) Size of the factory.

(b) Type of expenses, and

(c) The extent of control necessary.

An essential requisite for an effective system of standing order number is that such numbers should be clearly defined so that individuals responsible for booking expenditure may easily understand the classification into standing orders secondly, the classification into standing order number should have the quality of flexibility, so that as and when the need arises, suitable changes can be incorporated without seriously dislocating the existing system.

Methods of Allotting Standing Order Numbers :

Each standing order number is identified by a code number or symbol. The allocation of code numbers or symbols can be done by any of the following methods :

Methods of Coding :

(1) Serial number system
(2) Decimal system
(3) Alphabetical system
(4) Combination of alphabetical and numerical system.

(1) Serial number system

In this method, each type of expenditure is allotted a number in serial order as shown below :

S.O.Number	Expenditure
01	Farnase oil
07	Works Manager Salary
23	Power
34	Factory Lighting
52	Factory Rent

A group of numbers is set apart to classify the items under a broad head. For example, 1 to 20 for indirect materials, 21 to 40 for indirect labour, and so on.

2. Decimal System :

This is also a numerical system with the difference that instead of full numbers, decimals are used. The whole numbers are used to indicate the main group and the decimal represent the sub-groups. For example,

Sr. No.	Item	Sr. No.	Item
1.	Factory Overhead		
1.1	Indirect material	1.2	Indirect Labour
1.1.1	Farnace oil	1.2.1	Inspectors
1.1.2	Lubricating oil	1.2.2	Foremen
1.1.3	Cotton waste	1.2.3	Sweepers
1.1.4	Repairs and maintenance stores	1.2.4	Repair wages
1.1.5	Tools for general use	1.2.5	Idle time wages
Similarly			
2.	Administration Overhead		
2.1	Office expenses	2.2	Accounting Services
2.1.1	Travelling expenses	2.2.1	Salaries
2.1.2	Salaries / Honorarium	2.2.2	Depreciation of accounting
2.1.3	Maintenance of cars		Machine
2.1.4	Telephone expenses	2.2.3	Stationery, Xerox
		2.2.4	Postage / Courier

(3) Alphabetical System :

This system has the advantage that it may be formed into a mnemonic code.

For Example :
P = Purchases
PD = Purchase Discount
PM = Purchase Manager
PO = Purchase Outdoor
PR = Purchase of Raw Material
PI = Purchase Indoor
PC = Purchase - Components

On account of limited number of alphabets, this method has a limited coverage and lacks flexibility.

(4) Combination of Alphabets and Numbers System :

The alphabet denotes the main group and the sub-group or type of expenditure is indicated by the numerical 1.

The following codes illustrate this method :

R1	Repairs to Plant and Machinery	D1	Depreciation to plants and Machinery
R2	Repairs to Building	D2	Depreciation of Building
R3	Repairs to Delivery vans	D3	Depreciation of Delivery vans
R4	Repairs to Office cars	D4	Depreciation of Office cars

2.1 Collection of Overheads

The procedure of classification of overheads and of assigning standing order (code) numbers has already been discussed. Such classification and codification are prequisite to the collection of overhead.

Production overheads should be collected for understanding order numbers. The main sources from which overhead costs are collected are as follows :

(a) **Invoice :** For collection of indirect expenses like rent, insurance etc.

(b) **Stores Requisitions :** For collection of indirect materials.

(c) **Wages Analysis Sheet :** For collection of indirect wages.

(d) **Journal Entries :** For collection of those overhead items which do not result in current cash outlay and need some adjustment e.g. depreciation, charge in lieu of rent, outstanding rent etc.

Departmentalisation of Overheads :

After overhead costs have been collected under various standing order numbers, the second step is to allocate and apportion the overhead to production and service departments. This is also known as Departmentalisation or Primary Distribution of Overhead.

Departmentalisation of overhead is the process of allocation and apportionment of overhead to different departments or cost centres. For smooth and efficient working, a factory is sub-divided into a number of departments each of which denotes a particular activity of the factory e.g. Purchase Department, Stores Department, Time Keeping Department, Personnel Department, Crushing Department, Melting Shop etc. These departments are mainly of two types : (a) Production Departments, and (b) Service Departments.

The following factors are taken into account while organising a concern into a number ot departments.

(1) Similarity of operations, processes, machines and equipments in a department.

(2) Location of operations and processes and the sequence of operations.

(3) Division of responsibility for control of production and control of cost.

(4) Optimum number of centres. Too many cost centres make the system of cost accounting detailed and quite expensive whereas too few cost centres will not be able to provide requisite cost information and thus will fail to serve the main objectives of cost accounting.

Need for Departmentalisation of Overheads :

Departmentalisation of overheads is necessary for the reasons given below :

(1) Control of Overhead Costs : Effective control of overhead costs is possible because departmentalisation makes the incurrence of costs in a department or cost centre the responsibility of someone who heads the department or the cost centre. Thus, with the help of departmentalisation, responsibility accounting can be effectively introduced for control purposes.

(2) Forecasting and Estimating : Because of greater accuracy in cost ascertainment and cost control, departmentalisation ensures more accurate forecasting and estimating and decision-making.

(3) Ensures Greater Accuracy in Cost Ascertainment : By proper allocation and apportionment of overheads. For accurate costing of each function or operation, overhead absorption rates should be determined separately for each cost centres. This is possible only with the help of departmentalisation.

(4) Use of Different Methods of Absorption : Basis of absorption of overhead may be different for different cost centres. e.g. machine hour rate may be more appropriate for another cost centres. Different basis may be used for different cost centres only when overheads are departmentalised.

(5) **Valuation of Work-in-Progress** : Correct cost of work-in-progress cannot be ascertained unless overheads are departmentalised.

(6) **Cost of Service Departments** : Departmentalisation helps in ascertaining the cost of various service departments which is useful for making estimates and submitting quotations for those items which make use of the services of various cost centres.

2.2 Allocation of Overheads

Certain items of overhead costs can be directly identified with a particular department or cost centre as having been incurred for that cost centre. Allotment of such costs to departments or cost centres is known as allocation. Thus, allocation may be defined as "the allotment of whole items of cost to cost centres or cost units." In other words, allocation is charging to cost centre those overheads that result solely from the existence of that cost centre. A point to be clearly understood is that allocation can be made only when exact amount of overhead incurred in a cost centre is definitely known. For example, rent cannot normally be allocated since rent is payable for the factory as a whole and exact amount for each department cannot be known. Indirect materials, on the other hand, can be easily allocated to various departments in which they are incurred. Other items which are allocated include indirect wages, overtime and idle time cost, power (when sub-metres are installed in departments), depreciation of machinery, supervision etc. In brief, in order that an overhead can be allocated, it should meet both the following conditions :

(a) The cost centre must have caused the overhead to be incurred; and

(b) The exact amount incurred in a cost centre must be known.

2.3 Apportionment of Overheads

Certain overhead costs cannot be directly charged to a department or cost centre. Such costs are common to a number of cost centres or departments and do not originate from any specific department. Distribution of such overhead costs to various departments is known as 'apportionment'. Thus, apportionment may be defined as "The allotment of proportions of items of cost to cost centres or cost units." In other words, it is charging to a cost centre as fair share of an overhead. Where an item of overhead is common to various cost centres, it is allotted to different cost centres, proportionately on some equitable basis. Again taking the case of rent, as it cannot be allocated, it is apportioned to various departments on some equitable basis e.g. in the ratio of area occupied. Similarly, salary of a general manager cannot be allocated wholly to anyone department as he attends in general to all the departments. It should, therefore, be apportioned on some equitable basis. Other items which generally cannot be allocated but are apportioned include fire insurance, lighting and heating, time keeping expenses, canteen expenses, medical and other welfare expenses etc.

The distinction between allocation of overheads and apportionment of overheads can be shown as follows:

Production and Service Department : Departments are classified as either production or service department. A production department, is one that engages in the actual manufacture of the product

Allocation of Overhead	Apportioment of Overhead
(1) Allocation deals with the whole items of cost.	(1) Apportionment deals with proportions of items of cost.
(2) In allocation the cost is alloted with directly.	(2) In apportionment, the cost is distributed on the proportionate basis.
(3) Allocation is a direct process.	(3) Apportionment is an indirect process according to suitable bases.
(4) Overheads cannot be allocated directly to the products.	(4) It is possible to charge the expenses indirectly through apportionment and absorb the cost in the final products.
(5) Overheads should always be allocated if possible.	(5) If overhead cannot be allocated, it is apportioned.

(6) This is known as 'Departmentalisation of overheads' of 'Primary distribution of overheads.'	(6) This is also a part of primary distribution of overhead costs.
(7) It is the process of alloting or charging the whole amount of an item of overhead to a department or cost centre.	(7) It is the allotment of proportions or items of cost to cost centres or cost units. It is the distribution of common costs to different department on some suitable bases.

by changing the shape, form or nature of material worked upon or by assembling the parts into finished product. A service department, on the other hand, is one rendering a service that contributes in an indirect manner to the manufacture of the product but which does not itself change the shape, form or nature of material that is converted into the finished product. Examples are given below :

Production Department	Service Departments
Weaving Department	Stores Department
Crushing Department	Time Keeping Department
Mixing Department	Personnel Department
Grinding Department	Inspection Department
Annealing Shop	Canteen
Picking Shop	Labour Welfare Department
Polishing Department	Production Control Department
Finishing Department	Transport Department
Kiln Burning Shop	Tool Room
Melting Shop	Accounting Department

The distinction between Production Department and Srevice Department can be shown as follows :

Partly Producing Department : There may be certain departments which are normally treated as service departments, but

Production Department	Service Department
(1) It is one that is engaged in the actual manufacturing of the product by changing the shape, form or nature of material worked upon or by assembling the parts into finished product.	(1) It is one rendering a service that contributes in an indirect manner to the manufacture of product but which does not itself change the shape, form or nature of material, that is converted into finished product.
(2) Weaving department, spinning department, mixing department, grinding department, etc. are the examples of production department.	(2) Time-keeping department, canteen, stores department, labour welfare department, etc, are the examples of service department.
(3) It works on things.	(3) It works on people.
(4) It produces goods, which can be stored in inventory until sold at a later date.	(4) It produces on output that is, by nature, intangible. Its services are perishable, and cannot be stored.

sometimes they are also required to undertake direct production work. These may be known as **partly producing or partly service departments.** For example, a carpentry shop which is mainly engaged in the work of repairs and maintenance of fittings and fixtures, is a service department but may be occasionally required to manufacture wooden boxes for packing of goods which may be charged directly to output. Similarly tool room, though a service department, may manufacture special tools against job orders. As these departments are sometimes engaged in direct manufacturing activities, they are called partly producing departments.

Principles of Apportionment :

Apportionment of overheads to various production and service departments is based on the following principles:

(a) **Service or Use :** This is the most common basis of overhead costs. It is based on the theory that greater the amount of service or benefit received by a department, the larger should be the share of the cost to be borne by that department. For example, rent is apportioned to various departments according to the floor space occupied. Telephone cost according to the number of extension telephones in each department and so on.

(b) **Survey Method :** This method is used for those overhead costs that are not closely related to departments and whose remoteness necessitates an arbitrary distribution. For example, salary of a General Manager of a company may be apportioned on the basis of the results of a survey which may reveal that 30% of his salary should be apportioned to sales, 10% to administration and 60% to vatious producing departments. Similarly, lighting expenses may be apportioned on the basis of a survey of the number of lights, size, estimated hours of use etc.

(c) **Ability to Pay Method :** This is based on the theory of taxation which holds that those who have the largest income should bear the highest proportion of the burden. In overhead distribution, those departments which have the largest income may be charged the largest amount of overhead. This method is generally considered inequitable because it penalises the efficient and the profitable units of the business to the advantages of inefficient ones.

Bases of Apportionment :

The following are some of the common basis of apportionment of overheads.

The following table indicates the various basis of apportionment for the usual items of factory overheads.

Item of Factory overheads	Basis of Apportionment
(1) Rent	Area or volume of buildings
(2) Depreciation of Machinery	Percentage of original cost of machinery or machine hour rate.
(3) Power	Horse power multiplied by machine hours or KWH.
(4) Electric Lighting	Number of light points or area occupied.
(5) Canteen Expenses	Number of employees.
(6) Store-keeping and Materials Handling	Number of stores requisitions.
(7) Indirect Wages of maintenance department or inspection etc.	Estimated or actual time spent
(8) Delivery Expenses	Weight volume or tonne-kilometre.
(9) Repairs of plant	Value of plant.
(10) Supervision	Direct wages.
(11) Fire Insurance	Value of asset.
(12) Machine Shop Expenses	Machine hours or labour hours.
(13) General Expenses	Direct wages or number of employees.
(14) Audit Fees	Sales of total cost.
(15) Maintenance of Buildings	Area or labour hours.

Note : The basis of apportionment can be arrived at on a trial basis and reviewed annually.

It should be noted that some overheads in the above list can be apportioned on more thae than one basis. The choice of an appropriate basis is really a matter of judgement. For example, welfare expenses may be apportioned on the basis of employees or total wages. Similarly, lighting expenses may be apportioned on the basis of number of light points in each department or on the basis of technical estimates or on the basis of floor area.

Example

Hindustan Co. Ltd. Bangalore has three production departments X, Y and Z and two service departments, A and B. The following figures are extracted from the records of the company for the period ended on 31-3-2010.

	Rs.		Rs.
Rent and Rates	10,000	General Lighting	1200
Indirect Wages	3000	Power	3000
Depreciation of Machinery	20000	Sundries	20,000

The following further details are available.

Particulars	Total	X	Y	Z	A	B
Floor Space (sq.ft)	10,000	2,000	2,500	3,000	2,000	500
Light Points (Numbers)	60	10	15	20	10	5
Direct Wages (Rs)	10,000	3,000	2,000	3,000	1,500	500
H.P of Machines (H.P)	150	60	30	50	10	--
Value of Machinery (Rs.)	2,50,000	60,000	80,000	1,00,000	5,000	5,000

Apportion the costs to various departments on the most equitable basis.

Solution

In the Books of Hindustan Co. Ltd. Baroda
Primary Departmental Distribution Summary
for the Period Ended on 31-3-2010

Particulars	Basis of Apportionment	Total Rs.	X	Y	Z	A	B
Direct Wages	Actual	2,000	-	-	-	1,500	500
Rent and Rates	Floor space	10,000	2000	2500	3000	2000	500
General Lighting	Light point	1200	200	300	400	200	100
Indirect Wages	Direct wages	3000	900	600	900	450	150
Power	H. P. of Machines	3000	1200	600	1000	200	--
Dep. of Machinery	Value of machine	20000	4800	6400	8000	400	400
Sundries	Direct wages	20000	6000	4000	6000	3000	1000
Total		**59200**	**15100**	**14400**	**19300**	**7750**	**2650**

Accounting of Overhead (Part I) / 23

2.4 Re-apportionment of Overheads

Once the overheads have been allocated and apportioned to production and service departments and totalled, the next step is to re-apportion the service department costs to production departments. This is necessary because out ultimate object is to charge overheads to cost units, and no cost units pass through service departments. Therefore, the costs of service departments must be charged to production departments which directly comes in contact with cost units. This is called Secondary Distribution of Overheads.

The method of re-apportionment of service department costs is similar to apportionment of overheads discussed earlier. Some of the important bases of re-apportionment of service department costs are as follows.

Service Department	Basis of apportionment
(1) Stores keeping Department	Number of requisitions or value of quantity materials of each department.
(2) Purchase Department	Value of materials purchased for each department or number of purchase orders placed.
(3) Time-keeping Department, Payroll Department	Payroll Number of employees or total labour or machine hours.
(4) Personnel Department	Rate of labour turnover or number of employees in each department.
(5) Canteen, Welfare and Recreation Services	Number of employees.
(6) Maintenance Department	Number of hours worked in each department.
(7) Inspection Department	Direct labour hours or machine operating hours.
(8) Drawing Office	Number of drawings made or man-hours worked.
(9) Internal Transport Service	Value or Weight of goods transported, distance covered.

Thus, the costs of service departments are re-apportioned on the basis of service rendered i.e. the benefits received by the beneficiary departments.

The various methods of re-apportionment of service department Costs are summarised in the chart shown below

Methods of Re-apportionment of Service Department Overhead Costs

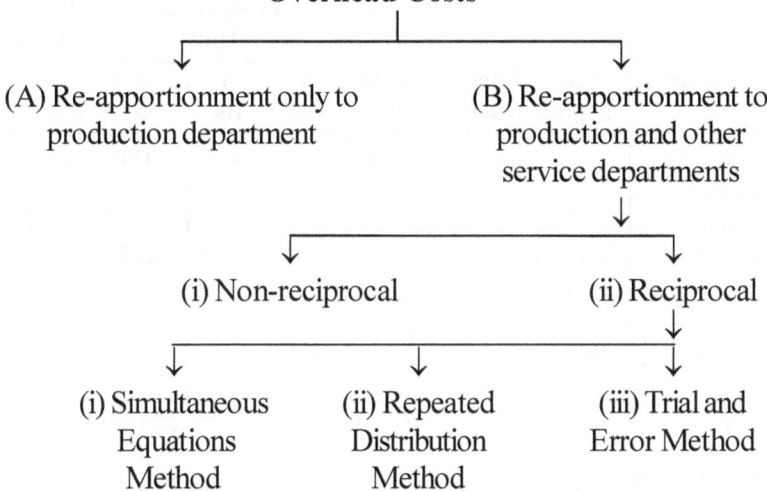

(A) Re-apportionment only to Production Departments:

In this case, cost of a service department is re-apportioned only to production departments without re-apportioning it to other service departments.

Example

Continuing above example by taking the total overhead as per departmental distribution summary and the following additional information, apportion the service department costs to production departments, ignoring inter-service department transfer.

	X	Y	Z
Number of Employees	75	30	45
Value of Materials Purchased	10,000	8,000	7,000

Further assume service department A is purchasing department and B is time-keeping department.

Answer :

In the books Hindustan Co. Ltd., Baroda
Secondary Distribution Summary for the
Period Ended 31-3-2010.

Particulars	Basic of Re-apportionment	Total Rs.	Production Depts.			Service Depts.	
			X Rs.	Y Rs.	Z Rs.	A Rs.	B Rs.
Total as per primary summary		59200	15100	14400	19300	7750	2650
Dept.A	Value of materials purchased		3100	2480	2170	-7750	
Dept.B	Number of employees		1546	442	662		-2650
Total		59200	19746	17322	22132	–	–

(B) Re-apportionment to production as well as service departments :

Quite often, a service department renders service not only on production department but also to ther service departments. For example, maintenance department looks after not only the plant and machinery of production department but also the equipment of other service departments like power house, materials handling, etc. Similarly, power house supplies eletricity not only to production departments but also to canteen, maintenance department etc.

This type of inter-service department apportionment may be either on reciprocal basis or non-reciprocal basis. :

(1) Re-apportionment of Non-reciprocal basis :

This is done when service departments are not interdependent. In this method, the service departments are arranged in descending order of their serviceability. The cost of the most serviceable department i.e. the department which serves the largest number of departments is first apportioned to other service departments. The service departments which serves the next largest number of departments is taken up next and its cost (including the prorated cost of the first service department) is apportined to other service and production departments except the first service department. In the same way, while apportioning the third service department in this order, the first two service departments are ignored. This process is continued till the cost of the last service department is apportioned. It should be note that the cost of the service department is apportioned only to production department.

Example

The method has been illustrated with assumed figures.

Secondray Distribution Summary of the Period Ended....

	Production Depts.			Service Depts.			
Total	X	Y	Z	A	B	C	D
Rs.	Rs.	Rs.	Rs.	Rs.	Rs.	Rs.	Rs.
25,350	8,000	7,250	5,600	1,200	1,000	800	1,500
	350	250	300	300	200	100	(-)1,500
	300	250	200	150	-	- 900	
	200	350	400	250	(-)1,200		
	600	700	600	(-)1,900			
25,350	**9,450**	**8,800**	**7,100**	--	--	--	--

It is assumed that the descending order of serviceability of service departments is D,C,B, and A. This means service department D is the most serviceable department i.e. it renders service to the largest number of production as well as other service departments. It does not receive any service from service department. Therefore cost of Rs. 1,500 of service department D is apportioned to other departments in the ratio it renders its services. The next most serviceable department is C which renders its services to all other departments except D. Therefore its cost is apprortioned to all departments except serivce department D. The cost of department B is apportioned which is next in the order of serviceability and lastly cost of A is approtioned.

(2) Re-apportionment on Reciprocal basis :

This method is used when service departments are mutually dependent. Thus, in the above example, position will be different if in addition to serving production departments, service department also renders services to each other service department. For example, service department B renders service to B, C and D, service department B renders service to A, C and D cannot allot any cost to B. Similarly, until A's charge to B, C and D is known, B, C and D cannot allot any costs to A. Thus, there are many unknown variables as the number of service departments, are several.

There are three methods for breaking this vicious circle which are given below :

(i) Simultaneous Equations Method
(ii) Repeated Distribution Method
(iii) Trial and Error Method

(i) Simultaneous Equations Method :

In this method, the following algebraic equations help in finding out the unknowns :

$X = a + by$
$Y = a + bx$

This is illustrated below :

Example

The departmental distribution summary showed the following departmental totals :

Departments	X	Y	Z	A	B
Amount Rs.	7,550	7,200	9,650	4,625	1,575

The costs of service departments A and B are to be charged on the basis of the following percentage :

	X	Y	Z	A	B
A	20%	30%	40%	-	10%
B	40%	20%	30%	10%	-

Find the total overheads of production departments.

Answer:

Let X denote total overhead of service department A
Y denote total overhead of service department B

$$X = Rs.\ 4,625 + \frac{10}{100}\ Y \qquad\qquad (i)$$

$$Y = Rs.\ 1,575 + \frac{10}{100}\ X \qquad\qquad (ii)$$

or
$$X = Rs.\ 4,625 + 0.10Y \qquad\qquad (i)$$
$$-X + 10Y = Rs.\ 15,750 \qquad\qquad (ii)$$

Again multiplying equation (ii) by 10 to eliminate X and adding :

$$10\ X - Y = Rs.\ 46,250$$
$$\underline{-10X + 100Y = Rs.\ 1,57,500}$$
$$90Y = Rs.\ 2,03,750$$

$$Y = \frac{Rs.\ 2,03,750}{99}$$

$$Y = Rs.\ 2,058$$

$\therefore$ Substituting the value of Y in equation (i)

$$10X - Rs.\ 2,058 = Rs.\ 46,250$$
$$10X = Rs.\ 46,250 + Rs.\ 2,058$$
$$10X = Rs.\ 48,308$$
$$X = Rs.\ 4,830.8\ or\ Rs.\ 4,831\ (Approx.)$$

Thus, X = Rs. 4,831 and Y = Rs. 2,058

Secondary Distribution Summary for the Period Ended...

Particulars	Total Rs.	Production Depts. X Rs.	Y Rs.	Z Rs.
Total as per Primary Distribution Summary	24,400	7,550	7,200	9,650
Service Department A (Rs. 4,831) **Less :** 10% to Dept. B.	4,348	966	1,450	1,932
Service Department B (Rs. 2,058) **Less :** 10% to Dept. A	1,852	823	411	618
Total	**30,600**	**9,339**	**9,061**	**12,200**

This method of simultaneous equations gives accurate results. But when the number of service departments exceeds two, calculations become cumbersome.

ii) Repeated Distribution Method :

In this method, following steps are taken to apportion the service departments costs :

(1) The costs of the first service department are apportioned in the normal way according to the given percentages. This will close the amount of the first service department.

(2) Then apply the given percentages to the apportionment of second service department costs which includes its own total plus amount apportioned from the first service department. This closes the account of the second service department but re-opens the account of the first service department.

(3) The same procedure should be followed in the case of all other service departments.

(4) The procedure should be repeated again starting with the first service department whose total now consists only of amounts apportioned from other service departments. In this way, service department costs keep on reducing with each process of distribution because each time a substantial amount is charged to the production departments.

(5) This process is continued until the amounts involved become insignificant.

The operation of this method is illustrated in the following illustration. The method of Repeated Distribution Method will be applied as follows.

Secondary Distribution Summary

Particulars	Production Depts.			Service Depts.	
	X Rs.	Y Rs.	Z Rs.	A Rs.	B Rs.
Total as per Primary Summary	7,550	7,200	9,650	4,625	1,575
Department A	625	1,387	1,850	-4,625	463
Department B	815	408	611	204	-2,038
Department A	41	61	82	-204	20
Department B	9	4	7	-	(-) 20
Total	**9,340**	**9,060**	**12,200**	**-**	

Working Note : In the above solution, first of all the cost of service department A is apportioned to X, Y, Z and B in the ratio given. Then the cost of service department B Rs. 2,038 (i.e. 1,575 + 463) has been apportioned to departments X, Y, Z and A in the given percentage. The account of department A is again opened with the amount of Rs. 204, which is distributed to X, Y, Z and B in the given ratio. Then the amount of Rs. 20 allotted to department B is distributed to departments X, Y, Z. Nothing is alotted to department A as the share of department A is quite negligible. In this way, the entire costs of service departments A and B are apportioned to production departments X, Y and Z.

It should be noted that, unlike simultaneous equations method, this method produces approximate results. But the advantage of this method is that it can be conveniently applied where the number of service department is more than two.

(iii) Trial and Error Method :

In this method, the cost of first service department is apportioned to other service departments in the given ratio. The cost of the next service department is apportioned to first and other service departments. In this way, when the costs of all service departments has been apportioned, the process is repeated till the service department costs are negligible. This is illustrated below :

Example

	Service Depts.	
Particulars	**A**	**B**
	Rs.	**Rs.**
Total as per Primary Summary	4,625	1,575
Service department A (10% to B)		463
Service department A (10% to B)	204	2038
Service department B (10% to B)		
Service department B (10% to A)	2	20

Thus, the total costs of service departments A and B are Rs. 4,831 and Rs. 2,038 respectively. Now a Secondary Distribution Summary can be prepared is the same way as was done in simultaneous equations method.

It will be seen that this is a modification of repeated distribution method where production departments are initially ignored for the purpose of redistribution. Like repeated distribution method, this method also gives approximate results and can be usefully employed where the number of service departments is more than two.

The distinction between 'Apportionment of Overheads' and 'Re-apportionment of Overheads' can be shown as follows.

Apportionment of Overheads	Re-apportionment of Overheads
1. It is the process to allot costs to the cost centres or cost units for ascertaining the total costs. Apportionment does not depends upon the nature of expenses to be incurred, but it depends upon the relationship with cost centre or cost unit to which it is required to be charged.	1. After "primary distribution' the cost of service department is borne by the production departments. The process of redistribution of the service department costs to the production department is known as "Re-apportionment" or secondary overhead distribution summary."
2. This is necessary because certain overhead costs cannot be directly charged to department or cost centre.	2. This is necessary because the ultimate aim is to charge overheads to cost units, and no cost unit pass through service department.
3. There is no hard and fast rule as regard the bases of apportionment of overheads. It depends on the nature of overhead incurred.	3. It is done on the basis of the benefits received by each department.
4. There are some common bases for apportionments of overheads costs on some equitable basis which is known as primary distribution method.	4. For selecting a suitable base for re-apportioning the cost of service department, the same principles of apportionment may be applied here also.

2.5 Illustrations on Primary Distribution

Illustration 1

Lucky Ltd. Ahmednagar provides the following particulars regarding Repairs and Maintenance Service Dept. for the month ended on 31st March, 2010

Particulars	Production Depts.		Service Depts.	
	X	Y	A	B
Standard labour hours required	500	250	200	300
Actual labour hours worked	400	200	150	250

The total expenses of Repairs and Maintenance Dept. for the period amounted to Rs. 50,000 out of which Rs. 40,000 were spent as marginal expenses.

You are required to allocate the expenses of Repairs and Maintenance Dept. to the Production Depts. and Service Depts.

Solution :

In the Books of Lucky Ltd., Ahmednagar

Statement Showing Allocation of Repairs and Maintenance Depts. Cost to the Production Depts. and Service Depts. for the Month Ended on 31-3-2010

Particulars	Basis of Apportionment	Ratio	Total Rs.	Production Depts. X Rs.	Production Depts. Y Rs.	Service Depts. A Rs.	Service Depts. B Rs.
Marginal i.e. Variable Expenses	Actual Labour Hours Worked	8:4:3:5	40,000	16,000	8,000	6,000	10,000
Fixed Expenses	Standard Labour Hours Required	10:5:4:6	10,000	4,000	2,000	1,600	2,400
Total			**50,000**	**20,000**	**10,000**	**7,600**	**12,400**

Illustration 2

The following are the figures obtained from the records of Sudarshan Chemicals Ltd., Pune for the month of March, 2010

Departments	Indirect Material Rs.	Indirect Labour Rs.
Production Depts -		
A	3650	2350
B	2425	1325
C	1200	1900
Service Depts -		
X	4150	2125
Y	2075	1300

Additional Informatins :

	Rs.
Lighting, Heating and Power	10000
Rent, Rates and Taxes	4000
Staff Welfare Charges	5000
Depreciation on Machinery	15000

Other information :

		Production Depts.			Service Depts.	
		A	B	C	X	Y
Area occupied	sq. ft.	3,000	2,000	1,000	1,500	500
Kilo watt-hours		6,000	5,000	4,500	2,500	2,000
Number of employees		80	100	60	130	30
Value of Machinery	Rs.	1,00,000	50,000	78,000	62,000	10,000

You are required to apportion the costs to various departments by considering the most suitable basis.

In the Books of Sudarshan Chemicals Ltd., Pune.
Statement showing Apporionment of Cost to Various Depts. for the Year Ended 31st March 2010

Particulars	Basis for Apportionment	Ratio	Total Cost	Production Dept.			Service Dept.	
				A Rs.	B Rs.	C Rs.	X Rs.	Y Rs.
Indirect Material	Actual	-	13,500	3650	2425	1200	4150	2075
Indirect Labour	Actual	-	9000	2350	1325	1900	2125	1300
Lighting, heating and power	kilowatt hours	12:10:9:5:4	10000	3000	2500	2250	1250	1000
Rent, rates and taxes	Area occupied	6:4:2:3:1	4000	1500	1000	500	750	250
Staff welfare charges	Number of employee	8:10:6:13:3	5000	1000	1250	750	1625	375
Depreciation on machinery	Value of Machinery	50:25:39:31:5	15000	5000	2500	3900	3100	500
Total :			56,500	16,500	11,000	10,500	13,000	5,500

Illustration 3

Prince Ltd., Nagpur has two production cost centres A and B and two service cost centres X and Y. The following is the summary of overhead costs for the month of March, 2010

	Rs.
Salary to Works Manager	6,000
Light and Power	36,000
Repairs to Plant	10,000
Rent of Factory Buildings	8,000
Meals to Working Staff	12,000
Deperciation on Machinery	25,000
Provident Fund Contribution	15,000

Additional Information :

Particulars		Production Depts.		Service Depts.	
		A	B	X	Y
Number of Workers		12	18	3	3
Area Sq. meter		1,000	2,000	500	500
Value of Plant and Machinery	Rs.	45,000	90,000	45,000	45,000
Direct Wages	Rs.	5,000	6,000	2,000	2,000
Horse Power		5	4	-	3

You are required to distribute the overhead costs to the Production and Service Depts. on the most equitable basis.

Solution :

In the Books of Prince Ltd., Nagpur
Statement Showing Distribution of Overhead Costos to the Prodction and Service Depts. for the Month Ended 31st March, 2010

Particulars	Basis of Apportionment	Ratio	Total Rs.	Productiond Depts.		Service Depts.	
				A Rs.	B Rs.	X Rs.	Y Rs.
Salary to Works Manager	Number of workers	4:6:1:1	6,000	2,000	3,000	500	500
Light and Power	Horse Power	5:4::3	36,000	15,000	12,000	--	9,000
Repairs to Plant	Value of Plant and Machinery	1:2:1:1	10,000	2,000	4,000	2,000	2,000
Rent of Factory Buildings	Area Sq. Meter	2:4:1:1	8,000	2,000	4,000	1,000	1,000
Meals to Working Staff	Number of Workers	4:6:1:1	12,000	4,000	6,000	1,000	1,000
Depreciation on Machinery	Value of Plant and Machinery	1:2:1:1	25,000	5,000	10,000	5,000	5,000
Provident Fund Contribution	Direct Wages	5:6:2:2	15,000	5,000	6,000	2,000	2,000
Total			**1,12,000**	**35,000**	**45,000**	**11,500**	**20,500**

Illustration 4

Kumaresh Ltd. has three production departments A, B and C and two service departments D and F. The following figures are extracted from the records of the company :

Rent and rates	Rs. 5,000
Indirect wages	1,500
Depreciation of machinery	10,000
General lighting	600
Power	1,500
Sundries	10,000

Following further details are available :

	Total	A	B	C	D	E
Floor space (sq. metres)	10,000	2,000	2,500	3,000	2,000	500
Light point	60	10	15	20	10	5
Direct wages (Rs.)	10,000	3,000	2,000	3,000	1,500	500
H.P. of machines	150	60	30	50	10	-
Value of Machinery (Rs.)	2,50,000	60,000	80,000	1,00,000	5,000	5,000

Apportion the costs to various departments on the most equitable basis by preparing a primary departmental distribution summary.

Accounting of Overhead (Part I) / 39

Soultion :

In the Books of kumaresh Ltd

Statement Showing Apportionment of Expenses to various Dept for the Year / Month Ended...

Particulars	Basis of Apportionment	Ratio	Total expenses	Productiond Depts. A Rs.	B Rs.	C Rs.	Service Depts. X Rs.	Y Rs.
Rent & Rates	Floor space	4:5:6:4:1	5000	1000	1250	1500	1000	250
Lighting	Light Points	2:3:4:2:1	600	100	150	200	100	50
Indirect wages	Direct wages	6:4:6:3:1	1500	450	300	450	225	75
Power	H.P.Basis	6:3:5:1	1500	600	300	500	100	-
Dep. of Machines	Value of machinery	12:16:20:1:1	10,000	2400	3200	4000	200	200
Sundries	Direct wages	6:4:6:3:1	10,000	3000	2000	3000	1500	500
Total			**28600**	**7550**	**7200**	**9650**	**3125**	**1075**

Illustration 5

Delta Ltd. Pune has four departments, three production departments viz. I, II and III and one service department viz. IV. The actual costs for the month of March, 2010 were as follows :

Indirect Expenses -	Rs.
Producing Departments :	
I	825
II	100
III	955
Service Department	
IV	620
Additional Expenses :	
Repairs	1,500
Depreciation	1,000
Rent, Rates and Taxes	5,000
Lighting	500
Insurance of Buildings	1,000
Supervision Charges	4,000
Employee's State Insurance-Contribution	
by the Employer	500
Motive Power	2,000

Other Information :

	Production Depts.			Service Depts.
	I	**II**	**III**	**IV**
Area Sq. Ft.	100	150	90	160
Number of Workers	15	10	9	16
Direct Wages Rs.	5,000	8,000	5,000	2,000
Value of Plant Rs.	25,000	10,000	8,000	7,000
and Machiery				
Number of light points	10	5	6	4
Kilo-watt hours	2,000	5,000	6,000	7,000

You are required to apportion the overhead costs to the various production and service departments on suitable basis.

Solution :

In the Books of Delta Ltd., Pune

Statement Showing Apportionment of Overhead Costs to the Production and Service Depts. for the Month Ended on 31st March, 2010

Particulars	Basis of Apportionment	Ratio	Total Rs.	Production Depts.			Service Depts.
				I Rs.	II Rs.	III Rs.	IV Rs
Indirect Expenses	Actual	-	2,500	825	100	955	620
Repairs	Value of Plant and machinery	25:10:8:7	1,500	750	300	240	210
Depreciation	Value of plant and machinery	25:10:8:7	1,000	500	200	160	140
Rent, Rates and Taxes	Area sq. ft.	10:15:9:16	5,000	1,000	1,500	900	1,600
Lighting	Number of light points	10:5:6:4	500	200	100	120	80
Insurance of Buildings	Area sq. ft.	10:15:9:16	1,000	200	300	180	320
Supervision	Number of workers	15:10:9:16	4,000	1,200	800	720	1,280
Employees state insurance contribution by the Employer	direct wages	5:8:5:2	500	125	200	125	50
Motive Power	Kilo-watt hours	2:5:6:7	2,000	200	500	600	700
Total			18,000	5,000	4,000	4,000	5,000

2.6 Illustration on Secondary Distribution

Illustration 1

Bharat forge Ltd., has three production departments and six service departments. the overhead expenses for the departments as per Primary Distribution Summary were as follows:

Production Depts :	Rs.
A	70450
B	19800
C	34750
Service Depts :	
Stores	5,000
Accounts	4,000
Power house	3,000
Cahteen	3,000
Time - keeping	5,000
Tool Room	8,000
Total	**1,30,000**

The following additional information was made available from the costing records as regards the production departments.

	Production Depts.		
	A	**B**	**C**
Number of workers	80	100	20
H.P. of machines	500	800	700
Value of stores requisitioned Rs.	6,000	2,000	2,000
Services rendered %	25	50	25

You are required to prepare a statement showing secondary distribution of service departments costs to production departments for the month ended 31st March, 2010.

Solution :

In the Books of Bharat Forge Ltd., Pune
Statement Showing Secondary Distribution of Service Depts, Costs to Prodution Depts. for the Month Ended on 31st March, 2010

Particulars	Basis of Re-apportionment	Ratio	Total Rs.	Production Depts. A Rs.	B Rs.	C Rs.
Overhead Expenses as per Primary Distribution Summary			1,25,000	70450	19800	34750
Service Depts. :						
(1) Stores Depts	Value of stores requestioned	3:1:1	5,000	3,000	1,000	1,000
(2) Accounts Dept.	Number of workers	4:5:1	4,000	1,600	2,000	400
(3) Power House Dept	H.P. of machines	5:8:7	3,000	750	1,200	1,050
(4) Canteen Dept.	Number of workers	4:5:1	3,000	1,200	1,500	300
(5) Time - keeping Dept.	Number of workers	4:5:1	5,000	2,000	2,500	500
(6) Tool room Dept	Services rendered	1:2:1	8,000	2,000	4,000	2,000
Total			1,53,000	81,000	32,000	40,000

Illustration 2

Loid Steel Ltd., Lonavala has three production Departments and has four service departments. The departmental overhead summary for the month of March, 2010 discloses the following results:

(A) Production Depts :

(i)	Cutting	7,000
(ii)	Milling	8,000
(iii)	Grinding	10,000

(B) Service Depts :

(i)	Stores	3,000
(ii)	Repairs	5,000
(iii)	Time - keeping	1,000
(iv)	Staff welfare	4,000

Additional Information :

	Production Depts.		
	Cutting	**Milling**	**Grinding**
Employee Numbers	40	70	90
Material Requisitions	10	16	14
Direst Labour Hours Worked	975	2,075	3,950

Yon are requirsd to work out the Overhead Absorption Rate.

Solution :

In the Books of Lloyd Steel Ltd., Lonavala

Statement Showing Secondary Distribution of Service Depts. Overhead Cost to Production Depts. for the Month Ended on 31st March, 2010

Particulars	Basis of Re-appartionment	Ratio	Total Rs.	Production Depts.		
				Cutting Rs.	Milling Rs.	Grinding Rs.
Overhead Expenses as Per Departmental Overhead Summary			25,000	7,000	8,000	10,000
Service Depts :						
(1) Stores Depts	Materials requisitions	5:8:7	3,000	750	1,200	1050
(2) Repairs Depts.	Direct labour hours worked	2:3:5	5,000	1,000	1,500	2,500
(3) Time -keeping Depts.	Employee numders	4:7:9	1,000	200	350	450
(4) Staff welfare Depts.	Employee numbers	4:7:9	4,000	800	1,400	1,800
Total			**38,000**	**9,750**	**12,450**	**15,800**

Working Notes :

1) Calculation of Overhead Absorption Rate (Base Direct Labour Hours Worked)

$$= \frac{\text{ProductionOverheads}}{\text{DirectLabourHoursWorked}} = \frac{\text{Rs.}9,750}{\text{Hrs. }975} = \frac{\text{Rs.}12,450}{\text{Hrs.}2,075} = \frac{\text{Rs.}15,800}{\text{Hrs.}3,950}$$

$$= \text{Rs.}10 \quad = \text{Rs.}6 \quad\quad = \text{Rs.}4$$

Illustration 3

The following data were obtained from the books of Vasanth Co. Ltd., for the half - year ended 30th September, 2010, Calculate the departmental overhead rate for each department assuming that overherds are recovered as a percentage on direct wages.

Items	Production Depts.			Service Depts.	
	A	B	C	X	Y
Direct wages (Rs)	7,000	6,000	5,000	1,000	1,000
Direct material (Rs)	3,000	2,500	2,000	1,500	1,000
Employees (N)	200	150	150	50	50
Electricity (KWh)	8,000	6,000	6,000	2,000	3,000
Light Points (Nos.)	10	15	15	5	5
Asset Value (Rs.)	50,000	30,000	20,000	10,000	10,000
Area occupied (Sq.m.)	800	600	600	200	200

Reapportionment : Service department y = in proportion to direct wages, x = ratio of 4 : 3 : 3 among production departments, A,B,C respectively.

The expenses for 6 months were : (a) stores overhead, Rs. 400; (b) motive power, Rs. 1,500; (c) Electric light, Rs. 200; (d) labour welfare, Rs. 3,000; (e) depreciation, Rs.6,000; (f) repairs, Rs.1,200; (g) general overheads, Rs.10,000; and (h) rent and taxes, Rs. 600.

B.Com., Kerala, April / May 86

Solution

Apportionment of Overheads & Calculation of Overhead Rate (Rs.).

Particulars	Basic	Total	Prodn. Dept			Service Dept.	
			A	B	C	X	Y
(a) Stores head	Over-Direct	400	120	100	80	60	40
(b) Motive Power	KWH	1,500	480	360	360	120	180
(c) Electric light	Light Points	200	40	60	60	20	20
(d) Labour welfare	Employees	3,000	1,000	750	750	250	250
(e) Depreciation	Asset Value	6,000	2,500	1,500	1,000	500	500
(f) Repairs	Asset Value	1,200	500	300	200	100	100
(g) General over heads	Direct Wages	10,000	3,500	3,000	2,500	500	500
(h) Rent & rates	Area	600	200	150	150	50	50
Total		22,900	8,340	6,220	5,100	1,600	1,640
Service Dept. Y.	Direct Wages		638	547	455	-	(-)1,640
Service Dept.X.	4:3:3		640	480	480	(-)1,600	
Total Overheads		**22,900**	**9,618**	**7,247**	**6,035**	**Nil**	**Nil**

Overhead rate :

$$\frac{\text{Overhead}}{\text{Direct Wages}} \times 100 \qquad \frac{9618}{7000} \times 100 \qquad \frac{7247}{6000} \times 100 \qquad \frac{6035}{5000} \times 100$$

$$= 137.41\% \qquad = 120.78\% \qquad = 120.7\%$$
$$\quad\text{A} \qquad\qquad \text{B} \qquad\qquad \text{C}$$

Illustration - 4

A factory has two service departments, S1 and S2 and three producing departments, P1, P2 and P3. The budgeted expenditure for a month was as follows :

Rs.	
Indirect Wages	4,000
Rent	2,100
Insurance	1,400
Power	2,800
Lighting	1,050
Depreciation	14,000
Other indirect expenses	8,000
Total	**33,350**

The other data available for the period were :

	S_1	S_2	P_1	P_2	P_3	Total
Direct Wages	2,000	3,000	15,000	8,000	12,000	40,000
Floor Space (sq. metres	300	300	300	500	600	2,100
Machine Value (Rs.)	6,000	4,000	40,000	50,000	40,000	1,40,000
Horse power	**5**	**5**	**40**	**50**	**40**	**140**

You are required to suitably apportion the expense to the various departments and determine the overhead recovery rates for each of the producing departments, assuming that the direct labour cost method of recovery is in use. The service department costs are to apportioned as follows :

Department S1 : 50% to P1,30% to P2 and rest to P3

Department S2 : 40% to P1,and 30% each to P2 and P3.

B.com., April/May 87

Solution :

Apportionment of Expense (Overheads) (Rs.)

Particulars	Basic of apportionment	Total	Service Dept. S₁	Service Dept. S₂	Producing Dept. P₁	Producing Dept. P₂	Producing Dept. P3
Indirect wages	Direct wages	4,000	200	300	1,500	800	1,200
Rent	Floor space	2,100	300	300	400	500	600
Insurance	Machine value	1,400	60	40	400	500	400
Power	Horse powerr	2,800	100	100	800	1.000	800
Lighting	Floor space	1,050	150	150	200	250	300
Depreciation	Machine value	14,000	600	400	4,000	5,000	4,000
Other indirect exp.	Direct wages	8,000	400	600	3,000	1,600	2,400
Total	....	33,350	1,810	1890	10,300	9,650	9,700
S1 Exp.	50:30:20		(-)1890		905	543	362
S2 Exp.	40:30:30			(-)1810	756	567	567
Total	....	33,350	Nil	Nil	11,961	10,760	10,629
Overhead recovery rate : % of wages (See Note below)					79.74	134.50	88.575

50 / Cost & Work Accounting (Paper II)

Note : Overhead recovery rate $= \dfrac{\text{Overhead}}{\text{Direct Wages}} \times 100$

$$P_1 = \frac{11,961}{15,000} \times 100 = 79.74\% \qquad P_2 = \frac{10,760}{8,000} \times 100 = 134.5\%$$

$$P_3 = \frac{10,629}{12,000} \times 100 = 88.57\%$$

2.7 Illustrations on Primary and Secondary Distribution

Illustration 1

In Bhel Ltd., Bhopal are two Production Depts. viz. A and B and two Service Depts.viz C and D. Department C provides service to A and B in the ratio of 2 : 3 whereas departmet D provides services to A and B in the ratio of 6 : 1

The other details as regards to the expenses and other charges for the period ended on 31-3-2010 are follows :

	Rs.
Rent, Rates and Taxes	40,000
Insurance	15,000
Electricity	5,000
Motive Power	20,000
Depreciation	2,00,000
Amenities to staff	13,000

Additional Information :

Particulars		Production Depts.		Service Depts.	
		A	B	C	D
Assets Values	Rs.	10,00,000	5,00,000	4,00,000	1,00,000
Floor Area	(sq.ft)	8,000	6,000	4,000	2,000
Number of Light Points	Numbers	40	30	15	15
H.P. of Machines	H.P	800	500	400	300
Number of Workers	Numbers	75	50	50	25
Direct Wages	Rs.	2,200	1,400	1,000	875

You are required to prepare a statement showing distribution of overhead cost and also find out the total overhead cost of each production department.

Solution :

In the Books of BHEL Ltd..,
Statement Showing Distribution of Overhead Cost
for the Period Ended 31ˢᵗ March,2010

Particulars	Basic of Apportionment	Ratio	Total Rs.	Production Depts		Service Depts	
				A Rs.	B Rs.	C Rs.	D Rs.
Rent, rates and taxes	Floor area sq.ft.	4:3:2:1	40,000	16,000	12,000	8,000	4,000
Insurance	Asset values	10:5:4:1	15,000	7,500	3,750	3,000	750
Electricity	Number of light points	8:6:3:3	5,000	2,000	1,500	750	750
Motive power	H.P. of machines	8:5:4:3	20,000	8,000	5,000	4,000	3,000
Depreciation	Asset value	10:5:4:1	2,00,000,	1,00,000	50,000	40,000	10,000
Amenities to staff	Number of workers	3:2:2:1	13,000	4,875	3,250	3,250	1,625
Direct wages	Actual		1,875	-	-	1,000	875
Total			**2,94,875**	**1,38,375**	**75,500**	**60,000**	**21,000**

Statement Showing Total Overhead Cost of Production Depts. for the In the books of BHEL Ltd. Period Ended 31ˢᵗ March, 2010

Particulars	Basic of Re-appor tionment	Ratio	Total Rs.	Prod'n A Rs.	Depts. B Rs.
Overhead costs as Per Primary Distribution Summary			2,13,875	1,38,375	75,500
Service Dept. C'	Actual	2:3	60,000	24,000	36,000
Service Dept. D'	Actual	6:1	21,000	18,000	3,000
Total			2,94,875	1,80,375	1,14,500

Illustration 2

Bharat Techno Ltd., Mumbai is having four departments A, B and C are the production department and D is the service department. The actual costs for the period ended 31-3-2010 are as follows :

Indirect Materials :	**Rs.**
Prodution Depts.	
A.	295
B.	535
C.	365
Service Depts.-	
D.	405
Rent	2,000
Repairs and Maintenance	1,200
Electric Lighting	200
Depreciation	900
Supervisor's salary	3,000
Employer's liability towards employee's insurance	300
Power	1,800
Insurance on Stock	1,000

The following additional data are also made available in respect of four departments.

Particulars		Production Depts.			Service Depts.
		A	B	C	D
Area sq.ft.		150	110	90	50
Value of stock	Rs.	15,000	9,000	6,000	
Number of employees		24	16	12	8
Value of plant	Rs.	24,000	18,000	12,000	6,000
Total Wages	Rs.	8,000	6,000	4,000	2,000

Apportion the costs to various departments on most equitable basis. Reapportion the overhead costs of Department D' to the Production Departments A, B and C in the ratio of 40%:40%:20% respectively.

Solution :

In the Books of Telco Engineering Ltd., Pune
Statement Showing Primary Distribution of overhead Expenses for the Month Ended 31st March, 2010

Particulars	Basis of Apportionment	Ratio	Total Rs.	Production Depts			Service Depts.	
				A Rs.	B Rs.	C Rs.	X Rs.	Y Rs.
Direct Materials	Actual	--	45,000	--	--	--	22,500	22,500
Direct Wages	Actual	--	45,000	--	--	--	15,000	30,000
Power	Electricity KWH	4 : 3 : 2 : 1 : 1	1,100	400	300	200	100	100
Lighting	Light Points	5 : 8 : 2 : 3 : 2	200	50	80	20	30	20
Stores Overheads	Direct Material	2 : 4 : 4 : 3 : 3	800	100	200	200	150	150
Staff Welfare	Staff Numbers	2 : 3 : 3 : 1 : 1	3,000	600	900	900	300	300
Depreciation	Asset Value	6 : 4 : 3 : 1 : 1	30,000	12,000	8,000	6,000	2,000	2,000
Repairs	Asset Value	6 : 4 : 3 : 1 : 1	6,000	2,400	1,600	1,200	400	400
General Overheads	Direct Wages	2 : 3 : 4 : 1 : 2	12,000	2,000	3,000	4,000	1,000	2,000
Rent and Taxes	Area Sq. Ft	3 : 5 : 1 : 1 : 1	550	150	250	50	50	50
Total			1,43,650	17,700	14,330	12,570	41,530	57,520

Statement Showing Secondary Distribution of Overhead Cost of Service Depts. to Production Depts. for the Month Ended 31ˢᵗ March 2010

Particulars	Basis of Re-apportionment	Ratio	Total Rs.	Production Depts. A Rs.	B Rs.	C Rs
Overhead Costs as per Primary Distribution Summary	-	-	44,600	17,700	14,330	12,570
Service Dept - X'	Actual	5:3:2	41,530	20,765	12,459	8,306
Service Dept - Y'	Direct Wages	2:3:4	57,520	12,782	19,173	25,565
Total			**1,43,650**	**51,247**	**45,962**	**46,441**

Working Notes :

(1) Calculation of departmental overhead rates of Production department as a percentage of Direct Wages

$$= \frac{\text{Production Overheads}}{\text{Direct Wages}} \times 100$$

$$\begin{array}{ccc} A & B & C \end{array}$$

$$= \frac{Rs.51,247}{Rs.30,000} \times 100 = \frac{Rs.45,962}{Rs.45,000} \times 100 = \frac{Rs.46,441}{Rs.60,000} \times 100$$

$$= 170.82\% \qquad = 102.14\% \qquad = 77.40\%$$

Repeated Distribution Method

Illustration 1

Sundar Paper Co Ltd. Akola has three production departments and two service departments. Their primary distribution summary discloses the results which are as follows :

Production Departments -

A - Rs.   7,810
B - Rs.   12,543

C - Rs.   4,547
Service Departments -
X - Rs.   4,000
Y - Rs.   2,600
The expenses of Service Departments are charged on a percentage basis as follows :

	A	B	C	X	Y
Service Dept. X	30%	40%	20%	-	10%
Service Dept. Y	10%	20%	50%	20%	-

You are required to prepare Secondary Distribution Statement as per Repeated Distribution Method for the period ended 31st March, 2010

Solution

In the Books of Sundar Paper Co Ltd., Akola

Statement Showing Secondary Distribution as per Repeated Distribution Method

for the Period Ended 31st March, 2010

Particulars	Ratio	Total Rs.	A Rs.	B Rs.	C Rs.	X Rs.	Y Rs.
Costs as per Primary Distribution Summary		31,500	7,810	12,543	4,547	4,000	2,600
Service Dept. X	3 : 4 : 2 : 1		1,200	1,600	800	(-) 4,000	400
						NIL	3,000
Service Dept. Y	1 : 2 : 5 : 2		300	600	1,500	600	3,000
						600	NIL
Service Dept. X	3 : 4 : 2 : 1		180	240	120	(-) 600	60
						NIL	60
Service Dept. Y	1 : 2 : 5 : 2		6	12	30	12	(-) 60
						12	NIL
Service Dept. X	3 : 4 : 2 : 1		4	5	3	(-) 12	-
						NIL	
Total		**31,500**	**9,500**	**15,000**	**7,000**	**NIL**	**NIL**

Illustration 2

The following information relates to the Production Departments A, B and C and the Service Departments X and Y for the month ended 31st March 2010

	Total	Production Depts			Service Depts	
		A	B	C	X	Y
	Rs.	Rs.	Rs.	Rs.	Rs.	Rs.
Heating and Lighting	3,600	500	500	500	700	1,400
Audit Fees	2,000	500	800	300	200	200
Depreciation	40,000	10,000	15,000	10,000	3,000	2,000
Time-Keeping Charges	4,000	800	1,600	600	600	400
Rates and Taxes	10,000	2,000	4,000	1,500	1,500	1,000
Total	**59,600**	**13,800**	**21,900**	**12,900**	**6,000**	**5,000**

Expenses of Service Departments are to be apportioned as follows

	A	B	C	X	Y
Dept. X	30%	40%	20%	-	10%
Dept. Y	10%	20%	50%	20%	-

Estimated Working Hours are as follows :

Dept. A : 8,257 hours

Dept. B : 8,633 hours

Dept. C : 5,729 hours

You are required to work out the production hour rate of recovery of overheads in departments A, B and C under Repeated Distribution Method of Mother Plant Ltd. Mumbai.

Solution

Statement Showing Secondary Distribution of Service Depts. Costs to Production Depts. as per Repeated Distribution Method for the Period Ended 31st March, 2010

Particulars	Ratio	Total Rs.	Production Depts.			Service Depts.	
			A Rs.	B Rs.	C Rs.	X Rs.	Y Rs.
Overhead Expenses as per Primary Distribution Summary		59,600	13,800	21,900	12,900	6,000	5,000
Service Dept. X	3 : 4 : 2 : 1		1,800	2,400	1,200	(-) 6000	600
Service Dept. Y	1 : 2 : 5 : 2		560	1,120	2,800	NIL	5,600
						1,120	5,600
Service Dept. X	3 : 4 : 2 : 1		336	448	224	(-) 1,120	122
						NIL	112
Service Dept. Y	1 : 2 : 5 : 2		11	22	57	22	-122
						22	NIL
Service Dept. X	3 : 4 : 2 : 1		7	9	6	(-) 22	-
Total		**59,600**	**16,514**	**25,899**	**17,187**	**NIL**	**NIL**

Working Notes :

(1) Calculation of Overhead rate of recovery in Production Depts. taking estimated working hours as a base.

$$= \frac{\text{Total Production Overheads}}{\text{Estimated Working Hours}}$$

$$\begin{array}{ccc} A & B & C \\ = \dfrac{\text{Rs. } 16,514}{\text{Hrs. } 8,257} = & \dfrac{\text{Rs. } 25,899}{\text{Hrs. } 8,633} = & \dfrac{\text{Rs. } 17,187}{\text{Hrs. } 5,729} \\ = \text{Rs. } 2 & = \text{Rs. } 3 & = \text{Rs. } 3 \end{array}$$

Illustration 3

Popular Co. Ltd., Mumbai has three production departments X, Y, and Z and two service departments A and B. The expenses incurred by them during the month of March 2010 were as follows:

	Rs.
Rent and Taxes	5,000
Canteen Expenses	1,300
Motive Power	4,000
Depreciation on Machines	5,000
Electric Lighting	2,000
Indirect Materials	1,500

Additional information provided for the month of March 2010

Particulars		Production Depts.			Service Depts.	
		X	**Y**	**Z**	**A**	**B**
Machine Values	Rs.	15,000	30,000	22,500	-	7,500
Direct Materials	Rs.	5,000	6,000	4,000	-	-
Direct Wages		4,000	5,000	3,000	-	-
Electricity KWH		5	10	10	6	9
Area occupied sq. ft		1,100	1,300	1,200	500	900
Light Point Numbers		8	12	10	4	6
Employee Numbers		50	10	40	10	20

Expenses of Service departments are to be apportioned as per Repeated Distribution Method as follows :

Particulars	X	Y	Z	A	B
Dept. A	20%	40%	30%	-	10%
Dept. B	30%	20%	30%	20%	-

Prepare a statement showing Primary Distribution of overhead expenses on most equitable basis. Also prepare a statement showing Secondary distribution of service dept. costs to production dept.

In the Books of Popular Co Ltd. Mumbai
Statement Showing Primary Distribution of Overhead Expenses
for the Month Ended 31st March, 2010

Particulars	Basis of Apportionment	Ratio	Total Rs.	Production Depts A Rs.	B Rs.	C Rs.	Service Depts X Rs.	Y Rs.
Rent and Taxes	Area occupied sq. ft	11:13:12:5:9	5,000	1,100	1,300	1,200	500	900
Canteen Expenses	Employee Numbers	5:1:4:1:2	1,300	500	100	400	100	200
Motive Power	Electricity K.W.H.	5:10:10:6:9	4,000	500	1,000	1,000	600	900
Depreciation on Machines	Machines Values	2:4:3::1	5,000	1,000	2,000	1,500	-	500
Electric Lighting	Light Point Numbers	4:6:5:2:3	2,000	400	600	500	200	300
Indirect Materials	Direct Materials	5:6:4:	1,500	500	600	400	-	-
Total			**18,800**	**4,000**	**5,600**	**5,000**	**1,400**	**2,800**

Accounting of Overhead (Part I) / 69

Solution

Statement Showing Secondary Distribution of Service Depts. Costs to Production Depts. as Per Repeated Distribution Method for the Month Ended 31st March, 2010

Particulars	Ratio	Total	Production Depts.			Service Depts.	
			X Rs.	Y Rs.	Z Rs.	A Rs.	B Rs.
Overhead Expenses as per Primary Distribution Summary	-	18,800	4,000	5,600	5,000	1,400	2,800
Service Dept. A'	2 : 4 : 3 : 1		280	560	420	- 1,400 NIL	140
Service Dept. B'	3 : 2 : 3 : 2		882	588	882	588	2,940 - 2,940 NIL
Service Dept. A'	2 : 4 : 3 : 1		118	235	176	588 -588 NIL	59
Service Dept. B'	3 : 2 : 3 : 2		18	11	18	12	59 -59 NIL
Service Dept. A'	2 : 4 : 3 : 1		2	6	4	12 -12 NIL	-
Total		**18,800**	**5,300**	**7,000**	**6,500**	**NIL**	**NIL**

Illustration 4

National Plastics Ltd. Nagpar has three production departments and two service departments. The overhead expenses for March, 2010 are as follows :

Particulars	Production Depts.			Service Depts.	
	A Rs.	B Rs.	C Rs.	D Rs.	E Rs.
Indirect Materials	800	2,000	900	400	200
Indirect Labour	1,500	1,600	1,300	350	1,900
Rent and Taxes					Rs. 10,000
Electricity Charges					Rs. 7,100
Plant Depreciation					Rs. 6,000
Supervisor's Salary					Rs. 3,200

The other details are as follows :

		A	B	C	D	E
Area occupied	Sq. Mtrs	800	1,000	900	700	600
Light Points	Numbers	15	35	8	7	6
Employee Numbers	Numbers	5	15	6	4	2
Capital value of Plant	Rs.	30,000	15,000	5,000	4,000	6,000
Working Hours	Hrs.	1,000	2,000	1,000	-	-

The expenses of Service Dept. D and E are to be charged as follows :

Particlars	A	B	C	D	E
Dept. D	20%	50%	20%	-	10%
Dept. E	10%	30%	40%	20%	-

You are required to find out the overhead rate per hour in production departments using Repeated Distribution Method.

Solution

In the Books of National Plastics Ltd., Nagpur
Statement Showing Primary Distribution of Overhead Expenses for the Months Ended 31st March, 2010

Particulars	Basis of Apportionment	Ratio	Total Rs.	Production Depts			Service Depts	
				A Rs.	B Rs.	C Rs.	X Rs.	Y Rs.
Indirect Materials	Actual	-	4,300	800	2,000	900	400	200
Indirect Labour	Actual	-	6,650	1,500	1,600	1,300	350	1,900
Rent and Taxes	Area occupied Sq.Mtrs.	8:10:9:7:6	10,000	2,000	2,500	2,250	1,750	1,500
Electricity charges	Light points	15:35:8:7:6	7,100	1,500	3,500	800	700	600
Plant Depreciation	Capital Value of Plant	30:15:5:4:6	6,000	3,000	1,500	500	400	600
Supervisor's Salary	Employee Numbers	5:15:6:4:2	3,200	500	1,500	600	400	200
Total			**37,250**	**9,300**	**12,600**	**6,350**	**4,000**	**5,000**

Statement Showing Distribution of Service Depts. Costs to Production Depts. as per Repeated Distribution Method for the Month Ended 31st March, 2010

Particulars	Ratio	Total Rs.	Production Depts. A Rs.	B Rs.	C Rs.	Service Depts. D Rs.	E Rs.
Overhead Expenses as per Primary Distribution Summary	-	37,250	9,300	12,600	6,350	4,000	5,000
Service Dept.D	2:5:2:1		800	2,000	800	(-)4,000	400
						NIL	5,400
Service Dept.E	1:3:4:2		540	1,620	2,160	1,080	(-)5,400
						1,080	NIL
Service Dept. D	2:5:2:1		216	540	216	(-)1,080	108
						NIL	108
Service Dept. E	1:3:4:2		11	32	43	22	(-)108
						22	NIL
Service Dept. D	2:5:2:1		5	12	5	-22	-
Total		**37,250**	**10,872**	**16,804**	**9,574**	**NIL**	**NIL**

Working Notes:

1) Calculation of Overhead rate per hour in Production Dept. taking working hours as a base :

$$= \frac{\text{Total Production Overheads}}{\text{Working Hours}}$$

A	B	C
$= \dfrac{\text{Rs.}10,872}{\text{Hrs.}1,000}$	$= \dfrac{\text{Rs.}16,804}{\text{Hrs.}2,000}$	$= \dfrac{\text{Rs.}9,574}{\text{Hrs.}1,000}$
$= \text{Rs.}10.87$	$= \text{Rs.}8.40$	$= \text{Rs.}9.57$

Simultaneous Equation Method

Illustration 1

A Ltd., Pune has have manufacturing Departments S_1, S_2 and S_3 and two service departments M_1 and M_2. The following are the total overhead expense as per primary distribution summary for the month ended 31st March, 2010

Manufacturing Depts :

S_1 = Rs. 2,000

S_2 = Rs. 1,800

S_3 = Rs. 1,600

Service Depts :

M_1 - Rs. 900, M_2 - Rs.400

The expenses of service depts. are charged on a percentage basis as follows.

Particulars	S_1	S_2	S_3	M_1	M_2
Service Dept. M_1	20%	30%	40%	-	10%
Service Dept. M_2	40%	20%	20%	20%	-

Prepare a statement showing apportionment of service departments by Simultaneous Equation Method.

Solution

Let x be the total overheads of Service Dept. M_1 and let y be the total overheads of Service Dept. M_2.

Then, x = Rs. 900 + 20% of y

$$\therefore \qquad x = \text{Rs. } 900 + \frac{y}{5}$$

$\therefore \qquad 5x = \text{Rs. } 4,500 + y$

$\therefore \qquad 5x\text{-}y = \text{Rs. } 4,500$

$\qquad\qquad y = \text{Rs. } 400 + 10\% \text{ of } x$

$$\therefore \qquad y = \text{Rs. } 400 + \frac{x}{10}$$

$\therefore \qquad 10y = \text{Rs. } 4,000 + x$

$\therefore \qquad 10y \text{ - } x = \text{Rs. } 4,000 \qquad\qquad (2)$

Multiplying Eq. No. 2 by 5, we get,

$\qquad 50y \text{ - } 5x = \text{Rs.} 20,000$

Now, the Equations are,

$\qquad 5x \text{ - } y = \text{Rs. } 4,500$

$\qquad \text{-}5x + 50y = \text{Rs. } 20,000$

$\qquad\qquad 49y = \text{Rs. } 24,500$

$$\therefore \qquad y = \frac{\text{Rs. } 24,500}{49}$$

$\therefore \qquad y = 500$

Substituting the value of y in Eq. No. 1, we get,

$\qquad 5x \text{ - Rs. } 500 = \text{Rs. } 4,500$

$\therefore \qquad 5x = \text{Rs. } 4,500 + \text{Rs. } 500$

$\therefore \qquad 5x = \text{Rs. } 5,000$

$$\therefore \qquad x = \frac{\text{Rs. } 5,000}{5}$$

$\therefore \qquad x = \text{Rs. } 1,000$

In the Books of A Ltd., Pune
Statement Showing Secondary Distribution of Service Depts. Overhead Expenses to Production Depts. by Simultaneous Equation Method for the Month Ended 31st March, 2010

Particulars	Total	Production Depts.		
	Rs.	S_1 Rs.	S_2 Rs.	S_3 Rs.
Overhead Expenses as per Primary Distribution Summary	5,400	2,000	1,800	1,600
Service Dept : M_1 90% of Rs. 1,000 : (2:3:4)	900	200	300	400
Service Dept. : M_2 80% of Rs. 500 : (4:2:2)	400	200	100	100
Total	6,700	2,400	2,200	2,100

Illustration 2

P Ltd., Patna has three Production Depts. viz. Assembly, Cutting and Mixing and two Service Depts. viz. Transport and Power. The following are the total overhead expenses as per departmental distribution summary for the month of March, 2010

A) **Production Depts :**

		Rs.
Assembly	-	2,000
Cutting	-	2,500
Mixing	-	3,000

B) **Service Depts.**

| Transport | - | 760 |
| Power | - | 700 |

The expenses of the Service Depts. are charged out on a percentage basis as follows :

Particulars	Assembly	Cutting	Mixing	Transport	Power
Service Dept. Transport	30%	30%	30%	-	10%
Service Dept. Power	20%	20%	30%	30%	-

Prepare a Statement showing the apportionment of Service department expenses to Production department by Simultaneous Equation Method.

Soltuion :

Let "x' be the total overheads of Service Dept. Transport and let y be the total overheads of Service Dept. Power.
Then,

$$x = Rs. 760 + 30\% \text{ of } y$$

$$\therefore \qquad x = Rs. 760 + \frac{3y}{10}$$

$$\therefore \qquad 10x = Rs. 7,600 + 3y$$

$$\therefore \qquad 10x - 3y = Rs. 7,600$$

$$y = Rs. 700 + 10\% \text{ of } y$$

$$y = Rs. 700 + \frac{x}{10}$$

$$10y = Rs. 7,000 + x$$

$$\therefore \qquad 10y - x = Rs. 7000$$

Multiplying Eq. No. 2 by 10 we get,

$$100y - 10x = Rs. 70,000$$

Now, the Equations are,

$$10x - 3y = Rs. 7,600$$

$$-10x + 100y = Rs. 70,000$$

$$97y = Rs. 77,600$$

$$\therefore \qquad y = \frac{Rs. 77,600}{97}$$

$$\therefore \qquad y = Rs. 800$$

Substituting the value of y in Eq. No. 1 we get,

10x - 3 × Rs. 800 = Rs. 7,600

∴ 10x - Rs. 2,400 = Rs. 7,600

∴   10x = Rs. 7,600 + Rs. 2,400

∴   10x = Rs. 10,000

∴ $x = \dfrac{Rs.10,000}{10}$

∴   x = Rs. 1,000

In the books of P Ltd. Patna
Statement showing Secondary Distribution of Service Depts. cost to Production Depts. by Simultaneous Equation Method for the Month Ended 31st March, 2010

Particulars	Total	Production Depts.		
	Rs.	Assembly Rs.	Cutting Rs.	Mixing Rs.
Overhead Expenses as per Departmental Distribution Summary	7,500	2,000	2,500	3,000
Service Dept. : Transport 90% of Rs. 1,000 : (3:3:3)	900	300	300	300
Service Dept. : Power 70% of Rs. 800 : (2:2:3)	560	160	160	240
Total	8,960	2,460	2,960	3,540

Illustration 3

You are supplied with the following information of Delux Ltd. Pune for the year ended 31st March 2010 from which work out the production hour rate of recovery of overheads in Depts. A, B & C.

| Particulars | Total | Production Depts. | | | Service Depts. | |
		A Rs.	B Rs.	C Rs.	D Rs.	E Rs.
Factory Rent	12,000	2,400	4,800	2,000	2,000	800
General Overheads	3,600	100	2,100	800	300	300
Indirect Materials	5,900	1,200	2,000	1,000	1,300	400
Machinery Depreciation	5,000	2,500	1,600	200	500	200
Electric Lighting	4,000	800	2,000	500	400	300
Total	**30,500**	**7,000**	**12,500**	**4,500**	**4,500**	**2,000**
Estimated Working Hours		17,500	3,000	1,125	-	-

Expenses of Service Depts. D and E are to apportioned as per Simultaneous Equation Method as under :

Particulars	A	B	C	D	E
Service Dept. D'	30%	40%	20%	-	10%
Service Dept. E'	10%	20%	50%	20%	-

Solution :

Let x be the total overheads of Service Dept. D and let y be the total overheads of service Dept. E

Then, $\quad$ x = Rs. 4,500 + 20% of y

∴ $\quad\quad$ x = Rs. $4,500 + \dfrac{y}{5}$

∴ $\quad\quad$ 5x = Rs. 22,500 + y

∴ $\quad\quad$ 5x - y = Rs. 22,500

$\quad\quad\quad$ y = Rs. 2,000 + 10% of x

∴ $\quad\quad$ y = Rs. $2,000 + \dfrac{x}{10}$

∴ $\quad\quad$ 10y = Rs. 20,000 + x

∴ $\quad\quad$ 10y - x = Rs. 20,000

Multiplying Eq. No. 2 by 5, we get,

$$50y - 5x = Rs. 1,00,000$$

Now, the Equation are,

$$5x - y = Rs. 22,500$$
$$-5x + 50y = Rs. 1,00,000$$
$$49y = Rs. 1,22,500$$

$$\therefore \quad y = \frac{Rs. 1,22,500}{49}$$

$$\therefore \quad y = Rs. 2,500$$

Substituting the value of y in Eq. No. 1 we get,

$$5x - Rs. 2,500 = Rs. 22,500$$
$$\therefore \quad 5x = Rs. 22,500 + Rs. 2,500$$
$$\therefore \quad 5x = Rs. 25,000$$

$$\therefore \quad x = \frac{Rs. 25,000}{5}$$

$$\therefore \quad x = Rs. 5,000$$

In the books of Delux Ltd. Pune Statement showing Secondary Distribution of Service Depts. Cost to Production Depts. as per Simultaneous Equation Method for the month ended 31st March, 2010

Particulars	Total	Production Depts.		
		A	B	C
	Rs.	Rs.	Rs.	Rs.
Overhead Expenses as per Primary Distribution Summary	24,000	7,000	12,500	4,500
Service Dept : D 90% of Rs. 5,000 : (3:4:2)	4,500	1,500	2,000	1,000
Service Depts. : E 80% of Rs. 2,500 : (1:2:5)	2,000	250	500	1,250
Total	30,500	8,750	15,000	6,750

Working Notes :

1) Calculation of Production hour rate of recovery of overheads taking estimated working hours as a base :

$$= \frac{\text{Total Production Overheads}}{\text{Estimated Working Hours}}$$

A	B	C
$= \dfrac{\text{Rs. } 8,750}{\text{Hrs. } 1,750}$	$= \dfrac{\text{Rs. } 15,000}{\text{Hrs. } 3,000}$	$= \dfrac{\text{Rs. } 6,750}{\text{Hrs. } 1,125}$
= Rs. 5.	= Rs. 5	= Rs. 6

Illustration 4

Pranav Co. Ltd., Pune has three Production Depts. viz. A, B and C and two Service Depts. viz. P and Q. The following figures are extracted from their books for the month ended 31st March, 2010.

Indirect Expenses :   **Rs.**

Production Depts.

A	100
B	600
C	300

Service Depts.

P	700
Q	300
Electric Lighting	2,000
Power	3,000
Plant Depreciation	9,000
Rent and Taxes	5,500

The other details are as follows :

Particulars	A	B	C	P	Q
Light Points	14	10	4	8	4
Electricity K.W.H.	50	30	20	30	20
Value of Plant Rs.	70,000	30,000	10,000	30,000	10,000
Floor Space Sq. ft.	4,000	3,000	1,000	2,000	1,000
Working Hours	2,500	2,250	2,375	-	-

The expenses of Service Department P and Q are to be allocatedd as follows :

Particulars	A	B	C	P	Q
Service Dept. P	30%	20%	40%	-	10%
Service Dept. Q	20%	30%	30%	20%	-

You are required to distribute the Service Depts. expenses to Production Dept. under Simultaneous Equation Method. Also calculate hourly rate of each Production Dept...

Solution

In the Books of Pranav Co. Ltd. Pune
Statement showing Primary Distribution of Overhead Expenses
for the Month Ended 31st March, 2010

Particulars	Basis of Apportionment	Ratio	Total Rs.	Production Departments			Service Depts.	
				A Rs.	B Rs.	C Rs.	P Rs.	Q Rs.
Indirect Expenses	Actual	-	2,000	100	600	300	700	300
Electric Lighting	Light Points	7:5:2:4:2	2,000	700	500	200	400	200
Power	Electricity K.W.H.	5:3:2:3:2	3,000	1,000	600	400	600	400
Plant Depreciation	Value of Plant	7:3:1:3:1	9,000	4,200	1,800	600	1,800	600
Rent and Taxes	Floor space Sq. ft.	4:3:1:2:1	5,500	2,000	1,500	500	1,000	500
Total			**21,500**	**8,000**	**5,000**	**2,000**	**4,500**	**2,000**

Let x' be the total overheads of Service Dept. P and Let y' be the total overheads of Service Dept. Q.

Then,

$$x = \text{Rs. } 4,500 + 20\% \text{ of } y$$

$$\therefore \quad x = \text{Rs. } 4,500 + \frac{y}{5}$$

$$\therefore \quad 5x = \text{Rs. } 22,500 + y$$

$$\therefore \quad 5x - y = \text{Rs. } 22,500 \qquad (1)$$

$$y = \text{Rs. } 2,000 + 10\% \text{ of } x$$

$$\therefore \quad y = \text{Rs. } 2,000 + \frac{x}{10}$$

$$\therefore \quad 10y = \text{Rs. } 20,000 + x \qquad (2)$$

$$\therefore \quad 10y - x = \text{Rs. } 20,000$$

Multiplying Eq. No. 2 by 5, we get,

$$50y - 5x = \text{Rs. } 1,00,000$$

Now, the Equations are,

$$5x - y = \text{Rs. } 22,500$$

$$-5x + 50y = \text{Rs. } 1,00,000$$

$$49y = \text{Rs. } 1,22,500$$

$$\therefore \quad y = \frac{\text{Rs. } 1,22,500}{49}$$

$$y = \text{Rs. } 2,500$$

Substituting the value of y in Eq. No. 1 we get,

$$5x - \text{Rs. } 2,500 = \text{Rs. } 22,500$$

$$\therefore \quad 5x = \text{Rs. } 22,500 + \text{Rs. } 2,500$$

$$\therefore \quad 5x = \text{Rs. } 25,000$$

$$\therefore \quad x = \frac{\text{Rs. } 25,000}{5}$$

$$\therefore \quad x = \text{Rs. } 5,000$$

In the Books of Pranav Co. Ltd., Pune.
Statement Showing Secondary Distribution of Service Depts.
Overhead Expenses to Production Depts. by Simultaneous
Equation Method for the Month Ended 31ˢᵗ March, 2010

Particulars	Total	Production Depts.		
	Rs.	A Rs.	B Rs.	C Rs.
Overhead Expenses as per Primary Distribution Summary	15,000	8,000	5,000	2,000
Service Dept : P' 90% of Rs. 5,000 : (3 : 2 : 4)	4,500	1,500	1,000	2,000
Service Dept : "Q' 80% of Rs. 2,500 : (2 : 3 : 3)	2,000	500	750	750
Total	**21,500**	**10,000**	**6,750**	**4,750**

Working Notes :

1) Calculation of hourly rate of Production Department -

$$= \frac{\text{Total Production Overheads}}{\text{Working Hours}}$$

A	B	C
$= \dfrac{\text{Rs. }10,000}{\text{Hrs. }2,500}$	$= \dfrac{\text{Rs. }6,750}{\text{Hrs. }2,250}$	$= \dfrac{\text{Rs. }4,750}{\text{Hrs. }2,375}$
= Rs. 4	= Rs. 3	= Rs. 2

Illustration : 5

From the following information, reapportion the service department's cost using repeated distribution method.

Production Departments				Service Departments	
	A	B	C	X	Y
As per Primary Distribution	8,000	6,000	10,000	800	500
Additional Information for Re-apportionment					
Dept. X	40%	20%	20%	-	20%
Dept. Y	30%	30%	30%	10%	-

Solution

Statement Showing the secondary distribution of Overheads - Repeated Distribution Method

Particulars	Production Depts.			Service Depts.	
	A (Rs.)	B (Rs.)	C (Rs.)	X (Rs.)	Y (Rs.)
Total Overheads	8,000	6,000	10,000	800	500
X overheads apportioned	+320	+ 160	+ 160	- 800	+ 160
40 % of 800	8,320	6,160	10,160	--	660
Y overheads apportioned	+ 198	+ 198	+ 198	+ 66	- 660
30% of 660	8,518	6,358	10,358	66	
X overheads apportioned	+ 27	+ 13	+ 13	- 66	+ 13
40 % of 66 =	8,545	6,371	10,371	--	+ 13
Y overheads apportioned	+ 5	+ 4	+ 4	--	- 13
Total	8,550	6,375	10,375	NIL	NIL

Illustration : 6

Overhead costs before distribution of costs of service departments are a follows.

Production Departments   A : 30,000
                                  B : 28,000
Service Departments   P : 35,000
                                  Q : 32,000

Service departments overheads to be allocated to the production departments are as follows.

	Production Departments		Service Departments	
	A	B	P	Q
Service departments				
P	55%	30%	-	15%
Q	25%	35%	40%	-

Compute the total overheads of production departments

Solution :

Statement showing secondary distribution of overheads Repeated Distribution (Rs.)

	Production Depts.		Service Depts	
	A	B	P	Q
Total over heads	30,000	28,000	35,000	32,000
P overheads (55 : 30 : 15)	+ 19,250	+ 10,500	(-) 35,000	+ 5, 250
	49,250	38,500	-	37,250
Q overheads (25 : 35 : 40)	+ 9,313	+ 13,037	+ 14,900	(-) 37,250
	58,563	51,537	14,900	-
P overheads	+ 8,195	+ 4,470	(-) 14,900	+ 2,235
	66,758	56,007	-	2,235
Q overheads	+ 558	+ 783	+ 894	(-) 2,235
	67,316	56,790	+ 894	-

	Production Depts.		Service Depts	
	A	**B**	**P**	**Q**
P overheads	+ 492	+ 268	(-) 894	- 134
Q overheads	+ 34	+ 47	+ 53	(-) 134
	67,842	57,105	-+ 53	+ -
P overheads	+ 29	+ 16	(-) 53	+ 8
	67,871	57,121	-	8
Q overheads	+ 4	+ 4	-	(-) 8
	67,875	57,125	-	-

Simultaneous Equation Method :

Let X, be the expenses of Service Dept. P

Let Y, be the expenses of Service Dept. Q

Then $\qquad X = 35,000 + \dfrac{2}{5}\ y$

(Since 40% of Q will be apportioned to P)

$$Y = 32,000 + \frac{3}{20}\ x$$

$$= 32,000 + \frac{3}{20}\left(35,000 + \frac{2}{5}y\right)$$

Substituting the Value of X

$$= 32,000 + 5,250\ \frac{6}{100} + y$$
$$= 37,250\ \frac{6}{100} + y$$
$$100y = 37,25,000 + 6y$$
$$100y - 6y = 37,25,000$$
$$94\ y = 37,25,000$$

$$y = \frac{37,25,000}{94} = 39,628$$
$$X = 35,000 + \frac{2}{5} \times 39,628$$
$$= 35,000 + 15,851$$
$$= 50,851$$

Statement showing secondary distribution of overheads

	Production Depts.		Service Depts	
	A	B	P	Q
Total overheads	30,000	28,000	35,000	32,000
Overheads of P				
(55 : 30 : 15)	+ 27,968	+ 15,255	(-) 50,851	+ 7,628
	57,968	43,255	- 15, 851	39,628
Overheads of Q				
(25 : 35 : 40)	9,907	+13,870	+ 15,851	(-) 39,628
	67,875	57,125	-	-

Illustration 7

A company has three production departments (P_1, P_2 and P_3) and two service departments (S_1 and S_2) and for a period the departmental distribution summary has the following towards P_1 Rs. 8000, P_2 Rs. 7000 : P_3 Rs. 5000, S_1 Rs. 2340, S_2 Rs. 3000. The expenses of S_1 and S_2 are allocated as follows.

Particulars	P_1	P_2	P_3	S_1	S_2
S_1	20%	40%	30%	-	10%
S_2	40%	20%	20%	20%	

Apportion the service departments expenses to production departments by simultaneous equation method.

Answer :

Simultaneous equation method.

Let x, the expenses of service dept. S_1

Let y, the expenses of service dept. S_2

Then $\qquad X = 2340 + \dfrac{1}{5}y$

(Since 20% of y will be apportioned to S_1)

$$y = 3000 + \dfrac{1}{10}x$$

$$= 3000 \; \frac{1}{10}\left(2340 + \frac{1y}{5}\right)$$

$$= 3000 + 234 + \frac{1y}{50}$$

$$= 3234 + \frac{1y}{50}$$

$$50y = 1,61,700 + y$$
$$49y = 1,61,700$$

$$y = \frac{161700}{49} = 3300 \text{ i.e. } S_2$$

$$x = 2340 + \frac{1}{5} \times 3300$$

$$= 2340 + 660 = \text{Rs. } 3000 \text{ i.e. } S_1.$$

Apportionment :

Particulars	Basis of Apportionment	P_1	P_2	P_3	S_1	S_2
Summary	Rs. 25,340	8000	7000	5000	2340	3000
S_1	3000 × 20%=	600	1200	900	(-) 3000	300
S_2	3300 × 40%=	1320	660	660	660	(-)3300
Total	Rs. 25,340	9920	8860	6560	-	-

2.8 Exercises

(a) State whether the following statements are True or False.

(1) Fixed overhead cost per unit remains fixed when output level changes.

(2) Reapportion of service departments cost is known as secondary distribution.

(3) Overheads are also known as indirect expenses.

(4) The time factor is ignored when the cost of material is used as the basis of apportionment of overhead.

(5) Basis of apportionment of depreciation of plant is the value of plants in each department.

Ans : (1) False, (2) True, (3) False, (4) True, (5) True

Theoritical questions.

(1) Define Overhead. Explain various classification of overheads.

(2) Explain with illustration the classification of fixed, semi fixed and variable items.

(3) Describe steps required in Accounting overheads.

(4) Discuss the secondary distribution of overheads.

(5) What do you understand by classification allocation and apportionment in relation to overhead expenses.

(6) Distinguish between allocation, apportment and absroption of overheads.

(7) Define cost allocation and cost apportionment. Explain fully the distinction between cost allocation and cost apportionment.

Practical problems :

1) Following cost information is available

Particulars		Production Department			Service Departments		
		A	B	C	Office	Stores	Work Shop
Direct Wages	Rs.	20,000	25,000	30,000	-	-	-
Direct Material	Rs.	30,000	35,000	45,000	-	-	-
Indirect Material	Rs.	2,000	3,000	3,000	1,000	2,000	2,000
Indirect Wages	Rs.	3,000	3,000	4,000	10,000	10,000	5,000
Area in Sq mtrs		200	250	300	150	100	250
Book value of Machinery	Rs.	30,000	25,000	25,000	-	-	15,000
Total H.P of Machine		15	20	25	-	-	5
Machine Hrs. Worked		10,000	20,000	15,000	-	-	5,000

Other items are as follows:

General Expenses	Rs.12,500
Rent	Rs.1,050
Depreciation	15% of value of Machine
Power	Rs. 3,800
Light	Rs.1,250

You are requested to prepare an overhead analysis sheet for the departments showing the apportionment of total cost of service departments to production departments on appropriate basis.

2) Surabhi Ltd, Surat is divided into two production departments A and B and two service departments X and Y The following is the summary of overhead costs for a particular period.

	Rs.
Works Manager's Salary	4,000
Power	21,000
Contribution to P.F	9,000
Plant Maintenance	4,000
Depreciation on Plant and Machinery	20,000
Rent paid	6,000
Canteen Expenses	12,000

Following information is also available from the various departments.

Particulars	A	B	X	Y
No. of employees	16	8	4	4
Area in Sq. meters	2,000	3,000	500	500
Value of plant (Rs.)	75,000	1,00,000	25,000	
Wages paid (Rs.)	40,000	20,000	10,000	5,000
H.P. Ratio	3	3	1	-

Apportion the cost to the various departments on the most suitable basis.

3) In Modern Enterprises, Mumbai there are three production department A, B, C and one service departments.

The Following figures are available for one month of 25 working days of 8 hours. each day All departments work all these days with full attendance.

Particulars		Service Depts.	Production Depts.		
		S	A	B	C
Power and Lighting	Rs.	240	200	300	360
Supervisor's Salary	Rs. 2,000	-	-	-	-
Rent	Rs.500	-	-	-	-
Welfare Expenses	Rs. 600	-	-	-	-
Other Expenses	Rs.	200	200	400	400
Supervisor"s Salary %		20%	30%	30%	20%
Number of workers	Numbers	10	30	40	20
Floor area in Sq mtrs	Sq. mtrs	500	600	800	600
Service rendered by Service Dept. to Production Dept.	%	-	50%	30%	20%

Claculate labour hour rate of the dept, A, B and C

4) **Nashik Enterprises Ltd, Nashik has three Production departments A, B, C and two Service departments D and E.**
The following figures are extracted from their racords.

	Rs.
Rent and Rates	5,000
General Lighting	600
Indirect Wages	1,500
Power	1,500
Depreciation of Machinery	10,000
Sundries	10,000

The Following Further details are available.

Particulars	Total	A	B	C	D	E
Floor Space (sq.ft)	10,000	2,000	2,500	3,000	2,000	500
Light Points	60	10	15	20	10	5
Direct Wages (Rs.)	10,000	3,000	2,000	3,000	15,00	500
H.P.of Machines	150	60	30	50	10	
Value of Machinery	2,50,000	60,000	80,000	1,00,000	5,000	5,000
Working Hours	-	6,226	4,028	4,066		

The expenses of D and E are allocated as follows:

Particulars	A	B	C	D	E
Dept D	20%	30%	40%		10%
Dept E	40%	20%	30%	10%	

Calculate the Labour Hour Rate for each of these departments. Sundry expenses are to be allocated on the basis of direct wages. What is the total cost of article if material cost is Rs. 30 and it passes through Dept. A, B and C for 4, 5 and 3 hours respectively.

5. **The primary distribution of expenses disclosed the following details in respect of production departments P_1, P_2 and P_3 and Service department S_1 and S_2.**

Departments	P_1	P_2	P_3	S_1	S_2
Overheads Rs.	6,300	7,400	2,800	4,500	2,000

The services given by S_1 and S_2 are as below :

Departments	P_1	P_2	P_3	S_1	S_2
S_1	40%	30%	20%	-	10%
S_2	30%	30%	20%	20%	-

Find out the overheads chargeable to Production departments by using Simultaneous equations method.

6. **Baramati Ltd., Baramati there are two Service departments P and Q and three Production departments A, B and C. In April 2006, the departmental expenses were :**

Departmens	A	B	C	P	Q
Rs.	75,000	60,000	50,000	12,000	10,000

The service department expenses are allotted on a percentage basis as follows :

Service	Production Depts.			Service Depts.	
Depts.	A	B	C	P	Q
P %	30	40	15	-	15
Q %	40	30	25	5	-

Prepare a Statment showing the distribution of the two Service Depts. expenses to the three depts. by
(a) Simultaneous Equation Method,
(b) Repeated Distribution Method.

7. **Work out overhead recovery rate under Repeated Distribution Method and Simultaneous Equation Method.**
Primary Overheads are as follows.

Productions Depts.		Service Depts.	
	Rs.		Rs.
A -	7,810	Transport P -	4,000
B -	12,540	Power Q -	2,700
C -	4,550		
D -	3,000		

Expenses of Service Depts. are apportioned as under -

	A	B	C	D	P	Q
P	10%	30%	20%	20%	-	20%
Q	30%	20%	30%	10%	10%	-

Estimated Labour Hours are : A - 900, B - 2,700, C - 1,500.

Chapter 3

Accounting of Overheads

3.1 Overhead Absorption - Meaning

After apportionment and re-apportionment of overheads to production departments, these can now be charged to cost units. In essence, the proceduse is to take each production department and distribute its overheads among all cost units passing through that particular department. This is technically known as "absorption' and is defined as charging of overheads to cost units.

We have seen in the earlier units, the methods of allocation and apportionment of overhead costs to cost centres. The next step in accounting of overheads is absorption of overheads in the cost of production i.e. recovery of overhead in the cost of production. All jobs, processes or services pass through one or more producing cost centre. The overhead expenses are ultimately charged to cost centre in such a manner that the cost of production of each unit includes an appropriate or equitable share of overhead of the cost centre. This method of apportionment of overhead expenses of the cost centres to cost units is called absorption of overheads. This is also known as application, levy or recovery of overheads.

The distinction between Apportionment of Overheads and Absorption of Overheads can be shown as follows :

Apportionment of Overheads	Absorption of Overheads
1. Apportionment may be defined as "allotment of proportions of items of cost to cost centre or cost units". In other words, 'distribution of common costs to different department on some suitable bases is called apportionment of overheads'.	1. After apportionment and re-apportionment of overheads to production departments, these can be charged to cost units. In essence the procedure is to take each production department and distribute its overheads among all cost units passing through that particular department. This is technically known as "absorption' and is defined as charging of overheads to cost units.
2. Apportionment of overheads is the second step in the distribution of overheads.	2. The abosorption of overheads is the last step in the distribution process of overheads.
3. Apportionment is the process to allot costs to the cost centre or cost units for ascertaining the total cost.	3. Overhead absorption is the charging of overheads to the cost units.
4. There are some common bases for apportionment of overheads cost on some equitable basis which is known as primary distribution method.	4. Absorption of overheads is known as levy, recovery or application of overheads.

3.2 Methods of Overhead Absorption

Following are the various methods of absorption adpted :
(1) Direct Labour Hour Rate
(2) Machine Hour Rate
(3) Combined Machine Hour Rate and Labour Hour Rate.
(4) Percentage of Direct Material Cost
(5) Percentage of Direct Labour Cost
(6) Percentage of Prime Cost Method

(1) Direct Labour Houre Rate :

This is also refered to as production hour rate method. This method is adopted in those factories where labour is prominent. Labour hour rate is calculated for each category of workers. The expenses incurred other than wages paid to workers on each category of works are listed and totalled for as certain period. The amount is divided by the number of hours put in by all the direct workers during the period to get the rate. Following formula may be used to decide the rate :

$$\text{Direct Labour Hour Rate} + \frac{\text{Factory Overheads}}{\text{Direct Labour hours during period}}$$

Effective working hours can be calculated by the following formula :

$$\begin{matrix} \text{Effective} \\ \text{working} \\ \text{hours} \end{matrix} = \begin{matrix} \text{Average no. of workers} \\ \text{employed during} \\ \text{a given period} \end{matrix} \times \begin{matrix} \text{No. of hours for which} \\ \text{the factory works} \\ \text{during each day} \end{matrix}$$

Advantages :

(1) The rate takes into account the time factor.
(2) It is suitable when most of the work is done by labour.
(3) It is not affected by the method of wage payment or the grade or rate of pay of the workers.

Disadvantages :

(1) It does not take into account factors of production other than labour. This may lead to faulty distribution of overheads to products.
(2) Many concerns do not maintain any record of time taken on job

when payment is not related to the time taken for production. Hence, more clerical work is involved in determination of rate.

(2) Machine Hour Rate :

This method of absorption is followed where work is performed predominantly on machines. The hourly machine rate is calculated departmentwise. A single machine rate is unsuitable because different types of machines may be used in various producing departments. In a department more than one rate may be computed. A separate rate is calculated for each machine. Each machine or a group of machines constitutes a cost centre for the purpose of absorption of overheads expenses. The machine hour rate is to be decided.

There are two ways of calculating the machine hour rate. As per first method, only indirect expenses directily or immediately connected with the operation of the machine are taken into account. e.g. power, depreciation, repairs, maintenance, insurance etc. The rate is calculated by dividing the total of these expenses by the number of operating hours of the machines during a stipulated period.

In addition to the above expenses, there may be still other manufacturing expenses such as supervision charges, Shop Cleaning and Lighting, Consumable Stores and lighting. Consumable stores and shop supplies, shop general labour, rent and rates etc. incurred for the department as a whole and hence not charged to any machine. In order to include such expenses of machine, the proportionate amount of such expenses applicable to the machine should be condidered to decide machine hour rate. Some people think that wages paid to the machine operator also should be considered while deciding the rate.

On the basis of the above discussion, it can be concluded that recovery of direct machine expenses without the proportion of the departmental expenses is likely to be more accurate than when these are made a part thereof because general departmental expenses are not connected with the actual operation of the machines.

Computation of Machine Hour Rate :

(a) Each machine or a group of machines is treated as a cost centre in order to identify the overhead expenses.

(b) Machine overhead expenses are of two types viz. standing charges (fixed) and machine expenses (variable or running)

Standing Charges or Fixed Expenses :

These expenses remain constant. They do not vary with the use of machines. These expenses include rent, rates, supervision etc. The standing charges are estimated for a given period for every machine. The estimated expenses divided by total working hours of the period will give an hourly rate for the standing charges.

Machine Expenses or Variable Expenses :

These are variable expenses which vary with the use of machines. These expenses include power, depreciation, repairs etc. The amount of machine expenses is divided by normal working hours to give hourly rate for each item. Normal working hours are calculated by taking into account idle time for maintenance, setting up etc.

(c) The sum of the standing rate and the machine expenses rate will give machine hour rate.

Bases for Apportionment of Expenses :

The standing charges are apportioned to each machine on a suitable basis. Following chart gives the basis of apportionment of expenses :

Items of Expenses	Basis of Apportionment
1. Depreciation on the machine	Life of the asset or number of machine hours.
2. Rent and rates	Area occupied by the machine
3. Lighting	No. of light points in the above mentioned area.
4. Repairs and Maintenance	Area occupied by the machine
5. Power	Actual allocation to the particular machine i.e. Horse power multiplied by Machine Hours
6. Insurance Premium	Machine value
7. Supervisory Labour	Time of Supervision
8. Miscellaneous Expenses	Actual or on any other reasonable basis
9. Operator Wages	Actual allocation

Hints for Calculation of Machine Hour Rate :

(1) Machine Hour Rate is an actual or pre-determined rate of cost apportionment or overheads absorption, which is calculated by dividing the cost to be apportioned or absorbed by the number of hours for which a machine or machines are operated or expected to be operated as per the ICMA definition. Machine Hour Rate is used where the cost centre is machine intensive and the work is performed predominantly on machines.

(2) A single machine hour rate may not be sufficient and in such cases, different machine hour rates may be worked out depending on the make, type, size or capacity, wattage, horsepower, value function and other technical factors. Each group of machines constitute a cost centre for the purpose of overhead absorption. The overhead expense of each machine are ascertained as above and machine hour rate is worked out on the basis of actual running hours of machine. Every job product using such machine will be debited by the machine hours rate multiplied by the number of machine hours taken by the such job or product. If the predetermined machine hours rate is required, it can be computed by dividing the estimted number of machine hours. Machine hour rates may be worked out separately for fixed and variable expense. Idle time also is taken into account for arriving at effective running hours.

(3) A rate may be worked out with or without operator. Similarly, it can be computed with or without set up time. Otherwise a separate rate also can be worked out for set-up time of machine. Combining these two or three above rates, we get a comprehensive machine hour rate.

Advantages :

(1) It is suitable where one operator uses several machines.

(2) Under absorption of overheads indicates that the machines were idle.

(3) It is the most appropriate method when machine is the main factor of production.

(4) It is a scientific and logical method as it takes into account time factor.

(5) Relative efficiencies of machines can be compared.

(6) The management can understand the difference between usefulness of machine work and manual work.

Disadvantages :

(1) It leads to more clerical work in finding out the working hours of machines.

(2) Expenses which are not proportional to the working hours of machines are not taken into account.

The distinction between Machine Hour Rate and Labour Hour Rate can be shown as follows.

Machine Hour Rate	Labour Hour Rate
1. In this method, the overheads charged to the production on the basis of number of hours for which the machines are used for a particular job. Machine hour rate means the cost or expenses incurred for running a machine for one hour.	1. This method is the oldest and most popular one. The percentage is arrived at by dividing the overhead costs by the amount of direct labour.
2. It gives due consideration to the time factor and thus produces more equitable results.	2. It gives full consideration to time factor.
3. From costing point of view, this is an accurate method of absorption of overheads. This is an ideal method where production is carried out on machine.	3. This method gives very satisfactory results in majority of cases except where machinery represents the predominating factor of production.
4. When separate rates are calculated for fixed and variable overheads, the cost of idle machines can be measured without difficulty.	4. This is not affected by the method of wage payment i.e. time rate or piece rate system.
5. This method is not universally applicable and can be used only for those cost centres where machine work is predominant.	5. This method necessitates the recording and analysing of time spent on each job by each worker and thus involves additional clerical labour. It does not take into account factors other than labour.

(3)Combined Machine Hour Rate and Labour Hour Rate :

This method can be used in the departments in which both machine work and manual work is involved. It is used for the purpose of absorbing works expenses. The expenses which are inseparable from the running of the machine are allocated on the basis of Machine Hour Rate and other expenses which are not directly related to the machines are allocated on the basis of the labour hour rate.

(4) Percentage on Direct Material Cost :

Under this method, the cost of material consumed in production is considered as a basis of absorption of overheads. The rate is determined by dividing the total overheads by cost of direct materials. Following formula may be used for the purpose :

$$\text{Rate} = \frac{\text{Factory Overheads}}{\text{Direct Material Cost}} \times 100$$

Advantages :

(1) It is suitable when material prices are stable.
(2) It is an equitable method of absorption of overheads.
(3) Calculation of the rate is simple as no additional records are required to be maintained.

Disadvantages :

(1) It ignores time factor.
(2) It is illogical and inaccurate as the incidence of overheads is not related to the cost of materials.
(3) Material prices are subject to constant fluctuations and hence, it may lead to high or low charges in respect of overheads.

(5) Precentage of Direct Labour Cost :

Under this method, overheads are recovered on the basis of pre-determined or actual rate. The formula for computation of the percentage is as follows :

$$\text{Rate} = \frac{\text{Factory Overheads}}{\text{Direct Labour Cost}} \times 100$$

This method is suitable where production is uniform and all the workers employed earn more or less the same hourly rate and labour is predominant.

Advantages :

(1) It is simple and less costly.

(2) Labour rates do not fluctuate much.

(3) The time factor is given fair consideration.

Disadvantages :

(1) It does not provide for varying skills of workers.

(2) When machinery is used to some extent in the process of manufactureing, no allowance is made for this.

(3) It gives rise to certain inaccuracies as time factor is not given adequate importance.

(6) Percentage of Prime Cost :

This is also a simple method of absorption of overheads. This method can be used where a standard product requiring a constant quantity of materials and a number of labour hours is produced. The rate is calculated by the following formula :

$$\text{Rate} = \frac{\text{Factory Overheads}}{\text{Prime Cost}} \times 100$$

This method does not take into account the time factor. The results of this method are liable to be more misleading because of the cumulative error of using of using both the material cost and labour cost.

Selection of Absorption Method :

Now the question arises as to which basis of absorption is an appropriate one out of six methods mentioned above. The direct labour hour method is usually the best method because most of the factory overheads are period costs as they relate to time and not to production If all the workers in a department / cost centre are paid with the same rate of wages, direct labour hour method is to be followed. If they are paid with different rates, direct wages percentage rate is to be adopted. Similarly, the circumstances under which each method is followed are indicated below :

Circumstances	Method to be used
1. If the cost centre is labour-intensive and workers are paid with the same rate of wages.	Direct labour hour method
2. If the cost centre is labour-intensive and workers are paid with different rates of wages.	Direct wages percentage rate
3. If the cost centre is machine intensive.	Machine hour rate
4. If the materials cost is predominant.	Direct materials cost percentage rate
5. If the prime cost is predominant.	Prime cost percentage rate.
6. If only a single product is in a cost centre.	Total number of units of output.

Further, the choice depends on the type of industry, nature of products, process of manufacture, nature of overheads expenses, organisational set-up and policy of management etc.

Essentials of a Good Absorption Rate :

Charging of overheads of cost centre to different cost units, products, jobs or processes is called as absorption of overheads. There are various methods of absorption of overheads. Each method has its own merits and limitations. While selecting an appropriate method, following points should be considered :

(1) It should be according to the nature of the product.

(2) The rate should be stable.

(3) It should be less costly.

(4) It should not increase clerical work.

(5) It should be according to the nature of the product.

(6) It should not differentiate much between absorbed overheads and actual overheads.

(7) It should be realted to time factor as far as possible.

(8) Departmental rates are better than blanket rates.

3.3 Overhead Rates

Overhead absorption rates are determined for the purpose of absorption of overheads in costs of job, process or products. There are several methods of determination of overheads absorption rates. These methods will be discussed in this chapter at a later stage. The basic procedure followed in these methods is to divide the amount of overheads by total number of units of the base selected. The base may be units of products, direct labour cost, labour hours, machine hours or direct material cost. The rate so determined is multiplied by the units of the base in each individual product or job to decide cost of each unit. The rate is given by the following formula :

$$\text{Rate} = \frac{\text{Amount of Overheads}}{\text{Quantity or value of base}}$$

Amount of overheads
absorbed in a product   = Units of the base x Overhead rate

Objectives :

The basic objectives of fixation of overhead rates are as follows :
(1) To facilitate absorption of overhead to cost units on a logical basis.
(2) To estimate overheads cost in advance of production.
(3) To even out the fluctuations in the overhead rates.
(4) To facilitate quick computation of cost on completion of production.
(5) To help in prompt calculation of cost of work in progress.

Types of Overhead Rates :

The main types of Overhead Rates are shown below :

(1) Actual rate :

This rate is determined by dividing actual overheads incurred during the accounting period by actual quantity or value of the base selected. The rate is calculated as follows :

$$\text{Actual Rate} = \frac{\text{Actual overheads expenses incurred during a certain period.}}{\text{Actual quantity or value of the base related to production during a certain period}}$$

As far as possible, recovery of overheads should be done on actual basis. However, in practice it is not possible due to the following reasons :

(1) Actual rate can be determined only after the accounting period is over. This may delay determination of cost.

(2) The incidence of some of the overhead expenses is not uniformly spread over all the accounting periods. Similarly, actual volume of activity of is affected by seasonal and cyclic factors.

(3) Actual rates do not provide any basis for cost control.

(2) Pre-determined Rate :

This rate is determined on the basis of budgeted overheads and the budgeted base for the period. It is calculated as follows :

$$\text{Pre-determined Rate} = \frac{\text{Budgeted overheads for the period}}{\text{Budgeted base for the period}}$$

Pre-determined rate facilitates computation of cost in advance. Quotations can be given in advance. This helps preparation of bills promptly. No extra clerical work is involved in determination of overhead rate in an organisation where budgetary control system is adopted.

(3) Blanket Rate :

This is the single or general overhead rate applicable to the whole factory. This is calculated as follows :

$$\text{Blanket Rate} = \frac{\text{Overhead cost for the entire factory}}{\text{Total quantum of the base selected}}$$

Blanket rate is suitable in those factories where only one major product is manufactured in a continuous process. It is also suitable where the work performed by every department is fairly uniform.

(4) Multiple Rate :

These are the rates for different departments in the factory. A separate rate is determined for each department. The rate is decided as follows :

$$\text{Overhead Rate} = \frac{\text{Overhead costs allocated and apportioned to each departments cost centre or product}}{\text{Corresponding base}}$$

Multiple rates are determined where the product lines are varied, or machinery is used to a verying degree in different departments i.e. the conditions in the factory are not uniform. The incidence of overhead cost of each department is different. Under such a circumstance, department rates are suitable.

Illustrations on Labour Rate Method

Illustration 1

Calculate direct labour-hour rate from the following :

Total number of workers	100
working days in a year	300
No. of hours worked per day.	8
Short and idle time	5%
Factory overheads	Rs. 11,400
Gift to workers	Rs. 1,000

Solution

Working Notes :

Total Labour Hours = 100 x 300 x 8	2,40,000
Less : Short & Idletime = 5%	12,000
Direct Labour Hours (DLH)	2,28,000

$$\text{Direct labour hour rate} = \frac{\text{Factory overheads}}{\text{DLH}}$$

$$= \frac{11,400}{2,28,000} = \text{Re. } 0.05$$

i.e. 5 paise per DLH

Note : Gift to workers Rs. 1,000, not considered as factory overheads. Gift might have been given as an administrative decision. Hence it may be treated as Admn. overheads.

Illustration 2

X Co. Ltd., has three manufacturing departments A, B and C and one service department S. The following particulars for one month of 25 working days for 8 hours each day. All Departments work all day with full attendance :

Expenses	Total	Service Department	Production Department		
		S	A	B	C
	Rs.	Rs.	Rs.	Rs.	Rs.
Power and lighting	1,100	240	200	300	360
Supervisor's salary	2,000				
Rent	500				
Overheads					
Welfare expenses	600				
Other	1,200	200	200	400	400
Supervisor's Salary		20%	30%	30%	20%
Floor area in sq.ft		10	30	40	20
Number of workers		500	600	800	600
Service rendered by					
Service Department to					
Production Department to					
			50%	30%	20%

Claculate the "Labour hour rate' for each of the Departments A, B and C

Answer :

Calculation of Labour Hour Rate (Rs.)
25 x 8 = 200 Hours in a Month

Expenses	Basis of Apportionment	Total	Production Dept.		Serivice Dept.	
			A	B	C	S
Power & Lighting	As given in question	1,100	200	300	360	240
Supervisor's salary	% as given	2,000	600	600	400	400
Rent	Floor area in sq. ft.	500	150	200	100	50
Welfare exp.	No. of workers	600	144	192	144	120
Others	As given in question	1,200	200	400	400	200
Total		5,400	1,294	1,692	1,404	1,010
Sevice Dept exp.	50:30:20		505	303	202	(-)1,010
Total		5.400	1,799	1,995	1,606	Nill
No. of Labour hours				600 x 200 = 1,20,000 1799	800 x 200 = 1,60,000 1995	600 x 200 = 1,20,000 1606
Labour Hour Rate				$\dfrac{120000}{} = 0.015$ A	$\dfrac{160000}{} = 0.012$ B	$\dfrac{120000}{} = 0.013$ C

Illustration 3

From the following information related to Asian Paints Ltd. compute labour hour rate, for the year 2008-2009

a) Total number of employees   35
b) Actual working for the period   300 days
c) Daily hourly working   8
d) Management overheads   Rs. 35,750
e) Short and Idle time   3.5%
f) Factory overheads   Rs. 6,14,250

Solution :

1) Actual Working days in a year   300 days
2) Calculation of actual number of working hours :
   Total number of working hours   2,400
   (300 Days × 8 Hours)
   Less : Short and Idle Time   60
   (2.5% of 2,400 Hours)

   Total   2,340

3) Calculation of total labour hours worked :
   = Actual labour hours worked x Number of employeess
   = 2,340 Hours x 35 Employees
   = 81,900 Hours
4) Calculation of Labour Hour Rate :

$$= \frac{\text{Total Factory Overheads}}{\text{Total Labour Hours worked}}$$

$$= \frac{\text{Rs. } 6,14,250}{\text{Hrs. } 81,900}$$

= Rs. 7.50 per hour

(**N.B. :** Management Overheads, as a part of Office and Administration Overheads is not to be considered while taking into account the total factory overheads).

Illustration 4

From the following information of a Production Department of "Knitting Machining" of Alok Textiles Ltd., Ajmer find out the labour hour rate for the year ended on 31st March 2008.

a) Number of hours worked per day   8
b) Number of workers in the department   500
c) Out of 305 working days 2.5% is treated to be the normal idle time
d) Department total works overhead   Rs. 71,37,000
e) Sunday is a holiday and during the year company has officially declared 9 other holidays.

Solution

1) Calculation of number of actual working days :

Total number of days in a year	366*
Less : Total Holidays	61
(i) Sundays - 52 + (ii) Officially declared - 9	(-)
Total	305

2) Calculation of total labour hours worked :

= Actual labour hours worked × Number of workers	2440
(305 Days x 8 Hours)	
Less : Normal idle time	61
(2.5% of 2,440 Hours)	
Total	2,379

3) Calculation of total labour hours worked :
= Actual labour hours worked × Number of Workers
= 2,379 Hours x 500 Workers
= 11,89,500 Hours

4) Calculation of Labour Hour Rate :

$$= \frac{\text{Total works Ovrhead}}{\text{Total Labour Hours Worked}}$$

$$= \frac{\text{Rs. } 71,37,000}{\text{Hrs. } 11,89,500}$$

= Rs. 6 per hour

(* **N.B.:** 2008 being a leap year, total number of days in a year were, 366)

Illustraion 5

The following figures are extracted from the accounts of Data Ltd. Pune for trhe month of March, 2009

Indirect Expenses :	Rs.
a) **Production Depts.-**	
i) A_1	250
ii) B_2	50
b) **Service Depts. -**	
i) A_2	650
ii) B_1	250
Power house expenses	2,000
Supervision charges	1,000
Rent and taxes	3,000
Insurance on plant	2,400
Depreciation on plant @ 12% p.a.	

From the above figures and the following additional information find out overhead recovery rate for the production Depts. A_1 and B_2 on the basis of labour hours. The expenses of Service Depts. should be apportioned in the ratio A_2 in 5 : 3 and B_1 in 1 : 1 to Production Depts. A_1 and B_2 respectively

Particulars		A_1	B_2	A_2	B_1
Electricity	K.W.H.	300	350	150	200
Space occupied	Sq. Ft.	4,000	3,000	7,000	1,000
Value of Plant	Rs.	80,000	40,000	70,000	50,000
Labour Hours		3,500	1,250	-	-
Employee Numbers		25	35	25	15

Solution

In the Books of Data Ltd, Pune
Statement Showing Primary Distribution of Overhead Expenses for the Month Ended on 31st march, 2009

Particulars	Basis of Apportionment	Ratio	Total Rs.	Production Depts. A₁ Rs.	B₂ Rs.	Service Depts. A₂ Rs.	B₁ Rs.
Indirect Expenses	Actual	-	1,200	250	50	650	250
Powerhouse Expenses	Electricity K. W.H	6:7:3:4	2,000	600	700	300	400
Supervision Charges	Employee Numbers	5:7:5:3	1,000	250	350	250	150
Rent and Taxes	Space Occupied sq. Ft.	4:3:7:1	3,000	800	600	1,400	200
Insurance on plant	Value of plant	8:4:7:5	2,400	800	400	700	500
Depreciation on Plant	@ 12% p.a. for one month	-	2,400	800	400	700	500
Total		-	12,000	3,500	2,500	4,000	2,000

Accounting of Overheads / 115

Working Notes :

1) Calculation of Overhead Recovery Rate on the basis of labour hours :

$$= \frac{\text{Total Production Overheads}}{\text{Labour Hours}}$$

A	B
$= \dfrac{\text{Rs. 7,000}}{\text{Hrs. 3,500}}$	$= \dfrac{\text{Rs. 5,000}}{\text{Hrs. 1,250}}$
= Rs. 2 per hour	= Rs. 4 per hour

Statement Showing Secondary Distribution of Dept. Overhead cost of Production Dept. for the Month Ended 31st March, 2009

Particulars	Basis of Reapport-ionment	Ratio	Total Rs.	Production Depts.	
				A$_1$ Rs.	B$_2$ Rs.
Overhead cost as per primary distribution Summary	-	-	6,000	3,500	2,500
Service Dept. - A$_2$	Actual	5:3	4,000	2,500	1,500
Service Dept. - B$_1$	Actual	1:1	2,000	1,000	1,000
Total			12,000	7,000	5,000

Illustration 6

X, Y, Z Ltd., Madras has three production departments, viz Milling, Cutting and Mixing and one Service Dept. viz Labour Welfare. The following details are available for the month of March, 2009 havings 25 working days for daily 8 hours. All these depts. work for all the days and with full attendance.

			Rs.
Power and Lighting -			

Power and Lighting -
a) **Production Depts : -**

	Rs.
i) Milling	400
ii) Cutting	700
iii) Mixing	860

b) **Service Depts. :-**

	Rs.
i) Labour welfare	340
Supervisor's salary	2,000
Rent, Rates and Tazes	500
Recreation Room Expenses	600

Additionall Information :

Particulars	Departments			
	Milling	Cutting	Mixing	Labour Welfare
Floor Area Sq. Ft.	6,000	8,000	6,000	5,000
Employee Numbers	30	40	20	10
Time devoted for supervision	30%	30%	20%	20%

Compute Labour Hour Rate for each of the Production Dept.

Solution

In the Books of XZY Ltd.
Statement Showing Primary Distribution of Overhead Expenses
for the Month ended on 31st March, 2009

Particulars	Basis of Apportionment	Ratio	Total Rs.	Production Depts.			Service Depts.
				Milling Rs.	Cutting Rs.	Mixing Rs.	Labour Welfare Rs.
Power and Lighting	Actual	-	2,300	400	700	860	340
Supervisor's Salary	Time Devoted for Supervision	3:3:2:2	2,000	600	600	400	400
Rent, Rates and Taxes	Floor Area Sq. Ft.	6:8:6:5	500	120	160	120	100
Recreation Room Exps.	Employee Numbers	3:4:2:1	600	180	240	120	60
Total			5,400	1,300	1,700	1,500	900

Statement Showing secondary Distribution of Overhead Cost of Service Dept. to Production Dept. for the Month Ended on 31st March, 2009

Particulars	Basis of Apportionment	Ratio	Total Rs.	Milling Rs.	Cutting Rs.	Mixing Rs.
					Production Depts.	
Overhead cost as per Primary Distribution Summary			4,500	1,300	1,700	1,500
Service Dept.- Labour Welfare	Employee Numbers	3:4:2	900	300	400	200
Total			5,400	1,600	2,100	1,700

Working Notes :

1) Calculation of Labour Hour Rate

$$= \frac{\text{Total Production Overheads}}{\text{Total Labour Hours Worked}}$$

(Number of Days × Number of Hours × Number of workers)

Milling

$$= \frac{\text{Rs. 1,600}}{25 \text{ Days} \times 8 \text{ Hrs.} \times 30 \text{ w}} = \frac{\text{Rs. 1600}}{\text{Hrs. 6,000}} = \text{Re. 0.27 per hour}$$

Cutting

$$= \frac{\text{Rs. 2,100}}{25 \text{ Days} \times 8 \text{ Hrs.} \times 40 \text{ w}} = \frac{\text{Rs. 2,100}}{\text{Hrs. 8,000}} = \text{Re. 0.26 per hour}$$

Mixing

$$= \frac{\text{Rs. 1,700}}{25 \text{ Days} \times 8 \text{ Hrs.} \times 20 \text{ W}} = \frac{\text{Rs. 1,700}}{\text{Hrs. 4,000}} = \text{Re. 0.43 per hour}$$

Illustrations on Machine Hour Rate Method

Illustration - 1

The following particulars relate to a new machine purchased in a manufacturing company.

Purchase price of the machine	Rs. 4,00,000
Rent and rates per quarter	Rs. 15,000
Installation expenses	Rs. 20,000
Monthly lighting charges for the total area	Rs. 1,000
Estimated value of scrap at the end of 10 th year	Rs. 20,000
Foreman's salary for the year	Rs. 30,000
Estimated life of the Machine - 10 Years	
Annual Insurance Premium for the machine	Rs. 3,000
Running of the Machine in its lifetime	Hrs. 2,00,000
Estimated Repairs and Maintenance for the machine for a period of 12 months.	Rs. 5,000

Machine occupies 25% of the total area.

Consumable Stores	Rs. 3,000 p.a.
Sundry Supplies	Rs. 1,000 p.a.

Time devoted by the foreman - $\frac{1}{6}$ th of his time.

Power consumption : 5 units per hour @Rs. 5 per 100 units.

Calculate Machine Hour Rate for new machine.

Your are required to prepare a statement showing computation of Machine Hour Rate .

Solution

Working Notes :

1) Depreciation :

$$= \frac{\begin{array}{c}\text{Purchase Price} \\ \text{of machine}\end{array} + \text{Installation Expenses} - \begin{array}{c}\text{Estimated Value} \\ \text{of Scrap}\end{array}}{\text{Estimated Working life of the machine}}$$

$$= \frac{\text{Rs. 4,00,000 + Rs. 20,000 - Rs. 20,000}}{\text{2,00,000 Hrs.}}$$

$$= \frac{\text{Rs. 4,00,000}}{\text{Hrs. 2,00,000}} = \text{Rs. 2}$$

2) Rent and Rates :
= Rs, 15,000 × 4 Quarters × 25% = Rs. 15,000

3) Lighting Charges :
= Rs. 1,000 × 12 months × 25% = Rs. 3,000

4) Foreman's Salary :

$$= \text{Rs. 30,000} \times \frac{1}{6} = \text{Rs. 5,000}$$

5) Repairs and Maintenance:

$$= \frac{\text{Rs. 5,000}}{\text{2,00,000 Hrs.}} = \text{Rs. 0.25}$$

6) **Power :**
= 54 units x Rs. 0.05 = Rs. 0.25

7) **Standing Charges :**

$$= \frac{Rs.\ 30,000}{Hrs.\ 20,000} = Rs.\ 1.50$$

In the Books of a Company
Statement Showing Computation of Machine Hour Rate

Machine No.......
Department .....

Particulars	Per Year Rs.	Per Hour Rs.
A) **Standing Charges :**		1.50
1) Rent and Rates	15,000	
2) Lighting Charges	3,000	
3) Foreman's Salary	5,000	
4) Insurance Premium	3,000	
5) Consumable Stores	3,000	
6) Sundry Supplies	1,000	
Total	**30,000**	
B) **Machine Expenses :**		
1) Depreciation		2.00
2) Repairs and Maintenance		0.25
3) Power		0.25
Machine Hour Rate		**4.00**

Illustration 2

From the following particulars, calculate Machine Hour Rate for a machine "Texmo".

Capital cost of the machine	Rs. 9,500
Rent and Rates of the shop per quarter	Rs. 900
Freight and installation charges	Rs. 1,500

Supervisor's Salary per month	Rs. 400
Estimated scrap value after 10 years of working life	Rs. 1,000
General lighting charges per month	Rs. 300
Sundry supplies per year	Rs. 40
Monthly insurance Premium	Rs. 30
Estimated cost of repairs and maintenance per annum	Rs. 200
Consumption of power 8 units per hour @Rs 5 per 100 units	
Effective running time per year,	Hrs. 2,000

Space occupied by the machine $\frac{1}{3}$ rd of the floor shop.

Time devoted by the superivsor for Texmo $1 - \frac{1}{4}$ th of his time.

Rent and Rates are to be apportioned in the ratio of floor space occupied by the machine on the floor shop. Out of 12 light points 4 points are being used for "Texmo" Machine.

Solution :

Working Notes :

1) **Depreciation :**

$$= \frac{\text{Capital cost} \atop \text{of machine} + \text{Freight and} \atop \text{Installation charges} - \text{Estimated Scrap} \atop \text{Value}}{\text{Estimated working life of the machine}}$$

$$= \frac{\text{Rs. } 9,500 + \text{Rs. } 1,500 - \text{Rs. } 1,000}{20,000 \text{ Hrs.} \times 10 \text{ years}} = \frac{\text{Rs. } 10,000}{\text{Hrs. } 20,000} \text{ Rs. } 0.50$$

2) **Rent and Rates :**
   = Rs. 900 x 4 Quarters x 1/3 = Rs. 1,200

3) **Supervisor's Salary :**
   = Rs. 400 x 12 Months x 1/4 = Rs. 1,200

4) **General Lighting charges :**
   = Rs. 300 x 12 months x 1/3 = Rs. 1,200

5) **Insurance Premium :**
   = Rs. 30 x 12 months = Rs. 360

6) **Repairs and Maintenance :**

$$= \frac{\text{Rs.200}}{2,000 \ \text{Hrs.}} = \text{Rs.0.10}$$

7) **Power :**
   = 8 units × Rs. 0.05 = Rs. 0.40

8) **Standing Charges :**

$$= \frac{\text{Rs. } 4,000}{2,000 \ \text{Hrs.}} = \text{Rs. 2}$$

In the Books of a Company
Statement Showing computation of Machine Hour Rate
Machine No.......
Department .....

Particulars	Per Year Rs.	Per Hour Rs.
A) Standing Charges :		2.00
1) Rent and Rates	1,200	
2) Supervisor's Salary	1,200	
3) General Lighting Charges	1,200	
4) Sundry Supplies	40	
5) Insurance Premium	(+) 360	
Total	**4,000**	
B) Machine Expenses :		
1) Depreciation		0.50
2) Repairs and Maintenance		0.10
3) Power		(+) 0.40
Machine Hour Rate		**3.00**

Illustration 3

Compute the Machine Hour Rate for the machine "Fowerluba'
From the following particulars.

1) Cost of the machine   Rs. 52,500
2) Machine fixation charge   Rs. 2,000
3) Octroi duty on import of machine   Rs. 3,500
4) Estimated scrap value at the end of 10 th year   Rs. 5,500
5) Estimated working life of the machine per annum   Hrs. 3,000
6) Estimated life of the machine   (10 years)
7) Rent, Rates and Taxes for the department   Rs. 28,500 p.a.
8) Monthly insurance charges for the machine   Rs. 75
9) Electric lighting   Rs. 8,000 p.a.
10) Consumable stores   Rs. 50 per month
11) Cotton, waste, oil etc.   Rs. 100 per quarter
12) Supervisor's salaries   Rs. 8,000 p.a.
13) Power - 13 units per hour @ Rs. 5 per 100 units
14) Repairs and Maintenance for the entire life of the machine   Rs. 18,000

Fowerluba occupies 1/3 rd space of the total area of the shop out of total number of light points in the shop 20 only 4 points are used by this machine. The supervisor devotes 1/4 th of his time on this machine.

Solution :

Working Notes :

1) Depreciation :

$$= \frac{\text{Cost of Machine} + \text{Machine fixation charges} - \text{Octroi duty} - \text{Estimated Scrap Value}}{\text{Estimated working life of the machine}}$$

$$= \frac{\text{Rs. } 52,500 + \text{Rs. } 2,000 + \text{Rs. } 3,500 - \text{Rs. } 5,500}{3,000 \text{ Hrs.} \times 10 \text{ yrs.}}$$

$$= \frac{\text{Rs. } 52.500}{\text{Hrs. } 30,000} = \text{Rs. } 1.75$$

2) Rent, Rates and Taxes :
= Rs. 28,500 = Rs. 9,500

3) Insurance charges :
= Rs 75 x 12 months = Rs. 900

4) Electric Lighting

$$= \text{Rs. } 8,000 \times \frac{4}{20} = \text{Rs. } 1,600$$

5) Consumable stores :
= Rs. 50 ×12 months = Rs. 600

6) Cotton, waste, oil etc.
= Rs. 100 × 4 quarters = Rs. 400

7) Supervisor's salaries :

$$= \text{Rs. } 8,000 \times \frac{1}{4} = 2,000$$

8) Repairs and Maintenance :

$$= \frac{\text{Rs. } 18,000}{30,000 \text{ Hrs.}} = \text{Rs } 0.60$$

9) Power :
= 13 units × Re. 0.05 = Rs. 0.65

10) Standing Charges :

$$= \frac{\text{Rs. } 15,000}{3,000 \text{ Hrs.}} = \text{Rs. } 5$$

In the Books of a Company
Statement Showing Computation of Machine Hours Rate
Machine No.......
Department .....

Particulars	Per Year Rs.	Per Hour Rs.
A) Standing Charges :		5.00
1) Rent, Rates and Taxes	9,500	
2) Insurance Charges	900	
3) Electric Lighting	1,600	
4) Consumable Stores	600	

5) Cotton, Waste, Oil etc.	400	
6) Supervisor's Salaries	(+) 2,000	
Total	**15,000**	
B) Machine Expenses :		
1) Depreciation		1.75
2) Power		0.65
3) Repairs and Maintenance		(+) 0.60
Machine Hour Rate		**8.00**

Illustration 4

From the following data compute the machine hour rate to be charged in respect of jobs carried out during the month of March, 2009

a) The cost of machine is Rs. 7,30,000, its anticipated residual value at the end of working life i.e. 15 years is Rs. 10,000

b) Monthly running hours - 375 hours spent on trial runs and job setting - 25, hours lost due to abnormal factors 40, hours lost due to normal repairs and maintenance - 25, overtime hours worked to complete the job in time - 75

c) Repairs and Maintenance   Rs. 1,000

d) Salaries to Supervisor   Rs. 8,000

e) Power   Rs. 2,500

f) Sundry Shop Expenses   Rs. 6,500

g) Departmental Overheads   Rs. 4,000

h) Production Service Charges   Rs. 1,500

i) Normal rate of wates per hour   Rs. 40

j) Rate of overtime : 50% extra over normal time wages.

Solution :

Working Notes :

1) **Calculation of effective working hours per month :**

		Hours
Monthly running hours		375
Less : Time allowed for -		
i) trial runs and job setting	25	
ii) normal repairs and maintenance	(+) 25	(-) 50
		325
Add : Time allowed for -		
i) overtime		(+) 75
∴ **Effective working Hours**		**400**

Effective working hours per year - 400 Hours × 12 months i.e. 4,800 Hours

2) **Depreciation :**

$$= \frac{\text{Cost of Machine} - \text{Residual value}}{\text{Estimated value}}$$

$$= \frac{\text{Rs. } 7,30,000 - \text{Rs. } 10,000}{4,800 \text{ Hrs.} \times 15 \text{ Years}} = \frac{\text{Rs. } 7,20,000}{\text{Hrs. } 72,000} = \text{Rs. } 10$$

3) **Overtime Wages :**
= 75 Hrs. × Rs. 60 (i.e. 50% extra over normal time wages of Rs. 40 per hour) = Rs. 4,500

4) **Repairs and Maintenance :**

$$= \frac{\text{Rs. } 1,000}{400 \text{ Hrs.}} = \text{Rs. } 2.50$$

5) **Power :**

$$= \frac{\text{Rs. } 2,500}{400 \text{Hrs.}} = \text{Rs. } 6.25$$

6) Standing Charges :

$$= \frac{\text{Rs. } 24{,}500}{400 \text{ Hrs.}} = \text{Rs. } 61.25$$

In the Books of a Company
Statement Showing Computation of Machine Hour Rate
During the Month March 2009.

Machine No.......
Department .....

Particulars	Per Month Rs.	Per Hour Rs.
A) Standing Charges :		61.25
1) Overtime Wages	4.500	
2) Salaries to Supervisors	6,000	
3) Sundry Shop Expenses	6,500	
4) Departmental Overheads	4,000	
5) Production Service Charges	(+) 1,500	
Total	**24,500**	
B) Machine Expenses :		
1) Depreciation		10,00
2) Repairs and Maintenance		2.50
3) Power		(+) 6.25
Machine Hour Rate		**80.00**

Illustration 10

From the following particulars related to a machine, calculate Machine Hour Rate

1) Original cost of the machine   Rs. 19,000
   Carriage and freight paid on purchase
   of machine   Rs. 1,200
   Residual value of machine after ten years   Rs. 200
   estimated life   10 years

In a year of 50 weeks the machine is operated for 48 hours, which includes 300 hours towards machine maintenance down - time and 100 hours towards setting up time.

2) Electric power used by the machine is 6 units per hour Rs. 5 per 100 units.
3) Repairs and Maintenance Rs. 75 per month.
4) Two operators attend the machine during operation alongwith three other machines, their total wages including fringe benefits amounted to Rs. 800 per month.
5) General overheads attributable to this machine Rs. 600 per year.
6) Rent and Taxes Rs. 1,500 p.a.

Solution

Working Notes :

1) Calculation of Deffective working hours per annum :

		Hours
Estimated yearly working hours		2,400
(50 weeks × 48 Hours)		
Less : Time allowed for -		(-) 400
a) Machine - Maintenance down time	300 hours	
b) Setting up time	(+) 100 hours	
∴ **Effective working hours**		2,000.

2) Depreciation :

$$= \frac{\text{Original cost of machine +Carriage and Freight paid on purchase of machine - Residual value of machine}}{\text{Estimated working life of machine}}$$

$$= \frac{\text{Rs. } 19,000 + \text{Rs. } 1,200 - \text{Rs. } 200}{2,000 \text{ Hours} \times 10 \text{ Years}} = \frac{\text{Rs. } 20,000}{\text{Hrs. } 20,000} \text{ Rs. } 1$$

3) Electric Power :
= 6 units × Rs. 0.05 = Rs. 0.30

4) Repairs and Maintenance :

$$= \frac{\text{Rs. } 75 \times 12 \text{ months}}{2,000 \text{ Hrs.}} = \text{Rs. } 0.45$$

5) Operators Wages :

$$= \frac{\text{Rs. }800 \times 12 \text{ months}}{4 \text{ machines}} = \text{Rs. }2,400$$

6) Standing Charges :

$$= \frac{\text{Rs. }4,500}{\text{Hrs. }2,000} = \text{Rs. }2.25$$

In the Books of a Company
Statement Showing Computation of Machine Hour Rate

Machine No.......
Department .....

Particulars	Per Year Rs.	Per Hour Rs.
A) Standing Charges :		2.25
1) Operators Wages	2,400	
2) General Overheads	600	
3) Rent and Taxes	(+) 1,500	
Total	**4,500**	
B) Machine Expenses :		
1) Depreciation		1.00
2) Electric Power		0.30
3) Repairs and Maintenance	(+)	0.45
Machine Hour Rate		**4.00**

Illustration 6

Calculate Machine Hour Rate from the following infomation relating to Machine No. 18

Purchase Price of the Machine	Rs. 97,000
Repair charges - 50% of depreciation	
Railway freight	Rs. 2,000
Lubrication Oil @ Rs. 2 per day per 8 hours (effective)	

Errection charges for the machine   Rs. 1,500
Consumable Stores @ Rs. 3 per day per 8 hours (effective)
Estimated Scrap Value of machine after 10 years of life   Rs. 500
Estimated working hours 2,150 per annum,
Cost of Supervision   1,500 p.a.
Hours lost due to normal tool setting   150
Rent and Taxes Rs. 11 per day per 8 hours (effective)
Electric Power   Rs. 1,000 P.a.

Labour cost of operating the machine No. 18 is to be ignored while calculating Machine Hour Rate.

Solution

Working Notes :

1) Calculation of effective working hours per annum :
Estimated working hours   2,150
Less : Hours lost due to normal tool-setting   -150

∴ **Effective working Hours**   2,000

2) Depreciation :

$$= \frac{\text{Purchase price of Machine + Railway Freight + Erection charges for the machine - Estimated Scrap Value}}{\text{Estimated working life of the Machine}}$$

$$= \frac{\text{Rs. } 97,000 + \text{Rs. } 2,000 + \text{Rs. } 1,500 - \text{Rs. } 500}{2,000 \text{ Hrs.} \times 10 \text{ Yeas}} = \frac{\text{Rs. } 1,00,000}{\text{Hrs. } 20,000}$$

= Rs. 5

3) Repair charges :
= 50% of depreciation i.e. Rs. 5 = Rs. 2.50

4) Electric Power :

$$= \frac{\text{Rs. } 1,000}{2,000 \text{ Hrs.}} = \text{Re. } 0.50$$

5) Standing charges :

$$= \frac{\text{Rs. } 16}{8 \text{ Hrs.}} = \text{Rs. } 2$$

6) Cost of supervision as related to labour cost operating the machine, hence, ignored while calculating machine hour rate.

In the Books of a company
Statement Showing Computation of Machine Hour Rate
Machine No. 18
Department .....

Particulars	Per Day Rs.	Per Hour Rs.
A) Standing Charges :		2.00
1) Lubricating Oil	2.00	
2) Consumable Stores	3.00	
3) Rent and Taxes	(+) 11.00	
Total	**16.00**	
B) Machine Expenses :		
1) Depreciation		5.00
2) Repair Charges		2.50
3) Electric Power		(+) 0.50
Machine Hour Rate		**10.00**

Illustration 11

From the following particulars calculate Machine Hour Rate for a Drilling Machine.

	Rs.
Cost of machine	1,00,000
Rent and Rates for the shop per month	350
Installation charges	7,500
General lighting for the shop per month	400
Carriage on purchase of machine	2,500
Shop Supervisor's salary per month	1,000
Estimated scrap value of machine after 15 years of working life	5,000

Quarterly insurance premium	337.50
Repairs and Maintenance per annum	1,000

Power Consumption 10 units per hour @ Rs.10 Per 100 units

Estimated working hours 2,200 per annum which includes setting up time of 200 hours.

The machine occupies 1/4 th area of the total area of the shop. The supervisor is expected to devote 1/5 th of this time for supervising the machine. General lighting charges and rent are to be apportioned in the ratio of floor space occupied

Solution

Working Notes :

1) Calculation of effective working hours per annum :

	Hours
Estimated working hours	2,200
Less : Setting up time - hours	(-) 200
∴ **Effective working Hours**	2,000

2) Depreciation :

$$= \frac{\text{Cost of Machine + Installation Charges + Carriage on Purchase of Machine - Estimates Scrap Value}}{\text{Estimated working life of the machine}}$$

$$= \frac{\text{Rs. } 1,00,000 + \text{Rs. } 7,500 + \text{Rs. } 2,500 - \text{Rs. } 5,000}{2,000 \text{ Hrs.} \times 15 \text{ Years}}$$

$$= \frac{\text{Rs. } 1,05,000}{\text{Hrs. } 30,000} = \text{Rs. } 3.50$$

2) Rent and Rates :
= Rs. 350 × 12 months × 1/4 = Rs. 1,050

3) General Lighting :
= Rs. 400 × 12 months × 1/4 = Rs. 1,200

4) Shop supervisor's Salary :
= Rs. 1,000 ×12 month x 1/5 = Rs. 2,400

5) Insurance Premium :
= Rs. 337.50 x 4 Quarters = Rs. 1,350

6) Repairs and Maintenance :

$$= \frac{\text{Rs. } 1,000}{2000 \text{ Hrs.}} = \text{Rs. } 0.50$$

7) Power :
= 10 units x Rs. 0.10 = Re. 1

8) Standing charges :

$$= \frac{\text{Rs. } 6,000}{2,000 \text{ Hrs.}} = \text{Rs. } 3$$

In the Books of a Company
Statement Showing Computation of Machine Hour Rate

Machine Drilling
Department .....

Particulars	Per Year Rs.	Per Hour Rs.
A) Standing Charges :		3.00
1) Rent and Rates	1,050	
2) General Lighting	1,200	
3) Shop Supervisor's Salary	2,400	
4) Insurance Premium	(+) 1,350	
Total	**6,000**	
B) Machine Expenses :		
1) Depreciation		3.50
2) Repair and Maintenance	0.50	
3) Electric power		(+) 1.00
Machine Hour Rate		**8.00**

Illustrations 8

Your are required to calculate a Machine Hour Rate from the following information.

1) Original Cost of Machine   Rs. 13,000
   Installation Charges   Rs. 1,700
   Carriage and freight on purchase of machine   Rs. 1,200
   Estimated scrap value after 10 years   Rs. 900
   Estimated working time per year is 2,400 hours i.e. 50 weeks of 48 hours each.
   Maintenance time treated as productive - 300 hours and staggering time treated as productive were 100 hours per annum
2) Electric power consumed by machine 13 units per hour @ Rs. 5 per 100 units.
3) Chemical solution required per week Rs. 20
4) Repairs and Maintenance for the entire life estimated to be Rs. 12,000
5) Consumable stores Rs. 50 per month.
6) Two attendants control the operation of the machine together with 4 other machines, their combined weekly wages were Rs. 240.
7) Lubricating oil Rs. 300 per quarter.
8) Annual Departmental Overheads Rs. 800

Solution :

Working Notes :

1) Calculation of effective working hours per annum :

		Hours
Normal working hours (50 weeks × 48 hours)		2,400
Less : Time allowed for -		
i) Maintenance time - Productive	300	
ii) Staggering time - productive	(+) 100	(-) 400
\ **Effective working Hours**		2,000

2) Depreciation :

$$= \frac{\text{Original cost of machine} + \text{Installation Charges} + \text{Carriage and freight on purchase of Machine} - \text{Estimated scrap value}}{\text{Estimated working life of the machine}}$$

$$= \frac{\text{Rs. 13,000} + \text{Rs. 1,700} + \text{Rs. 1,200} - \text{Rs. 900}}{2,000 \text{ Hrs.} \times 10 \text{ Years}}$$

$$= \frac{\text{Rs. 15,000}}{\text{Hrs. 20,000}} = \text{Re. 0.75}$$

3) Electric Power :

= 13 units x Re. 0.05 = Re. 0.65

4) Chemical Solution :

= Rs. 20 x 50 weeks = Rs. 1,000

5) Repairs and Maintenance :

$$= \frac{\text{Rs. 12,000}}{20,000 \text{ Hrs.}} = \text{Re. 0.60}$$

6) Consumable stores:

= Rs. 50 x 12 months = Rs. 600

7) Attendant's wages :

= Rs. 50 x 12 months = Rs. Rs. 2,400

$$\frac{\text{Rs. 240 x 50 weeks}}{5 \text{ machines}}$$

8) Lubricating Oil :

= Rs. 300 x 4 Quarters = Rs. 1,200

9) Standing charges :

$$= \frac{\text{Rs. 6,000}}{2,000 \text{ Hrs.}} = \text{Rs. 3}$$

In the Books of a Company
Statement Showing Computation of Machine Hour Rate
Machine No. ...
Department .....

Particulars	Per Year Rs.	Per Hour Rs.
A) **Standing Charges :**		3.00
1) Chemical Solution	1,000	
2) Cosumable Stores	600	
3) Attendant's Wages	2,400	
4) Lubricating Oil	1,200	
5) Departmental Overheads	(+) 800	
Total	**6,000**	
B) **Machine Expenses :**		
1) Depreciation		0.75
2) Electric Power		0.65
3) Repairs and Maintenance	(+)	0.60
Machine Hour Rate		**5.00**

Illustration 9

The following expenses have been incurred in respect of a shop having four identical machines.

	Rs.
Rent and Taxes for the year	6,000
Power consumed by the shop @ Re. 0.10 per unit	4,800
Annual repairs for four machines	1,200
Lighting for the shop for 12 months	500
Yearly charges for Lubricants	160
Depreciation per machine for the year	600
Supervisor looking after four machines and is paid with a monthly salary	600
Hire purchases installments for machines (Including Rs. 300 for hire purchase interest)	6,300

Attendants : two attendants looking after four machines paid Rs. 60 per month, each

Each machine consumes 10 units of power per hour.

Calculate the machine hour rate.

Solution :

Working Notes :

1) **Calculation of effective working hours in a year taking power consumption as a base :**

a) Calculation of power units consumed by the shop per year -

If Re. 0.10 = 1 unit

∴ Rs. 4,800 = ?

$$= \frac{Rs. 4,8000 \times 1}{Re. 0.10} = 48,000 \text{ units}$$

b) Calculation of power units consumed by each machine in a shop

If 4 Machines = 48,000 units

∴ 1 Machine = ?

$$= \frac{1 \times 4,8000 \text{ units}}{4} = 12,000 \text{ units}$$

c) Calculation of actual working hours in a year-

If 10 units = 1 hour

∴ 12,000 units = ?

$$= \frac{12,000 \text{ units} \times 1}{10} = 1,200 \text{ Hours.}$$

(2) **Rent and Taxes :**

$$= \frac{Rs. 6,000}{4 \text{ Machines}} = Rs. 1,500$$

(3) **Power:**

= 10 units × Re. 0.10 = Re. 1

(4) **Repairs:**

$$= \frac{Rs. 1,200}{4 \text{ Machines}} = \frac{Rs. 300}{1,200 \text{ Hrs.}} = Re. 0.25$$

(5) Lighting:

$$= \frac{Rs.500}{4 \text{ Machines}} = Rs.125$$

(6) Lubricants:

$$= \frac{Rs.160}{4 \text{ Machines}} = Rs.40$$

(7) Depreciation :

$$= \frac{Rs.160}{1,200 \text{ Hrs.}} = Re.0.50$$

(8) Supervisor's Salary:

$$= \frac{Rs.600 \times 12 \text{Months}}{4 \text{ Machines}} = Rs.1,800$$

(9) Hire Purchase Interest:

$$= \frac{Rs.300}{4 \text{ Machines}} = Rs.75$$

(10) Attendant's Salary:

$$= \frac{Rs.60 \times 12 \text{ Months} \times 2 \text{Attendants}}{4 \text{ Machines}} = Rs.360$$

(11) Standing Charges:

$$= \frac{Rs. 3,900}{1,200 \text{ Hrs.}} = Rs.3.25$$

(**N.B.:** Out of total hire purchase installments for machines, only hire purchase interest is to be considered.)

In the books of a Company
Statement Showing Computation of Machine Hour Rate
Machine No. 18
Department .....

Particulars	Per Year Rs.	Per Hour Rs.
A) Standing Charges:		3.25
1) Rent and Taxes	1,500	
2) Lighting	125	
3) Lubricants	40	
4) Supervisor's Salary	1,800	
5) Hire Purchase Interest	75	
6) Attendant's Salary	+ 360	
Total	**3,900**	
B) Standing Charge		
1) Power		1.00
2) Repairs		00.25
3) Depreciat		00.50
Machine hour rate		**5.00**

Illustration 10

Calculate the machine-hour rate:

Cost of the machine	Rs.16,000
Estimated scrap value	Rs. 1,000
Effective working life	10,000 hours
Running time per four-weekly period	160 hours
Average cost of repairs and maintenance	Rs.120
Standing charge allocated to machine per four-weekly period	Rs. 40
Power used by machine	4 Units per hour at a cost of 5 Paise per unit.

Solution :

Statement of Machine Hour Rate

(Running time per four-weekly period: 160 hours)

Particulars	Basis	Per hour (Rs)
Depreciation	$\dfrac{16,000-1,000}{10,000 \text{ hours}}$	1.50
Repairs	$\dfrac{Rs.\,120}{160}$	0.75
Standing charges (allocated)	$\dfrac{40}{160}$	0.25
Power	4 Units at 5 paise per Unit	0.20
Machine hour rate		2.70

Illustration 11

From the following particulars compute Machine Hour Rate:

	Rs.
Cost of machine	1,14,800
Installation charges	5,400
Anticipated life of machine	10 years
Residual value at the end of 10 yrs.	5,000
Rent and rates per annum	12,000
Insurance of the machine p.a.	3,000
Repairs and maintenance p.a.	8,640
Consumable stores p.a.	1,200
Total production services p.a.	1,080
Power cost is 5 units per working hour @ 40 paise per unit	
Setting up time (Non-productive)	400 hrs.p.a.

There are 300 working days each of eight hours in a year.

Soution

Calculation of Machine Hour Rate
Fixed costs

	P.A.	Per hour
Rent and rates	12,000	
Insurance	3,000	
Consumable stores	1,200	
Repairs and maintenance	8,640	
Production services	1,080	
	25,920	
Fixed cost per hour		12.96
(25, 920/ 2,000) (Note 1)		12.96
Depreciation (Note 2)		5.76
Power 5 × 0.40		2.00
Machine hour rate		20.72
Note: 1. 300 × 8 = 2400 - 400 = 2000 hours.		
Note: 2		
Depreciation		1,14,800
Cost		5,400
Add : Installation		5,400
		1,20,200
Less : Scrap value		5,000
Net cost		1,15,200

$$\text{Depreciation per hour} = \frac{1,15,200}{10 \text{ years} \times 2,000 \text{ hours}} = 5.76$$

Illustration 12

Compute the machine-hour rate from the following data:

Cost of machine	1,00,000
Installation charges	10,000
Estimated scrap value after the expiry	

of its life (15 years)

Rent and rates for the shop per month	200
General lighting for the shop per month	300
Insurance premium for the machine per annum	960
Repairs and maintenance expenses per annum	1,000
Power consumption - 10 units per hour	
Rate of power per 100 units	20
Estimated working hours per annum	2,200
This includes setting up time of 200 hours.	
Shop supervisor's salary per month	600

The machine occupies 1/4th of the total area of the shop. The supervisor is expected to devote 1/5th of his time for supervising the machine.

Solution

Computation of Machine Hour Rate
Net Working Hours per Annum 2,200-200 for Setting Up = 2,000

Particulars	Basic of apportionment	Amount per annum (Rs.)	Rate per hour (Rs.)
A. Fixed : Cost			
Depreciation	$\dfrac{1,00,000+10,000-5,000}{15 \text{ years}}$	7,000	
Rent and rates	$200 \times 12 = \dfrac{2400}{4}$	600	
General lighting	$300 \times 12 = \dfrac{3600}{4}$	900	

Particulars	Basic of apportionment	Amount per annum (Rs.)	Rate per hour (Rs.)
Insurance premium	As given	960	
Repairs & Maintenance	As given	1,000	
Shop Supervisor's salary	$600 \times 12 = \dfrac{7,200}{5}$	1,440	
Total A :		11,900	
Rate per hour	$\dfrac{11,900}{2,000}$		5.95
B. Variable Cost Power	10 units at 20 paise per unit		2.00
Machine Hour Rate	A+B		7.95

Illustration 13

Compute the machine hour rate from the information given below relating to Machine X,

Cost of machine	Rs.13,500
Expected working life	10 years
Scrap value (after 10 years)	Rs.2,000
Working hours (per annum)	Rs.1,800
Insurance (per annum)	Rs.45
Cotton waste (per annum)	Rs.75
Rent for the department (per annum)	Rs.975
Foreman's salary (per annum)	Rs.7,500
Lighting (per annum)	Rs.360
Repairs for entire life	Rs.1,406
Power - 10 units @ 7 1/2 paise	per unit

Machine occupies 1/5th of the area and the foremen devotes 1/4th of his time to Machine X. Machine X has two points out of the total 12 for lighting in the department.

Solution   **Statement of Machine Hour Rate**
(Working hours per annum 1800)

Particulars	Basic of Per annum	Amount per annum (Rs.)	Rate per hour (Rs.)
Fixed Cost			
Depreciation	$\dfrac{13,500-2,000}{10}=$	1,150.00	
Insurance	as given in question	45.00	
Cotton waste	as given in question	75,00	
Rent	1/5 of 975	195.00	
Foreman's salary	1/4 of 7,500	1,875.00	
Lighting	2/12 of 360	60.00	
Repairs	1406/10 =	140,60	
Total		3,540.60	
Per hour	$\dfrac{3,540.60}{1,800}=$		1.97
Variable Cost			
Power	10 Units at		0.75
Machine Hour Rate			2.72

Illustration 14

From the following information, find out the machine hour rate :

	Rs.
Cost of Machine	10,000
Estimated scrap value	1,000
Repairs for one month	120
Fixed expenses for one month	40
Effective life of machine	10,000 hours
Power - 5 units per hour	
Rate per unit of power	Re.0.10
Working hours for one month	160 hours

B.Com., 1989

Solution

Computation of Machine Hour Rate
Working Hours for one Month : 160 Hours

Particulars	Basic of apportionment	Amount per month (Rs.)	Per hour (Rs.)
Repairs	As given in question	120	
Fixed exp.	As given in question	40	
			160
Per hour	160 ÷ 160		1.00
Power	5 units at Re. 0.10		0.50
Depreciation	$\dfrac{10,000-1,000}{10,000 \text{ hours}}$		0.90
Machine Hour Rate			2.40

Illustration 15

In a light engineering factory, the machine shop consists of three cost centres (A, B and C) each having three distinct sets of machines. The following are the details of estimates for a period:

(Amounts are in lakh of rupees)

	A	B	C
(i) Number of Workers - 800	200	200	400
(ii) Number of machine hours - 1,00,000	30,000	30,000	40,000
(iii) Percentage of horse-power-100%.	40%	25%	35%
(iv) Value of assets Rs.40.00	Rs.10.00	Rs.16.00	Rs.14.00
(v) Direct wages - Rs.30.00	Rs.8.00	Rs.10.00	Rs.12.00
(vi) Depreciation-Rs.4.00			
(vii) Indirect labour - Rs.9.00.			

	A	B	C
(viii) Insurance charges - Rs.2.00 (ix) Electricity - Rs.3.00 (x) Supervisory Salary - Rs.1.60 (xi) Staff welfare expenses - Rs.3.00 (xii) Other expenses - Rs.6.00			

Work out a composite machine-hour rate for each of the three cost centres and show clearly the basis of apportionment of expenses between the cost centres.

B.Com., April/May 88

Composite Machine Hour Rate for Each Cost Centre (Rs.in lakhs)

Particulars	Amount	Basis of apportionment	Cost centre A	Cost centre B	Cost centre C
Depreciation	4.00	Value of assets i.e.10:16:14	1.00	1.60	1.40
Indirect labour	9.00	Number of workers 2:2:4	2.25	2.25	4.50
Insurance	2.00	Value of assets 10:16:14	0.50	0.80	0.70
Electricity	3.00	Horse-power. 40%, 25%, 35%	1.20	0.75	1.05
Supervisory Salary	1.60	Number of workers 2:2:4	0.40	0.40	0.80
Staff Welfare exp.	3.00	Direct wages 8:10:12	0.75	0.75	1.50
Other exp.	6.00		1.60	2.00	2.40
Direct wages	30.00	Actuals	8.00	10.00	12.00
Total:	58.60	---	15.70	18.55	24.35
No. of Machine Hours		1,00,000	30,000	30,000	40,000
			15,70,000	18,55,000	24,35,000
Composite Machine Hour rate			30,000	30,000	40,000
			= Rs.52.33	= Rs. 61.83	= Rs.60.88

Illustration 16

From the following annual careges incurred in respect of a machine in a shop where labour is almost nil and where work is done by menas of five machines of exactly similar type, calculate machine hour rate for one machine :

		Rs.
(i)	Rent and Rates (Proportional to the floor space occupied) for the shop	4,800
(ii)	Depreciation of each machine	500
(iii)	Repairs and maintenance for five machines	1,000
(iv)	Power consumed (as per meter) @ 25 paise per unit for the shop	5,000
(v)	Electric charges for light in shop	540
(iv)	There are two attendants for the five machines and they are each paid Rs. 160 per month	
(vii)	For the five machines in the shop, there is one supervisor whose emoluments are Rs. 500 per month	
(viii)	Sundry supplies such as lubricants cotton waste etc. for the shop	450
(xi)	Hire purchase installments payable for the machine (including Rs. 300 as interest)	1,200
(x)	The machine uses 10 units of power per hour	20

Solution

Working Notes

(iv) Power consumed in the shop: Rs. 5,000
per unit = 25 paise

$$\text{No. of Units } \frac{5,000}{0.25} = 20,000 \text{ Units}$$

$$\text{For one machine} = \frac{20,000}{5} = 4.000 \text{ Units.}$$

(x) Machine uses 10 units of power per hour.

$$= \frac{4,000}{10} = 400 \text{ hours.}$$

Calculation of Machine Hour Rate

Particulars	Basic	Amount charges for one machine(Rs.)	Machine hour rate (Rs.)
(i)Rent and Rates	$\dfrac{4,800}{5}$	960	
(ii) Depreciation		500	
(iii) Repairs & Maintenance	$\dfrac{1,000}{5}$	200	
(v) Electric charges	$\dfrac{540}{5}$	108	
(vi) Attendant's Salary	$\dfrac{160 \times 2 \times 12 \text{ Months}}{5}$	768	
(vii) Supervisor's Salary	$\dfrac{500 \times 12}{5}$	1,200	
viii) Sundry supplies	$\dfrac{450}{5}$	90	
		3,826	
Total Annual Charges per hour	$\dfrac{3,826}{400}$	9.57	
(iv) & (x) power	10 Units of power per hour = 10 x 0.25		2.50
Machine Hour Rate			12.07

Note : Hire purchase Installments:
Interest   300   Does not from part of cost.
Repayment of principal   900
Installment Amount1,200These need not be included for calculation of machine hour Rate.

Illustrations on other Methods

Sunshine Ltd. gives the following information for the year 2009

Process Materials	Rs.50,000
Factory Overheads	Rs.20,000
Productive Expenses	Rs.10,000
Operating Labour	Rs. 40,000
Machine Hours	Hrs. 5,000
Direct Labour Hours	Hrs. 10,000

Company has undertaken a Job No. 204 in the year 2006 for which the following cost data is estimated-

Direct Materials required	Rs.2,000
Estimated Direct Labour	Rs.1,000
Estimated Direct Expenses	Rs.200
Machine Hours	Hrs.100
Direct Labour Hours	Hrs.300

Prepare a statement showing the total cost of Job No. 204 under the following method of absorption of overheads.

(A) Percentage of Direct Material Cost
(B) Percentage on Direct Labour Cost
(C) Percentage on Prime Cost
(D) Labour Hour Rate
(E) Machine Hour Rate

Solution

In the Books of sumstive Ltd.
Statement of Cost for the Year 2009

Particulars			Amount Rs.	Amount Rs.
	Process Materials		50,000	
Add :	Operating Labour		40,000	
Add :	Productive Expenses	(+)	10,000	
	Prime Cost		1,00,000	1,00,000
Add :	Factory Overheads	(+)	20,000	
	Total Cost		1,20,000	1,20,000

Working Notes :

(1) **Calculation of percentage of factory overheads to direct material cost**

If   Rs. 50,000 D.M. = Rs. 20,000 F.O

∴   100   = ?

$$= \frac{100 \times Rs.\,20,000}{Rs.\,50,000} = 40\%$$

(2) **Calculation of percentage of factory overheads to direct labour cost :**

If   Rs. 40,000 D.L. = Rs. 20,000 F.O.

∴   100   = ?

$$= \frac{100 \times Rs.\,20,000}{Rs.\,40,000} = 50\%$$

(3) **Calculation of percentage of factory overheads to prime cost:**

If   Rs. 1,00,000 p.c. = Rs. 20,000 F.O.

∴   100   = ?

$$= \frac{100 \times Rs.\,20,000}{Rs.\,1,50,000} = 20\%$$

(4) **Calculation of Labour Hour Rate :**

$$= \frac{Factory\ Overheads}{Direct\ Labour\ Hours} = \frac{Rs.\,20,000}{Hrs.\,10,000} = Rs.\,2\ per\ labour\ hour$$

(5) **Calculation of Machine Hour Rate :**

$$= \frac{Factory\ Overheads}{Direct\ Hours} = \frac{Rs.\,20,000}{Hrs.\,5,000} = Rs.\,4\ per\ machine\ hour$$

(A) Percentage on Direct Material Cost Method
Statement Showing Job Cost for Job No. 204 for Year 2006

Particulars		Amount Rs.
Direct Materials required		2,000
Add : Estimated Direct Labour		1,000
Add : Estimated Direct Expenses	(+)	200
Prime Cost		**3,200**
Add : Factory Overheads		
(40% of Direct Materials i.e. Rs. 2000)	(+)	800
Job Cost		**4,000**

(B) Percentage on Direct Labour Cost Method :
Statement Showing Job Cost
for Job No. 204 for the Year 2006

Particulara		Amount Rs.
Direct Materials required		2,000
Add : Estimated Direct Labour		1,000
Add : Estimated Direct Expenses	(+)	200
Prime Cost		**3,200**
Add : Factory Overheads		
(50% of Direct Labour i.e. Rs. 1,000)	(+)	500
Job Cost		**3,700**

(c) Percentage on Prime Cost Method :
Statement Showing Job Cost
for Job No. 204 for the Year 2006

Particulars		Amount Rs.
Direct Materials required		2,000
Add : Estimated Direct Labour		1,000
Add : Estimated Direct Expenses	(+)	200
Prime Cost		**3,200**
Add : Factory Overheads		
(20% of Prime Cost i.e. Rs. 3,200)	(+)	640
Job Cost		**3,840**

D) Labour Hour Rate Method :
Statement Showing Job Cost for No. 204 for the Year 2006

Particulars		Amount Rs.
Direct Materials required		2,000
Add : Estimated Direct Labour		1,000
Add : Edtimated Direct Expenses	(+)	200
Prime Cost		**3,200**
Add : Factory ovreheads		
(Labour Hours 300 x Rs. 2)	(+)	600
Job Cost		**3,800**

E) Machine Hour Rate Method :
Statement Showing Job Cost
for Job No. 204 for the Year 2006

Particulars		Amount Rs.
Direct Materials required		2,000
Add : Estimated Direct Labour		1,000
Add : Estimated Direct Expenses	(+)	200
Prime Cost		**3,200**
Add : Factory Overheads (Machine Hours 100 × Rs.4)	(+)	400
Job Cost		**3.600**

3.4 Under-absorption and over absorption of overhead
meaning, reasons and accounting treatment

We know that, overheads may be asbsorbed either on the basis of a actual rates or predetermined rates. When actual rates are used, the overheads absorbed must, if all the calculations are correctly made, exactly equal to the overheads incurred. In such a case, there is no problem of under or overabsorption of overheads. But when a predetermined rate is employed, overheads abosorbed may not be equal to the amount of actual overheads incurred. Thus, whenever the overheads absorbed are not equal to the amount of actual overheads, it is a case of either under-absorption or over absorption overheads.

It should be noted that the overhead absorption rates are predetermined.

$$\text{Pre-determined rate} = \frac{\text{Factory Overheads Estimated}}{\text{Basis i.e. units of output etc.}}$$

Where a pre-determined rate is adopted, the overhead absorption may not be the same as overhead incurred actually.

Factory overheads incurred : Rs. 5,500

Factory overheads absorbed : Rs 5,000 @ Rs. per unit on the actual output of 2,500 units.

Thus there is under absorption of factory overheads to the extent of Rs. 500.

Meaning

Under - Absorption :

When the amount of overheads absorbed is less than the amount of overheads incurred. It is called under-absorption or under-recovery. This has the effect of under-stating the cost because the overheads incurred are not fully recovered in the cost of jobs, processes etc.

Over-Absorption :

When the amount of overhead absorbed is more than the amount of overhead incurred, it is known as over-absorption or over-recovery. It has the effect of over stating the cost of jobs processes etc.

Reasons for under or Over-Absorption

Under or over-absorption of overheads may arise due to one or more of the following reasons.

(1) Faulty estimation of overheads costs or overhead incurred exceed the estimates or outputs is less than anticipation.
(2) Faulty estimation of the quantity of output.
(3) Seasonal fluctuation in the amount of overhead in certain industries.
(4) Unforeseen changes in the production capacity.
(5) Unexpected changes in the method of production affecting changes in the amount of overhead.
(6) Non-utilisation of normal capacity.

Whatever be the reason, under or over-absorption is caused mainly due to wrong estimation either of the costs incurred or of the production over which they are to be absorbed.

The distinction between under Absorption of Overheads and Over Absorption of Overheads can be shown as follows :

Under Absorption of overheads	Over Absorption of Overheads
(1) When the amount of overheads absorbed is less than the amount of overhead incurred it is called "under-absorption or under recovery."	(1) When the amount of overhead abssorbed is more than the amount of overhead incurred it is known as "over-absorption or over recovery"
(2) This has the affect of understating the cost because the overthead incurred are not fully recovered in the cost of jobs, processes, etc.	(2) This has the overtating the cost of jobs, processes, etc.
(3) In case of under absorption, supplementary rate is computed by dividing the under absorbed production overheads by the actual value of the base. This is supplementary rate may be formed positive supplementary rate as the under absorbed overheads is to be added.	(3) In case of over-absorption, supplementary rate is computed by dividing the over-absorbed production overheads by the actual value of the base. This supplementary rate may be called negative supplementary rate as over absorbed amount is to be substracted.
(4) In case of under absorption, under absorbed production overheads are to be added. applying positive supplementary rate, to the cost of various categories.	(4) In case of over absorption, over-absorbed proudction overheads are to be deducted from the cost of work in progress, unsold stock and units sold.

Example

It was estimated that the annual overhead in department would be

Fixed	Rs.14,000
Variable	Rs. 26,000

and that machine hours would be 10,000. The rates for charging overhead to production orders passing through department was therefore set up as follows :

Fixed Overheads   Rs.14,000 ÷ Hrs.10,000 = Rs 1.40
Variable Overheads   Rs.26,000 ÷ Hrs.10,000 = Rs. 2.60

Acutual machine hours worked were 9,850 and the overheads incurred were :

Fixed	Rs.14,950
Variable	Rs.25,340

Answer

	Actual Overhead Rs.	Overhead Asorbed at pre determined rate Rs.	Over Absorbed Rs.	Under Absorbed Rs.
Fixed Overheads	14,950	13,790	-	1,160
Variable Overheads	25,340	25,610	270	-
	40.290	39,400	270	1,160

Working Notes

(1) Calculation of Overhead absorbed at pre-determined rate :
Hrs. 9,850 x Rs. 1.40 = Rs. 13,790
Hrs. 9,850 x Rs. 2,60 = Rs. 25,610

Accounting Treatment :

The under or over recovered amounts are disposed of in accordance with any of the following methods depending upon the circumstances.

(1) Use of Supplementary Rates :

Where the amount of under or over-absorbed overhead is not negligible, a supplementary overhead absorption rate is calculated to adjust this amount in the cost. However, adjustment is made in the cost of i) work-in-progress, ii) finished stock and iii) cost of sales.

In the case of under-absorption the overhead is adjusted by a plus rate since the amount is to be added whereas over absorption is adjusted by a minus rate since the amount is to be deducted.

Example

Pre-determined overhead rate	:	Rs. 10 per machine hour
Actual machine hours	:	Hrs. 1.500
Actual overheads	:	Rs. 18.000

Answer

Overhead-absorbed	= Hrs. 1,500 x Rs. 10 = 15,000
Under-absorption	= Rs. 3,000
	i.e. 18,000 - Rs. 15,000

Under Supplementary Rate Rs.3,000 × Rs. 1,500 = Rs.2

This is a plus rate because it is for under absorbed overheads and will be used to add to the overhead already recovered.

Supplementary Overhead Rate

$$= \frac{\text{Under absorption of Factory Overheads}}{\text{Units of Output}}$$

$$= \frac{\text{Rs. } 3,000}{1,500 \text{ Units}}$$

= Rs. 2.00 per unit.

Accounting entry :

Work-in-Progress A/c	Dr.	Rs.3,000
To Factory Overhead Control A/c		Rs.3,000

(2) Writing-off to Costing Profit and Loss Account or Transfer to Current year's Costing Profit and Loss Account :

The method is used when the under or over-absorbed amount is quite negligible and it is not worth-while to absorb it by supplementary rates. Under-absorption due to abnormal factors like idle capacity, defective planning etc. is also transferred to Costing profit and Loss Account.

This method suffers from the shortcoming that stocks of work-in-progress and finished goods remain under or-over-valued and are carried over to the next accounting period at such values.

Considering the above example, the accounting entry will be as follows:

Costing profit and Loss A/c	Dr.	Rs.3,000
To Factory Overhead Control A/c		Rs.3,000

(3) Carry over to the next year :

Under this method, the under or over-absorbed amount is transferred to Overhead Reserve Account or Suspense Account for carry over to the next accounting year. This procedure is open to criticism on the ground that it is not logical carry over the overhead of one year to the subsequent years for absorption. But, this method can be usefully employed where normal business cycle extends over more than one year and overheads are determined on a long-term basis.

Example

In a Manufacturing unit. overhead was recovered at a per-determined rate of Rs. 25 per man day. The total factory overhead expenses incurred and the man-days actually worked were Rs. 41.50 lakhs and 1.50 lakh days respectively.

Out of the 40,000 units produced during a period, 30,000 were sold.

On analysing the reasons, it was found that 60% of the unabsorbed overheads were due to defective planning and the rest were attributable to increase in overhead costs.

How would unabsorbed overheads to be treated in cost accounts?

Answer **Rs. (in lakhs)**

Actual overhead expenses incurred		41.50
Overhead expenses absorbed		
(Rs. 25 x 1.50 lakhs days)	(-)	37.50
Unabsorbed overheads		4,00

60% of this amount of unabsorbed overheads which is due to defective planning (controllable reasons) should be charged to Costing profit and Loss Account and the remaining 40% should be adjusted to the Cost of sales and Closing stock in the ratio of units sold and units in stock respectively.

Thus, **Rs.(in lakhs)**

Charge to Costing profit and Loss A/C		2.40
(60% of Rs. 4 lakhs)		
Adjustment to the Cost of sales		1.60
(40% of Rs. 4 lakhs)		
Rs. 1.60 lakhs $\times \dfrac{30,000 \text{ units}}{40,000 \text{ units}}$		
Adjustment to Closing Stock :		0.40
Rs. 1.60 lakhs $\times \dfrac{10,000 \text{ units}}{40,000 \text{ units}}$	(+)	
Unabsorbed overhead		4.00

Example

A manufacturing company absorbs overheads on pre-determined rates, for the year ending 31st Dec. 2009, Factory overhead absorbed were Rs. 3,66,250. Actual amount of overheadd incurred totalled Rs. 4, 26,890. The following figures are also derived from the trial balance.

	Rs
Finished Stock	2,30.732
Cost of goods sold	8,40,588
Work-in-progress	1,41,480

Give two methods for the disposal of under-absorbed overhead and show the profit implications of each method.

Answer

Under-absorbed overhead = Rs. 4,26,890 - Rs. 3,66,250
= Rs. 60,640

This under-absorbed amount may be disposed off by any of the following two methods.

i) Use of Supplementary Rate :

Here under absorbed amount will be charged to finished stock, cost of goods sold and work in progress.

$$\text{Supplementary Rate} = \frac{\text{Unabsorbed amount}}{\text{Total cost}} \times 100$$

$$= \frac{\text{Rs. } 60,640}{\text{Rs.} 12,12,800} \times 100$$

$$= 5\%$$

Rs. 2,30,732 + Rs. 8,40,588 + R s.1,41,480 = Rs.12,12, 800

The following journal entry will be made :

Work-in-progress Ledger Control A/c   Dr.   7,074.00
Finished Goods Ledger Control A/c   Dr.   11,536.00
Cost of Goods sold A/c   Dr.   42,029.49
To Factory Overhead Control A/c   60,640

(Being the apportionment of under-absorbed factory overhead to work-in-progress, finished goods and cost of goods sold @ 5% of cost)

The cost of goods sold increased by Rs. 42,029.40. Since, this is debited to profit and Loss Account, the profit will decrease by this amount. On the other hand, credit to profit & Loss A/c on account of increase in the value of closing stocks of work-in-progress and finished stock will be Rs. 18, 610.60 (i.e. 7,074 + 11,536.60). Thus, the net effect of using this method is that profit for the year will reduce by Rs. 23,868.80 (i.e. Rs. 42,029.40-18,610.60)

ii) Carry over to next year :

Alternatively, entire amount of under absorbed overhead may be carried over to next year. This will have no effect on the current year's profit or loss.

ILLUSTRATIONS

Illustrations 1

Star Co. Ltd., Satara distribute their estimated overhead expenses to departments and recover each departmental overhead expenses in various jobs on the basis of the direct labour hour method. The estimates are made on the basis of the normal working capacity of the factory. The following figures relate to the estimates prepared for the year 2009 in respect of the finished department.

Overhead expenses estimated	Rs.60.000
Direct labour hours	Hrs.15,000

The actual overhead expenses incurred was found to be Rs. 30,000 and the actual direct labour hours 9,000 at the end of the half year. Due to heavy orders, the factory had to work overtime for 3,000 hours and incurred an additional overhead expenses of Rs. 8,000

Calculate the actual over-absorbed overhead expenses for normal capacity working and explain how the over-absorbed overhead expenses should be treated.

The estimates from 1ˢᵗ July 2009 to 31ˢᵗ December 2009 are as follows :

	Normal capacity	Actual working
Overhead expenses	Rs.27,000 (estimated)	Rs.35,000
Direct labour hours	9,000 hrs. (estimated)	12,000 hrs.

What should be the overhead recovery rate for the period 1ˢᵗ July 2009 to 31ˢᵗ December 2009

Solution

Estimated overhead rate per hour

$$= \frac{Rs.\ 60,000}{Hrs.15,000} = Rs.4 \text{ per hour}$$

Amount of overhead expenses recovered for the half year ended June 2009 on actual working hours.

= Hrs. 9,000 × Rs. 4 = Rs.36,000

Amount of overabsorbed overhead

= overheads recovered on actual hours

- Actual overhead expenses incurred

= Rs. 36,000 - Rs. 30,000

= Rs. 6,000.

Normal working hours for the half year ended 30th June 2009 was-

Actual working hours - Overtime hours

= Hrs.9,000 - Hrs. 3,000

= 6,000 hours

Overhead recovered on normal hours -

= Hrs.6000 ×Rs.4

= Rs. 24,000

Actual overheads incurred for normal hours -

= Actual overhead expenses - Additional overhead for working overtime

= Rs. 30,000 - Rs.8,000

= Rs. 22,000

Amount of over absorbed overhead on normal hours -

= Overhead recovered on normal hours

- Actual overhead for normal hours

= Rs. 24,000 - Rs. 22,000

= Rs. 2,000

Treatment of Overabsorbed overhead expenses :

The amount of overabsorbed overhead expenses should be adjusted through the value of work in progress and value of finished goods (if shown at cost), and it should not be reduced from the overhead expenses of the next half year.

In order to remove the anamoly of over or under absorption of overheads, the overhead recovery rate should be calculated afresh for the period from 1ˢᵗ July 2009 to 31ˢᵗ December 2009 gives as follows.

Overhead rate for normal working hours

= Overhead expenses (estimated)

+ Direct labour hours (estimated)

$$= \frac{Rs.\ 27,000}{9,000\ hrs.}$$

= Rs. 3 per hour

Overhead rate for excess working hours

$$= \frac{\begin{array}{c}\text{Overhead for} \\ \text{actual working}\end{array} - \begin{array}{c}\text{Overhead} \\ \text{(estimated)}\end{array}}{\begin{array}{c}\text{Direct labour hours} \\ \text{for Actual working}\end{array} - \begin{array}{c}\text{Direct labour hours} \\ \text{(estimated)}\end{array}}$$

$$= \frac{Rs.35,000 - Rs.27,000}{Hrs.12,000 - Hrs.9,000}$$

$$= \frac{Rs.\ 8,000}{Hrs.3,000}$$

= Rs. 2.67

Overhead rate for actual hours -

$$= \frac{\text{Overhead for actual working}}{\text{Direct labour hours for Actual working}}$$

$$= \frac{Rs.35,000}{Hrs.12,000}$$

= Rs. 2.91

Hence, the overhead rate for actual hours i.e. Rs. 2.91 should be used for all calculations of costs for the period from 1ˢᵗ June 2009 to 31st December 2009.

Illustration 2

Madan industries provide the following information from their costing records :

Actual hours worked	2,00,000hrs.
Actual overhead incurred	Rs.5,00,000
Estimated rate of recovery of overheads	Rs.2 per hour
Number of units produced	9,500
Number of units in work-in-progress	500
Number of units in sold	7,500

The Cost Accountant found that 35% of the unabsorbed overhead expenses were due to the increase in the cost of indirect material and indirect labour. 65% of the unabsorbed overhead expenses were due to the inefficiency of the factory staff.

You are required to show how the unabsorbed overhead expenses would be treated?

Solution **Rs.**

Actual overhead incurred	5,00,000
Actual overhead recovered	(-) 4,00,000
(Actual Hrs. worked x Estimated	
recovery rate = Hrs. 2,00,000 x Rs.2	
Unabsorbed Overheads	1,00,000

Since 35% of the unabsorbed overheads was due to the increase in the cost of indirect material and indirect labour, supplementary rate should be charged i.e.

$$\frac{35}{100} \times \frac{Rs.1,00,000}{1} = 35,000$$

∴ Rs.35,000 should be recovered as follows.
Units produced (including work-in-progress)
$$= 9,500 \text{ units} + 500 \text{ units}$$
$$= 10,000 \text{ units}$$

∴ Supplementary rate $= \dfrac{Rs.\ 35,000}{units\ 10,000}$

$$= Rs.\ 3.50 \text{ per unit}$$

Therefore, Rs. 35,000 should be recovered using the supplementary rate of Rs. 3.18 per unit is as follows :

				Rs.
Cost of absorbed	-	7,500 units ×Rs.3.50	=	26,250
Work-in-progress	-	500 units × 3.50	=	1,750
Finished goods	-	2,000 units × Rs. 3.50	=	(+)7,000
				35,000

The remaining 65% of Rs. 1,00,000 i.e. 65,000 is due to one inefficiency of the factory. Hence, this amount should be charged to the Costing Profit and Loss Account.

3.5 Exercises

(a) State whether the following Statement are True or False.

(1) The time factor is ignored when the cost of material is used as the basis for absorption of overhead.

(2) Direct labour hour rate of absorption of overhead is suitable where most of the production is done by using machines.

(3) Basis of apportionment of cost of steam is wages of each department.

(4) When under or over-absorbed overhead is a significant amount. It should be transferred to Costing profit and loss Account.

(5) Machine hour rate method of absorption should be used in only those cost centre in which work is dominantly done by machines.

(6) Cost of after sales services is the part of Selling and distribution overhead.

(7) Apportionment of overhead on reciprocal basis is known as step ladder system.

Ans : (1) True (2) False (3) False (4) False (5) True (6) True (7) False.

(b) Fill in the blanks.

(1) ...... is the allotment of proportion of items of cost to cost centre or cost unit.

(2) Under / over absorption of overhead arises only when overhead absorption is based on.... rate.

(3) ..... is the cost of seeking to create and stimulate demand.

(4) under overhead of absorption is minimum when the overhead rate is based on.....

(5) In..... machine hour rate, wages of operator are included.

(6) Factory rent should be apportioned to various department on the basis of .....

(7) Basis of apportionment of store service expenses is.....

(8) Basis of apportionment of welfare department expenses is.....

(9) Basis of apportionment of creche expenses is....

(10) Machine hour rate is obtained by dividing the total running expenses of machine during the particular period by the .... the machine is estimate work during the period.

Ans : (1) Apportionment (2) Predetermined (3) Selling overhead (4) Normal (5) Comprehensive (6) Area occupied. (7) Value of material counsumed (8) number of employees (9) number of female employees. (10) number of hours.

Practical Problems

(1) From the following particulars compute a Machine Hour Rate. Consider the base period as one year.

(1)	Name of Equipment	-	Crane
(2)	Date of Purchase	-	1st April 2005
(3)	Make	-	L & T Co. Ltd., Mumbai
(4)	Cost of Equipment	-	Rs. 25,000
(5)	Power	-	Diesel 10 H. P. Engine
(6)	Estimate Life	-	10 years
(7)	Depreciation	-	15% p.a. on Original Cost
(8)	Insurance	-	Rs. 25 per quarter
(9)	Repairs	-	Rs. 50 per month
(10)	Consumable Stores (Oil, Grease etc.)	-	Rs. 150 per term of six months
(11)	Rent paid for space allotted to Crane	-	Rs. 125 for 2 months
(12)	Overheads for 5 Similar machines	-	Rs. 1, 300 P.a.
(13)	Cost of Diesel per hour	-	Rs. 1.50

(14) Hire purchase installment paid   -   Rs.5,960 including
     for one year   Rs. 960 as interest.
(15) Assume Crane works normally for 200 hours per month but
     actually works for only 80% fo the normal hours.

**(2) From the following particulars compute Machine hour rate
for a machine for the month of November, 2009**

	Per Annum Rs.
Rent and Taxes	12,000

($\frac{1}{4}$ space is occupied by the machine)

Lighting and Heating	3,000

(10 workers are engaged in the department,
out of them 4 are working on this machine

Supervisor's Salary	6,000

($\frac{1}{3}$ time is devoted for this machine)

Insurance	600
Lubricants and Cotton waste	60

The cost of machine is Rs. 16,000 and its scrap value is estimated
at Rs. 1,000.

From the past experience it has been ascertained
(a) That the working life of the machine is 20,000 hours.
(b) That the machine will work 2,000 hours annually.
(c) That the estimated cost of repairs and maintenance is
Rs. 1,000 for the whole life.
(d) That the machine consumes 4 units per hours, rate of power
is 5 paise per unit.

**(3) The following particulars relate to a processing machine
treating a typical material :**

(1) The cost of machine	Rs.10,000
(2) Estimated life	10 years
(3) Scrap Value	Rs. 1,000
(4) Yearly working time	2,200 hours
(50 weeks of 44 hours each)	

(5) Machine maintenance   200 hours P.a.

(6) Setting up time estimated at 5% of total productive time is regarded as productive time.

(7) Electricity is 16 units per hour @ 10 paise per unit.

(8) Chemical required weekly   Rs.20

(9) Maintenance cost per year   1,200

(10) Two attendants control the operations of machine together with 6 other machines.
Their combined weekly wages are-   Rs.140

(11) Departmental overhead allocated to this machine per annum   Rs.2,000
you are required to calculate the Machine Hour Rate.

(4) The following expenses have been incurred in respect of a shop having 4 identical machines-

		Rs.
(1)	Rent and Rates	9,000 p.a.
(2)	Power consumed by the shop @ 10 paise per unit	4,800 p.a.
(3)	Repairs	1,000 p.a.
(4)	Lighting for the shop	1,800 p.a.
(5)	Attendants two each getting Rs. 60 p.m.	
(6)	Supervisor Salary	6,000 p.a.
(7)	Lubricants etc. per machine	100 p.m.
(8)	Depreciation per machine	900 p.a.
(9)	Hire-Purchase Installment for the machines (including Rs. 300 for interest)	
(10)	Each machine consumes 10 units of power in an hour	

(5) In a machine department of factory there are five identical machines from the particulars given below, prepare a machine hour rate for one of the machine.

(1) Space of department 10,000 sq. meters.

(2) Effective space occupied by this machine 2,000 sq. mtrs.

(3) Cost of machine Rs. 20,000.

(4) Estimated scrap value of the machine Rs. 300.

(5) Effective life of machine 13 years. Depreciation is to be charged at $7\frac{1}{2}$% p.a. on original cost.

(6) Normal running hours of machine 2000 hours p.a.

(7) Power consumed by the machine as shown by meter Rs. 3,000 p.a.

(8) Estimated repairs and maintenance throughout working life of the machine Rs.5,200.

(9) Sundry supplies including oil etc. charged direct to the machine amounted to Rs. 600 p.a. an average.

(10) Other expenses of the department are as follows:

Rent and Taxes	9,000
Lighting to be apportioned to workers employed	400
Supervision	1,250
Other charges	5,000

It is ascertain that the degree of supervision requires by the machine 2/5th and 3/5th being devoted to other machines.

There are 16 workers in the department of which 4 attend to the machine and remaining to other machines.

(6) The following information relates to the activities of a production department of a factory for certain period.

Direct material used	4,000
Direct wages	6,000
Direct labour hours worked	24,000
(including 2,000 hrs. of machine operation)	
Overheads chargeable to department	5,000

for order No. 204 carried out in the department, the relevant figures were:

Direct material used	200
Direct wages	165
Direct labour hours	820
(including 800 machine hours)	

You are required to calculate the overheads chargable to order No. 204 by four different methods.

(7) The following figures have been extracted from the books of a manufacturing concern. All jobs, pass through the company's two departments..

	Production Dept.	Finishing Dept.
Materials	6,000	-
Direct labour	3,000	2,000
Factory overheads	1,800	1,200
Direct hour hrs.	12,000	1,000
Machine hrs	10,000	600

The following information pertains to work order No.III

	Production Dept.	Finishing Dept.
Materials used	240	30
Direct labour	130	60
Direct hour hours	530	150
Machine hours	510	90

You are required to prepare a statement showing the different cost results for work order No. III under the three commonly used methods.

(8) From the following budgeted figures of the Bajaj Ltd. Bangalore.

(a) Prepare normal overhead application rate using:

(1) Direct Labour Hour Rate Method.

(2) Direct Labour Cost Method, and

(3) Machine Hour Rate Method.

Estimated Factory Overheads for year	1,00,500
Estimated Direct Labour Hours for the year	1,34,000
Estimated Direct Labour Cost for the year	67,000
Estimated Machine Hours	50,250

(b) Prepare a Comparative Statement of cost showing the result of application of each of the above rates to Job No. 321 from the data given below:

Cost of Direct Material consumed   250

Direct Labour cost	120
Direct Labour Hours	80
Machine Hours	36

(9) Following data is available relating to a company for a certain month.

		Territory		
		I	II	III
Selling Expenses	Rs.	7,600	4,200	6,240
Distribution Costs	Rs.	4,000	1,800	2,000
Number of units sold	Numbers	16,000	6,000	10,000
Sales	Rs.	76,000	28,000	52,000

The company adopts sales basis and quantity basis for application of selling and distribution costs respectively.

Compute-
  (a) The territorywise overhead recovery rates separately for Selling and Distribution costs.
  (b) The amounts of Selling and distribution cost chargeable to a consignment of 2,000 units of a product, sold in each territory at Rs. 4.50 per unit.

(10) The budgeted working conditions of a cost centre are as follows:

Normal working per week	42 hours
Number of machines	14
Normal weekly loss of hours on maintenance etc.	5 hrs. per machine
Number of weeks worked per year	48
Estimated annual overheads	Rs.1,24,320
Estimated direct wage rate	Rs. 4 Per hour
Actual result in respect of a 4 week period are	
Wages incurred	Rs.9,000
Overheads incurred	Rs.10,200
Machine hours Produced	2,000

You are required to calulate

(a) The overhead rate per machine hour
(b) The amount of under or over absorption of wages and overheads.

(11) **A small scale unit has three producing departments I,II,III and IV and one service department.the cost of service department S is apportioned to the other departments on the basis of direct wages. The unit incurred the following costs during the year 31st March, 2009.**

Repairs to Plant	7,000
Repairs to Buildings	9,000
Depreciation of Plant	15,000
Rent paid	5,000
Lighting	2,800
Electric power	6,600
Supervisor's salary	2,000

Further Information

Depts	No. of employees	Wages	Value of Plant	Area sq.ft.
I	22	58,000	5,60,000	2,000
II	8	62,000	2,40,000	1,500
III	6	84,000	52,000	500
IV	9	16,000	88,000	800
S	5	80,000	60,000	200

You are required to apportion the overhead costs to the producing departments.

(12) **A medium scale unit has three producing departments A, B and C and one service department X.**

The records show the following costs incurred for the year 2009.

Lighting	10,000
Depreciation on Plant and Machinery	1,50,000
Rent of Factory Building	15,000
Servicing and Repairing cost of Plant	56,000
Painting and Repairing of Building	9,000

Further information:

	A	B	C	X
			Departments	
No.of workers	50	20	20	10
Floor Area (sq.ft)	2,000	1,500	1,000	500
Direct wages Rs.	59,000	61,000	98,000	32,000
Value of Plant and Machinery Rs.	5,60,000	3,40,000	2,00,000	

The cost of department X is apportioned on the basis of the value of Plant and Machinery.

(13) Calculate the machine hours of machine "M' from the following particulars.

Cost of machine	25,000
Estimated and residual value	1,500
Estimated life of the machine	20,000 hours
Utility of machine a 4 weekly period	200 hours
Cost of repairs and renewals for a 4 weekly period	
Power consumed	400
	6 units per hour @ 70 ps. per unit
Standing charges for a 4 weekly period	50

(14) Calculate the machine hour rate from the following particulars :

Rs.

Lighting charges (No. of light points in the dept. 20 5 light points are utilized by this machine "M").	360
Rent of the dept. (area occupied by the machine, 1/4th of the dept.)	800
Sundry materials viz, oils and lubricants, cotton waste, etc.	50
Insurance charges	45
Repairs and maintenance (value of machine "M" Rs. 2,00,000	800
Total value of all machines	8,00,000

Supervision (1/5 th of supervisor's time is
    spent for machine "M")   15,000
The estimated residual value of the machine is Rs.20,000
The following are the further estimates.
(a) The machine will work for 2,000 hours per year.
(b) There will be an expenditure of Rs. 1,300 as regards overhauling of the machine.
(c) Its consumption of electric power is 10 units per hour @ 70 ps. per unit.
(d) The life of the machine will be 20,000 hours.

(15) A department is having three machies. The figures indicate the departmental expenses. Calculate the machie hour rate in respect of these machins from the information given below:

Depreciation of Machinery	12,000
Depreciation of Buildings	2,880
Repair to Machinery	4,000
Insurance of Machinery	800
Indirect Wages	6,000
Power	6,000
Lighting	800
Miscellaneous Expenditure	4,200
Total	**36,680**

		Machine I	Machine II	Machine III
Direct wages	Rs.	1,200	2,400	2,400
Power	Units	30,000	10,000	20,000
Number of workers	Number	4	8	8
Light points		8	24	48
Space	sq.ft.	400	800	800
Cost of machine	Rs.	3,00,000	1,20,000	1,80,000
Hours, worked		200	300	300

(16) The following are the figures of Kirloskar Ltd. Kirloskarwadi for the month of may 2006.

	Cutting Dept.	Finishing Dept.
Raw Material	15,000	4,000
Direct Labour	20,000	3,000
Works Overhead	5,000	1,000
	40,000	8,000
Direct labour hours worked	30,000	5,000

The details of Job. No. 64 are given below

	Cutting Dept.	Finishing Dept.
Raw Material	300	40
Direct Labour	400	30
Direct Labour Hours	900	80
Machine Hours worked	850	25

Find out the overhead rates for department using the following methods:

(1) Direct Labour Hours

(2) Direct Labour Cost

(3) Machine Hour Rate

You are required to prepare a statement for Job. No. 64, under each of the above methods, showing thereby the total cost.

(17) From the following particulars, calculate Machine Hour Rate :

(i) Cost of machine   Rs.1,00,000

   Estimated life   10 Years

   Scrap value   Rs.10,000

(ii) Estimated working time : 50 weeks od 44 hours each.

   It includes the following :

   1. Time taken up in maintenance   200 hours

   2. Setting up time   100 hours

However setting up time is rsgarded as productive time.

(iii) power used during production is 16 units per hour at 9 paise per unit. No current is taken during maintenance or setting up time.

(iv) the machine requires a chemical solution which is replaced at the end of each week at a cost of Rs. 20 each time.

(v) Cost of maintenance : Rs 1,200 per annum.

(vi) Two attendants control the opreations of the machine together with five other identical machines. The combined weekly wages amount to Rs. 120

(vii) General works overheads to the machine for the year amount to Rs. 2,000

(18) The following particulars relate to a new machine :

	Rs.
Purchase price	4,00,000
Installation expenses	1,00,000
Rent per quarter	3,750
General lighting for the total area	1,000 per month
Foreman's salary	30,000 per annum.
Insurance premium for the machine	3,000 per annum
Estimated repairs for the machine	5,000 per annum
Consumable stores	4,000 per annum

Power - 2 untis pre hour at Rs. 50 per 100 units.

The estimated life of the machine is 10 years and scrap value at the end of 10th year is Rs. 1,000,000 the machine is expected to run 20,000 hours in its lifetime. The machine occupies 25% of total area. The foreman davotes 1/6th his time for the machine.

Chapter 4

Activity Based Costing Technique

4.1 Meaning and Definition
4.2 Stages in Activity Based Technique
4.3 Purpose and Benefits of Activity Based Technique
4.4 Cost Drivers
4.5 Exercise

Introduction

In any system of costing direct costs are easier to handled as they are directly charged to the end product but indirect costs are difficult to handled because they need to be allocated to the end product by following suitable basis of allocation. It is the indirect costs, which are also known as overhead, which create problem for the cost accountant in determining the accurate product cost. Traditionally indirect cost have been allocated at the end the product in three steps : Firstly from ledger accounts to production and service departments taken from service department to production department following reapportionment method of allocation and then finally allocating the indirect costs of production, department to the end product. In traditional costing there is no general basis of allocation of indirect cost and it is left to the judgement of cost accountant to select the most appropriate basis of allocation. Indirect costs so allocated do not truely reflect the resources consumed by the end product and unnecessarily result in inflated or reduced cost of the end product. In the computer age of advanced technologies and automation, the importance of indirect cost in manufacturing operation is increasing and direct cost being relegated to the background. In order relegated to determine total cost of the end product, under the traditional approach the indirect cost are allocated and apportioned. Activity based costing is an upcoming and more refined approach for charging indirect cost to product and computing more accurate product cost.

4.1 Meaning and Definition

Activity based costing (ABC) is a new and scientific approach by Cooper and Kalpan (1988) for assigning overhead to end products, job or process. It aims to rectify the problem of inaccurate cost information due to selecting of wrong base of indirect cost apportionment. In the words of **Cooper and Kalpan.** "ABC system, calculate the costs of individual activities and assign costs to cost object such as product and services. on the basis of activities undertaken to produce each product or service." In this system overheads are assigned to activities or grouped into cost pools before they are charged to cost object i.e. job or product.

According to **Horngren, Foster and Datar** "ABC is not an alternative costing system to job costing or process costing. Rather ABC is an approach to developing the cost number used in job costing or process costing systems. The distinctive feature of ABC is its focus on activities as the fundamental cost object. In constrast more traditional approach to developing the cost numbers used in job or process costing system rely on general purpose (generic) accounting system not tailored to the activities found in individual organisation. The ABC approach is more expensive than traditional approaches. ABC has the potential, however, to provide managers with information they find more useful for costing purposes." It is an effective method of exercising cost control and can be used indesigning either a job costing system or process costing system.

According to CIMA, London, activity based costing is "Cost attribution to cost units on the basis of benefit received from indiret activities i.e. ordering, setting up, assuring quality etc."

Activity based costing is not an alternative to job costing or process costing.Rather it is a modern tool of charging overhead cost in which costs are first traced to activities and then to products or jobs. Its main focus is on activities performed in the production of goods or service. Thus activities become the focal point for cost consumption. Costs are charged to products or services based on individual product's consumption of each activity. It recognises that job, product, services etc. do not directly consume resources but consume activities which consume resources. In short in ABC costing, overheads are first assigned to activities and then absorbed by cost objects on the basis of activities consumed by these cost objects.

Activities based costing aims at rectifying the inaccurate cost information.It is a modern approach of indirect cost allocation. ABC does not restrict itself to the allocation of indirect costs to departments as is done in the traditional approach but it recognises individual activity as the lower unit for indirect cost allocation. Cost allocated to each activity represents the resources consumed by it.

4.2 Stage or Steps in Activity Based Technique

Following are the stages or steps in activity based technique.

(1) Identification of main activities :

First of all, major activities in the organisation or factory are identified. The number of activities in an organisation should neither be too large or too small. Too large number will be costly and will add to the complexity of the system while too small number of activities will compromise with the accuracy of the cost. Total cost involved in the activity should be sighificant enough to justify to give an activity a separate treatment.

(2) Creation of Cost Pool :

Cost Pool is grouping of individual cost items. Cost Pool should be created for each activity. Cost Pool is like cost centre around which cost are accumulated. For example : the total cost of machine set ups might constitute one cost pool for all setup related costs.

(3) Determination of activity cost drivers :

The factors that influence the cost of a particular activity is known as cost dirvers. In other words cost drivers signify the factors or events that determine the cost of activity. Number of orders placed, Number of units, Number of research projects, Number of services calls etc. are some of the examples of cost drivers.

(4) Calculation of the activity cost driver rate :

Just as an overhead absorption rate is calculated in traditional cost system, in ABC a cost driver rate is calculated as follows.

$$\text{Activity cost driver rate} = \frac{\text{Total cost of activity}}{\text{cost drivers}}$$

(5) Charging the cost of activities to product :

The cost of activities are traced to product on the basis of demand by products. The cost drivers are used to measure product demand of activities. For example : the total cost allocuted to cost centre for machine setup related cost is 100,000 and that there 100 set ups during the period Thus the rate per set up is Rs. 100,000 ÷ 100 = Rs. 1000. If a particular product needs 10 setups, charge to that product will be Rs. 1000 x 10 = Rs. 10000. If so units of product are produced, cost per unit will be Rs. 10000 x 50 = Rs. 2000. In this way cost of other activitis also will be charged to product.

4:3 Purposes and Benefits of Activity Based Technique

(i) Purposes : Following are the purposes of ABC.

(1) To remove the inaccurate allocation of indirect expenses.

(2) To determine the product of service cost.

(3) To provide basis for make or buy decision.

(4) To improve the performarce of organisation.

(5) To fix the price of product or service.

(ii) Benefits : (Advantages / Merits)

The following are the main benefits of activity based technique.

(1) Determination of product service cost :

Now a days, non manufacturing costs can no longer be negelected as they constitute a substantial portion of the total cost, for example. Softdrink giants of the world, coke or pepsi have huge marketing and advertising cost. On the contrary manufacturing cost coustitute a very small proportion of the total cost these non-manufacturing cost can be allocated easily using ABC because the relationship between cost and its causes is better understood.

(2) Make or buy decision :

ABC enables the manager to decide whether he should get the activity done with in the firm or buy outside agency. Subcontracting may be done if the firm is incurring higher overhead cost as compared to the subcontractor. On the coutrary if the cost is not going to decrease or the resources fed by sub-coutracting can not be economically dirverted elsewhere, the company should get the activity done internally.

(3) Cost management and downsizing :

ABC reduce the cost by providing meaningful information on the opportunities available for reducing costs. If company's financial performance is not satisfactory, it may have to resort to extreme measure like layoffs. ABC helps in making the right decisions as it clearly defines the various activities. Thus one can focus on value adding activites and eliminating the non-value adding activities.

(4) Transfer pricing :

ABC helps to determine the cost of each activity. Thus when finished goods of department 'X' is transferred to department 'y', the cost of product of department 'y' can be easily known. Moveover, accuracy of indirect cost allocation to the product being transferred is very important as the performance evaluation of both department 'x' and 'y' depends on the proportion of indirect cost being passed on to department 'y.' ABC provides accurate cost information to evaluate the performance of the tranfer or and transferee department.

(5) Product / service pricing :

ABC enables the management to fix the product / service prices by formulating an effective pricing policy. ABC helps in price fixation by providing information about product / service cost.

(6) Improvements in performance :

ABC involves perparing the statement of expenditure

activity-wise and comparing it with the corresponding value addition to know the activities which are to be eliminated. ABC provides accurate cost information which is essential for most of the recent productivity improvement approaches like Total Quality Management and Business process Reengineering kaizen.

4.4 Cost drivers :

Cost driver is a factor that caused a changes in the cost of activity. Cost driver is of two types-resource, cost driver and activity cost driver.

(i) Resouree cost driver :

It is the measure of cost the quautity of resource consumed by an activity. For example, number of purchase orders placed will determine the cost of purchasing the material. Similarly, the number of times machines are setup will determine the cost of setting up of machines. Resource cost driver is used to assign the cost of resource to an activity or cost pool.

(ii) Activity cost driver :

It is a measure of the frequency and intersity of demand placed on the activities by cost objects. It is used for assigning activity costs to cost objects consuming the activity.

Examples of cost drivers for various business functions are given on next page.

Functional Areas	Activities Involved	Cost Driver
a) Material Management	1) Issuing Tenders 2) Receiving of indents 3) Analysis of offers from suppliers 4) Issue of purchase order 5) Inspection of materials 6) Information to stores for receeving the materials	No. of Tenders issued No. of indents No. of purchase orders No. of purchase orders No. of purchase orders No. of purchase orders
b) Stores Management	1) Storing of materials 2) Servicing of requisitions. 3) Inspection and verifications 4) Taking perpetual stock-taking.	Value of materials stored No. of requisitions. No. of times inspected Value of stock handled
c) Personel Management	1) Recruitment 2) Maintenance of records of attendance, leave, increment etc. 3) Training 4) Industrial relations 5) Settlement of industrial disputes 6) labour turnover	No. of employees recruited No. of employees No. of employees No. of employees No. of employees No. of employees replaced
d) Marketing	1) Demand creation 2) Advertising efforts. 3) Analysis of feed back from sales 4) Preparation of sales forecasts	% increase in sales % increcrase in sales Time spent with distributors, consumers Time spent
e) Quality Control.	1) Receipt of samples 2) Testing of samples 3) Issue of test certificales	No. of batches produced No. of batches product No. of batches produced

4.5 Exercises

State whether the following statement or True or False.

1) Traditional method of costing may result in undercosting and overcosting of product.
2) Machine hour rate is used in traditional method of overhead costing but not in activity based costing.
3) Activity based costing is one of the best tools for refining a costing system.
4) An activity is an item for which separate cost measurement is required.
5) Cost pool is like cost centre.
6) Identifying less number of activities result is more accurate cost.
7) Purchasing of large quantity of materials is a cost driver.

Ans : True 1, 3, 4, 6 False 2, 5, 7, 8.

Theoretical question.

1) Briefly explain the meaning and purposes of activity based costing.
2) Describe the main features of activity based costing.
3) Explain the steps in activity based costing.
4) Explain the following in relation to ABC.
   (a) Cost object   (b) cost driver   (c) Cost pool

Chapter 5

Methods of Costing

5.1 Introduction to Methods of Costing
5.2 Job Costing - Meaning and Features
5.3 Advantages and Limitations
5.4 Exercises

5.1 Introduction to Methods of Costing

The method of cost accumulation and identifying them to products and services depends upon the nature of operations in an enterprise. Therefore, cost accounting procedure varies from one company to another company. For example, a non-manufacturing enterprise may not follow the procedure of accumulating costs with specific customer orders. Similarly, a hospital may prefer to accumulate costs in a manner as to provide the cost of outpatient treatment or a specific medical treatment. A concern organising exhibitions and fairs may be interested in knowing the cost of an exhibition to be organised in a particular season. On the contrary, a contractor accumulates costs for each separate contract. Although the procedure of accumulating costs may differ among different types of organisations, the basic principles underlying cost accumulating procedures are applicable to all types of organisations. Each cost accounting procedure or system aims to provide information that is needed by the management.

Meaning

Cost Accounting is the process of accounting for cost, from the point at which expenditure is incurred or to be incurred to the point of charging to the cost centres and cost units. It has many uses which includes the preparation of statistical data, the application of cost control methods and the ascertainment of the profitability of activities carried out or planned. It is the means which consists of concepts, methods and procedures used to measure, analyse or estimate the cost, profitability and performance of individual products, departments and other sectors of a company's operations. It has internal and external use or both and it answers to all the questions to the concerned parties. Thus, Cost Accounting is the process and technique of determination of a product cost. It is a system of cost accumulation, ascertainment and classification for product costing and managerial planning, control and decision-making process. In short, Cost Accounting is a dynamic and diverse field of activity.

Need

Methods of Costing indicates a systematic procedure established for ascertaining cost of a product, job process or services by using the principles of costing. A cost Accounting method is merely the process of "Collecting and presenting cost." The nature of industries differs. Some are very simple and produce only one product e.g. brick-making. Some industries may produce only one product but it may really be an assembly of numerous components e.g. bicycle, motor car etc. Again there may be a homogeneous product but involving many distinct stages and processes such as vegetable oil. In some case there may be important by - products or joint products e.g. petrolium products, sugar etc. It is therefore, natural that the exact method employed to ascertain cost per unit should depend on the nature of the industry. The general principle of ascertaining cost of production per unit are the same, but the methods ascertaining and presenting the costs vary with the type of production. Hence, various methods are required for ascertaining the costs because every business is different in its nature, in its type of products, in methods of production etc.

Various Methods of Costing

In manufacturing organisations, the principles of cost accumulation and their identification with products are more clear and visible and therefore the principles used by a manufacturing enterprise is often used by other organisations also for accumulating costs. In manufacturing concerns, costs are accumulated and assigned to products on the basis of the following cost accounting methods.

    1) Specific Order Costing and

    2) Operation Costing.

    But according to Mr. Batty, "Many costing systems do not fall neatly into the category of either job or process costing. Often, systems use some features of both the main costing systems." It is, for this reason, that he uses the term "hybrid costing systems" for all those methods that combine the features of the basis methods. The Figure indicated below shows various Methods of Costing.

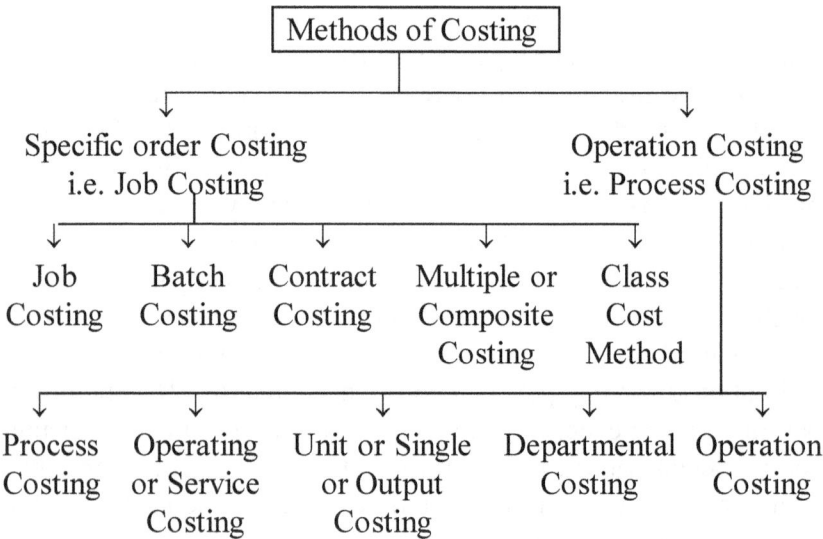

Specific Order Costing :

    The terminology of ICMA defines Specific Order Costing as "the category of basis costing methods applicable where the work consists of separate contracts, jobs or batches each of which is authorised by a special order or contract." This method is adopted in made-to-order type of standardisation in the production process for want of uniformity.

This method may take any of the following :

1) Job Costing : The terminology of ICMA defines Job Costing as "that form of specific order costing which applies where work is undertaken to customers' special requirements." Under this method, costs are collected and accumulated for each job, work order or project separately. Each job can be separately identified, so it becomes essential to analyse the cost according to each job. A job card is prepared for each job for cost accumulation. This method is applicable to printers, machine tool manufacturers, foundaries and general engineering workshops, interior decorator, painters, repair shops etc.

2) Batch Costing : The terminology of ICMA defines Batch Costing as "'that form of specific order costing which applies where similar articles are manufactured in batches either for sale or use within the undertaking." This method is a variation of Job Costing. In this method, the cost of a batch or group of identical products is ascertained and, therefore, each batch of products is a unit of cost for which costs are accumulated. This method is used in biscuit factories, bakeries, ready-made garments, hardwares like nuts, bolts, screws, shoes, toys, drugs and pharmacuticals etc.

3) Contract Costing : The terminology of ICMA defines Contract Costing as "that form of specific order which applies where work is undertaken to customers' special requirements and each order is of long duration." The cost unit here is a contract which is of a long duration and may continue over more than one financial year. A separate account is kept for each contract. This method is used by builders, civil engineering contractors, constructional and mechanical engineering firms etc.

4) Multiple or Composite Costing : It is an application of more than one method of cost ascertainment in respect of the same product. This method is used in industries where a number of components are separately manufactured and then assembled into a final product. In such industries each component differs from the others as to price, material used and process of manufacture undergone. So it will be necessary to ascertain the cost of each component for this purpose, for which process costing may be applied. To ascertain the cost of the final product, batch costing may be applied. This method used in factory's manufacturing cycles, automobiles, engines, radioes, TVs, typewriters, aeroplanes etc. This method has been completely dropped from the latest ICMA Terminology.

5) Class Cost Method : It is the method of Job Costing where the costing of goods is done by classes instead of the unit or price. Instead of the cost being separately accumulated for each article or piece, the cost will cover a group of orders of the same class of product.

Operation Costing :

The terminology of ICMA defines Operation Costing as "the catagory of basic costing methods applicable where standardised goods or services result from a sequence of repetitive and more or less continuous operations or process to which costs are charged before being averaged over the units produced during the period."

The following are the different methods of costing which fall under this category.

1) Process Costing : The terminology of ICMA defines Process Costing as "That form of operation costing which applies where the standardised goods are produced." It is a method of costing where cost is ascertained at the stage of every process and also after completing the finished production. It is used in concerns where production follows a series or sequential process. Process type of industries do not manufacture individual items to the specific requirements of customers. As such, production is not intermittent but continuous. Each process represents a distinct stage of manufacture and the output of one process becomes the input of the following process. The unit cost is arrived at by averaging the cost over the units produced, and cost per unit of each process is ascertained. Process Costing is used in a variety of industries such as chemicals, oil refining, paper making, flour milling, cement manufacturing, sugar, rubber, textiles, soap, glass, food processing etc.

2) Operating or Service Costing : The terminology of ICMA defines Service Costing as "that form of Operation Costing which applies where - standardised services are provided either by an undertaking or by a service cost centre within an undertaking." This method of costing is used by those undertakings which render service as against manufacturing and supply of tangible products. It is an essential method of costing where only the services are rendered. It ascertains the cost of one unit of service rendered. This method is applicable to transport undertakings, electricity supply undertakings, hospitals, hotels, canteen, water works, gas companies, educational institutions etc. The cost unit depends upon the service provided. Usually, a composite cost unit is used. For example tonne km, passenger km, patient day or bed day, KWH, meal served, student hours etc.

3) Unit or Single or Output Costing : It is a method of costing by the unit of production, where manufacturing is continuous and the units are identical. In some cases the units may differ in terms of size, shape, quality etc. This method is also called as Single Costing because only one type of product alone is manufactured. Examples of industries where this method is applicable are : Collieries, quarries, flour-mills, paper mills, textile mills, brick-making, radio, cameras, pencils, slates, dairy products etc. No separate set of books is generally required and costing information is presented in the form of a statement known as Cost Sheet.

4) Departmental Costing : A factory may be divided into a number of departments and sometimes good results are obtained by allocating expenditure first to different departments and then to different products manufactured in that department. Under this method, the cost incurred in maintaining a particular department is ascertained. There are two objectives for using this method viz. to control the cost of department and to charge the cost of a department on to the finished product.

5) Operation Costing : It is a special type of Process Costing. It refers to the determination of cost of operations, the cost unit is the 'operation' instead of the number of units completed in the operation centre. For large undertakings it is frequently necessary to ascertain the cost of various operations. Cost control can be exercised more effectively with operation costing.

5.2 Job Costing

Meaning and Features

The industries which manufacture articles or products or render services against specific orders, use the Job Costing method for ascertaining the cost per job or service. e.g. specific requirement of a customer, fabrication, repairs etc. Each job has a separate identity. Under this method, individual jobs are identifiable and each job becomes a separate cost centre. ICMA London defines Job Costing as "it is that category of basic costing method which is applicable where the work consists of separate contract, jobs or batches each of which is authorised by specific order or contract." Examples of Job order industries are printing press, construction of buildings, bridges, ship-building, furniture making, machine tool manufacturing, repair shops, painting works etc.

Features

1) Production is made or services are rendered against specific orders.
2) A job is clearly identifiable throughout the production process.
3) Each job has its own characteristics and requires special attention.
4) A distinguishing number is allotted to each job order undertaken.
5) Each of the job becomes a separate cost centre.
6) Costs are charged directly to individual job orders.
7) The manufacturing cost of a job order can be found out only after the job order is completed irrespective of the time taken for the same.
8) Production is not made in anticipation of demand and for storing purpose.

5.3 Job Costing Advantages and Limitations

Advantages

1) Cost of each job as per order is ascertained separately. This helps in finding out the profit or loss on each individual job.
2) It enables management to detect those jobs which are more profitable and those which are not profitable.
3) It provides a basis for determining the cost of similar jobs undertaken in future. It thus helps in future production planning.
4) It enables the management to know the trends in costs.
5) Profitability ratio of different jobs can be found out.
6) It helps the management to fix selling price of specific job on the basis of costs.
7) It enables the management to provide quotations for similar type of jobs.
8) Spoilage and defective work can be easily identified with specified jobs or products.
9) It enables the management to take corrective steps for improving the efficiency in future.
10) It is essential for cost plus contracts.

Limitations

1) Calculations are more and hence there is possibility of errors which may cause a serious loss.
2) A system of budgetory control may not be used effectively.
3) The system does not indicate any standard of performance efficiency.
4) Comparison of cost of a job over any period of time cannot be made if certain economic changes takes place in between.
5) It is expensive to operate as there is increase in clerical work.
6) Job costing is a historical costing which ascertains the cost of job or product after it has been manufactured.

Procedure followed in Job Costing :

Job Costing is designed to show in detail their cost components of the total cost executing a job. A Job Cost sheet is prepared for every job which is undertaken. Material Cost is accounted for in the job cost sheet on the basis of material requisition concerned. Labour cost on the basis of time clocked in respect of the job with the help of time tickets and factory overheads are added to those cost components according to some reasonable methods of overhead absorption. Thus, the total cost of the job consists partly of direct cost and partly of costs arrived at by assignments, allocation, apportionment and finally by absorption. Thus, the procedure followed in Job Costing may be summarised as follows :

1) Receiving an Enquiry : Before placing an order with the manufacturer, usually the customer will enquire about the price, quality to be maintained, the duration within which the order is to be executed and other specifications of the job.

2) Estimation of the Price of the Job : The cost accountant estimates the cost of Job after considering the various elements of cost and keeping in mind the specification of customers. This is based on the cost of execution of similar job in the previous year and considering the possible changes in the various elements of cost. The estimated cost of the job is then communicated to the prospective customer.

3) Receiving of Order : If the prospective customer accepts the quotation, the intention of acceptance is forwarded to the respective departments so that preparation work may begin even before the issue of the formal Production Order. The production control department receives the order.

4) Job Number : When an order has been accepted, an individual work order number must be assigned to each such job so that separate orders are capable of being identified at all stages of production. Assignment of Job numbers also facilitates reference for costing purposes in the ledger and convenient for use in various forms and documents.

5) Production Order : Once the job is accepted the Planning Department prepares Production Order. The Production Order is nothing but a form of instructions issued to the foreman to proceed with the manufacture of the articles. Several copies of Production

Order are prepared and passed on to the following :
  i) All departmental foremen connected with the job.
  ii) Store-keeper for issuance of materials.
  iii) Tool room - an advance notification of tools required.

A Production Order contains all the information that is relevant to the job or products or service. It gives information about the following :
  a) Particulars of job, product or service.
  b) Quantity to be produced.
  c) Date of starting and required date of completion of the job.
  d) Particulars of materials required.
  e) Particulars of various operations involved in the performance and execution of the job.

The Figure indicated below shows a specimen form of Production Order for a Job.

ABC Co. Ltd., Pune Production Order			
Name of Customer .... Job No. .... Date of Commencement .... Date .... Date of Completion .... Bill of Material No. .... Special Instructions .... Drawing attached-Yes/No.			
Quantity (Units)	**Description**	**Machines to be used**	**Tools required**
sd./- ..... Production Authorised by : Head of Production Control Dept.			

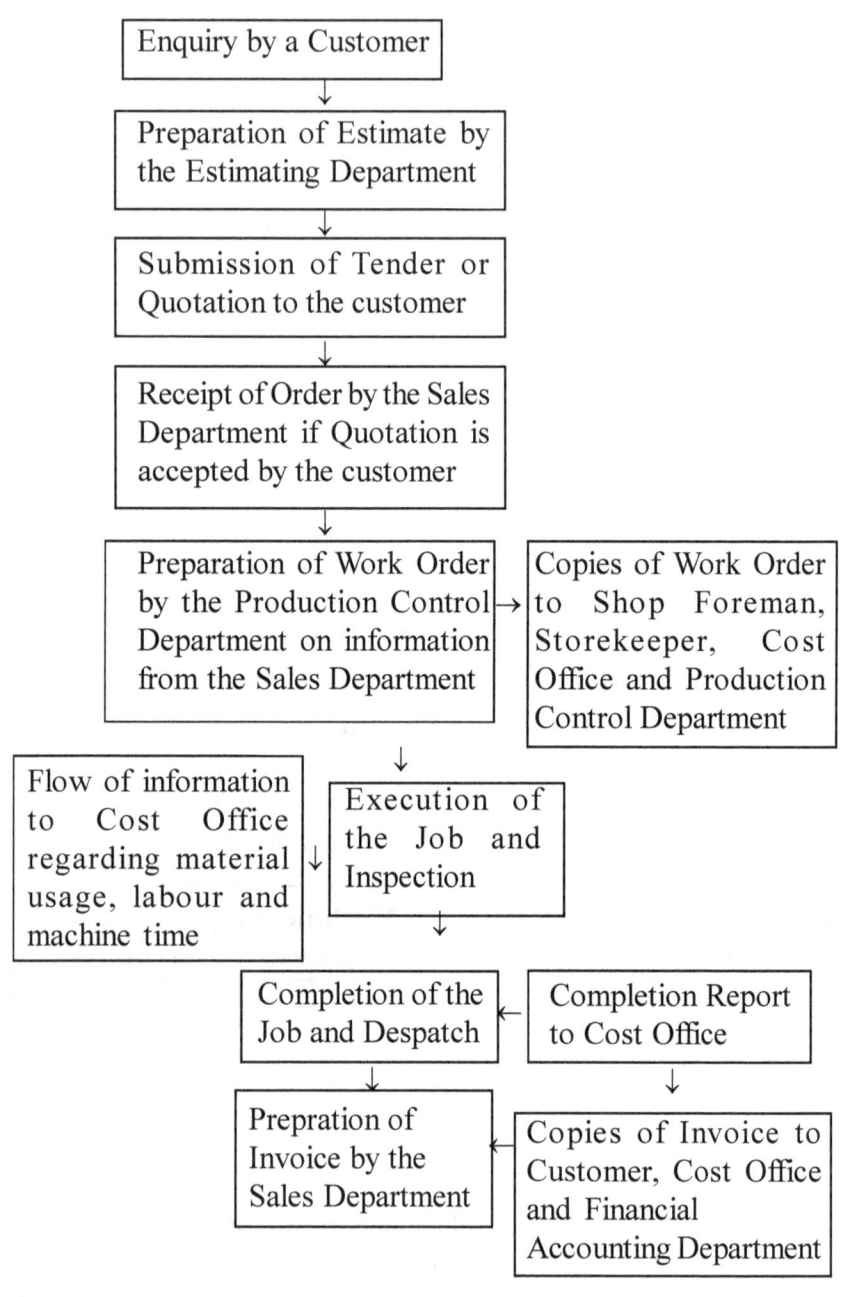

Diagram showing Job Order Execution Procedure

Production Order for a Job

The columns provided in the Production Order differ widely, depending largely upon the nature of production. Some such orders are accompanied by the blue prints and contain a bill of materials and detailed instructions as to which tools and machineries are to be used.

6) Recording of Costs : There are various costs required for the job. The raw materials, the labour costs, overhead charges etc. are directly chargeable to that particular production order number. General Job Cost Sheet is prepared for each job.

The basis of collection of costs are :

a) **Materials :** Materials Requisition, Bills of Materials or Material Issue Analysis Sheet.

b) **Wages :** Operation Schedule, Job Card or Wages Analysis Sheet.

c) **Direct Expenses :** Direct Expenses Vouchers.

d) **Overheads :** Standing Order Number or Cost Account Number.

e) **Completion of Job :** On completion of a Job report is sent to Costing Department. The expenditure under each element of cost is totalled and the total Job cost is ascertained.

7) Profit or Loss on Job : It is determined by comparing the actual expenditure of cost with the price obtained.

The figure above indicated is a diagram showing Job Order Execution Procedure.

Preparation of Job Cost Sheet

A job cost sheet is a cost statement prepared to analyse and ascertain the actual cost incurred with respect to the individual jobs. Thus, a card for each job is maintained wherein the total cost of the job is accumulated. A separate job Cost Sheet is prepared to find out profit or loss on each job. It records the actual costs incurred on direct material, direct labour, direct expenses and overheads job that passes through the factory and that the total constituent's of cost of the job Order or Operation. Cost of Material Consumed

ABC Co. Ltd., Pune.
Job Cost Sheet

Customer .... Job No. ....

Date of Commencement .... Date of Completion ....

Material Cost

Date	Material Req. No.	Amount Rs.
Total		

Labour Cost

Date	Hours	Rate Rs.	Amount Rs.
Total			

Factory Overheads (Absorbed)

Date	Hours	Rate Rs.	Amount Rs.
Total			

Cost Summary

	Rs.
Material	
Add : Labour	(+)
Add : Factory Overheads	(+)
Add : Administration Overheads	(+)
Add : Selling Overheads	(+)
Total Cost	

Profit or Loss

	Rs.	
Price Quoted	....	
Less : Cost (–)	....	....
Profit or Loss	....	....

Job Cost Sheet

is collected from invoices and material requisition note. The Direct Labour Cost is found out by operating each workmen's wages according to the time he spends on each job, as recorded on job sheets. Overheads may be allocated as a simple percentage of material cost or by some such other method as is appropriate and practicable for the organisation concerned. On completion of a job the various elements of costs are summed together and the total cost is ascertained. The total cost is then divided by the number of jobs completed or units produced to ascertain the cost per job or unit.

The figure indicated below shows a specimen of Job Cost Sheet.

Forms used in Job Costing :

Following are the various forms used in Job Costing method :

1) **Production Order :** It is a written authority to factory foreman to proceed with a job.

2) **Bill of Materials :** It is a complete schedule of materials, parts etc. required for a particular Job or Production order.

3) **Operation Schedule :** There are various operations of a job e.g. turning, drilling, milling, assembling etc. It contains name of job, name of operation, description of operation, starting time and completion time etc.

4) **Tool List :** It is a list of all types of tools required for a particular job. It is given alongwith schedule and instruction cards.

5) **Planning Board :** It is nothing but a time-table of a particular job to be done. It sets the time for processing the various jobs.

6) **Move Tickets :** There are various steps in completion of the job. There is a progress of each job which is checked off on the operations schedule. The move tickets are sent alongwith each lot at the time of transfer to the next department.

Illustration 1

Dawson India Ltd., Dombivali provides the following information in respect of Job No. 346, you are required to prepare a Job Cost Sheet for the period ended 31st March, 2006 showing the cost of job and selling price to give a profit of 20% on sales.

	Rs.
Productive Wages	90,000
Materials used directly for Job	90,000
Sundry Work Expenses	3,400
Selling Commission	1,200
Machinery Repairs	5,700
Advertising	2,500
Coal and Coke	3,000
Consumable Stores	12,800
Directors Fees	3,000
Factory Insurance	1,400
Carriage Outward	9,200
Unproductive Wages	24,200
Chargeable Expenses	4,500
Depreciation on Office Furniture	3,700
Selling on Cost	10,000
Motive Power	10,100
Packing Charges	7,500
Technical Directors Fees	1,700
Salary to Works Manager	5,400
Heating and Lighting	700
Office Rent	9,500
Direct Expenses Payable	500

Solution

Working Notes :

1) Calculation of Profit i.e. 20% on Sales

SP = CP + P

100 = 80 + 20

If 80 CP = 20 P

∴ Rs. 3,00,000 = ?

$$\frac{Rs. 3,00,000 \times 20}{80}$$

$$= Rs.\ 75,000$$

In the books of Dawson India Ltd., Dombivali
Job Cost Sheet for Job No. 346 for the period ended
31ˢᵗ March, 2006

Particulars	Amount Rs.	Amount Rs.
Materials used directly	90,000	
Add : Productive Wages	90,000	
Add : Direct Expenses :		
i) Chargeable expenses	4,500	
ii) Direct expenses payable (+)	500	
PRIME COST	**1,85,000**	1,85,000
Add : Factory Overheads :		
i) Sundry Works Expenses	3,400	
ii) Machine Repairs	5,700	
iii) Coal and Coke	3,000	
iv) Consumable Stores	12,800	
v) Factory Insurance	1,400	
vi) Unproductive Wages	24,200	
vii) Motive Power	10,100	
viii) Technical Directors Fees	1,700	
ix) Salary to Works Manager	5,400	
x) Heating and Lighting (+)	700	
WORKS COST	**2,53,400**	2,53,400
Add : Administration Overheads :		
i) Directors Fees	3,000	
ii) Depreciation on Office Furniture	3,700	
iii) Office Rent (+)	9,500	
COST OF PRODUCTION	**2,69,600**	2,69,600

Add : Selling and Distribution Overheads :			
i) Selling Commission		1,200	
ii) Advertising		2,500	
iii) Carrige Outward		9,200	
iv) Selling on Cost		10,000	
v) Packing Charges	(+)	7,500	
COST OF JOB	(1)	**3,00,000**	3,00,000
Add : Profit (20% Sales) +	(+)	75,000	
SELLING PRICE	(2)	**3,75,000**	3,75,000

Illustration 2

Following information relates to two different jobs of a manufacturing concern Bharat Engineering Co. Ltd., Bharatpur for the month of March, 2008.

	Job No. 367	Job No. 376
	Rs.	Rs.
Chargeable Expenses Payable	250	400
Process Materials	6,200	7,500
Cost of Special Designs	700	650
Direct Labour	4,800	1,700
Other Direct Expenses	2,050	3,950
Operating Labour	1,300	5,200
Prime Cost Materials	3,800	10,500
Productive Wages Outstanding	900	100

Additional Information :
  i) Distribution on Cost - 3% on Office Cost
  ii) Management Expenses - 20% on Works Cost
  iii) Works Overheads - 50% on Basic Cost
  iv) Selling Expenses - 7% on Cost of Production
     Find out the Cost of Sales and Value of Sales to get a profit of 25% on Value of turnover.

In the books of Bharat Engineering Co. Ltd., Bharatpur

Job Cost Sheet for the month of 31st March, 2008

Particulars	Job No. 367 Amount Rs.	Job No. 367 Amount Rs.	Job No. 376 Amount Rs.	Job No. 376 Amount Rs.
Direct Materials :				
i) Process Materials	6,200		7,500	
ii) Prime Cost Materials (+)	3,800	10,000 (+)	10,500	18,000
Add : Direct Wages :				
i) Direct Labour	4,800		1,700	
ii) Operating Labour	1,300		5,200	
iii) Productive Wages Outstanding (+)	900	7,000 (+)	100	7,000
Add : Direct Expenses :				
i) Chargeable Expenses Payable	250		400	
ii) Cost of Special Designs	700		650	
iii) Other Direct Expenses (+)	2,050	3,000 (+)	3,950	5,000
PRIME COST/BASIC COST		**20,000**		**30,000**
Add : Works Overheads (50% on Basic Cost)	(+)	10,000	(+)	15,000

Particulars		Job No. 367		Job No. 376	
	Amount Rs.	Amount Rs.	Amount Rs.	Amount Rs.	Amount Rs.
WORKS COST/FACTORY COST			30,000		45,000
Add : Management Expenses (20% on Works Cost)	(+)		6,000	(+)	9,000
COST OF PRODUCTION/OFFICE COST			36,000		54,000
Add : Selling Expenses (7% on Cost of Production)	(+)		2,520	(+)	3,780
Add : Distribution on Cost (3% on Office Cost)	(+)		1,080	(+)	1,620
Cost of Sales	(1)		39,600		59,400
Add : Profits (25% on value of turnover)	(+)		13,200	(+)	19,800
VALUE OF SALES	(2)		52,800		79,200

Solution

Working Notes :

1) Calculation of Profits i.e. 25% on value of turnover

$$SP = CP + P$$

(i.e. value of turnover)

$$100 = 75 + 25$$

a) Job No. 367 : If 75 CP = 25 P

∴ Rs. 39,600 C.P. = ?

$$= \frac{Rs.39,600 \times 25}{75} = Rs.\ 13,200$$

b) Job No. 376 : If 75 CP = 25 P

∴ Rs. 59,400 CP = ?

$$= \frac{Rs.59,400 \times 25}{75} = Rs.\ 19,800$$

5.4 Exercises

Job costing

A) State whether following statements are True or False :

i) Job costing is used in industries which produce against specific orders.

ii) job order is issued by cost accounting department.

iii) A job ticket gives details of cost incurred for a job.

iv) Setting-up costs are of the nature of fixed costs.

v) Job costing can be used in industries using standard costing.

vi) Job costing is applied only in small concerns.

vii) Job costing can be used in conjunction with marginal costing.

Ans. : i) True; ii) False, iii) False, iv) True, v) True   vi)   False, vii) True.

B) Select the most appropriate answer.

i) Job costing is suitable for –
   a) specific order concerns   b) mass producing concerns
   c) all concerns.

ii) With every increase in the size of the batch –
   a) setting-up cost per unit decreases

b) setting-up cost per unit increases

c) setting-up cost per unit remains constant.

iii) The document which provides information regarding the progress of each job at each operation is known as –

a) Progress Advice   b) Job ticket   c) Job order.

iv) Which of the following would not be used in Job order costing?

a) Standards

b) Averaging of direct labour and material rate

c) Direct costing

v) A job order cost sheet normally does not contain which of the following?

a) Direct materials   b) Direct labour

c) Actual factory overhead.

Ans. : i) a, ii) a, iii) b, iv) b, v) c

C) Fill in the blanks :

i) Job order is a .... order issued to the manufacturing depts.

ii) Each job becomes a separate .....

iii) A particular ..... is allotted to each job order undertaken.

iv) Job costing helps the management to fix .... of specific job.

v) Costs are charged directly to ...... job orders.

vi) Job costing helps the management to provide .... for similar type of jobs.

Ans : i) written, ii) cost centre, iii) number, iv) selling price, v) individual, vi) quotation.

Eassy type

1) What is "method of costing"? Explain the need of various methods of ascertaining cost.

2) How would you classify methods of ascertaining cost?

3) Explain the term "Job costing". State the important features of Job costing.

4) What are the advantages and limitations of job costing?

5) What is job costing? Give a specimen form of job cost sheet.

Practical Exercises

1) From the following particulars prepare Cost-Sheet for job No. and find out the selling price of the job.

	Rs.
Materiaks directly issued for the job	21,400
Direct Expenses	5,000
Productive Wages	8,000

Provide 70% on production wages for works overheads, 10% on Works Cost for office cost and 5% on Cost of Production and Selling and Distribution overheads. Profits shall be 25% on the Selling Price.

2. From the following information in respect on Job No. 3663 you are required to prepare a job cost sheet showing the cost of the job and also calculate the selling price to give a profit of 20% on Selling price.

Chapter 6

Contract Costing

Introduction

Contract or Terminal Costing is a special type of Job Costing where the unit of cost is a single contract. It is a further development of Job Costing. In this method it is desired to find out the cost of carrying out a complete contract for a customer involving numerous jobs and batches of jobs. The costs are ascertained and analysed with respect to the contract accepted for execution. This method of costing is adopted by those concerns undertaking definite contracts e.g. builders, contractors and civil engineers who undertake long-term projects like construction of roads, bridges, houses, large estates, irrigation schemes etc. It is also adopted by the concerns where the unit of output is heterogenous e.g. ship building companies, turbines and boilers manufacturing company, motion pictures etc.

6.1 Meaning and Features of Contract Costing

Definition :

The terminology of ICMA defines Contract Costing as "that form of specific order costing which applies where work is undertaken to customers special requirements and each order is of long duration. It is also known as 'Terminal Costing' because when the work is terminated the Job Cost sheet has to be completed.

Features

1) The work is carried out away from contractor's premises.
2) A conract is usually of long-duration and may continue over more than one accounting period.
3) As the contracts are of large size, a contractor usually carries out a small number of contracts in the course of a year.
4) Cost unit in contract costing is a contract.
5) A separate account is prepared for each contract to ascertain profit or loss on each contract.
6) Most of the materials are specially purchased for each contract.
7) Expenses chargeable to contracts are direct in nature, e.g. electricity, telephone charges, insurance etc.
8) Specialists sub-contractors may be employed for say, electrical fittings, welding works, glass work, plumbing work etc.
9) Plant and equipment may be purchased or hired for the duration of the contract.
10) Nearly all labour will be direct.
11) The payment is received depending on the stage of completion of work.
12) A contract usually includes clause for 'penalty' for delayed completion.
13) A contract usually includes 'Escalation Clause' under which the contractor is compensated for increase in costs on account of inflation.
14) A percentage of the value of work done is deducted from the progress payment as 'Retention Money.'

Difference between Job Costing and Contract Costing

Job Costing	Contract Costing
1) A job is small in size.	1) A contract is big in size.
2) Work under job costing is performed in the premises of manufacturer.	2) A contract is executed generally in the premises of customer i.e. (contractee).
3) A job usually takes less time to complete.	3) A contract takes more time to complete.
4) The selling price is paid after completing the job in full.	4) The price is paid in various instalments depending upon the progress of work.
5) Job costing involves heavy investment on assets initially.	5) Investment of assets in Contract costing is less than compared to Job costing.
6) Expenses under job costing takes the form of both direct and indirect.	6) Under contract costing most of expenses are direct in nature.
7) Profit carried on Job is entirely taken to Profit and Loss Account.	7) In case of incomplete contract, only proportionate profit is taken to Profit and Loss Account.
8) A number of Jobs in hand may be large.	8) Number of contracts that may be undertaken at a time may be few.

Costing Procedure

The preparation of Contract Account is the essence of Contract Costing. The Contract Account is prepared by the contractor in his books. In addition to this account he prepares contractee's Account also. A separate account is opened for each contract. The purpose of contract Account is to know the profit or loss on every contract executed. The basic procedure for costing of contract is as follows:

1) Contract Account Number : Each contract is allotted a distinct number in order to distinguish it from other contracts. A separate account is opened for each contract.

2) Direct Costs : Most of the costs of a contract can be allocated directly to the contract. All such direct costs are debited to the Contract Account.

Direct costs for contracts include :

i) Materials,

ii) Labour Cost,

iii) Direct Expenses,

iv) Depreciation of Plant and Machinery,

v) Sub-Contract Costs

3) Indirect Costs :

Contract Account is also debited with overheads which tend to be small in relation to direct costs. Such costs are often absorbed on some arbitraty basis as a percentage of prime cost, materials, wages etc. Overheads are normally restricted to head office and storage costs.

4) Transfer of Materials or Plant :

When materials, plant or other items are transferred from the contract, the Contract Account is credited by that amount.

5) Contract Price :

The Contract Account is also credited with the contract price. In case of incomplete contract, the Contract Account is credited with the value of work-in-progress as on that date.

6) Profit or Loss on Contract :

The balance of Contract Account represents profit or loss which is transferred to Profit and Loss Account. In case of incompleted contract, only a part of profit arrived is taken into account and remaining profit is kept as reserve to meet any contigent loss on the incomplete portion of the contract.

Basic Concepts :

1) Material Costs : The material required for the contract are debited to Contract Account which includes :

a) Materials specially purchased for the contract.

b) Materials issued from stores against requisition.

c) Materials urgently required transferred from another contract.

On completion of the contract the following types of materials should be credited to Contract Account.

a) Materials returned to store.

b) Materials in hand on site at the end of the accounting period.

c) Materials transferred to another contract.

d) Sale of materials.

Any profit or loss arising out of such materials transactions must be recorded from Profit and Loss Account. Following are certain items of losses which should be debited to Profit and Loss Account and should be credited to Contract Account.

a) Loss on sale of materials

b) Materials which are stolen or destroyed by fire.

c) Materials lost in accidents.

d) Cost of defective materials.

2) Labour Cost :

All labour actually engaged at contract site is regraded as direct labour, irrespective of the mature of the tasks performed by the workers concerned and is charged to the contract. The extact labour cost that should be debited to a Contract Account thus includes the total remuneration paid and payable to all workers engaged on contract at the end of the accounting period.

3) Other Direct Expenses :

All other expenses incurred for directly for the contract should be debited to Contract Account e.g. Architect's or Surveyor's fee, Sub-contract costs, hire charges of Plant and Machinery etc.

4) Overhead Costs :

There are some common indirect expenses incurred for various contracts, which cannot be charged directly to the individual contract. These expenses are divided into works expenses, office expenses and are distributed on various contracts on some appropriate basis. The ultimate proportionate industry expenses paid or payable should be debited to Contract Account i.e. head office expenses, expenses of central stores, establishment charges etc.

5) Plant and Machinery Costs :

In every Contract work some special plant, heavy machines and special tools are usually employed. The plant and Mechinery cost represents the cost for the use of Plant and Machinery and tools for the contract. These costs are treated in Contract Account with the following alternative methods.

i) If Plant and Machinery and tools are used for the contract only for a short period, Contract Account may be debited with the amount of depreciation on it.

ii) If Plant and Machinery and tools are used for the contract for a long period, the full amount of it may be debited to contract Account and at the end of the accounting period or completion of the contract, the residual or written down value of it may be credited to the Contract Account.

6) Sub-Contract Cost :

If the contractor has entrusted some special work to some expert sub-contractor, the costs incurred for such sub-contract is treated as a direct charge to the contract and hence should be debited to Contract Account e.g. a building contractor may entrust the following types of specialised jobs to a sub-contractors e.g. task of digging foundations, electrical installation, specialised flooring, installation of lifts, painting work, plumbing work etc.

7) Cost of Additional Work :

If a contractor is asked to do some extra work or alteration in the work which is not included in the original contract, the cost of such additional work may be charged separately to the contract as follows :

i) If the additional work is substantial and the amount involved is large, it is better to treat the same as a subsidiary contract and a separate contract account should be operated for the same.

ii) If the additional work is not substantial, its cost should be debited to contract account and should be added to the contract price.

6.2 Work Certified and Uncertified

(A) Work Centified : It is the cost of that part of the contract work which is being completed by the contractor for which a completion certificate has been issued by the contractee's account and credited to Contract Account.

(B) Uncertified Work : It is the cost of that part of the contract work which is being completed by the contractor but not certified by the architects because of the faulty work or the work not according to the specifications. In respect of such work there will be no payment from the contractee. The cost price of each work is debited to Work-in-Progress Account and credited to Contract Account.

The distinction between Work Certified and Work Uncertified can be shown as follows:

Work Certified	Work Uncertified
1) It is the cost of that part of the contract work which is being completed by the contractor for which a completion certificate has been issued by the contractee's architect.	1) It is the cost of that part of the contract work which is being completed by the contractor but not certified by the architects because of the faulty work or the work not according to the specifications.
2) The amount of work certified is debited to Contractee's A/c and credited to Contract A/c.	2) The amount of work uncertified is debited to Work-in-Progress A/c and credited to Contract A/c.
3) The cost of work certified represents the total expenditure incurred on the contract to date, less cost of work-uncertified, material in hand, plant at site, etc.	3) The cost of work uncertified represents the cost of the work which has been carried out by the contractor but has not been certified by the architect. It is always shown at cost price.

4) Cost of work certified may be ascertained as follows : Cost of work Certified = Cost of Work to date - (Cost of Work Uncertified + Materials on Hand + Plant at Site.)	4) The cost of Works Uncertified may be ascertained as follows: Cost of Work Uncertified = Total Cost to date ..... (Cost of Work Certified) + ... Materials on Hand + ... Plant at Site) ....

6.3 Escalation Clause

Escalation clause is usually provided in the contract as a safeguard against likely changes in price and utilization of material and labour. By adding this clause, the contractor makes it clear to his customer that price quoted is dependent on prevailing market prices of cost elements. If the prices of cost elements rise beyond a certain percentage over the price prevailing at the time of tendering, the customer has to bear the additional cost. The escalation clause may also be added to cover the risk involved due to change in utilization of material and labour, where the quantity of material or labour time cannot be properly assessed under the work that has sufficiently advanced. Thus, the term of contract specify the procedure for making the adjustment to avoid all further disputes. Properly constructed escalation clauses should cover the following points :

a) Description of the elements of cost that are subject to escalation.

b) Stipulation of the index to be applied to each cost category.

c) Indication of the frequency with which the contract price will be adjusted.

d) Definition of the limits to which the cost elements concerned may be increased or decreased during specific periods or over the length of the contract.

e) The contract should indicate whether changes mean only rises or also falls in prices. The benefit of lower prices should be trasferred to the consumer.

f) Prices / rates variances normaly means the purchase price of material or wage rates incurred by the contractor from time to time. It is imperative that the contractee should have power to investigate or audit the relevant invoices or pay roll. It may also need certain provisions in the contract, whether the contractor is incurring such expense prudently at prevailing rates in the market.

8) Architect's Certificate :

In case of large contract which takes a long period, it is normal practice for the contractor to get interim advanced payments against to actual portion of contract completed by him. The contractee appoints the architects survey or engineer who works as a technical assessor and issues the certificate as the value of work so far performed. Thus, as per the contract agreement, the periodic payment is made to the contractor on the basis of such an architects certificate.

10) Retention Money :

It is a common practice to include the clause of retention money in the contract agreement. Under this clause the contractee will not make payment of the work certified by the architect, but a certain protion thereof shall be retained by him which is called "Retention Money'. The object of this retention money is to place the contractor in a safer position. This amount will be paid to the contractor after the satisfactory completion of the work depending upon the terms of contract.

Profit on Incomplete Contracts :

If contracts are started and completed during the same accounting year there is no problem as regards profit computation. But in case of those contracts which take more than one accounting year, a problem arises whether profit on such contracts should be worked out only on the completion of the contract or at the end of each accounting year on the partly completed work. If profit is computed only on the completion of the contract profit will be high in the year of completion of contract, whereas in other years of working on contract, profit will be nil. This would result not only in distorted profit patterns, but also higher tax liability on Income Tax at higher rates may have to be paid. Hence, when contract extends beyond a year, it becomes necessary to take into account the profit earned (or loss incurred) on the work preformed during each year. This helps in avoiding distortion of the year to year profit trend of the business.

There are two aspects of profit computation.

a) Computation of estimated or notional profit at the end of the year when contract is not complete.

b) Computation of the portion of such profit to be transferred to Profit and Loss A/c.

The amount of profit that is to be credited to Profit and Loss A/c depends upon the fact that how far the contract has advanced.

There are no hard and fast rules in this regard. However, the following are the conventional norms for determining the profit to be taken to the Profit and Loss A/c at different stages of completion.

a) It should be noted that the profit should be considered in respect of work certified only. Work certified should always be valued at cost.

b) If a very small portion of the work has been done, it is neither desirable nor sound to take into account profit on the work done and the Contract Account must then be **closed by balance.** In such a case, the amount expended on account of the contract to the date of balancing will be shown as **Work-in-Progress** on the asset side of the Balance Sheet and any cash received from the contractee on account of work will be shown by way **deduction** therefrom.

No definite rule can be laid down as to what stage of the work it would be safe to take credit for the profit on incomplete contracts. But the general rule may be laid down is that **no profit should be ascertained unless at least one fourth or more of the whole work has been completed.**

c) When the work certified is 25% or more but less than 50% of the Contract Price, profit to be taken to the credit of Profit and

Loss Account will be computed follows :

$$= \text{Notional Profit} \times \frac{1}{3} \times \frac{\text{Cash Received}}{\text{Work Certified}}$$

d) When the work certified is 50% or more but less then 90% of the Contract Price, profit to be taken to the credit of Profit and Loss Account will be computed follows :

$$= \text{Notional Profit} \times \frac{2}{3} \times \frac{\text{Cash Received}}{\text{Work Certified}}$$

e) When contract is **near completion,** then the estimated profit should be calculated as the whole contract. This is computed as follows :

Rs.

Contract Price
Less : Total Expenditure to date   ......
Less : Estimated Additional Expenditure   ....
Estimated Profit   ......

The profit to be taken to the credit of Profit and Loss Account will be computed by applying any of the following formula:

i) $\text{Estimated Profit} \times \dfrac{\text{Work Certified}}{\text{Contract Price}}$

ii) $\text{Estimated Profit} \times \dfrac{\text{Work Certified}}{\text{Contract Price}} \times \dfrac{\text{Cash Received}}{\text{Work Certified}}$

OR

$\text{Estimated Profit} \times \dfrac{\text{Cash Received}}{\text{Contract Price}}$

iii) Estimated Profit $\times \dfrac{\text{Cash of Work to date}}{\text{Estimated Total Cost}}$

iv) Estimated Profit $\times \dfrac{\text{Cash of Work to date}}{\text{Estimated Total Cost}}$
$\times \dfrac{\text{Cash Received}}{\text{Work Certified}}$

f) **For Loss on incompleted contracts :** If the cost of work certified exceeds the value of such certificate or loss is incurred the whole amount of such loss is to be charged to Profit and Loss Account. The entry will be passed as follows:

Profit and Loss A/c .... Dr.

To Contract A/c

g) According to AS2 "Accounting for construction contracts." a foreseable loss on the entire contract should be provided for in the financial statements irrespective of the amount of work done and the method of accounting followed.

6. 4. Cost Plus Contracts

This is a modified method of Contract Costing. Under this the contractee agrees to pay to the contractor the actual cost of work done plus an agreed percentage thereof to cover overhead expenses and profits. Cost plus contract method is generally employed in those cases.

i) Where the estimated cost of contract cannot be ascertained accurately because of the frequent changes in the prices of materials and labour rates.

ii) Where the work to be done is not fixed at the time of placing the contract.

iii) When the contract is totally new to the contractor.

iv) Where the contract requires a fairly long period to complete the same.

This method is commonly used in the manufacturing of exceptional articles produced very rarely e.g. aircraft component, urgent repairing of power house, contructions during war time etc.

Advantages to the Contractor :

i) The Contractor will not suffer any risk of loss as he will receive the contract price as is assured by the contractee.

ii) There is bargain in the contract price in future under this type of contract.

iii) The contractor is relieved from the botheration of preparing quotation price for the sake of submitting it to the contractee.

Advantages to the Contractee :

i) Since the contract price is governed by the contract, the contractee will also not suffer from risk of loss.

ii) The contractee also stands to benefit in a period of uncertain market condition as he is expected to pay only a reasonable price after satisfying the ruling prices.

Disadvantages to the Contractor :

i) No efforts are taken by contractor for cost reduction. Hence, he becomes inefficient.

ii) The profit percentage, though fixed, will necessarily very in amount since it depends upon the increase in cost.

iii) The percentage of profit may either be excessive or inadequate to cover to overhead expenses also.

Disadvantages to the Contractee :

i) This method is not desirable from the point of view of the contractee because the price to be paid depends upon the cost of contract.

ii) Till complete execution of the contract, he cannot estimate his commitment accurately.

6.5 Work-in-Progress

Contracts in progress mean contracts which have not yet been completed. Such uncompleted contracts are also referred to as Work-in-Progress. All the expenditure incurred on the uncompleted contracts should be shown on the asset side of the Balance Sheet under the heading 'Work-in-progress'. Where profit is taken in respect of incompleted contract, the work-in-progress stated in the Balance Sheet should also include the profit i.e. valuation of work-in-progress is done by addition the profit to the cost to the contract. It should be shown as follows :

Balance Sheet - Asset Side

Work-in-Progress :
Cost of Contract till date -
   i) Cost of Work Certified   ....
   ii) Cost of Work Uncertified   ....
Add : Profit taken to Profit and Loss A/c (+).......

            ....
Less : Cash Received from the contractee (-) ....

OR

Work-in-Progress Account :
   i) Cost of Work Certified   (+).......
   ii) Cost of Work Uncertified   (-).......
Less : Reserve for unrealised profit   (-)....... ....
Less : Cash received from contractee   (-)....... ....

Accounting Procedure in Contract Costing (i.e. Journal Entries)

1. **For materials issued to Contract :**
   Contract A/c   .... Dr.
    To Materials A/c

2. **For surplus materials transferred to another Contract :**
   Receiving Contract A/c   .... Dr.
    To Supplying Contract A/c

3. **For expenses incurred or payable on contract :**
   Contract A/c   .... Dr.
    To Expenses A/c
    To Outstanding Expenses A/c

4. For Plant and Machinery and Equipments (at cost) issued to contract :

Contract A/c   .... Dr.

To Plant and Machinery / Equipment A/c

5. For share of apportioned Overhead Expenses :

Contract A/c   .... Dr.

To Overhead A/c

6. For sub-contract cost :

Contract A/c   ... Dr.

To Sub-contract A/c

7. For materials at site at the end / materials returned to stores / supplier :

Materials A/c or Materials Returned A/c   ... Dr.

To Contract A/c

8. For Plant and Machinery and Equipment at site at the end at written down value :

Plant and Machinery A/c   .... Dr.

Equipment A/c   .... Dr.

To Contract A/c

9. For Work Certified :

Contractee's A/c   .... Dr.

To Contract A/c

10. For Work Uncertified :

Work-in-Progress A/c   .... Dr.

To Contract A/c

11. For cash received against work-certified from Contractee:

Bank A/c   ... Dr.

To Contractee's A/c

12. For materials / plant sold at site at profit :

Bank A/c ... Dr.

To Contract A/c (cost of materials / plant)

To Profit and Loss A/c (with profit on sale)

If there is a loss, the above entry will be reversed.

13. **For materials stolen or lost and Insurance Co. admitted claim for certain account :**

Bank A/c .... Dr. (Recovery for Insurance Co).
Profit and Loss A/c ... Dr. (Loss on material)
    To Contract A/c

14. **For abnormal Loss of materials, Plant etc. on site :**

Profit and Loss A/c ... Dr.
    To Contract A/c

15. **For Sale of scrap :**

Bank A/c ... Dr.
    To Contract A/c

16. **For profit transferred to Profit and Loss A/c Profit to be reserved :**

Contract A/c ... Dr.
    To Profit and Loss A/c (with profit credited)
To Work-in-Progress / Profit Reserve A/c (with profit kept as Reserve)

The Specimen of various Ledger Accounts in the Books of a Contractor may be shown as follows.

Dr.   Contractee's Account   Cr.

Particulars	Rs.	Particulars	Rs.
To Balance C/D	.....	By Bank (part payment)	.....
	.....		.....
To Contract (Contract Price)	.....	By Balance B/D	.....
		By Bank (Final Payment)	.....

Dr. **Contract Account** Cr.

Particulars	Rs.	Particulars	Rs.
To Work-in Progress (Opening) :		By Materials :	
Work-certified		Returned to Store	
Work uncertified		Transferred to	
Plant at Site		other contracts	
Materials at Site			
....		By P & L A/c	....
		(Loss on Sale if any)	
Less : Reserve	....	By Plant returned to stores	....
		Less : Depreciation	
To Materials :		By Profit and Loss A/c	
		(For items stolen / lost)	....
From Stores		**By Work-in-Progress**	
From outside		**(Closing)** :	
(purchases)		Work Certified	
From other contracts		Work Uncertified	
To wages (including		Plant at site	
Outstanding)	....	Materials at site	....
To Direct Expenses			
(including Outstanding)			
To Plant as Cost /		**OR**	
Tools at Cost		Contractee's A/c (with total	
To Overheads		contract price) (in case of	
(including outstanding)	....	contracts completed)	
To Sub-contract costs	....		
To Cost of extra-work done	....		
To Profit and Loss A/c	....		
(Profit on sale, if any)			
To Notional Profit C/D	....		
	....		....
To Profit and Loss A/c		By Notional Profit B/D	....

$\left(\dfrac{1}{3} \text{ or } \dfrac{2}{3}\right)$ x Notional profit	...		
$\text{x} \dfrac{\text{Cash Received}}{\text{Work Certified}}$ To Work-in-Progress A/c (Reserve)	....		....
	....		....

6.6 Illustration :

The following are the informations relating to a Contract Account No. 123.

Illustration 1 :

	Rs.
Contract Price	6,00,000
Wages	1,64,000
General Expenses	8,600
Raw Materials	1,20,000
Plant	20,000

As on date, cash received was Rs. 2,40,000 being 80% of work certified. The value of materials remaining at site was Rs. 10,000. Depreciate plant by 10%.Prepare the contract account.

Solution :

Contract Account No. 123

Particulars	Rs.	Particulars	Rs.
To Raw Materials	1,20,000	By Work-in-progress :	
To Wages	1,64,000	Work certified	3,00,000
To General Expenses	8,600	By Materials at site	10,000
To Plant	20,000	By Plant at site	18,000
To P & L A/c	8,213		
To Work-in-Progress (Reserve)	7,187		
	3,28,000		3,28,000

Working Note :

Profit taken to P & L. Account has been arrived at as follows:

Profit to date x $\dfrac{2}{3} \times \dfrac{80}{100}$

$= 15,400 \times \dfrac{2}{3} \times \dfrac{80}{100}$

$= $ Rs. 8,213

Illustration 2 :

The Hindustan Construction Company Ltd. have undertaken the construction of a bridge over the river Yamuna for the Municipal Corporation. The value of the contract is Rs. 12,50,000, subject to a retention of 20% until one year after the certified completion of the contract, and final approval of the Corporation's engineer. The following are the details as shown in the books on 30th June, 2008.

	Rs.
Labour on site	4,05,000
Materials direct to site less returns	4,20,000
Materials from store	81,200
Hire and use of plant - plant unkeep account	12,100
Direct Expenses	23,000
General overhead allocation to the contract	37,100
Materials in hand on June 30, 2008	6,300
Wages accrued on June, 2008	7,800
Direct expenses accrued on June 30, 2008	1,600
Work not yet certified at cost	16,500
Amount certified by the Corporation Engineer	11,00,000
Cash received on account	8,80,000

Prepare (a) Contract Account, (b) Contractee's Account and (c) show the relevant items would appear in the Balance Sheet.

Solution :

Contract Account

Particulars	Rs.	Particulars	Rs.
		By Work-in-progress :	
To Materials -		By Materials in hand	6,300
direct to site 4,20,000		By Work-in-Progress	
from store 81,200	5,01,200	Work certified	11,00,000
To Labour at			
site 4,05,000		Work uncertified	16,500
Add : Accrued 7,800	4,12,800		
To Direct			
Expenses 23,000			
Add : Accrued 1,600	24,600		
To Hire and use of plant	12,100		
To General Overhead	37,100		
To Profit c/d	1,35,000		
Rs.	11,22,800	Rs.	11,22,800
To Profit and Loss A/c	72,000	By Profit b/d Rs.	1,35,000
To Balance carried			
forward as Reserve	63,000		
Rs.	1,35,000	Rs.	1,35,000

* The Profit taken to Profit and Loss Account has been arrived at, as follows :

$$1,35,000 \times \frac{2}{3} \times \frac{80}{100} = \text{Rs. } 72,000$$

If it is desired that the contract account should show the value of work-in-progress, and only the amount of profit be taken to the Profit and Loss Account, the Contract Account will appear as given below :

Contract Account

Particulars	Rs.	Particulars	Rs.
To Materials - direct to site 4,20,000 from store 81,200	5,01,200	By Materials in hand By Work-in-Progress	6,300 10,53,500
To Labour at site 4,05,000 Add : Accrued 7,800	4,12,800		
To Direct Expenses 23,000 Add : Accrued 1,600	24,600		
To Hire and use of plant	12,100		
To General Overhead	37,100		
To Profit c/d Profit and Loss A/c	72,000		
Rs.	10,59,800	Rs.	10,59,800

Contractee's Account

Particulars	Rs.	Particulars	Rs.
To Balance c/d Rs.	8,80,000	By cash	8,80,000

Extracts from Balance Sheet as on 30th June, 2008

Liabilities	Rs.	Assets	Rs.
Wages accrued	7,800	Work-in-Progress : Rs.	
Direct Expenses accrued	1,600	Value of work	
		certified 11,00,000	
		Cost of work	
		uncertified 16,500	
		11,16,500	
		Less Reserve 63,000	
		10,53,500	
		Less : Amount	
		received from the	
		contractee 8,80,000	1,73,500

Working Notes :

1) The amount of profit has been ascertained as follows : Rs.

Total Expenditure on the contract   9,87,800

Less : Value to materials in hand   6,300

                                                                             9,81,500

Value of work certified   11,00,000

Value of work uncertified   16,500   11,16,500

Total profit made to date   Rs. 1,35,000

Profit to be transferred to Profit and Loss Account

$$= 1,35,000 \times \frac{2}{3} \times \frac{80}{100}$$

$$= \text{Rs. } 72,000.$$

Profit to be carried
forward as a Reserve = Rs. 63,000

2) The value of work-in-progress has been ascertained as
follows :

		Rs.
Value of work certified		11,00,000
Cost of work uncertified		16,500
		11,16,500
Less : Reserve		63,000
		Rs. 10,53,500

Illustration 3 :

Deluxe Limited undertook a contract for Rs. 5,00,000 on 1st July, 2007. On 30th June, 2007 when the accounts were closed, the following details about the contract were gathered :

	Rs.
Materials Purchased	1,00,000
Wages Paid	45,000
General Expenses	10,000
Plant Purchased	50,000
Materials on hand 30.6.08	25,000
Wages Accrued 30.6.08	5,000
Work Certified	2,00,000
Cash Received	1,50,000
Work Uncertified	15,000
Depreciation of Plant	5,000

The above contract contained an escalation clause which read as follows :

"In the event of prices of materials and rates of wages increase by more than 5%, the contract price will be increased accordingly by 25% of the rise in the cost of materials and wages beyond 5% in each case."

It was found that since the date of signing the agreement the prices of materials and wage rates increased by 25%. The value of the work certified does not take into account the effect of the above clause.

Prepare the contract account. Your workings should form part of the answer.

Solution :

Contract Account

Particular	Rs.	Particulars	Rs.
To Materials	1,00,000	By Work-in-Progress :	
To Wages		Work	
(45,000 + 5,000)	50,000	Certified 2,00,000	
To General Expenses	10,000	Work	
To Depreciation on Plant	5,000	Uncertified 15,000	2,15,000
To Profit transferred to		By Contract Escalation	5,000
P & L Account	20,000	(Working Note - 1)	
Work-in-Progress	60,000	By Materials in hand	25,000
(Working Note - 2)			
	2,45,000		2,45,000

Working Notes :

1. Escalation Charges :

a) Materials

Effect of increase in price of materials :

Total increase (Rs.)   Up to 5% (Rs.)   Beyond (Rs.)

$$75,000 \times \frac{25}{125}$$ $$75,000 \times \frac{5}{125}$$

$= 15,000$ $= 3,000$ $= 12,000$

b) Wages

Effect of increase in wage rate

$$50,000 \times \frac{25}{125}$$ $$50,000 \times \frac{5}{125}$$

$= 10,000$ $= 2,000$ $= 8,000$

Total Increase (a) + (b)

$= 25,000$ $= 5,000$ $= 20,000$

Increase in Contract

Price (25% increase beyond 5%) $= 20,000 \times \dfrac{25}{100} = $ Rs. 5,000

2. Computation of profit transferred to Profit & Loss Account: Since more than 1/4th but less than 1/2 of the contract has been completed. 1/3 or the profit earned as reduced on cash basis has been transferred to Profit & Loss Account.

$$80,000 \times \frac{1}{3} \times \frac{1,50,000}{2,00,000} = \text{Rs. } 20,000$$

Illustration 4 :

A firm of building contractors began to trade on 1st April 2007. The following was the expenditure on the contract for Rs. 4,00,000

	Rs.
Materials issued to contract	50,000
Plant used for contract	20,000
Wages	71,000
Other expenses	10,000

Cash received on account to 31st March, 2010 amounted to Rs. 1,44,000. The work certified was of Rs. 1,80,000. Of the plant and materials charged to the contract, plant which cost Rs. 4,000 and materials which cost Rs. 3,000 were lost. On 1st March, 2010 plant which cost Rs. 3,000 was returned to stores. The cost of work done but uncertified was Rs. 1,500 and material costing Rs. 2,500 were in hand on site.

Charge 15% depreciation on plant and take to the Profit and Loss Account 2/3 of the profit received. Prepare a Contract Account, Contractee's Account and Balance Sheet from the above particulars.

Solution :

Contract Account

Particulars	Rs.	Particulars	Rs.
To Materials	50,000	By P. & L. A/c (Plant	
To Plant	20,000	and Materials lost)	7,000
To Wages	71,000	By Plant returned to	
To Other Expenses	10,000	stores (3,000 - 450)	2,550
		By Materials at site	2,500
To Profit c/d	53,600	By Work-in-Progress :	
		Work uncertified	1,500
		Work certified	1,80,000
		By Plant at site	
		(13,000 - 1,950)	11,050
	2,04,600		2,04,600
To P. & L. Account	28,587	By Profit b/d	53,600
To Reserve	25,013		
	53,600		53,600

Working Notes :

1) Profit to be taken to P. & L. A/c has been calculated as follows :

$$\text{Rs. } 53,600 \times \frac{2}{3} \times \frac{1,44,000}{1,80,000} = \text{Rs. } 28,587$$

2) Value of plant at site -

Cost of Plant		Rs. 20,000
Less : Plant lost	Rs. 4,000	
Plant returned	3,000	Rs. 7,000
		13,000
Less - Depreciation - 15%		1,950
		11,050

Contractee's Account

Particular	Rs.	Particulars	Rs.
To Balance c/d	1,44,000	By Cash	1,44,000

Balance Sheet
as on 31st March, 2010

Liabilities	Rs.	Assets	Rs.
		Work-in-Progress : Value of Work Certified 1,80,000 Cost of Work Uncertified 1,500	
		1,81,500	
		Less : Reserve 25,013	

* It has been presumed that plant was cost before it could be used. In case of loss of plant after being used for some period, contract account would be credited with the depreciated value of plant.

Illustration 5

Bharat Constructions, Baroda undertook a Contract No. 54 for Rs. 4,00,000 on 1st April, 2007. They incurred the following expenses during the year 2007-08.

	Rs.
Materials issued from stores	36,600
Materials transferred from Contract No. 45	3,400
Materials directly purchased for the Contract	10,000
Materials in hand on site	2,500
Plant issued for contract	20,000
Wages paid directly	70,000
Architect's Fees	3,000

Wages due but not paid	1,000
Direct expenses outstandings	600
Cash received from contractee	1,44,000
Work Certified	1,80,000
Cost of Work uncertified	1,500

Of the Plant and Materials charged to contract, Plant costing Rs. 4,000 and Materials costing Rs. 3,000 were lost. On 31-3-2008 Plant costing Rs. 3,000 was returned to stores. Charge depreciation on Plant @ 15% p.a. as per written down value method.

Prepare Contract Account for the year ended 31-3-2008.

Solution

Working Notes :

1) **Calculation of amount of Notional profits to be credited to Profit and Loss A/c**

As the value of Work Certified (Rs. 1,80,000) is more than $\dfrac{1}{4}$ but less than $\dfrac{1}{2}$ of the contract price (Rs. 4,00,000), the following formula is to be applied to find out the amount of notional profits to be credited to Profit and Loss A/c.

$$= \frac{1}{3} \times \text{Notional Profits} \times \frac{\text{Cash Received}}{\text{Work Certified}}$$

$$= \frac{1}{3} \times \text{Rs. } 60,000 \times \frac{\text{Rs.} 1,44,000}{\text{Rs.} 1.80,000}$$

$$= \text{Rs. } 16,000$$

In the Books of Bharat Constructions, Baroda
Contract Account for Contract No. 54
Dr.   **for the Year Ended 31ˢᵗ March, 2008**   Cr.

Particular	Rs.	Particulars	Rs.
To Materials issued from stores	36,600	By Materials in hand on site	2,500
To Materials transferred to Contract No. 45	3,400	By Work Certified	1,80,000
To Materials directly purchased for the Contract	10,000	By Cost of Work Uncertified	1,500
To Plant issued for contract	20,000	By Costing Profit and Loss A/c :	
To Wages paid directly	70,000	(i) Plant lost	4,000
To Architect's Fees	3,000	(ii) Materials lost	3,000
To Wages due but not paid	1,000	By Plant returned to stores :	
To Direct Expenses Outstanding	600	Original Cost 3,000 Less : Depr. @ 15% p.a. (-) 450	2,550
		By Plant in Hand : Original Cost 13,000 Less : Dep. @ 15% p.a. (-) 1950	11,050
To Notional Profits c/d	60,000		
	2,04,600		2,04,600
To Profit and Loss	16,000	By Notional Profits b/d	60,000
To Reserve	44,000		
	60,000		60,000

Illustration 6

Reliable Constructions Ltd., Raipur undertook a contract of Rs. 8,00,000 for the construction of a sports Gymkhana on 1ˢᵗ April, 2007. The following information is taken up from the contract ledger as on 31-3-2008 in respect of the above.

	Rs.
Materials directly issued from stores	1,30,000
Materials purchased	70,000
Scrap materials sold	8,000
Materials transferred to other contract	10,000
Materials in hand on site	11,000
Materials returned to stores	6,000
Direct wages paid and payable	85,000
Direct charges	45,000
Overheads charged to contract	40,000
Sub-contract cost	9,000
Cost of additional work	3,400
Outstanding direct expenses	1,600
Plant purchased on 1-4-2007 and issued directly	80,000
Annual depreciation on plant	8,000
Plant transferred on 1-4-2007 to other contract	40,000
Cash received being 90% of Work Certified	3,60,000
Uncertified Work being 8% of certified work	

You are required to prepare :

i) Contract Account and ii) Contractee's Account

Solution

Working Notes :

1) Calculation of Value of Work Certified :

Work Certified = Cash Received + Retention Money

100 = 90 + 10

? = Rs. 3,60,000

If 90 CR = 100 WC

∴ Rs. 3,60,000 CR = ?

$$= \frac{Rs. 3,60,000 \times 100}{90}$$

= Rs. 4,00,000

2) Calculation of Cost of Work uncertified

= 8% of Work Certified i.e. Rs. 4,00,000

= Rs. 32,000

3) Calculation of amount of notional profits to be credited to Profit and Loss A/c.

As the value of Work Certified (Rs. 4,00,000) is exactly half of the contract price (Rs. 8,00,000) the following formula is to be applied to find out the amount of notional profits to be credited to Profit and Loss A/c.

$$= \frac{2}{3} \times \text{Notional Profits} \times \frac{\text{Cash Received}}{\text{Work Certified}}$$

$$= \frac{2}{3} \times \text{Rs. } 75,000 \times \frac{\text{Rs.3,60,000}}{\text{Rs.4,00,000}}$$

$$= \text{Rs. } 45,000$$

In the Books of Reliable Constructions Ltd., Raipur
Contract Account for the Year Ended

Dr.   **31ˢᵗ March, 2008**   Cr.

Particulars	Rs.	Particulars	Rs.
To Materials directly issued from stores	1,30,000	By Scrap materials sold	8,000
To Materials purchased	70,000	By Materials transferred to other contract	10,000
To Direct wages paid and payable	85,000	By Materials in hand on site	11,000
To Direct charges	45,000		
To Overheads charged to contract	40,000	By Materials returned to stores	6,000
To Sub-Contract cost	9,000	By Plant at site 40,000	
To Cost of additional work on hand	3,400	**Less :** Depreciation (-) 8,000	32,000
To outstanding direct expenses	1,600	By Plant transferred to other contract on 1-4-2007	40,000

Particular	Rs.	Particulars	Rs.
To Plant purchased and issued directly	80,000	By Value of work certified	4,00,000
		By Cost of Work Uncertified	32,000
To Notional Profits C/D *	75,000		
	5,39,000		**5,39,000**
To Profit and Loss	45,000	By Notional Profits B/D	75,000
To Reserve	30,000		
	75,000		**75,000**

Dr.   **Contractee's Account**   **Cr.**

Particular	Rs.	Particulars	Rs.
To Work Certified	4,00,000	By Cash received	3,60,000
		By Balance C/D * (Balancing figure i.e. Rentention money)	40,000
	40,000		**40,000**

Illustration 7

Porwal Builders, Patna undertook several large contracts. The following are the particulars relating to Contract No. 22 for the year ended 31-3-2008.

	Rs.
Materials issued from storehouse	90,000
Materials purchased	40,000
Materials transferred from Contract No. 27	25,000
Materials returned to storehouse	500
Materials at site on 31-3-2008	1,000
Plant purchased and installed at site	72,000
Freight and installation charges of plant	8,000
Operating Wages	1,22,000
Process labour outstandings	5,000
Other direct expenses	12,000

Operating expenses payable	2,000
Establishment on cost	27,000
Office expenses accrued	1,500
Work uncertified	6,000
Contract price	16,00,000
Cash received from contractee	3,20,000

(represented the full amount of Work Certified less 20% as retention money). Provide depreciation on Plant @ 10% p.a as per Reducing Balance Method.

You are required to prepare :

a) Contract Account, b) Contractee's Account and c) Balance Sheet (extracts only) as on 31st March, 2006.

Solution

Working Notes :

1. Calculation of Value of Work Certified :

Work Certified = Cash Received + Retention Money

$$100 = 80 + 20$$

$$? = Rs. 3,20,000$$

If 80 CR = 100 WC

$$\therefore \quad Rs. 3,20,000 \ CR = ?$$

$$= \frac{Rs. 3,20,000 \times 100}{80}$$

$$= Rs. 4,00,000.$$

2) Calculation of amount of notional profits to be credited to Profit and Loss A/c.

As the value of Work Certified (Rs. 4,00,000) is exactly 1/4 of the Contract Price (Rs. 16,00,000) the following formula is to be applied to find out the amount of notional profits to be credited to Profit and Loss A/c

$$= \frac{1}{3} \times \text{Notional Profits} \times \frac{\text{Cash Received}}{\text{Work Certified}}$$

$$= \frac{1}{3} \times Rs. 75,000 \times \frac{Rs. 3,20,000}{Rs. 4,00,000}$$

$$= Rs. 20,000$$

3) Calculation of depreciation on Plant @ 10% p.a. as per Reducing Balance Method:

	Rs.
Plant purchases and installed	72,000
Add : Freight and installation charges	(+) 8,000
	80,000
Less : Depreciation @ 10% p.a.	(-) 8,000
	72,000

Contract Account for Contract No. 22

Dr. **for the Year Ended 31ˢᵗ March, 2008** Cr.

Particulars	Rs.	Particulars	Rs.
To Materials issued from storehouse	90,000	By Materials returned to storehouse	500
To Materials purchased	40,000	By Materials at site on 31-3-2006	1,000
To Materials transferred from Contract No. 27	25,000	By Work Certified	4,00,000
To Depreciation on Plant	8,000	By Work Uncertified	6,000
To Operating Wages	1,22,000		
To Process Labour outstandings	5,000		
To Other Direct Expenses	12,000		
To Operating Expenses Payable	2,000		
To Establishment on cost	27,000		
To Office Expenses Accrued	1,500		
To Notional Profits c/d	75,000		
	4,07,500		**4,07,500**
To Profit and Loss	20,000	By Notional Profits b/d	75,000
To Reserve	55,000		
	75,000		**75,000**

Dr.   **Contractee's Account**   Cr.

Particular	Rs.	Particulars	Rs.
To Work Certified	4,00,000	By Cash received	3,20,000
		By Balance C/D*	80,000
		(Balancing figure i.e.	
		Rentention money)	
	4,00,000		**4,00,000**

In the books of Porwal Builders, Patna
Balance Sheet (Extracts Only)
Dr.   **as on 31st March, 2008**   Cr.

Liabilities	Rs.	Rs.	Assets	Rs.	Rs.
Profit and Loss :		20,000	Materials site		1,000
Outstanding			Plant installed	72,000	
Lisabilities :		8,500	**Add :** Freight &		
1) Process Labour	5,000		Installation		
2) Operating			charges +	8,000	
Expenses	2,000			80,000	
3) Office Expenses			**Less :** Depreci-		
(+)	1,500		ation 10% p.a. (-)	8,000	
			Work-in-Progress :		72,000
			Work Certified	4,00,000	
			Add : Work		
			Uncertified (+)	6,000	
				4,06,000	
			Less : Cash		
			received (-)	3,20,000	
				86,000	
			Less : Reserve (-)	55,000	31,000

Illustration 8

The following information relates to a building contract for Rs. 10,00,000 :

	2007	2008
Materials issued	3,00,000	84,000
Direct wages	2,30,000	1,05,000
Direct expenses	22,000	10,000
Indirect expenses	6,000	1,400
Work certified	7,50,000	10,00,000
Materials at site	8,000	–
Plant issued	5,000	7,000
Cash received from contractor	6,00,000	10,00,000

The value of plant at the end of 2007 and 2008 was Rs. 7,000 and Rs. 5,000 respectively.

Prepare (i) Contract Account, and (ii) Contractee's Account for two years 2007 and 2008 taking into consideration such profit for transfer to Profit and Loss Account as you think proper.

Solution :

Contract Account for 2007

Particulars	Rs.	Particulars	Rs.
To Materials issued	3,00,000	By Materials at site	5,000
To Direct wages	2,30,000	By Plant at site	7,000
To Direct Expenses	22,000	By Work-in-progress :	
To Indirect Expenses	6,000	By Work centified	7,50,000
To Plant issued	14,000	Work uncertified	8,000
7,58,000			
Profit c/d	1,98,000		
	7,70,000		**7,70,000**
Profit & Loss A/c	1,05,600	By Profit b/d	1,98,000
Work-in-Progress	92,400		
	1,98,000		**1,98,000**

Profit taken to Profit & Loss A/c :

$$= \text{Total Profit} \times \frac{2}{3} \times \frac{\text{Cash Received}}{\text{Work Certified}}$$

$$= \text{Rs. } 1,98,000 \times \frac{2}{3} \times \frac{6,00,000}{7,50,000} = \text{Rs. } 1,05,600$$

Contractee's Account

Year	Particulars	Rs.	Year	Particulars	Rs.
2007	To Balance c/d	6,00,000	2007	By Cash	6,00,000
2008	To Contract A/c	10,00,000	2008	By Balance b/d	6,00,000
				By Cash	4,00,000
		10,00,000			10,00,000

Contract Account for 2008

Particulars	Rs.	Particulars	Rs.
To Material at site b/d	5,000	By Materials at site	7,000
To Plant at site b/d	7,000	By Plant at site	5,000
To Work-in-Progress	6,65,600	By Contractee A/c	10,00,000
(Rs.7,58,000 - Rs.92,400)			
To Materials issued	84,000		
To Direct Wages	1,05,000		
To Direct Expenses	10,000		
To Indirect Expenses	1,400		
To Plant issued	2,000		
To Profit & Loss A/c	1,32,000		
	10,12,000		10,12,000

Illustration 9

Mr. Richardson undertook a contract for Rs. 75,00,000 on an arrangement that 80% of the value of the work done, as certified by the architects of the Contractee, should be paid immediately, the remaining 20% be retained until the contract was completed.

In 2006 the amounts expended were : Materials Rs. 9,60,000. Wages Rs. 8,50,000, Carriage Rs. 30,000. Cartage Rs. 5,000, Sundry Expenses Rs. 35,000. The work was certified for Rs. 18,75,000 and 80% of this was paid as agreed.

In 2007 the amounts expended were : Materials Rs. 11,00,000, Wages Rs. 11,50,000, Carriage Rs. 1,15,000, Cartage Rs. 10,000, Sundry Expenses Rs. 20,000. Three-Fourths of the contract was certified as done by the 31st December and 80% of this was receized accordingly. The value of the unused stock and work-in-progress uncertified was ascertained at Rs. 1,00,000.

In 2008 the amounts expended were : Materials Rs. 6,30,000, wages Rs. 8,50,000, Cartage Rs. 30,000, Sundry Expenses Rs. 15,000. The whole contract was completed on 30th June.

Show how the contract account, work-in-progress account and the contractee's account would appear in each of these years in the books of the contractor assuming that balance due to him was received on completion of the contract. Also show the relevant items in the Balance sheet.

Solution :

Contract Account

Particulars	Rs.	Particulars	Rs.
2006			
To Materials	9,60,000	By Work-in-progress :	
To Wages	8,50,000	Work Certified	18,75,000
To Carriage	30,000	By Profit and Loss A/c	
To Cartage	5,000	(loss transferred)	5,000
To Sundry Expenses	35,000		
	18,80,000		18,80,000
To Work-in-Progress :		By Work-in-progress :	
Work cerified	18,75,000	Work Certified	56,25,000
To Materials	11,00,000	Work Uncertified	1,00,000
To Wages	11,50,000		
To Carriage	1,15,000		
To Cartage	10,000		
To Sundry expenses	20,000		
To Profit and Loss A/c*	7,76,000		
To Work-in-Progress			
A/c (Reserve)	6,79,000		
	57,25,000		57,25,000
2008			
To Work-in-Progress :		By Contractee's	
Work certified 56,25,000		Account	75,00,000
Work			
uncertified 1,00,000			
57,25,000			
Less : Reserve 6,79,000	50,46,000		
To Materials	6,30,000		
To Wages	8,50,000		
To Cartage	30,000		
To Sundry Expenses	15,000		
To Profit and Loss A/c	9,29,000		
	75,00,000		75,00,000

Working Notes

* Profit to date   Rs. 14,55,000

Work certified is more than $\frac{2}{3}$ of the contract price.

$\frac{2}{3}$ of profit made to date as reduced on cash basis has been transferred to Profit and Loss Account.

$$14,55,000 \times \frac{2}{3} \times \frac{80}{100} = \text{Rs. } 7,76,000$$

Work-in-Progree Account

Particulars	Rs.	Particulars	Rs.
2006 To Contract Account	18,75,000	By Balance b/d	18,75,000
2007 To Balance b/d	18,75,000	By Contract A/c (transfer)	18,75,000
To Contract Account	57,25,000	By Contract Account (Reserve)	6,79,000
		By Balance c/d	50,46,000
	76,00,000		76,00,000
2008 To Balance b/d	50,46,000	By Contract Account (transfer)	50,46,000

Contractee's Account

Particulars	Rs.	Particulars	Rs.
2006		By Cash (80% of	
To Balance c/d	15,00,000	Rs. 18,75,000)	15,00,000
2007			
To Balance c/d	45,00,000	By Balance b/d	15,00,000
		By Cash (80% of	
		Rs. 37,50,000)	30,00,000
	45,00,000		45,00,000
2008			
To Contract Account	75,00,000	By Balance b/d	45,00,000
		By Cash	30,00,000
	75,00,000		75,00,000

Illustration 10 :

The following information is relating to building contract of Rs. 50,00,000 undertaken by Nirman Builders Jalgoan. The contractee has agreed to pay 90% of the work certified in cash.

Particulars	2005-06 Rs.	2006-07 Rs.	2007-08 Rs.
Materials	7,00,000	8,00,000	4,00,000
Labour	3,20,000	4,80,000	5,00,000
Expenses - Direct	20,000	30,000	10,000
Expenses - Indirect	10,000	7,000	3,000
Work Certified	10,00,000	30,00,000	50,00,000
Work Uncertified	-	40,000	-
Plant issued	2,00,000		-
Value of Plant on 31-3-2006	1,80,000	1,60,000	1,30,000

Prepare Contract Account for the year Account mentioned.

Solution

Working Notes :

1. 2005-06

The entire amount of loss suffered during the year 2003-04 is to be transferred to Profit and Loss Account.

2. 2006-07

As the value of Work Certified (Rs. 30,00,000) is more than $\frac{1}{2}$ of Contract Price (Rs. 50,00,000), the following formula is to be applied to find out the amount of notional profits to be credited to Profit and Loss Account.

$$= \frac{2}{3} \times \text{Notional Profits} \times \frac{\text{Cash Received}}{\text{Work Certified}}$$

$$= \frac{2}{3} \times \text{Rs.} 7,03,000 \times \frac{\text{Rs.} 27,00,000}{\text{Rs.} 30,00,000}$$

$$= \text{Rs. } 4,21,800$$

3. 2007-08

As entire contract is completed during the year 2007-08, the total amount of profit is to be transferred to Profit and Loss Account.

In the books Nirman Builders, Jalgaon.

Dr.   **Contract Account for the year ended 31ˢᵗ March, 2006**

Cr.

Particulars	Rs.	Particulars	Rs.
To Materials	7,00,000	By Work-in-Progress :	
To Labour	3,20,000	i) Work Certified	10,00,000
To Expenses - Direct	20,000	ii) Work Uncertified	-----
To Expenses - Indirect	10,000	iii) Plant in hand	1,80,000
To Plant issued	2,00,000	(Closing Balance c/d.)	
		By Profit and Loss*	70,000
		(Balancing figure	
		i.e. Actual loss)	
	12,50,000		12,50,000

Dr.   **Contract Account for the year ended 31st March, 2007**
Cr.

Particulars	Rs.	Particulars	Rs.
To Work-in-Progress :		By Work-in-Progress :	
i) Work Certified	10,00,000	i) Work Certified	30,00,000
ii) Work Uncertified	-	ii) Work Uncertified	40,000
iii) Plant in hand	1,80,000	iii) Plant in hand	1,60,000
(Opening Balance b/d.)		(Closing Balance c/d.)	
To Materials	8,00,000		
To Labour	4,80,000		
To Expenses - Direct	30,000		
To Expenses - Indirect	7,000		
To Notional Profits c/d*	7,03,000		
	32,00,000		32,00,000
To Profit and Loss	4,21,800	By Notional Profits b/d	7,03,000
To Work-in-Progress			
(Reserve c/d)	2,81,200		
	7,03,000		7,03,000

Dr.   **Contract Account for the year ended 31st March, 2008**   Cr.

Particulars	Rs.	Particulars	Rs.
To Work-in-Progress :		By Work-in-Progress :	
i) Work Certified	30,00,000	(Reserve b/d)	2,81,200
ii) Work Uncertified	40,000	By Contractee's A/c	50,00,000
iii) Plant in hand	1,60,000	(Work Certified)	
(Opening Balance b/d.)		By Plant in hand	1,30,000
To Materials	4,00,000		
To Labour	5,00,000		
To Expenses - Direct	10,000		
To Expenses - Indirect	3,000		
To Profit and Loss	12,98,200		
(Balancing figure			
i.e. actual Profit)	54,11,200		54,11,200

Working Notes :

		2005-06	2006-07	2007-08
Contract Price		50,00,000	50,00,000	50,00,000
Work Certified	100%	10,00,000	30,00,000	50,00,000
Work Uncertified		---	40,000	---
Cash Received	90%	9,00,000	27,00,000	---
Retention Money	10%	1,00,000	3,00,000	---
Notional Profits / Actual Loss / Actual Profit		70,000 (AL)	70,300 (N.P.)	12,98,200 (A.P.)

Illustration 11

The following is the Trial Balance of Premier Construction Company engaged on the execution of contract No. 747, for the year ended 31st December 2008.

	Rs.	Rs.
Contractee's Account - amount received		3,00,000
Buildings	1,60,000	
Creditors		72,000
Bank Balance	35,000	
Capital Account		5,00,000
Materials	2,00,000	
Wages	1,80,000	
Expenses	47,000	
Plant	2,50,000	
	8,72,000	8,72,000

The work on Contract No. 747 was commenced on 1st January, 2008. Materials costing Rs. 1,70,000 were sent to the site of the contract but those of Rs. 6,000 were destroyed in an accident. Wages of Rs. 1,80,000 were paid during the year. Plant costing Rs. 50,000 was used on the contract all through the year. Plant with a cost of

Rs. 2 lakhs was used from 1st January to 30th September and was then returned to the stores. Materials of the cost of Rs. 4,000 were at site on 31st December 2008.

The contract amount was Rs. 6,00,000 and the contractee paid 75% of the work certified. Work certified was 80% of the total contract work at the end of 2008. Uncertified work was estimated at Rs. 15,000 on 31st December 2008.

Expenses are charged to the contract at 25% of Wages. Plant is to be depreciated at 10% for the entire year.

Prepare Contract No. 747 Account for the year 2008 and make out the Balance Sheet as on 31th December, 2008 in the books of Premier Construction Co.

Solution :

Contract No. 747 Account for the year ended 31st Dec. 2008

Particulars	Rs.	Particulars	Rs.
To Materials	1,70,000	By P. & L A/c (Ab. loss)	6,000
To Wages	1,80,000	By Plant retd. to stores	
To Expenses		Rs. (2,00,000	
(25% of wages)	45,000	- 15,000)	1,85,000
To Plant	2,50,000	By Plant at site	
To P. & L (Note 1)	45,000	(Rs. 50,000-5,000)	45,000
To W.I.P (being Reserve)	45,000	By Material at site	4,000
		By Work-in-progress	
		Work certified	4,80,000
		Work uncertified	15,000
	7,35,000		7,35,000

Working Notes

1. The profit taken to Profit & Loss Account has been arrived at as follows :

$$90,000 \times \frac{2}{3} \times \frac{3}{4} = Rs.\ 45,000$$

The profit to be taken to P & L Account may also be calculated on the basis of actual cash received. In such a case the amount will be Rs. 37,500 calculated as follows :

$$90,000 \times \frac{2}{3} \times \frac{3,00,000}{4,80,000} = \text{Rs. } 37,500$$

2. Depreciation is to be charged @ 10% on plant for the whole year. Plant costing Rs. 1,50,000 has been used only for 9 months on the contract. Depreciation for 9 months Rs. 15,000 has been charged to the contract and the rest Rs. 5,000 to P & L Account.

Balance Sheet
as on 31ˢᵗ Dec. 2008

Liabilities		Rs.	Assets		Rs.
Capital		5,00,000	Buildings		1,60,000
Profit & Loss			Plant		
Account Rs.	45,000		in store		1,80,000
Less Ab. Loss	6,000		at contract site		45,000
Less Depreciation			Materials		
on plant	5,000		in store		30,000
Less Unabsorbed			at contract site		4,000
expenses	2,000	32,000	Work-in-Progress		
Creditors		72,000	Work certified	4,80,000	
			Work uncertified	15,000	
				4,95,000	
			Less Reserve	45,000	
				4,50,000	
			Less Cash		
			received from		
			Contractee	3,00,000	1,50,000
			Bank Balance		35,000
		6,04,000			6,04,000

*Alternatively, they may be carried forward.

Illustration 12 :

Construction Ltd. is engaged on two contracts A and B during the year. The following particulars are obtained at the year end (Dec. 31) :

	Contract A	Contract B
Date of Commencement	**April 1**	**September 1**
	Rs.	**Rs.**
Contract Price	6,00,000	5,00,000
Materials issued	1,60,000	60,000
Materials returned	4,000	2,000
Materials on site (Dec. 31)	22,000	8,000
Direct Labour	1,50,000	42,000
Direct Expenses	66,000	35,000
Establishment Expenses	25,000	7,000
Plant istalled at cost	80,000	70,000
Value of Plant (Dec. 31)	65,000	64,000
Cost of Work not yet Certified	23,000	10,000
Value of Work Certified	4,20,000	1,35,000
Cash received from Contractees	3,78,000	1,25,000
Architect's Fees	2,000	1,000

During the period materials amounting to Rs. 9,000 have been transferred from contract A to contract B. You are required to show :
a) Contract accounts,
b) Contratee's accounts, and
c) Extract of Balance sheet as on December 31, clearly showing the calculation of work-in-progress.

Solution :

Contract Account

Particulars	Rs.	Particulars	Rs.
To Materials used	1,60,000	By Materials returned	4,000
To Direct Labour	1,50,000	By Materials transf-	
To Direct Expenses	66,000	erred to Contract B	9,000
To Establishment Expenses	25,000	By Stock of materials	22,000
To Depreciation on Plant	15,000	By Work-in-Progress:	
To Architect's Fee	2,000	Work certified 4,20,000	
To Balance c/d	60,000	Work uncertified 23,000	4,43,000
	4,78,000		4,78,000
To Profit and Loss A/c	*36,000	By Balance b/d	60,000
To Work-in-Progress			
A/c (Reserve)	24,000		
	60,000		60,000

*The figure has been arrived at as follows :

$$\left[60,000 \times \frac{2}{3} \times \frac{3,78,000}{4,20,000} \right] = Rs.\ 36,000$$

Contract B Account

Particulars	Rs.	Particulars	Rs.
To Materials issued	60,000	By Materials returned	2,000
To Materials from Contract A	9,000	By Stock of materials	8,000
To Direct labour	42,000	By Work-in-Progress :	
To Direct Expenses	35,000	Work certified 1,35,000	
To Establishment Expenses	7,000	Work uncertified 10,000	1,45,000
To Depreciation on Plant	6,000	By P. & L. A/c	
		(Loss on contract)	5,000
To Architect's Fees	1,000		
	1,60,000		1,60,000

Contractee A

Particulars	Rs.	Particulars	Rs.
To Balance c/d	3,78,000	By Cash	3,78,000
	3,78,000		3,78,000

Contractee B

Particulars	Rs.	Particulars	Rs.
To Balance c/d	1,25,000	By Cash	1,25,000
	1,25,000		1,25,000

Balance Sheet as on 31st December (Extracts)

Liabilities	Rs.	Assets	Rs.
Profit and Loss A/c : Profit of A 36,000 Less Loss of B 5,000	31,000	Fixed Assets : Plant 1,50,000 Less : Depreciation 21,000	1,29,000
		Stock of Materials Contract A 22,000 Contract B 8,000	30,000
		Work-in-Progress Contract A 41,000 Contract B 20,000	61,000

Calculation of Work-in-Progress :

Contract A

	Rs.
Work Certified	4,20,000
Work Uncertified	23,000
	4,43,000
Less : Reserve for unrealised profit	24,000
	4,19,000
Less : Cash received	3,78,000
Work-in-Progress	41,000

Contract B

	Rs.
Work Certified	1,35,000
Work Uncertified	10,000
	1,45,000
Less : Cash received	1,25,000
Work-in-progress	20,000

Illustration 13:

Jain and Company obtained a contract for building an office for Rs. 3,00,000. Building operations started on 1st April 2007. At the end of the financial year, i.e. 31st March 2008, they received from the party a sum of Rs. 1,20,000 being 80% of the amount on work certified. The following additional information is given below:

	Rs.
Stores issued to contract	60,000
Stores on hand (31-3-2008)	2,500
Wages paid	80,000
Plant purchased for the contract	60,000
Direct expenses	11,000
Overhead allocated to the contract	5,500
Work finished but not yet certified at cost	25,000
Plant to be depreciated at	10%
Materials lost at site	3,000
Wages accqued and due	2,000
Material return	3,000

Prepare the contract account and show how much profit share he carried on to the Profit and Loss Account of Jain and Company.

Soultion

Contract A./c. for the Year Ended 31-3-2008

Particulars	Rs.	Particulars	Rs.
To Stores issued	60,000	By WIP-Stores on hand	2,500
To Wages 80,000		By Materials returned	3,000
Accured 2,000	82,000	By P & L A/c (Materials	
		lost)	3,000
To Direct exp.	11,000	To Cost of contract c/d.	1,56,000
To Dep. on plant			
10% on 60,000	6,000		
To overheads	5,500		
	1,64,500		1,64,500
To cost of contract b/d.	1,56,000	By Contract a/c	
To National Proift	19,000	work certified	1,50,000
		1,20,000 x 100 /80	
		By WIP-Work not	
		certified	25,000
	1,75,000		1,75,000
To P&L A/c	10,133	By National Profit	19,000
(See Note)			
To Profit provision	8,867		
	19,000		19,000

Note : Contract Price Rs. 3,00,000 Work Certified Rs. 1,50,000 i.e. 50% of work has been completed Hence the following formula has been applied for transferring Profit and Loss A/c.

$$= \frac{2}{3} \times \text{Notional Profits} \times \frac{\text{Cash Received}}{\text{Work Certified}}$$

$$= \frac{2}{3} \times 19,000 \times \frac{1,20,000}{1,50,000} = \text{Rs.}10,133$$

Illustration 14

A contractor undertook a contract for constructing a building. The contract price was Rs. 15,00,000 and the contract commended on 1st January 2009. During the year, the following expenses were incurred on the contract.

	Rs.
Materials issued from stores	10,000
Materials purchased	3,00,000
Labour	2,50,000
Indirect expenses	90,000
Plant	3,50,000
Materials returned to stores	20,000
Materials lost by fire	5,000
Materials at site	15,000
Plant at site	3,00,000
Work certified	7,00,000

Cash received from contractee (80% of work certified). Prepare contract account and show how work-in progress will appear in the Balance Sheet.

Solution

Contract A/c for 2009

Particulars	Rs.	Particulars	Rs.
To Materials issued	10,000	By Materials returned	20,000
To Material purchased	3,00,000	By P & L Material lost	5,000
To Labour	2,50,000	By WIP-materials at site	15,000
To Indirect exp.	90,000	By Plant at site	3,00,000
To plant	3,50,000	By Cost of contract c/d	6,60,000
	10,00,000		10,00,000
To Cost of contract b/d	6,60,000	By Contractee A/c	7,00,000
To Notional Profit	40,000	work certified	
	7,00,000		7,00,000
To P & L A/c (see note)	10,667	By National Profit	40,000
To Profit Provision	29,333		
	40,000		40,000

WIP :	Rs.
Contractee's Balance 20% of 7,00,000	1,40,000
Materials at site	15,000
	1,55,000
Less : Profit provision	29,333
W. I. P. as on 31-12-2009	1,.25,667

Note : Contract Price Rs. 15,00,000. Work certified Rs. 7,00,000 i.e. less than 50% of work has been completed. Hence, the following formula is applied for transferring Profit to P & L A/c.

$$= \frac{1}{3} \times \text{Notional Profits} \times \frac{\text{Cash Received}}{\text{Work Certified}}$$

$$= \frac{1}{3} \times 40,000 \times \frac{5,60,000}{7,00,000} = \text{Rs.}10,667$$

Illustration 15

Annual Construction Ltd., have obtained a contract for building a bridge. The value of the contract is Rs. 12,00,000 and the work commenced on 1st October 2008. The following details are shown in their books for the year ended 30th September 2009.

	Rs.
Plant purchased	60,000
Wages paid	3,40,000
Materials issued	3,36,000
Direct expenses	8,000
General overheads apportioned	32,000
Wages due as on 30-9-09	2,800
Materials at site on 30-9-09	4,000
Direct Expenses due on 30-9-09	1200
Work not yet certified (at cost)	14,000
Cash received being 80% of work certified	6,00,000

Life of plant purchased is 5 years and scrap value is nill.

(a) Prepare the Contract Account for the year ended 30th Sep.09

(b) Show the proportion of the profit that can be taken to the P. & L. Account on 30th Sep. and explain how you have calculated it.

Solution

Contract A/c for the year ended 30-9- 2009

Particulars	Rs.	Particulars	Rs.
To Materials issued	3,36,000	By Contract A/c.	
Less : Material at site	4,000	work certified	
Material Consimed	3,32,000	$\left(\dfrac{6,00.000 \times 100}{80} \right)$	7,50,000
To wages paid + O/s.			
3,40,000 + 2,800	3,42,000		
To Direct Exp.			
8,000 + 1,200 =	9,200	By WIP :	
To Depreciation on Plant		Cost work not certified	14,000
(60,000 / 5)	12,000		
To General Overheads	32,000		
Total Cost	7,28,000		
To National Profit	36,000		
	7,64,000		7,64,000
To P & L A/c.	19,200	By Notional Profit	36,000
(see(b) below)			
To Profit in Reserved c/d.	16,800		
	36,000		36,000

(b) Contract Price : Rs. 12,00,000

Value of work certified : Rs. 7, 50,000

i.e. 62.5% of work has been completed.

Hence, the following formula is used for Proift to be taken to P.& L. A/c.

$$= \frac{2}{3} \times \text{Notional Profits} \times \frac{\text{Cash Received}}{\text{Work Certified}}$$

$$= \frac{2}{3} \times 36,000 \times \frac{6,00,000}{7,50,000} = \text{Rs.}19,200$$

Illustration 16

A civil engineering company has undertaken the construction of a bridge. The following particulars relate to this work for the year ended 31-12-2008.

	Rs.
Materials	
Direct purchase	50,000
Issued from stores	10,000
Wages	45,000
General plant in use (written down value)	1,00,000
Depreciation thereon	10,000
Direct expenses	3,500
Share of general overhead	2,000
Material on hand (31-12-08)	1,000
Material lost by fire	500
Salvage value thereon	150
Wages accrued (31-12-08)	5,000
Direct expenses accrued	500
Value of work certified	1,59,000
Value of uncertified work	4,500

The value of the contract was Rs. 2,15,000 and it is a practice of the contractee, as per the terms of the contract, to retain 10% of the work certified.

From the abouve particulars, prepare the following

(i) Contract Account.

(ii) Showing how the items would appear in the Balance Sheet.

Solution

Contract A/c for the year ended 31-12- 2008

Particulars	Rs.	Particulars	Rs.
To Materials Purchase	50,000	By P. & L. A/c.	
To Materails issued from		Materials lost by fire	
stores	10,000	500-150	350
To wages	45,000	To Materials on hand	1,000
To wages accrued	5,000	(31.12.08)	
To Direct exp.	3,500	By cost of contrac c/d.	1,24,650
To " accrued	500		
To Dep. on plant	10,000		
To share of general	2,000		
overhead			
	1,26,000		1,26,000
To cost of Contract b/d.	1,24,650	By contractee a/c	
To National Profit	38,850	By work certified	1,59,000
		Uncertified work	4,500
	1,63,500		1,63,500
To P. & L. A/c.	23.310	By National Profit	38,850
(see Note below)			
To Profit in Reserve c/d.	15,540		
	38,850		38,850

Note : 1. Value of work certified   1,59,000
Retained amount 10%   15,900
Cash received   1,43,100

2. Contract Price   2,15,000
Work certified   1,59,000
i.e. 74% of work has been completed. Hence, the following formula is applied for the profit to be taken to P. & L. A/c.

$$= \frac{2}{3} \times \text{Notional Profits} \times \frac{\text{Cash Received}}{\text{Work Certified}}$$

$$= \frac{2}{3} \times 38.850 \times \frac{1,43,000}{1,59,000} = 23,310$$

3. Work-in-progress

Uncertified work	4,500
Contractee's balance	15,900
Materials on hand	1,000
	21,400
Less : Profit in Reserve	15,540
Work-in progress	5,860

(ii) Balance Sheet as on 31-12-08 (Extract)

	Rs.			Rs.
P & L. A/c 23,310 Less : Materials 350 lost by fire	22,960	Plant 1,10,000 Less : Dep. 10,000 Work-in-progress		1,00,000 5,860
Accured Wages & Direct Exp.	5,500			

6.7 Exercises

A) State whether the following statement are True or False

i) A contract is a big job while job is a small contract.

ii) Work-in-progress includes both work certified and uncertified work.

iii) Work-in-progress is valued at cost plus profit which has not been taken to the profit and loss account.

iv) Work uncertified is valued at cost.

v) Escalations clause is inserted in the contract for the benefit of the contractee.

vi) Contract costing is a basic method of specific order costing.

vii) Most of the items of cost are direct in contract costing than in job costing.

viii) In cost plus contract, the contract runs a risk of incurring loss.

ix) Final contract price to be paid is certain in cost plus contracts.

x) Escalation clause in a contract provides that the contract price is fixed.

xi) In contract costing credit is taken only for a part of the profit or incomplete contract.

Ans. : i) True, ii) True, iii) False, iv) False, v) False, vi) True, vii) True, viii) False, ix) False, x) False, xi) True

B) Select the most appropriate answer :

i) Cash received on contract is credited to
   a) work-in-progress account
   b) contract account
   c) contractee's account

ii) Work certified at the end of accounting year is valued at
   a) cost
   b) cost-plus profit made to date
   c) cost-plus profit taken to profit and loss account.

iii) The degree of completion of work is determined by

comparing the work certified with

a) contract price

b) work-in-progress

c) cash received on contract

iv) Essential feature of a long-term contract

a) It has a duration of more than 12 months.

b) It is in progress at a financial year-end and has a significant effect on the activity of the contractor for the period under review.

c) It has a duration in excess of 6 calender months.

v) A debit balance on the contractee account should be incorporated in the balance sheet as :

a) A current liability ar contract balances outstanding

b) Set off against stock valuation.

c) In debtors as "amount recoverable on contracts.'

Ans. : i) c, ii) c, iii) a iv) b, v) c

C) Fill in the blanks :

i) Contract costing is that form of ..... order costing.

ii) Contract costing is also known as ..... costing.

iii) In contract costing the work is carried out ..... from contractor's premises.

iv) Cost unit in contract costing is a .....

v) Direct costs are ...... to the contract account.

vi) Escalation clause is generally provided to .... against possible changes in price.

vii) Work certified is debited to ..... account and credited ..... account.

viii) The value of work-uncertified is debited to ...... account.

ix) When the work certified is more that 50% but less than 90% of contract price the profit taken to the credit of P. & L. Accounts will be computed as :

$$= \text{Notional Profit} \times \frac{2}{3} \times \frac{6,00,000}{7,50,000} = \text{Rs.19,200}$$

x) ..... is related to accounting for construction contracts.

Ans. : i) Specific, ii) Terminal, iii) away, iv) contract, v) debited, vi) safeguard, vii) contractee's, contract, viii) work-in-progress, ix) work certified, x) AS-2

Essay Type

1) Define 'contract costing.' Give some examples where this system of costing would be suitable.
2) Explain the principles involved in taking profits on incomplete contracts.
3) What is a 'Sub-Contractor.' How is he related to the contractee.
4) What is 'contract costing?' State the important features of contract costing.
5) Explain the costing procedure involved in contract costing.
6) What is 'Escalation clause?' State the importance of escalation clause to the contractor.
7) What is work-in-progress? How to make valuation of work-in-progress in contract costing?
8) What are the advantages and limitations of contract costing.
9) Distinguish between job costing and contract costing.
10) Write short notes on :
    a) Escalation clause
    b) Work certified and work uncertified
    c) Sub-contract costs
    d) Retention Money
    e) Profit on incomple contract
    f) Cost plus contract
    g) Work-in-progress

Practical Exercises

1) A contractor obtained a contract for Rs. 6,00,000 on 1st January, 2008. The expenses incurred during the year ended 31st December, 2008 were as under :

	Rs.
Materials	1,80,000
Wages paid	1,60,000
Wages accrued	10,000
Other expenses	25,000

The plant, specially installed for the contract worth Rs. 45,000 was returned to the stores subject to a depreciation of 20%. Materials on 31st December, 2008 were valued at Rs. 24,000.

Up to 31st December, 2008 the contractor had received Rs. 3,60,000 in cash representing 80% of the work certified. Work uncertified was estimated at Rs. 4,000. Prepare the contract account, showing the profit for the year. Also show how the value of work-in-progress would appear in the balance sheet as on 31st December, 2008.

(**Ans.** Total Profit Rs. 94,000; Profit taken to P & L A/c Rs. 50,133)

2) Mr. Vasanth commenced his contract on 1st April, 2007. The following was the expenditure on the contract for Rs. 3,00,000:

	Rs.
Materials issued	51,000
Plant used	15,000
Wages	81,000
Other expenses incurred	5,000

Cash received on account of contract up to 31st March, 2008 amounted to Rs. 1,28,000, being 80% of the work certified. Of the plant and materials charged to the contract, plant which costs Rs. 3,000 and materials worth Rs. 2,500 were lost. On 31st March, 2008 the cost of the work done but not certified was Rs. 1,000. Materials in hand were Rs. 2,300. Charge 15% depreciation on plant. Ascertain the profit of the contract up to 31st March 2008 and also show the relevant entries in the balance sheet.

(**Ans.** Total Profit Rs. 27,000; Profit taken to P. & L. A/c Rs. 14,400)

3) A company of builders undertook a contract to construct a multistoreyed structure for Rs. 20,00,000 estimating the cost to be Rs. 18,40,000. At the end of the year the company had received Rs. 7,20,000 being 90% of work certified. Work done but not certified was Rs. 20,000. Following expenditure were incurred :

Materials	Rs. 2,00,000
Labour	Rs. 5,00,000
Plant	Rs. 40,000

Materials costing Rs. 10,000 were damaged. Plant is considered as having depreciated 25%.

Prepare contract account and show the profit that can reasonably be taken to Profit & Loss Account.

(**Ans.** Total Profit Rs. 1,20,000, Taken to P & L A/c only $\frac{1}{3}$ after reducing on cash basis Rs. 36,000)

4) Jain & Co. obtained a contract for the building of an office for Rs. 3,00,000. Building operations started on 1st April, 2007 and at the end of the financial year, i.e., 31st March, 2008, they received from the party a sum of Rs. 1,20,000 being 80% of the amount of the surveyor's certificate. The following additional information is available from the books of Jain & Co.:

	Rs.
Stores issued to contract	60,000
Stores on hand as on 31-3-2008	5,000
Wages paid	82,000
Plant purchased for the contract	10,000
Direct Expenses	4,300

Plant to be depreciated at 10%.

You are required to prepare an account showing profit on contract up to 31-3-2008. Also discuss whether Jain & Co. would be justified in taking the full amount of this profit to the credit of their Profit and Loss Account.

(**Ans.** Total Profit Rs. 7,700, Profit taken to P & L A/c Rs. 4,107)

5) A contract account in the books of Contractors Ltd. appears as follows :

2008	Rs.
Materials issued to site	5,000
Plant issued to site	12,500
Direct Labour	4,600
Indirect Labour	640
Overhead Expenses	1,950

You are informed that it is the practice of the firm to take credit for two-thirds of the profit earned on the contracts in progress after taking into account the value of the work certified for payment by architects. You are required to-

a) complete the contract account to June 30,
b) show the amount which you would transfer to Profit and Loss Account along with necessary calculations.
c) show relevant entries in the Balance Sheet as on 30th June. For this purpose you are supplied with the following further information as at that date :

	Rs.
Value of work certified for payment	10,000
Cost of work carried out, but not certified	3,800
Stock of materials not used	950
Value of plant on sit after depreciation	11,875

(**Ans.** Transferred to Profit and Loss A/c Rs. 1,290)

6) A firm of builders carrying out large contracts kept in contract ledger separate account for each contract. On 30th June, 2008 the following was shown as being the expenditure in connection with contract No. 777.

	Rs.
Materials purchased	58,063
Materials from Stores	9,785
Plant which had been used on other contracts	12,523
Additional plant purchased	3,610
Wages	73,634
Direct Expenses	2,026
Production and Establishment Charges	8,720

The contract which had been commenced on 1st Feb., 2008, was of Rs. 3,00,000 and the amount certified by the architect after deduction of 20% retention money, was Rs. 1,20,800 representing 80% of work certified up to 30th June, 2008. The materials on the site at that date was valued at Rs. 9,858.

A contract plant ledger was also kept, in which depreciation was dealt with monthly, the amount debited in respect of plant on contract No. 777 to 30th June was Rs. 1,130. You are required to prepare an account showing the profit on the contract upto 30th June, 2008.

(**Ans.** Profit transferred to P. & L. A/c Rs. 4,000; to Reserve Rs. 3,500)

7) Two contracts, commenced on 1st January and 1st July 2008, respectively, were undertaken by a contractor and their accounts on 31st December, 2008 showed the following position.

	Contract 1 Rs.	Contract 2 Rs.
Contract price	4,00,000	2,70,000
Expenditure :		
Materials	72,000	58,000
Wages paid	1,10,000	1,12,400
General charges	4,000	2,800
Plant installed	20,000	16,000
Materials on hand	4,000	4,000
Wages accrued	4,000	4,000
Work certified	2,00,000	1,60,000
Cash received in respect thereof	1,50,000	1,20,000
Work done but not certified (at cost)	6,000	8,000

The plant was installed on the date of commencement of each contract; depreciation thereon is to be taken at 10% per annum.

Prepare the Contract Accounts in the tabular form and ascertain the profit or loss to be taken to Profit and Loss Account.

(**Ans. :** Contract 1 - Total Profit Rs. 18,000, Profit taken to P. & L. A/x Rs. 9,000, Contract 2 - Loss Rs. 6,000)

8) A Contractor secured a contract to supply and erect machinery for the sum of Rs. 7,50,000. He was to receive payments an account from time to time equal to 90% of the certified value of the work done.

He commenced work on 1st January, 2007 and incurred the following expenditure during the year :- Plant and Tools Rs. 70,000; Machinery and Stores Rs. 2,00,000. Wages Rs. 1,50,000. Sundry Expenses Rs. 30,000; and Establishment Charges Rs. 40,000.

A part of the machinery costing Rs. 20,000 was unsuited to the contract and was immediately sold at a profit of Rs. 5,000.

In order to calculate the profit made on the contract up to 31st December, 2008 the contractor estimated the further expenditure that would be incurred in completing the contract and took to the credit of Profit and Loss A/c for the year that proportion for the estimated net profit to be realised on contract which the certified value of the work done bore to the contract price. He estimated :

a) That the contract would be completed in a further period of six months.

b) that Plant and Tools would have a residual value of Rs. 10,000 upon the completion of the contract.

c) That the cost of Machinery and Stores required in addition to those in stock on 31st December, 2008 would be Rs. 1,00,000 and that further Sundry Expenses of Rs. 20,000 would be incurred.

d) That the wages on the contract for the six months up to 30th June, 2008 would amount to Rs. 80,000.

e) That the Establishment would cost the same sum per month as in the previous year.

f) That 2½% of the total cost of the contract (excluding this percentage) should be provided for contingencies.

Prepare the (i) Contract Account for the year ended 31st December, 2008 and show your calculations of the profit to be credited to Profit & Loss A/c for the year.

ii) Will your answer be different in case reserve for contingencies?

Ans : (i) Total profit Rs. 53,000; amount credited to P. & L. A/c Rs. 34,450; (ii) Yes, the Reserve for contingencies will be Rs. 17,436 in place of Rs. 17,000 as in the (i) case

Hint. Profit has not been reduced on cash basis, since the words used are 'Profit realised' and not 'profit received'; Reserve for contingencies in (ii) case $\frac{5}{2} \times \frac{2}{195} \times 6,80,000$)

9) Thekedar accepted a contract for the construction of a building for Rs. 10,00,000; the contractee agreeing to pay 90% of work certified as complete by the architect. During the first year, the amounts spent were :

Material Rs. 1,20,000		Machinery Rs. 30,000	
Labour 1,50,000		Other expenses 90,000	

At the end of the year, the machinery was considered to be of Rs. 20,000 and materials at site were of the value of Rs. 5,000. Work certified during the year totalled Rs. 4,00,000. In addition,, work-in-progress but not certified at the end of year had cost Rs. 15,000. Prepare Contract Account in the books of Thekedar. Also show the various figures of profit that can be transferred reasonably to the Profit and Loss Account. (B.Com. Delhi)

Ans : Transfer to P & L A/c Rs. 15,000; Reserve Rs. 35,000.

(Hint : Work certified is less than half the price of the contract. Hence 1/3 of the contract. Hence 1/3 of the profit on cash basis has been transferred to P & L A/c.)

10) Nable Contractors Ltd. undertook a contract on 1-4-2008. From the following particulars for the year ending 31-3-2005 prepare a Contract account.

	Rs.		Rs.
Contract Price	6,00,000	Plant istalled	80,000
Material issued	1,60,000	Plant value	65,000
Material returned	4,000	[on 31-3-2009]	
(on 31-3-2009)	22,000	Uncertified work	23,000
Lahour	1,50,000	Engineer's fees	4,20,000
Establishment expen.	25,000	Engineer's fees	2,000

Dire expenses	66,000	Cash received from	
		contractee	3,78,000

(B. Com. Bangalore)

Ans : National Profit Rs. 51,000, Transfer, to P & L A/c Rs. 30,600)

11) The following information relates to contract No. 58. Prepare the Contract Account.

	Rs.
Direct Materials	45,600
Direct wages	24,400
Special plant	18,400
Stores issued	6,040
Loose Tools	3,560
Expenses of Tractor	
Running materials	3,500
Wages of drives etc.	4,540
Other direct charges	2,560

The contract was completed in 26 weeks at the end of which the plant was returned subject to depreciation at 15% p. a. on the original cost. The value of loose and stores returned were Rs. 2,260 and Rs. 840 resectively. The value of tractor was Rs. 40,000 and depreciation was to be charged to this contract at 20% p. a. Administration expenses at 10% on total works cost. The contract price was Rs. 1,25,000.

(B.Com., Bangalore)

Ans : Works cost Rs. 92,480; Profit Rs. 23,272, Adm. exp. Rs. 9,248)

12) The Indian Construction Company undertakes large contracts. The following particulars to contract No. 125 carried out during the year ended on 31st March, 2009

	Rs.
Work certified by architect	1,43, 000
Cost of work not certified	3,400
Plant installed at site	11,300
Value of plant on 31 March, 2009	8,200

Material sent to site	64,500
Labour	54,800
Establishment charges	3,250
Wages accrued on 31 March, 2009	1,800
Direct expenditure	2,400
Materials on hand on 31 March, 2009	1,400
Materials returned to store	400
Direct Expenditure accrued on 31 March, 2009	200
Contract price	2,00,000
Cash received from contractee	1,30,000

Prepare a Contract Account for the period ending 31 March, 2009 and find out the profit. It was decided to transfer 2/3 of the profit on cash basis to Profit and Loss Account.

(B.Com. Andhra; Poona)

Ans : Transfer to P & L A/c, Rs. 11,000 Reserve Rs. 7,150)

13) The Hindustan Construction Co. Ltd. has undertaken the construction of a bridge over River Yamuna for a Municipal Corporation. The value of the contract Rs. 12,50,000. subject to a retention of 20% until one year after the certified completion of the contract, and final approval of the Corporation's engineer. The following are the details as shown in the books on 30 June, 2009.

	Rs.
Labour on site	4,05,000
Materials direct to site less returns	4,20,000
Materials from stores	81,200
Hire and use of plant (plant upkeep a/c)	12,100
Direct expenses	23,000
General overhead allocated to the contract	37,100
Materials on hand June 30,2009	6,300
Wages accrued on June, 30,2009	7,800
Direct expenses accrued on June 30,2009	1,600
Works not yet certified - at cost	16,500
Amount certified by the Corporation's engineer	11,00,000
Cash received on account	8,80,000

Prepare (a) Contract Account, (b) Contracter's Account and (c) Show how it would appear in the Balance sheet (B.Com., Delhi).

14) Tata Construction Ltd. is engaged on two contracts A and B during the year. The following particulars are obtained at year ending 31ˢᵗ Dec.

Date of Commencement	Contract A 1 April Rs.	Contract B 1 Sept. Rs.
Contract price	6,00,000	5,00,000
Materials issued	1,60,000	60,000
Material returned	4,000	2,000
Materials on site (Dec. 31)	22,000	8,000
Direct labour	1,50,000	42,000
Direct expenses	66,000	35,000
Establishment expenses	25,000	7,000
Plant installed at cost	80,000	70,000
Value of plant (Dec. 31)	65,000	64,000
Cost of contract not yet certified	23,000	10,000
Value of contract certified	4,20,000	1,35,000
Cash received from contractees	3,78,000	1,25,000
Architects fees	2,000	1,000

During the period materials amount to Rs. 9,000 have been transferred from contract A to contract B. You are required to show : (a) Contract Accounts, (b) Contracter's accounts and (c) Extracts from Balance sheet as on 31ˢᵗ December. Clearly showing the calculation of work-in-progress. (B. Com, Pune)

Ans : Contract A Transfer to P & L A/c Rs. 36,000 : Reserve Rs. 24,000; Contract B. Loss Rs. 5,000

Chapter 7

Process Costing

7.1. Meaning and Features of Process Costing
7.2 Normal Loss and Abnormal Loss
7.3. Joint Product and By-Product
7.4 Illustrations
7.5 Exercises

7.1 Meaning and Features of Process Costing

Process costing is the most widely costing method. It represents a type of costing procedure for mass production industries producing standard product. It is the method in which costs are collected according to departments or process and the cost of each department or process is divided by the quantity or production to arrive at the cost of product at each stage of production or at each process. Thus, process costing is used where the production moves from one process or department to next until its final completion and there is a continuous mass production of identical units through a series of processing operation.

7.1.1 Definition and Meaning of Process Costing.

1) **KOHLER** difines process costing as, 'a method of cost accounting where by cost are charged to processes or operations and averaged over units produced'.

2) ICMA defines process costing as follows - 'The costing method is applicable where goods or services result from a sequence of continuous or repetitive operations or processes.

Costs are averaged over the units produced during the period'. Alternatively process costing is that form of operation costing which applies where standardised goods are produced.

From the above definitions, the main FEATURES of process costing can be explained as follows.

1) There is a continuous flow of production.

2) The process cost centres are clearly defined and all cost relating to each process cost centre are accumulated.

3) The production process is devided in number of processes as per requirement.

4) The finished product of one process becomes the raw material of next process or operation, and so on until final product is obtained.

5) Products are not distinguishable in process stage.

6) The finished products are uniform in all respect such as weight, quality, size, shape, colour etc.

7) The products are standardised and homogeneous.

8) The sequence of operations or processes is specific and predetermined.

9) The cost per unit produced is the average cost which is calculated by dividing the process cost by the number of units produced.

10) Avoidable and unavoidable losses usually arise at different stage of manufacture for various reasons. For example chemical action wastage, spoilage, evoparation etc. These losses may be normal or abnormal losses.

11) Appropriate method is used in absorption of overheads to the process cost centres.

12) The costs incurred in the earlier process are transferred to the later process along with the output.

13) Since the production is continuous in nature, there will be closing work-in-progress which must be valued separately.

14) The output from the process may be a single product but there may also be a by product or joint products.

15) Costs are accumulated by processes.

16) Sometimes goods are transferred from one process to another

process not at cost price but at transfer price just to compare this with the market price and losses occuring in a particular process.

Application of process costing :

Process costing is suitable for industries involving continuous production of the same product or products through the same process or processes. Generally, process costing system can be usually devised in all industries except where job, batch or unit operation costing is necessary. In particular, the following are the examples of the industries where process costing is applied.

Chemical works, oil refining, Textile mills, Cement manufacture, Food Processing, Paint manufacture, Distilleries, Soap making, Breweries, Sugar industries, Canning factory etc.

Advantages of process costing ;

The advantages of process costing are as under.

1) Process cost can be determined periodically at short interval.
2) It is simple and less expensive to find out the process cost.
3) It involves less clerical work as compared to job josting.
4) Allocation of expenses can be easily made and this results in a more accurate costing.
5) Actual costs and budgeted costs are available in detail. Thus, managerial control is possible by evaluating performance of each process.
6) It is earier to establish the standards in case of continuous production, hence standard costing system can be followed easily in process costing.
7) Quotations can be submitted more promptly with standardisation of processes.

Disadvantages or limitations of process costing :

The following are the disadvantages of process costing.

1) Process costing is based on historical cost and costs are obtained at the end of the period. Hence, managerial control may not be effective.
2) Due to the average cost, process cost may not be accurate

for analysis, evaluation and control of performance.

3) Valuation of closing stock becomes more difficult, when output of one process is transfered to another process at market price.

4) It is often very difficult to estimate normal quantity loss in process.

5) The method does not permit evaluation of efforts of individual workers or supervisors.

6) In case of joint product or by-product, the apportionment of expenses is difficult and due to this accurate cost may not be calculated.

Basis of distinction	Job costing	Process costing.
1) Production	Production is undertaken as per specific orders from the customers.	Production is in continuous flow. It is carried out uniformly because it is homogeneous product.
2) Cost Determination	Cost for each job is determined separately.	Costs are compiled for each process and the output cost of the process becomes the input costs of the subsequent process.
3) Suitability	It is suitable where jobs are made according to the orders of customer.	It is suitably employed where production is continuous.
4) Transfer	There are usually no trnsfers from one job to another except in case of surplus material.	Cost of one process is transferred to next or subsequent process.

Basis of distinction	Job costing	Process costing.
5) Form and details	It requires more forms and documents.	It requires less paper work.
6) Entity	Each process is separate and independent of others.	It is in continuous flow and hence the product lose their individuality.
7) Cost calculation	Costs are ascertained only after completion of job.	Costs are calculated at the end of cost period.
8) Unit cost	Total cost of a job is divided by the number of units produced in the job in order to calculate unit cost of a job.	Total cost of each process is divided by total production for the process to calculate the average cost per unit for the period.
9) Work-in-progress	There may or may not be work-in-progress at the beginning or end of the accounting period.	There is always some work-in-progress at the beginning as well as at the end of accounting period.
10) Control	More control is required as each job is different and according to specification of the customer. Thus, are non-standardised jobs.	Proper control is comparatively easier as the production is standardised and is more stable.

7) It may not always be possible to indicate the suitable units for showing quantity figures in process cost statements.

Difference between job costing and process costing.

Fundamental principles of process costing.

The fundamental principles of process costing are.

1) Cost of materials, direct wages and overheads are collected for each process or operation in a particular period.
2) Sufficient record is kept in respect of output and scrap for each process.
3) The cost per finished output of each process is obtained by dividing the total cost incurred during a period by the number of units produced during the period after considering the losses and amount realised from sale of scrap.
4) The finished product alongwith its cost is transferred from one process to another, till the production is manufactured.

Process Cost Accounting Procedure :

The essential stages in process costing are :

1) The factory is divided into number of processes and a separate account is maintained for each process.
2) Each process account is debited with material cost, labour cost, direct cost and overheads or expenses apportioned to the process.
3) Output is recorded in terms of units i.e. tons, kgs, litres, units etc. on a suitable periodical basis depending upon the processing time.
4) The output of a process is transfered to the next process in the sequence. Thus, finished product of one process becomes the raw material or input of next process.
5) Average cost per unit is found out by dividing the total cost of each process per unit by total production of that process after considering scrap value and normal and abnormal losses.
6) The principle that the cost of normal loss is borne by good output is to be applied.

7) Generally, following formula is applied for ascertaining the cost per unit.

$$\text{Cost per unit} = \frac{\text{Total Cost of each process less value of normal scrap}}{\text{Input quantity less normal loss quantity}}$$

8) The finished output of last process or final process is transferred to Finished Goods Account.

9) When there is work-in-progress at the commencement of the period or at the end of the period, it is also to be valued by computing equivalent production units in regard to material labour, factory, administrative overheads and accounted for in the process account.

10) The value of abnormal loss is debited to costing profit and loss Account where as the value of abnormal gain is credited to costing profit and loss Account.

Process Losses and Wastages.

The process loss contains wastage or scrap. These terms are defined by ICMA as under.

Waste : "Discarded substances having no value"

Scrap : "Discarded material having some recovery value which is usually disposed off without further treatment or re-introduced into the production process in place of raw materials."

It is usual that a certain amount of material introduced into the processes are lost, scrapped or wasted. Such a loss may arise due to evaporation, shrinkage, breakages, spoilage, chemical reaction, inefficiency etc.

It is therefore necessary to keep accurate records of both input and output. The concerned supervisor or foreman must keep control on the losses, otherwise the production cost will increase. Materials which have been processed and are then found to be defective and scrapped have incurred their share of labour and variable overheads upto the point of rejection, so obviously the loss to the firm increases with each stage of production. It is desirable that scrap should be disposed off immediately as it is usually valued higher than the loose scrap and needs less storage space. Process loss may be classified into normal and abnormal.

7.2 Normal Loss and Abnormal Loss

The amount of loss which cannot be avoided because of the nature of the material or process is a normal loss. This loss is expected during the normal course of operation. It is unavoidable on account of its inherent nature. In other words such loss is quite expected under normal conditions. It is caused by factors like evaporation, shrinkages, chemical change, withdrawals for tests or sampling etc. The normal loss can be estimated in advance on the basis of past experience or data. For example, 100 Kgs are introduced into the production process and on an average 95 kgs. comes out after the process, so we can say that the normal process loss is 5% or 5 kgs.

Accounting Treatment of Normal loss : It is a fundamental costing principle that the cost of normal losses should be borne by the good production. It is generally determined as a percentage of input. Very often such a loss is due to loss in weight, say, due to evaporation or chemical action. Since such a wastage is not physically present, it **cannot have any value**. However, when normal loss is physically present in the form of scrap it may have some value, i.e. it may be sold at some price. Wherever scrapped material has any value, it is credited to normal output. Process loss is shared by usable or saleable units. The normal process cost is borne by the good units produced as under.

unit cost = Total process cost - Value of Normal Wastage
Good units produced.

Accounting entries in respect of normal loss are as under.
a) For arising normal loss.
    Normal loss A/c   ...... Dr.
      To Process A/c
b) For Sale of Scrap (if any)
    Cash / Bank A/c   ...... Dr.
      To Normal loss A/c
c) For adjustment of deficiency in the sale of normal loss :
    Abnormal gain A/c   ...... Dr.
      To Normal loss A/c

Abnormal Loss / Abnormal Wastage.

The loss which arises due to abnormal factors and represents a loss which is over and above the normal loss is called abnormal loss. It may arise due to unforeseen factors or abnormal conditions such as carelessness, machine break-down, accident, use of defective material, power failure, bad design, strike, fire etc. abnormal loss is avoilable and can be controlled by management calculated as follows. For example, if 100 kgs. material introduced into the process and the expected normal loss is 5% and if the actual output of the process is 92 kgs, the abnormal loss is calculated as under.

	Kgs.
Units introduced (Input)	100
Less : Normal loss	5
(5% of input)	
Expected output / Normal output	95
Less Actual output	92
Abnormal loss	3

In short the difference between normal output and actual output is the abnormal loss or wastage.

Accounting Treatment : Unlike normal loss, abnormal loss is not absorbed by good production. Abnormal process loss should not be allowed to affect the cost of production as it is caused by abnormal loss Account and the balance is ultimately written off to costing profit and loss Account. For disclosing the cost of abnormal loss, following procedurre is adopted.

i) Allow the normal loss in the manner described earlier.

ii) After considering the normal loss, total value of abnormal loss is calculated by using the following formula.

Value of Abnormal Loss

$$= \frac{\text{Total cost} - \text{Value of normal loss}}{\text{Units introduced} - \text{Normal loss units}} \times \text{Units of abnormal loss}$$

iii) Credit the relevant process account with the quantity and value of abnormal loss.

iv) The balance figure in the process account is the cost of good units produced in the process.

v) Open and Abnormal loss Account and debit it with quantity and value of abnormal loss shown in the process account. Any balance left in this account is net loss and transferred to costing profit and loss account.

The accounting entries in respect of Abnormal Loss may be passed as follows.

1) For the value of Abnormal loss.

Point of Distinction	Normal Loss	Abnormal Loss
1) Condition	Normal loss is expected under normal conditions.	Abonormal loss is arised due to abonormal or unexpected conditions.
2) Avoidable	Normal loss is unavoidable	Abnormal loss is avoidable.
3) Cause	Normal loss is caused by the factors like evoporation, shrinkage, chemical changes etc.	It may arise due to unforeseen factors such as carelessness, use of defective material, power failure, strike, fire etc.
4) Estimation	Normal loss can be estimated in advance on the basis of past experience	Abnormal loss can not be estimated in advance.
5) Borne or Suffered by	The normal loss in a process is borne by good units produced.	The abnormal loss is valued at the end at which good units would be valued if there were only normal loss

Abnormal loss A/c .... Dr.
To Process A/c
2) If any amount is received from sale of scrap.
Cash / Bank A/c .... Dr.
To Abnormal loss A/c
3) For closing Abnormal Loss Account.
Costing profit and loss A/c .... Dr.
To Abnormal loss A/c.

**Difference Between Normal Loss and Abnormal Loss :
Abnormal Gains / Abnormal Effectives.**

Normal process loss is expected under normal condition. It is an estimated figure. The actual loss may be greater or less than the normal loss. If actual loss is greater than normal loss, it is known as abnormal loss. But if the actual loss is less than normal loss, the gain is obtained which is known as abnormal gain or abnormal effectives. In short, if the loss is less than normal expected loss the difference is considered as abnormal gain. For example, if 100 kgs material is introduced into the process and expected normal loss is 5% and if the actual output of the process is 97 kgs, the abnormal gain is calculated as under.

	Kgs.
Units introduced (input)	100
Less : Normal loss (5% of input)	5
Normal output	95
Actual output is	97
Less : Normal output	95
Abnormal Gains / Effectives	2

Accounting Treatment

Like abnormal loss, abnormal gain also does not affect the cost of normal production, as this is also valued in the same manner as abnormal loss. It is shown on the debit side of process account and credit side of Abnormal Gain Account. Finally, it is seen that the process account is credited with quantity and value of normal scrap. But the actual quantity is less. Hence, the difference is credited to normal loss account by debiting the normal gain account. Then the balance to the credit of abnormal gain account is transferred to costing profit and loss account as abnormal gain.

The value of abnormal gain is calculated as under

Value of abnormal gain =

$$\frac{\text{Total cost - Normal loss}}{\text{Units introduced} - \text{Normal loss units}} \times \text{Units of gain.}$$

Accounting Entries in respect of Abnormal gain may be passed as follows.

1) For Value of Abnormal Gain :
   Process A/c   ...... Dr.
       To Abnormal Gain A/c
2) For closing Abnormal Gain Account :
   Abnormal gain A/c   ...... Dr.
       To Costing profit & loss A/c.
3) For adjustment of scrap value of Abnormal Gain :
   Abnormal Gain A/c   ...... Dr.
       To Normal loss A/c.

7.3 Joint Product and By-Product

There are certain industries where two or more products of equal importance are simultaneously produced. Such products are known as joint product. In joint products, two or more product of equal economic value are produced in the same manufacturing process. Joint products, thus represent two or more products separated in the course of same processing operation usually requiring further processing, each product being in such proportion that no single product can be designated as a major product.

ICMA defines joint product as "two or more products separated in course of processing, each having sufficiently high value to merit recongisation as a main product.

In short joint products have equal value in manufactuing process following is an example of Joint product. In oil industry, gasolive, fuel oil, paraffin asphalt, lubricants, coaltar, and kerosene all are produced from crude pertroleum other examples are in flour mill where joint products are white flour, brown flour, animal feeding stuff, in meat canning where joint product are wides, cannot meat, fertilizers etc. The term joint product is also used to describ various qualities of the same products, as far example, many grades of coal which may be produced in coal mining. The main features of joint products are as follows .

1) They are produced simultaneously by a common process
2) They are comparatively of almost equal value.
3) Joint products may be saleable after separation or may be further processed by incuming addition at cost to make them saleable or an improfed product.

Typical Example of Joint Product

Industry	Joint Product
a) Oil refining	Petrol, diesal, kerosene, grease, Lubricating oils etc.
b) Dairy	Skimmed milk, butter
c) Meat processing	Meat or hides
d) Mining	serveral metals from the same ore i.e. copper, silver, zink etc.

By Products

According to ICMA terminology, a by-product is, "a product which is recovered incidentally from the material used in the manufacture of recognised main product such as having either a net realisable value or a usable value which is relatively low in comparision with the saleable value of the main products. By-product may be further processed to increase their realisable value."

In short by-productss are the products of relatively small value which are incidentally and unavoidably produced in the course of manufacturing the main product. By-products are of a lesser value. In many processes by-products and /or scrap are produced. The main product of one industry may be the by product of another industry. In sugar mills, the main product is sugar. But baggasse and molasses of comparatively smaller value are incidentally produced and these are by-products. In cake ovens of steel plants, coke is the main product and gas which is incidentally produced becomes a by-product. These by-products are unavoidably produced are secondary value. The sales value of these by products is much less as compared to the main product. For example, sales value of by-product bhagasse and molasses is much less than that of the main product sugar.

Some typical examples of by-products are given below :

Industry	Main product	By Product
1) Sugar	sugar	molasses and bayosse
2) Flour	flour	bran, pollard, semolina etc.
3) Meat	dressed carcases	hides, tongues, liver, bones, grease and tallow.
4) Ginning process	cotton	cotton seed
5) Coke ovens	coke	coaltar, benzol, ammonia
6) Dairy	milk	butter, cheese

Distinction between Joint Product and By-Product

There is no hard and fast rules to distingwish between joint product and by product. A product may be treated as a joint product in one business and the same product may be treated as by-product in another business. The differences between joint-product and by product is as follows.

Point	Joint Product	By-Product
Sales Value	The sales value of all joint product is equal.	The sales value of by-product is relatively low as compared to main product
Objective of	While producing joint product, the objective is to produce two or more products.	By-product is incidentally and unavoidably produced.
Policy of Management	Management may consdier two or more products as joint products.	Management may consider one product as main product and remaining as by-product.

In the book of a ..... company

Process Account

Dr.   Cr.

Particulars	Quantity Units	Cost per unit Rs.	Amount Rs.	Particulars	Quantity Units	Cost per unit Rs.	Amount Rs.
To Earlier Process A/C	-	-	-	By Normal loss	-	-	-
To Units Introduced	-	-	-	By loss in weight	-	-	-
To Direct Material	-	-	-	By sale of scrap	-	-	-
To Direct Labour	-	-	-	By sale of			
To Direct Expenses	-	-	-	By-product	-	-	-
To Indirect Expenses	-	-	-	By Abnormal loss	-	-	-
(Production or				By Next process	-	-	-
Maunfacturing or				or warehouse			
office & Adm Exp)	-	-	-	(in case of last			
To Abnormal gains	-	-	-	process)	-	-	-
To profit	-	-	-	or Closing stock A/c	-	-	-

Dr.   **Normal Loss Account**   Cr.

Particulars	Quantity (Units)	Amount (Rs.)	Particulars	Quantity (units)	Amount (Rs.)
To Process A/c	-	-	By Abnormal gain A/c By Cash / Bank A/c Sale	- -	- -
	-	-		-	-

Dr.   **Abnormal Loss Account**   Cr.

Particulars	Quantity (Units)	Amount (Rs.)	Particulars	Quantity (units)	Amount (Rs.)
To Process A/c	-	-	By Cash / Bank A/c (sale) By Costing profit & loss A/c	- -	- -
	-	-		-	-

Dr.   **Abnormal Gain / Effectives Account**   Cr.

Particulars	Quantity (Units)	Amount (Rs.)	Particulars	Quantity (units)	Amount (Rs.)
To Normal loss A/c To Costing profit & loss Account	-		By Process A/c	-	-
	-	-		-	-

Illustrations on process costing

Illustration 1:

A product passes through three distinst processes for completion, viz A, B and C. During the month ended 31st, January 2008, 1000 units are produced. The following information is obtained.

Particulars	Process A Rs.	Process B Rs.	Process C Rs.
Material	6,000	3,000	2,000
Labour	5,000	4,000	5,000
Direct Expenses	1,000	200	1,000

Indirect expenses for the period were Rs. 2800 apportioned to the processes on the basis of wages.

Prepare process accounts showing total cost and cost per unit.

Solution :

Dr.   **Process 'A' Account**   Output 1000 units   Cr.

Particulars	Cost per units (Rs.)	Total (Rs.)	Particulars	Cost per units (Rs.)	Total (Rs.)
To Materials	6 = 00	6,000	By output		
To Labour	5 = 00	5,000	transferred to		
To Direct			"B' process	13 = 00	13,000
Expenses	1 = 00	1,000			
To Indirect					
Expenses					
$(2800 \times \frac{5}{14})$	1 = 00	1,000			
	13 = 00	13,000		13 = 00	13000

Dr.   **Process 'B' Account**   Output 1000 units   Cr.

Particulars	Cost per units (Rs.)	Total (Rs.)	Particulars	Cost per units (Rs.)	Total (Rs.)
To Process 'A' A/c (transfer)	13 = 00	13,000	By output transferred		
To Materials	3 = 00	3,000	To process 'C' A/c	21 = 00	21,000
To Labour	4 = 00	4000			
To Direct Expenses	= 20	200			
To Indirect Expenses $(2800 \times \frac{4}{14})$	= 80	800			
	21 = 00	**21,000**		**21 = 00**	**21000**

Dr.   **Process 'C' Account**   Output 1000 units   Cr.

Particulars	Cost per units (Rs.)	Total (Rs.)	Particulars	Cost per units (Rs.)	Total (Rs.)
To Process 'B' A/c (transfer)	21 = 00	21,000	By output transferred Finished stock or goods A/c	30 = 00	30,000
To Materials	2 = 00	2,000			
To Labour	5 = 00	5,000			
To Direct Expenses	1 = 00	1,000			
To Indirect Expenses $(2800 \times \frac{5}{14})$	1 = 00	1,000			
	30=00	**30,000**		**30 = 00**	**30,000**

Dr.   **Finished stock Account**   Cr.

Particulars	Cost per units (Rs.)	Total (Rs.)	Particulars	Cost per units (Rs.)	Total (Rs.)
To Process 'C' A/c (transfer)	1000	30,000			

Note : Indirect expenses are opportioned on the basis of wages i.e 5000
: 4000 : 5000 or 5:4:5

Illustration 2:

Prepare process cost Accounts from the following.

	Process 'X'	Process 'Y'
Material used Ton	100	162
Cost per tons Rs.	120	200
Loss in weight	2%	4%
Scrap in tons	10%	10%
Scrap realisation per tonnd Rs.	100	200
Wages	20,000	30,000
Production Expenses	10,000	15,000

Solution :

Dr.   **'X' Process Account**   Cr.

Particulars	Tons	Total cost (Rs.)	Particulars	Tons	Total cost (Rs.)
To Material used	100	12,000	By loss in weight		
To Wages		20,000	(2% of 100 tonnes)	2	
To Manufacturing		10,000	By Scrap (sold)		
Expenses			(10% of 100 tonne		-
			(10 tonnes×100)	10	1,000
			By Output		
			transferred to		
			process 'Y'	88	41,000
		42,000			**42,000**

$$\text{Cost per ton} = \frac{\text{Process cost - Amount realised by scrap}}{\text{Input quantity - Normal loss quantity with sorap}}$$

$$= \frac{42,000 - 1,000}{100 - 12} = \frac{41,000}{88} = \text{Rs. } 465.90$$

$$= 465.90 \text{ per tonne}$$

Dr.			'Y' process Account		Cr.
Particulars	**Tonne**	**Total cost (Rs.)**	**Particulars**	**Tonne**	**Total cost (Rs.)**
To transfer from process 'X'	88	41,000	By loss in weight 4% of 250 tons	10	-
To Materials	162	32,400	By Scrap (sold) 10% of 250	25	5,000
To Wages		30,000	(25 tons × 200)		
To Manufacturing Expenses		15,000	By Finished goods A/c	215	1,13,400
	250	1,18,400		250	1,18,400

Cost per tonne = $\dfrac{\text{Process cost} - \text{Amount realised by scrap}}{\text{Input quantity} - \text{Normal loss quantity with scrap}}$

$$= \frac{1,18,400 - 5000}{250 - 35} = \frac{1,13,400}{215}$$

= Rs. 527.44 per ton.

Finished goods = 527.44 × 215

= Rs. 1,13,400

Illustration 3:

Maharashtra Chemical Co Ltd produced three chemicals during the month of october 2008 by three consecutive processes. In each process 2% of the total weight put in is lost and 10% scrap from processes I and II realised Rs. 100 a tonne and from process III Rs. 20 a tonne.

The product of three processes are dealt with as follows.

	process I	process II	process III
Passed on to next process	75%	50%	-
Sent to warehouse for sale	25%	50%	100%

	process I		process II		process III	
	Rs.	tonnes.	Rs.	tonnes	Rs.	tonnes
Raw materials	1,20,000	1000	28,000	140	1,07,840	1348
Manufacturing Wages	20,500	-	18,520	-	15,000	-
General Expenses	10,300	-	7,240	-	3,100	-

Prepare Process Cost Accounts Showing the cost per ton of each product.

Solution :

Dr.   **Process 'I' Account**   Cr.

Particulars	Tonne	Total cost (Rs.)	Particulars	Tonne	Total cost (Rs.)
To Raw Materials	1000	1,20,000	By loss in weight (2% of 1000 tonne)	20	-
To Mfg. wages		20,500			
To General Expenses		10,300	By sale of scrap (10% of 1000 tonne) (100 tonne ×100)	100	10,000
			By Transfer to warehouse	220	35,200
			By Transfer to process II	660	1,05,600
	1,000	1,50,800		1,000	1,50,800

$$\text{Cost per tonne} = \frac{\text{Cost of goods transferred to process II}}{\text{Tonnes sent to process II}}$$

$$= \frac{1,05,600}{660}$$

= Rs. 160 per tonne

Dr.   **Process "II' Account**   Cr.

Particulars	Tonne	Total cost (Rs.)	Particulars	Tonne	Total cost (Rs.)
To Transfer from Process I	660	1,05,600	By loss in weight (2% of 800 tonne)	16	---
To Raw Materials	140	28,000			
To Mfg. wages	-	18,520	By sale of scrap (10% of 800 tonne) (80 tonne × 100)	80	8,000
To General Expenses	-	7,240			
			By Transfer to warehouse	352	75,680
			By Transfer to process III	352	75680
	800	1,59,360		800	1,59,360

$$\text{Cost per tonne} = \frac{75,680}{352}$$

Output transferred to process III
= Rs. 215 per tonne

Dr.   **Process 'III' Account**   Cr.

Particulars	Tonne	Total cost (Rs.)	Particulars	Tonne	Total cost (Rs.)
To Transfer from process II	352	75,680	By loss in weight (2% of 1700 tonne)	34	-
To Raw Material	1348	1,07,840	By sale of scrap (10% of 1700 tonne) (170 tons ´ 20)	170	3400
To Mfg. wages	-	15,000			
To General Expenses	-	3,100	By Finished good A/c (Transferred to ware house for sales)	1496	1,98,220
	1700	2,01,620		1700	2,01,620

Cost per tonne (Finished goods) $= \dfrac{1,98,220}{1,496}$

$= $ Rs. 132.50 per tonne

Illustration 4:

The following details are extracted from the costing record of Bharat Oil Mill for the year 31st March 2008.

Purchase 500 Tons of copra   Rs. 200,000

Particulars	Crushing (Rs.)	Refining (Rs.)	Finishing (Rs.)
Cost of Labour	2,500	1,000	1,500
Electric Power	600	360	240
Sundry Materials	100	2,000	-
Steam	600	450	450
Repairs of Machinery	280	330	140
Factory Expenses	1,320	660	220
Cost of Casks	-	-	7,500

300 Tonne of crude oil were produced.

250 Tonne of oil were produced by the refining process.

248 Tonne of refined oil were finished for delivery.

Copra sacks sold for Rs. 140

175 tonne of copra residue sold for Rs. 11,000

Loss in weight in crushing 25 tons.

45 tonne of by-product obtained from refining process Rs. 6,750.

You are required to prepare the accounts in respect of each of the following stages of manufacture for the purpose and the total cost per tonne of each process and the total cost per ton of finished oil.

a) Copra crushing process b) Refining process c) Finishing process including casking.

Solution :

Dr.   **Crushing Process Account**   Cr.

Particulars	Tonne	Total cost (Rs.)	Particulars	Tonne	Total cost (Rs.)
To purchase of			By loss in weight	25	-
copra	500	2,00,000	By sale of copra		
To labour	-	2,500	Residue	175	11,000
To Electric Power	-	600	By sale of		
To Sundry			copra sacks	-	400
Material	-	100	By Refining	300	1,94,000
To Steam		600	Process A/c at		
To Repair of		280	Rs. 646.67		
machinery			per tonne		
To Factory					
Expenses		1,320			
	500	2,05,400		500	2,05,400

Calculation of loss in weight   tonne   tonne

Tonne introduced		500
Loss Sale of Residue	175	
Transfer to refining process	300	475
Loss in Weight =		25 tonne

Dr.   **Refining Process Account**   Cr.

Particulars	Tonne	Total cost (Rs.)	Particulars	Tonne	Total cost (Rs.)
To Crushing			By loss in		
process	300	1,94,000	weight	5	----
To Labour		1,000	By sale of		
To Electric Power		360	by-product	45	6,750
To Sundry			By Finished		
Materials		2,000	Process A/c	250	1,92,050

302 / Cost & Work Accounting (Paper II)

		450	(2@ Rs. 768.20		
To Steam			per tonne)		
To Repairs to					
Machinery		330			
To Factory					
Expenses		660			
	300	2,05,400		300	2,05,400

Dr.   **Finishing Process Account**   Cr.

Particulars	Tonne	Total cost (Rs.)	Particulars	Tonne	Total cost (Rs.)
To Refining			By loss in		
Process A/c	250	1,92,050	weight	2	-
To Labour		1,500	By Finished		
To Electric Power		240	Goods A/c	248	2,02,100
To Steam		450	(at Rs. 814.92		
To Repairs of			per tonne)		
Machinery		140			
To Factory					
Expenses		220			
To Cost of Casks		7,500			
	250	2,02,100		250	2,02,100

1) **Loss in Weight in Refining Process**   Tonne   Tonne
    Tons transfer from crushing process   300
    Loss sale of by-products   45
    Transfer to finishing process   250   295

    Loss in Weight   05

2) **Loss in Weight in Finishing Process**   Tonnes
    Tons transfer from refining process loss   250
    Transfer to finished goods   248

    Loss in Weight   2

Ilustration 5:

The products of a manufacturing concern passes through two processes A and B and then to finished stock. It is ascertained that in process A, normally 5% of the total input is scrap which realises Rs. 80 per tonne.

From the following information relating to process.

A for the month of April, 2010, prepare process account :

	Process A
Material in tonnes	500 tonnes
Cost of materials	Rs. 125 per tonne
Wages	Rs. 14,000
Mfg. overheads	Rs. 4,000
Output	415 tonnes

Dr.   **Process A Account**   Cr.

Particulars	Tonnes	Rs.	Particulars	Tonnes	Rs.
To materials	500	62,500	By Normal Loss (Rs. 80 x 25)	25	2,000
To wages	-	14,000	By Abnormal Loss	60	9,916
To Mfg. ohds.		4,000	By Output transfer to process B	415	68,584
	500	80,500		500	80,500

$$\text{Cost per tonne} = \frac{80,500 - 2,000}{500 - 25} = \frac{78,500}{475} = \text{Rs. } 165.26315$$

Cost of output = 415 x 165.26315 = Rs. 68,584

Value of abnormal loss = 60 x 165.26315 = Rs. 9916

Illustration 6:

From the information given below prepare -

(i) Process A Account

(ii) Abnormal Loss Account :

1,0000 tonne @ Rs. 125 per tonne were initially introducted in the process.

Wages   Rs. 28,000

Factory Overheads Rs. 8,000

Normal Wastage   5% of total weight of material initially introducted

Output   830 tonnes

Normal Scrap   10% of the initial quantity introduced

The scrap realises at Rs. 80 per tonne.

Soulution

Process A Account

Dr.   Cr.

Particulars	Tonnes	Rs.	Particulars	Tonnes	Rs.
To materials	1,000	1,25,000	By Normal wastage	50	---
To wages	-	28,000	By Normal scrap	100	8,000
To factory	-	8,.000	By abnormal loss	20	3,600
overheads			By process B A/c	830	1,49400
	1000	1,61,000		1000	1,61,000

Abnormal Loss Account

Dr.   Cr.

Particulars	Tonnes	Rs.	Particulars	Tonnes	Rs.
To Process A	20	3,6000	By sale of scrap	20	1,600
			By costing P&L A/c	-	2,000
	20	3,600		20	3,600

Note : Cost per unit $= \dfrac{161000 - 8000}{1000 - 150}$

$= \dfrac{153000}{850} = $ Rs.180

Value of Output = 830 x 180 = Rs. 1,49,400
Abnormal Loss = 20 x 180 = Rs. 3600

Illustration 7:

250 units are introduced into a process at a cost of Rs. 5.00 each. Direct labour cost was Rs. 125 and manufacturing expenses Rs. 400. Normal Loss is 10% input. Scrap is saleable at 50 paise per unit. Output was 200 units. Prepare Process Account and Abnormal Loss Account.

Solution

Dr.   **Process A Account**   Cr.

Particulars	Units	Rs.	Particulars	Units	Rs.
To Process A	250	1,250	By Normal Loss	25	12.50
			By Abnormal Loss	25	196.00
To Direct labour		400	By Tr. to next		
To Mfg. exp.	250	1,775	process (output)	200	1566,50
	250	**1,775**		**250**	**1,775**

Note : Cost per unit = $\dfrac{\text{Total cost - Value of Normal Loss}}{\text{Input Qty. - Normal Loss Quality}}$

$$= \frac{1775-12.50}{250-25} = 7.833$$

This rate is to be applied to the output and abnormal loss
Value of output : 200 × 7.833 = Rs. 1566.50
Value of Abnormal Loss : 25 × 7.833 = Rs. 196 (rounded off)

Dr.   **Abnormal Loss A/c**   Cr.

Particulars	Units	Rs.	Particulars	Units	Rs.
To Process A	25	196	By sale of scrap	25	12.50
			By costing P & L A/c (Abnormal Loss)		183.50
	25	196		25	196

Illustration 8 :

2,000 units costing Rs. 4 per unit were introduced to Process I. Labour Costs and other expenses were Rs. 1,080 and Rs. 120 respectively. Its output was 1,900 units. The Normal Scrap was 10% of the input and had a realisable value of Rs. 1 per unit. Prepare Process I Account, Normal Loss Account and Abnormal Gain Account.

Solution

Process I Account

Dr.   Cr.

Particulars	Units	Rs.	Particulars	Units	Rs.
To Materials	2,000	8,000	By Normal Loss	200	200
To Labour		1,080			
To Other Costs		120	By Transfer to		
To Abnormal	2,000	9,200	Process II	1,900	9,500
Grain	100	500			
	2,100	9,700		2,100	9,700

$$\text{Cost per unit} = \frac{9200 - 200}{2000 - 200} = \text{Rs.5.00}$$

Value of output = 1900 x 5 = Rs. 9500
Value of abnormal gain = 100 x 5 = Rs. 500

Normal Loss Account

Dr.   Cr.

Particulars	Units	Rs.	Particulars	Units	Rs.
To Process I	200	200	By Sales of Scrap	100	100
			By Abnormal Gain (Shortfall in scrap sale)	100	100
	200	200		200	200

Abnormal Gain Account

Particulars	Units	Rs.	Particulars	Units	Rs.
To Normal Loss	100	100	By Process I	100	500
To P & L A/c. (Abnormal gain)	--	400			
	100	500		100	500

Illustration 9 :

The product of a company passes through two processes. From past experience its ascertained that loss is incurred in each process as Process-I-2%, Process II- 5%. The lost of each process possesses scrap value. The loss of Process I is sold at Rs. 10 per 100 Units that of Process II at Rs. 20 per 100 units.

The following information is available for the year ended December 31, 2010.

40,000 units of crude materials were introduced in Process I at a cost of Rs. 16,000.

Wages paid Rs. 8,000

Overheads Rs. 6,000

Output of Process I 39,000 units, Process II 37,100 Units.

Prepare process I Account and Abnormal Loss Account

Solution

Dr.   **Process I Account**   Cr.

Particulars	Units	Rs.	Particulars	Units	Rs.
To Raw materials	40,000	16,000	By Normal Loss	800	80
To Wages		8,000	By Abnormal Loss	200	152
To Overheads		6,000	By Process II A/c	39,000	29,768
	40,000	30,000		40,000	30,000

Normal loss $40000x = \dfrac{2}{100} = 800$ Units at 10 pasie = Rs. 80

Abnormal loss = Estimated output - Actual output

= 39200 - 39000 = 200 Units

Cost of normal production =

$$\dfrac{\text{Total Cost in Process- Abnormal realised by scrap}}{\text{Estimated Production}}$$

$$= \dfrac{30,000\text{-}80}{39,200}\,0.7633$$

Abnormal loss = 200 x 0.7633 = Rs. 152/-

Abnormal Loss Account

Particulars	Rs.	Particulars	Rs.
To Process I A/c	152	By Bank (200 x 0.10) =	20
		By P & L A/c - Loss	132
	152		152

Value of output = 39,000 x 0.7633
= Rs. 29,768

Note : Process II could not be done in the absence of particulars regarding wages paid and overheads etc. are not given.

Illustration 10 :

A product passes through two distinct processes A and B. From the following information you are required to prepare : Process A, Process B, Account, Normal Loss Account, Abnormal Loss Account and Abnormal Gain Account.

Particulars	Process A Rs.	Process B Rs.
Materials	30,000	3,000
Labour	10,000	12,000
Overheads	7,000	8,600
Input units	20,000	17,500
Output units	17,500	17,000
Normal Loss	10%	4%
Sale value of waste unit	Rs. 1	Rs. 2

Solution

Dr.   **Process 'A' Account**   Cr.

Particulars	Units	Total cost (Rs.)	Particulars	Units	Total cost (Rs.)
To Materials	20,000	30,000	By Normal Loss (10% of 20,000 units) (units2000 × Rs. 1)	2,000	2,000
To Labour		10,000			
To Overheads		7,000			
			By Abnormal Loss	500	1250
			By process B A/c (transfer)	17,500	43,750
	20,000	47,000		20,000	47,000

Note : Calculation of Abnormal Loss

Abnormal Loss = Total unit - Normal loss = Expected units - Actual units

in Units   = 20,000 - 2,000 = 18,000 - 17,500 = 500

$$\text{Cost per unit} = \frac{\text{Total cost - value of normal loss}}{\text{Input - Normal loss (in units)}}$$

$$= \frac{47{,}000 - 2{,}000}{20{,}000 - 2000} = \frac{45{,}000}{18{,}000}$$

= Rs. 2.50 per unit

Abnormal Loss = 500 × 2.50 = 1,250

Cost of output of process = 17,500 × 2.50 = 43,750

Dr.   **Process 'B' Account**   Cr.

Particulars	Units	Total cost (Rs.)	Particulars	Units	Total cost (Rs.)
To transfer from process 'A'	17,500	43,750	By Normal loss 4% of 17,500 (700 × 2)	700	1,400
To Materials		3,000	By finished		
To Labour		12,000	goods/stock A/c	17,000	66,735
To Overheads		8,600			
To abnormal gain	200	785			
	17,700	68,135		17,700	68,135

Note : Calculation of Abnormal Gain / Effectives

Abnormal gain in units	Total unit	17,500
	Normal loss	700
	Expected units	16,800
	Actual units	17,000
Less -	Expected units	16,800
	Abnormal gain in units	200

$$\text{Abnormal gain per unit} = \frac{\text{Total cost - Value of normal loss}}{\text{Input - Normal loss in unit}}$$

$$= \frac{67{,}350 - 1{,}400}{16{,}800}$$

$$= 3.9256$$

Abnormal gain $= 200 \times 3.9256 = $ Rs. 785

Cost of output of process $= 17,000 \times 3.9256 = $ Rs. 66,235

Dr.   **Normal Loss A/c**   Cr.

Particulars	Units	Total cost (Rs.)	Particulars	Units	Total cost (Rs.)
To process A	2,000	2,000	By Bank A/c	2,000	2,000
To process B	700	1,400	By Bank A/c	500	1,000
			By Abnormal gain A/c (See Note)	200	400
	2,700	3,400		2,700	3,400

Note : Actual loss in process 'B' is 17500-17000 = 500 units. But normal loss account has been debited by 700 units. Hence, excess debit of 200 units should be transferred to Abnormal gain account. 500 units have been sold for Rs. 1000.

Dr.   **Abnormal loss A/c**   Cr.

Particulars	Units	Total cost (Rs.)	Particulars	Units	Total cost (Rs.)
To process A	500	1,250	By Cash / Bank A/c	500	500
			By costing P&L A/c		750
		1,250			1,250

Dr.			Abnormal gain / effective A/c		Cr.
Particulars	Units	Total cost (Rs.)	Particulars	Units	Total cost (Rs.)
To Normal loss A/c	200	400	By process B	200	785
To Costing P&L A/c (gain)		385			
		785			785

Illustration 11:

The following details have been extracted from the costing record of an oil mill for the year ended 30th, June 2008. The product passes through two distinct processes x and y and then to finished stock. It is known from the past experience that wastage occurs in the processes as under.

In process X, 5% of the units entering and in Y, 10% of the units entering.

The scrap value of wastage in process X is Rs. 8 per 100 units and process Y is Rs. 10 per 100 units.

The process figures are as follows.

	X Rs.	Y Rs.
Material	25000	10,000
Wages	30,000	20,000
Manufacturing Expenses	10,000	10,000
Factory Lighting	5,000	5,000
Sundry Expenses	5,000	-

5,000 units were introduced in process 'X'
Costing Rs. 25,000.
The output were :
From process x - 4,700 units
From process y - 4,150 units
Prepare process cost accounts showing cost of output per unit.

Solution :

In the books of Oil Mill

Dr.   **Processs 'X' Account**   Cr.

Particulars	Units	Total cost (Rs.)	Particulars	Units	Total cost (Rs.)
To Units introduced	5,000	25,000	By Normal wastage		
To material		25,000	(5% of 5,000)	250	20
To wages		30,000	By Abnormal		
To Mfg.Expenses		10,000	loss (see note)	50	1,052
To Factory			By output trans-		
Lighting		5,000	ferred to 'Y'	4,700	98,928
To Sundry					
expenses		5,000			
	5,000	1,00,000		5,000	1,00,000

Note : Abnormal loss

Units introduced	5,000
Normal Wastage	250
Expected output	4,750
Actual output	4,700
Abnormal loss	50 units.

$$\text{Cost per unit} = \frac{\text{Total cost - Value of Wastage}}{\text{Input - Normal loss in units}}$$

$$= \frac{1,00,000 - 20}{5000 - 250} = \frac{99,980}{4,750}$$

$$= 21.04842$$

Abnormal loss $= 21.04842 \times 50 = $ Rs. 1052

Cost of output $= 21.04842 \times 4700 = $ Rs. 98,928

Dr.   **Processs 'Y' Account**   Cr.

Particulars	Units	Total cost (Rs.)	Particulars	Units	Total cost (Rs.)
To Transfer from 'X' process	4,700	98,928	By Normal Wastage (10% of 4700)	470	47
To Materials		10,000	By Abnormal		
To Wages		20,000	loss (see note)	80	2,721
To Mfg. Expenses		10,000	By finished		
To Factory lighting		5,000	goods / stock	4,150	1,41,160
	4,700	1,43,928		4,700	1,43,928

Note :   Abnormal loss

Units introduced	4,700
- Normal wastage	470
Expected output	4,230
- Actual output	4,150
Abnormal loss	80

$$\text{Cost per unit} = \frac{\text{Total cost} - \text{Value of Wastage}}{\text{Input} - \text{Normal loss in units}}$$

$$= \frac{1,43,928 - 47}{4,700 - 470} = \frac{1,43,881}{4,230}$$

Cost per unit   = 34.0144

Abnormal loss   = 34.0144 × 80 = Rs. 2,721

Cost of output   = 34.0144 × 4,150 = 1,41,160

Illustration 12 :

Product A is obtained after it passes through three distinct processes, I, II and III. The following information is obtained from the accounts for the month of Dec. 2008.

Items	Total	Process		
	(Rs.)	I (Rs.)	II (Rs.)	III (Rs.)
Direct Material	15,084	5,200	3,960	5,924
Direct Wages	18,000	4,000	6,000	8,000
Production overhead	18,000			

1000 units at Rs. 6 each were introduced into process I. There was no stock of material or work-in-progress at the beginning or at the end. The output of each process passes directly to the next process and finally to the finished stock. Production overhead is recovered at 100% of direct wages. The following additional data are obtained.

Process	Output during the month units	Percentage of normal loss to input	value of scrap per unit.
I	950	5%	4
II	840	10%	8
III	750	15%	10

Prepare Process Accounts and Abnormal loss, Abnormal effective and Normal loss Account.

Solution :

Dr.   **Process 'I' Account.**   Cr.

Particulars	Units	Total cost (Rs.)	Particulars	Units	Total cost (Rs.)
To Units inroduced	1,000	6,000	By Normal loss (5% of 1000 units)	50	200
To Direct Material		5,200	By Output trans-		
To Direct Wages		4,000	ferred to process		
To Production overheads (100% of wages)		4,000	II (See note)	950	19,000
	1,000	19,200		1,000	19,200

Cost Per Unit $= \dfrac{\text{Total cost - Value of normal loss}}{\text{Input - Normal loss in units}}$

$= \dfrac{19,200-200}{1,000-50} = \dfrac{19,000}{950}$

$=$ Rs. 20 per unit.

Dr.   **Process 'II' Account.**   Cr.

Particulars	Units	Total cost (Rs.)	Particulars	Units	Total cost (Rs.)
To Transfer from Process I	950	19,000	By Normal loss (10% of 950)	95	760
To Direct Material		3,960	By Abnormal		
To Direct wages		6,000	loss (see note)	15	600
To Production overhead (100%			By output transferred to		
of wages)		6,000	process III	840	33,600
	950	34,960		950	34,960

1) Abnormal loss

   Normal output   950 - 95 = 855

   Less Actual output   840

   Abnormal loss   15

2) Cost Per Unit $= \dfrac{34,960-760}{950-95} = \dfrac{34,200}{855}$

   $=$ Rs. 40 per unit

   Abnormal loss / Wastage $=$ Rs. 40 × 15 = Rs. 600

   Cost of output $=$ Rs. 40 × 840 = Rs. 33,600

Dr.   **Process 'III' Account.**   Cr.

Particulars	Units	Total cost (Rs.)	Particulars	Units	Total cost (Rs.)
To Transfer from process II	840	33,600	By Normal loss (15% of 840 unit)	126	1,260
To Direct Material		5,924	By Finiished stock	750	57,000
To Direct wages		8,000			
To Production overheads (100% of wages)		8,000			
To Abnormal gain (see note)	36	2,736			
	876	58,260		876	58,260

Note :   Abnormal gain / effective

Units introduced	840 units.
- Normal loss	126 units.
Normal / expected Production	714 units.
Actual Production	750 units.
- Normal production	714

Abnormal gain   = 36 units.

Cost Per Unit $= \dfrac{\text{Total cost - Normal loss}}{\text{Input - Normal loss units}}$

$$= \frac{55,524 - 1,260}{860 - 126} = \frac{54,264}{714}$$

= Rs. 76

Abnormal loss   = Rs. 76 × 36 = Rs. 2,736.

Cost of output of process   = Rs. 76 × 750 = Rs. 57,000

Dr.   **Abnormal loss A/c**   **Cr.**

Particulars	Units	Total cost (Rs.)	Particulars	Units	Total cost (Rs.)
To Process II A/c	15	600	By Cash / Bank A/c	15	120
			By Costing P & L. A/c		480
		600			600

Dr.   **Abnormal Gain / Effective A/c**   **Cr.**

Particulars	Units	Total cost (Rs.)	Particulars	Units	Total cost (Rs.)
To Normal A/c (See note)	36	360	By Process III A/c	36	2,736
To Costing P & L A/c		2,376			
	36	2,736		36	2,736

Note : Actual loss in process III = 840 - 750 = 90 units. But normal loss account has been debited with 126 units. Hence, excess debit of 36 units has been cancelled by transfer from Abnormal gain account.

Dr.   **Normal loss A/c**   **Cr.**

Particulars	Units	Total cost (Rs.)	Particulars	Units	Total cost (Rs.)
To Process I A/c	50	200	By Cash / Bank A/c	50	200
To Process II A/c	95	760	By Cash / Bank A/c	95	760
To Process III A/c	126	1,260	By Cash / Bank A/c	90	900
			By Abnormal gain A/c	36	360
	271	2,220		271	2,220

Note : Actual scrap in process III is 90 units only which are sold at Rs. 10 Per unit.

Illustration 8

A product of a company passes through three dintinct processes to completion. They are known as A, B and C. From past experience it is ascertained that loss is incurred in each process as process A - 2%, Process B - 5%, Process C - 10%.

In each case the percentage of loss is computed on number of units entering the process concerned.

The loss of each process possesses a scrap value. The loss of processes A and B is sold at Rs. 5 per 100 units and that of process C at Rs. 20 per 100 units.

The output of each process passes immediately to next process and finished units are passed from process C into stock.

	Process A	Process B	Process C
	Rs.	Rs.	Rs.
Material Consumed	6,000	4,000	2,000
Direct labour	8,000	6,000	3,000
Manufacturing expenses	1,000	1,000	1,500

20,000 units have been issued to process A at a cost of Rs. 10,000. The output of each process has been as under.

Process A 19,500, Process B 18,800, Process C 16,000

There is no work-in-progress in any process.

Prepare Process Accounts Normal loss A/c. Abnormal loss A/c and Abnormal gain account. Calculations should be made to the nearest rupee.

Solution :

Dr.   **Process A Account**   Cr.

Particulars	Units	Rs.	Particulars	Units	Rs.
To Unit Introduced	20,000	10,000	By Normal Loss A/c		
To Material		6,000	(2% of 20,000 units)	400	20
To Direct labour		8,000	By Abnormal loss A/c		
To Mfg. Expenses		1,000	(See Note)	100	127
			By transfer to B		
			Process	19,500	24,853
	20,000	25,000		20000	25,000

Dr.   **Process 'B' Account**   Cr.

Particulars	Units	Rs.	Particulars	Units	Rs.
To Transfer from			By Normal loss A/c		
Process A	19,500	24,853	(5% of 19,500 units)	975	49
To Material		4,000	By Transferred to		
To Direct labour		6,000	Process 'C'	18,800	36,336
To Mfg Expenses		1,000			
To Abnormal gains					
(See Note 2)	275	532			
	19,775	36,385		19,775	36,385

Dr.   **Process 'C' Account**   Cr.

Particulars	Units	Rs.	Particulars	Units	Rs.
To Transfer from			By Normal loss A/c		
process "B'	18,800	36,336	(10% of 18,800		
To Material		2,000	units)	1,880	376
To Direct labour		3,000	By Abnormal loss A/c	920	2,309
To Mfg. Expenses		1,500	By Finished		
			stock A/c	16,000	40,151
	18,800	42,836		18,800	42,836

Dr.   **Finished Stock A/c**   Cr.

Particulars	Units	Rs.	Particulars	Units	Rs.
To Process 'C'A/c	16,000	40151			

Working Notes :

1) Process A, Abnormal loss

Units introduced - Normal loss = Normal output

20,000   - 400   = 19,600

$$\text{Cost per unit} = \frac{\text{Total cost - Normal loss}}{\text{Input - Normal loss unit}}$$

$$= \frac{25,000 - 20}{20,000 - 400} = \frac{24,980}{19,600}$$

$$= \text{Rs. } 1.274$$

Abnormal loss $= 1.274 \times 100 = 127$
Cost of output of process $= 1.274 \times 19500 = 24,853$

2) Process "B'

Abnormal gain = Units introduced - Normal loss
= Normal output
= 19,500 - 975
= 18,525

Actual output - Normal output
= 18,800 - 18,525
= 275 Abnormal units.

$$\text{Cost Per Units} = \frac{\text{Total cost - Normal loss}}{\text{Input - Normal loss unit}}$$

$$= \frac{35,853 - 49}{19,500 - 975} = \frac{35,804}{18,525}$$

= Rs. 1.9327
Abnormal gain = Rs. $1.9327 \times 275 = 532$
Cost of Output = Rs. $1.9327 \times 18,800 = 36,335$

3) Process 'C'

Abnormal loss.

Units Introduced - Normal loss = Normal output
18,800 - 1,880 = 16,920
Normal output - Actual output
16,920 - 16,000 = 920
Abnormal loss = 920 units.

$$\text{Cost per unit} = \frac{\text{Total cost - Normal loss}}{\text{Input - Normal loss unit}}$$

$$= \frac{42,836 - 376}{18,800 - 1,880} = \frac{42,460}{16,920}$$

= Rs. 2.5094
Abnormal loss = Rs. $2.5094 \times 920 = 2,309$
Cost of output = Rs. $2.5094 \times 16,000 = 40,151$

Dr. **Normal Loss A/c** Cr.

Particulars	Units	Rs.	Particulars	Units	Rs.
To process A A/c	400	20	By Abnormal gain	275	14
To process B A/c	975	49	By Cash / Bank A/c	2,980	431
To process C A/c	1,880	376			
	3255	445		3255	445

Dr. **Abnormal Loss A/c** Cr.

Particulars	Units	Rs.	Particulars	Units	Rs.
To Process A A/c	100	127	By Cash / Bank A/c (100 at Rs. 20 Per 100)	1,020	189
To Process C A/c	920	2,309	By Costing P & L A/c		2,247
	1,020	2,436		1,020	2,436

Dr. **Abnormal Gain A/c** Cr.

Particulars	Units	Rs.	Particulars	Units	Rs.
To Nominal loss A/c (loss to income)	275	14	By Process B A/c	275	532
To Costing P. & L. A/c		518			
	275	532		275	532

7.5 Exercise

Objectives type questions

a) State which of the following statements are True or False.
1) Process costing is one aspect of operation costing.
2) Process costing is applied in garment industry.
3) Process costing is used in chemical works.
4) Normal loss does not increase the cost per unit of usual production.
5) Abnormal loss is spread on good units of production.
6) Process costing is ordinarily applied where all operations are performed on one department.
7) In process costing generally no distinction is made between direct and indirect material.
8) The cost of one process may be transferred to next process at cost or at market price.
9) In process costing each process is a cost unit.
10) Process costing is generally used in small scale industry.
11) Abnormal gain arising in process is transferred to costing profit & loss account.
12) Process costing is suitable for use in automobile industry.

Ans : 1) True, 2) False, 3) True, 4) False, 5) False, 6) False, 7) True, 8) True, 9) False, 10) False, 11) True, 12) False.

b) **Fill in the blanks.**
1) Two examples of industries in which process costing is used are .... and ...
2) Two items that appear on the debit side of process account are ... and .....
3) Normal process loss may arise due to reasons like .. and .....
4) In inter process profits, output of one process is transferred to next process not at ... but at...
5) Abnormal loss is written on the ..... side of process account.
6) Average process cost for each process is calculated by dividing ...... by .....
7) Where raw material is to pass certain stage before it is

converted into finished goods, the method of costing used is ....

8) When actual loss is more than the estimated loss, the difference between the two is considered to be...

9) When actual loss is .... than the estimated loss, the difference between loss is considered as abnormal loss.

10) When 1,000 units are 60% complete in process it is equivalent to .... completed units.

11) ..... process loss should be transferred to costing profit and loss account.

12) The cost of ..... process loss is absorbed in the cost of production of good units.

13) Where actual loss in a process is less than the anticipated loss, the difference between the two is considered to be .....

Ans. : 1) steel, textile; 2) materials, wages; 3) Evaporation, scrap; 4) cost, market price; 5) credit; 6) total process cost, no of units in process; 7) process costing; 8) abnormal loss; 9) less; 10) 600; 11) abnormal; 12) normal; 13) abnormal gain.

c) **Short Answer type :**

1) What is process costing?

2) Name five industries in which process costing is used.

3) Distinguish between job costing and process costing.

4) State the features of process costing.

5) What is normal loss? How is it treated in cost accounts?

6) How does abnormal gain arise? How will you treat these in cost accounts?

7) Give the advantages and disadvantages of process costing.

8) Define normal and abnormal losses, explaining the possible cases.

9) How will you deal with (i) abnormal wastage and abnormal gain in process cost accounts?

10) Write short note on inter process profit.

Practical Problems :

1) An article under goes three processes. From the following information show the cost of each process of manufacture and cost per article produced during the month of January, 2008.

	Process A	Process B	Process C
Materials consumed	37,500	12,500	5,000
Wages	20,000	50,000	15,000
Other Direct Expenses	6,500	18,000	6,250

The indirect expenses amounted to Rs. 21,250. These are apportioned on the basis of wages. Articles produced during the month were 240.

Ans : cost per article A-Rs. 287.50; B-Rs.675; C-Rs. 800.

2) The product of a manufacturing company passes through two processes viz. x and y. It is ascertained that in each process 10% of the total weight is lost and 20% is scrap. The realisation from scrap amounted to Rs. 160 per tonne and Rs. 400 Per tonne from process x and process y respectively. The cost figures relating to processes are as follows :

	Process x	Process y
Material consumed	2,000 tonne	1400 tonne
Cost of material per tonne	Rs. 250	Rs. 400
Direct wages	Rs. 36,000	Rs. 24,000
Chargeable expenses	Rs. 11,000	Rs. 12,960

Prepare process account showing the cost per tonne in each process.

Ans. : Cost per tonne process x Rs. 345 per tonne
Process y Rs. Rs.420 per tonne.

3) The following details are taken from the books of an oil mill for the month of Oct. 2008. Purchase of 100 tonne of oil seeds at Rs. 1,000 per tonne.

	Crushing	Refining	Finishing
Wages	1,000	700	900
Sundry stores	200	600	100
Electricity	400	350	200

Steam	300	250 200
Factory Expenses	500	400 300
Containers		2,350

60 tonne of cude oil were produced. 51 tonne of oil were produced in the refining process. 50 tonne of refining oil were furnished for delivery. Empty bags of oilcake were sold at Rs. 60 per tonne. Loss in weight in crushing was 5 tonne. 8.5 tonne of by product from refining process were valued at Rs. 2,250

Make out accounts in respect of each process and calculate the cost of the product per tonne at the end of each process.

Ans : Cost per tonne - crushing Rs. 1,670; Refining Rs. 1,959.80; Finishing Rs. 2,080.

4) A product of a manufacturing company passes through two processes A & B and then to finished goods. It is ascertained that in each process normally 5% of the total weight is lost and 10% is scrap which from process A & B realises Rs. 80 per tonne and Rs. 200 per tonne respectively. The following are the figures relating to both the process.

Particulars	Process A Rs.	Process B Rs.
Cost of material perton	125	200
Wages	28,000	10,000
Manufacturing Expenses	8,000	5,250
Materials in tonne	1,000	70
Output in tonne	830	780

Prepare process cost accounts showing cost per tonne of process. There was no stock or work-in-progress in any process.

Ans. Process A abnormal loss 20 tonne Rs. 3,600. Cost per tonne Rs. 180 process B - Abnormal gains 15 ton Rs. 3150, cost per ton Rs. 210.

5) A product passes through three processes A, B and C. The normal loss of each process is as follows process A - 3%, process B - 5%, process C - 8%

Loss of process A was sold at 25 paise per unit, that of B at 50 paise per unit and that of C at Rs 1 = 00 per unit. 10,000 unit were introduced in process A at Rs. 1 = 00 per unit. The other expenses are as follows.

	Process 'A' Rs.	Process 'B' Rs.	Process 'C' Rs.
Materials	2,050	2,688	2,509
Labour	5,000	8,000	6,500
Actual output (in units)	9,500	9,100	8,100

Prepare Process Accounts assuming that there were no opening or closing stock.

Ans. : Process A - Transfer 9,500 units at Rs. 16,625, Anormal loss 200 units at Rs. 350. Process B - Transfer units 9,100 units at Rs. 27,300, Abnormal gain 75 units at Rs. 225. Process C - Transfer to finished goods, 8100 units at Rs. 34,425, abnormal loss 272 units at Rs. 1156.

6) A product passes through two Processes A and B and thereafter it is transferred to finished stock. The output of A passes to B and of B to finished stock. From the following information you are required to prepare process accounts.

	A Rs.	B Rs.
Materials consumed	24,000	14,000
Direct labour	28,000	18,000
Manufacturing expenses	23,100	26,468
Input in process A	Units 20,000	--
Input in process A	20,000	--
Output	Units 18,000	16,000
Normal wastage% of input	5%	10%
Value of normal wastage	Rs. 10 per 100 units	Rs. 10 per 100 units

(B.Com.)

Ans. Abnormal loss in Process A = 200 units @ Rs. 5; Process B = 320 units @ Rs. 9; Tr. to finished stock = Rs. 1,49,400]

7) In a factory, the product passes through two Processes, A and B. A loss of 5% is allowed in Process A and 2% in Process B, nothing realised by disposal of the wastage. During April, 10,000 units of material costing Rs. 6 each were introduced in Process A, The other costs were as follows :

	Process A Rs.	Process A Rs.
Material	--	6,140
Labour	10,000	6,000
Overheads	6,000	4,600

The output was 9,300 units from Process A. 9,200 units were produced by Process B which were transferred to warehouse.

8,000 units of the finished product were sold @ Rs. 15 per unit, the selling and distribution expenses being Rs. 2 per unit.

Prepare (i) Process Accounts, and (ii) a Statement of Profit or Loss of the firm for April assuming there were no opening stock on any type. (B.Com.)

Ans Net Profit Rs. 23,260

8) The product of a company passes through three distinct processes to completion. From the past experience it is ascertained that wastage is incurred in each process as under :

Process A 2% Process B 5% and Process C 10%

The wastage of Process A and B is sold at Rs. 10 per 100 units and that of Process C at Rs. 80 per 100 units.

Following is the information regarding the production of March 2009.

	Process A Rs.	Process B Rs.	Process C Rs.
Materials	12,000	8,000	4,000
Direct labour	16,000	12,000	6,000
Machine expenses	2,000	2,000	3,000
Other factory expenses	3,500	3,800	4,200

20,000 units have been issued to Process A at a cost of Rs. 20,000. The output of each process has been as under :

Process A 19,500 units

Process B 18,800 units

Process C 16,000 units

There was no stock of work-in-progress in an process in the beginning and in the end of March. Prepare Process Accounts. (B.Com)

[Ans. Tr. Process B 19,500 units at Rs. 16,000 units at Rs. 90,550]

9) The product of manufacturing concern passes through two Processes A and B and then to finished stock. It is ascertained that in each process normally 5% of the total weight is lost and 10% is scrap which from Processes A and B realises Rs. 80 per tonne and Rs. 200 per tonne respectively.

The following are the figures relating to both the processes :

	Process A	Process B
Materials in tonnes	1,000	70
Cost of materials in rupees per tonnes	125	200
Wages in rupees	28,000	10,000
Manufacturing expenses in rupees	8,000	5,250
Output in tonnes	830	780

Prepare Process Accounts showing cost per tonne of each process. There was no stock of work-in-progress in any process. (B.Com)

[**Ans.** Cost per tonne A. Rs. 180, B Rs. 210]

10) Department A of ABC Chemicals conducts a process which required mixing of materials loss of weight of the mixture. Also, past experience shows that two batches out of every ten started in the process are spoiled. The production records for March 2009 the following :

(i) Production started in the Process : 50 batches of 1,000 kg each.

(ii) Production completed and transferred to finished goods : 34,200 kg.

(iii) There is no inventory of work-in-progress at the beginning or at the end of the month.

Costs recorded during the month totalled Rs. 70,000

Prepare the Account of the Process conducted by Department A. (B.Com)

[**Ans.** Cost per unit Rs. 2; Abnormal Loss 800 units @ Rs. 2 - Rs. 1,600; Tr. to finished stock 34,200 units @ Rs. 2 - Rs. 68,400]

11) A product is completed in three consecutive processes. During a particular month, the input to Process I of the basic raw material was 5,000 units at Rs. 2 per unit. Other information for the month was as follows :

| | Processes | | |
	I	II	III
Output (units)	4,700	4,300	4,050
Normal loss as % of input	5	10	5
Scrap Value per unit (Rs.)	1	5	6
Direct wages (Rs.)	3,000	5,000	8,000
Direct expenses (Rs.)	9,750	9,910	15,560

Overhead total Rs. 32,000 chargeable as percentage of direct wages. There were no opening or closing work-in-progress stock. Compite three process accounts and finished stock account with details of abnormal loss and gain, where applicable.

[Ans. Cost per unit at Process I Rs. 6, at II Rs. 12 and at III Rs. 22, Abnormal loss I 50 units Rs. 300, III. 35 units at Rs. 770, Abnormal gain II 70 units at Rs. 840.]

12) A Product is obtained after passing it through three processes. The following information is collected for Januany 2009.

| | Processes | | |
	I	II	III
Direct material (Rs.)	5,200	3,960	5,924
Direct wages (Rs.)	4,000	6,000	8,000
Output in the month (units)	950	840	750
Normal Loss	5%	10%	15%
Value of scrap per unit (Rs.)	4	8	10

Additional data :

1,000 units at Rs. 6 each were introduced in Proces. There was no stock of materials of work-in-progress at the beginning or at the end of the month. Production overhead was Rs. 18,000 for the month. Prepare process accounts indicating normal loss, abnormal loss and abnormal gain. (B. Com)

[Ans. Cost per unit - Process I Rs. 20, II Rs. 40 and III Rs. 76, Abnormal loss 15 units in Process II. Abnormal gain 36 units in Process III]

13) A product passes through three processes to completion. In January 2005 the cost of production was given below Processes

	I	II	III
	Rs.	Rs.	Rs.
Material	2,000	3,020	3,462
Wages	3,500	4,226	5,000
Prodution overheads	1,500	2,000	2,500

1,000 units were issued to process I @ Rs. 5 each.

Normal loss in Proces I 10% Process II 5% and Process III 10%. Wastage realises Rs. 3 per unit. Rs. 5 per unit and Rs. 6 per unit in Processes I, II, III respectively. Actual production. Process I-920 units. Process II-870 units and Process III-800 units. Prepare the necessary accounts.

[Ans. Tr. to finished stock 800 units @ Rs. 40 - Rs. 32,000]

14) A product is finally obtained after it passes through three distinct processes. The following information is available from the cost records.

	Proces I	Process II	Process III	Total
	Rs.	Rs.	Rs.	Rs.
Materials	2,600	2,000	1,025	5,625
Direct Wages	2,250	3,680	1,400	7,330
Production overheads --	--	--	7,330

500 units @ Rs. 4 per unit were introduced in process I. Production overheads are absorbed as a percentage of direct wages.

The actual output and normal loss of the respective processes are given below :

Output	Normal Loss as a	Value of scrap
(units)	percentage of input	(per unit)
Process I	450	10% Rs. 2
Process II	340	20% Rs. 4
Process III	270	25% Rs.5

Prepare the Process accounts and the abnormal gain/loss accounts. (I.C.W.A. Inter)

[Ans. Tr. to Process II 450 units at Rs. 9,000 to Process III 340 units at Rs. 17,000 Tr. to finished goods 270 units at Rs. 21,600]

15) A product passes through three process - A, B and C. The details of expenses incurred on the three processes during the year 2009 were as under :

Processes	A	B	C
Units issued	1,000		
	Rs.	Rs.	Rs.
Cost per unit	50	--	--
Sundry materials	1,000	1,500	500
Labour	2,600	8,000	6,392
Direvt expenses	600	8,815	2,720
Sale price of output (per unit)	70	100	200

Actual outout of the three processes was --

Process A : 930 units : Process B : 540 units : Process C : 210 units.

Two-thirds of output of Process A and one half of the output of Process B was passed on to the next process and the balance ws sold, The entire output of Process C was sold.

The normal loss of the three processes, calculated on the input of every process was : Process A : 5%; Process B : 15% and Process C : 20%

The loss of Process A was sold at Rs. 1 per unit that of Process B at Rs. 3 per unit, and that of Process C at Rs. 6 per unit.

Selling and distribution expenses during the year were Rs. 10,000. These are not allocabel to the processes but to be considered while drawing the income statement. Prepare the three process accounts and a statement of income. (C. S., Inter)

[Ans. Net Profit Rs. 6.243, Cost per unit A Rs. 57, B Rs. 88, C Rs. 153]

16) Product X in a manufacturing unit passes through processes - A, B and C. The expenses incurred in the three processes during the year 2009 were as under :

	A	B	C
Units of input inssed	9,000		
	Rs.	Rs.	Rs
Cost per unit	150	--	--
Sundry materials	23,500	25,000	15,000
Direct Labour	80,000	2,07,200	26,110
Direct expenses	2,250	7,200	8,100
Selling price per unit of output	200	280	600

The actual outputs obtained vis-a-vis normal process losses from the three processes were :

	Output (units)	Process loss (%)
Process A	8,400	5
Process B	5,700	10
Process C	3,660	3

During the year, three-fourth of the output of process A and two-third of the output of process B were transferred to the next process and the balances were sold outside. The entire output of process C was however, sold outpute. The losses of the three processes were sold at Rs. 5 per unit for proces A, Rs. 10 per unit for process B and Rs. 15 per unit for process C.

Prepare the three process accounts and a statement of income considering a total selling and distribution expenses of Rs. 45,000 which is not allocated to processes. (I. C. W. A., Inter)

[Ans. Cost per unit : Process A Rs. 170, B Rs. 230, C Rs. 250, Net Profit Rs. 13,69,7401]

Chapter 8

Services Costing

8.1. Meaning, Definition, Features and Application
8.2. Cost Unit - Simple and Composite
8.3. Cost Sheet for Transport Service (Illustrations)
8.4. Exercises

8.1. Meaning, Definition, Features and Application

Operating costing is also known as service cost. This system is applied to those industries, where standardised services are provided either by an undertaking or by a service cost centre within undertaking. These units render or offer services and no items are produced. This system is useful to service organisation rather than manufacturing organisation. In short, operating or service costing method is applied in those undertakings which provide services and are not engaged in manufacturing tangible products. The cost of providing service is termed as operating or service cost. In many manufacturing companies operating costing is used in certain departments which render services. e.g. internal transport, power house, personnel department etc.

ICMA defines operating costing as "Operating costing which applies where standardised services are rendered either by an undertaking or by a service cost centre within undertaking."

Operating costing should not be confused with operation costing. Operating costing is applied to determine the cost of providing service whereas operation costing is a process costing. In may industries, a manufacturing process is sub-divided into number of parts and each of the part is known as operation. Operating costing is the determination of the cost of each operation of a process. Thus, operating costing is the part of process costing.

Operating costing is generally used where uniform and standardised services are rendered by an undertaking. Sometimes this method may be used where services are not completely standardised but where it is convenient to calculate the average cost in relation to the standardised unit of measurement.

Features of operating costing.

The main features of operating costing are as follows.

1) Services rendered to customers are of unique type.

2) In operating costing, cost unit differs from undertaking to undertaking. So selection of cost unit is difficult in this method.

3) A large proportion of total capital is invested in fixed asset and comparatively less working capital is required.

4) An undertaking, where operating costing system is applied, provides standardised and uniform services.

5) Usually large plants are involved and concerns are either large monopolistic unit or public untility undertakings.

6) The distnction between fixed and variable cost is of particular importance because the economics of scale of operation considerably affect the cost per unit of service rendered. For example, fixed cost per passenger will be lower if buses in transport company run capacity packed.

7) In operating costing, there is no need to distinguish the cost into direct and indirect. The costs and expenses are traced to the individual plant or facilities which render the services.

8) Operating costing requires a more detailed but simpler statistical data for proper costing.

9) As compared to other industries, there is no difficulty in respect of valuation of work-in-progress or closing stock.

10) Costs are usually computed period-wise. However, under special circumstances costs are computed otherwise such as in the case of utilisation of vehicles, use of road-rollers etc.

11) In service sector instead of manufacturing tangible product, generally services are rendered to society or public.

12) It is a cost of producing and maintaining a service.

Application of operating costing.

Operation or service costing is applied to those organisations which render services internally or externally. In big manufacturing industries many services are provided by service department to production departments. These are internal services. For example, canteen for staff, Hospital for staff, boiler house or supplying steam to production department, captive power generation unit, internal transport system, computer department services used by other departments.

There are some organisations which provide external services to customers. For example, supply of gas, water, electricity, lodging and boarding, transport facilities etc. The objective of organisation which supply external services, is to know the manufacturing cost and the profit on the provision of such services. In short, Operating Costing is applied to the following undertakings.

1) Transport undertakings such as Roadways, Railways, Airways, Tramways, Shipping transport.
2) Electricity companies or undertakings.
3) Supply of water or water works.
4) Gas supply companies.
5) Educational institutions like school and colleges.
6) Hospital
7) Hotels covering lodging and boarding
8) Cinemas
9) Canteen
10) Local authority like Municipality or Corporation.
11) Personnel department in a factory.
12) Service departments in big factories.
13) Services such as supply of crane, road-roller fire extinguishers, etc.
14) Sports and recreational clubs.

8.2 Cost unit - Simple and Composite

All costs incurred during a period are collected and analysed and then expressed in terms of a cost per unit of service. The selection of cost unit is very important. Selection of cost unit depends upon the nature of business. Each undertaking is having a freedom to choose its cost unit. However, a common cost unit by similar undertakings facilitate cost comparison. The cost unit may be of the following two types.

1) Simple or single cost unit. - In single cost unit, generally a single or one feature of cost unit is taken into account. A few examples of single cost units are as given below.

Undertaking	Cost unit
1) Transport	Per kilometre or per tonne
2) Water works	Per 1000 Litres
3) Canteen	Per meal / Per dish / Per cup of tea
4) School or College	Per Student
5) Gas supply	Cubic metre of gas
6) Hospital	Per Bed
7) Cinemas	A seat per show
8) Boiler Home	Quantity of steam raised (kg)

2) Composite cost unit : In composite cost unit, generally two characteristics are measured simultaneously. In operating costing, in some undertakings, two types of services are compounded together to express cost per unit. This is called composite unit. For example, in a transport company weight of goods as well as distance covered should be taken into account in evolving the cost unit i.e. tonne-kilometre. A few examples of composite unit cost are as under.

Undertaking	Cost Unit.
1) Transport	Per passenger kilometre (For passenger)
2) Electricity	Per kilowatt hour (KWH)
3) Hotel	Per room per bed.
4) Cinema	Per seat per show
5) Hospital	Per bed per day.

Difference between output costing and service costing.

Output costing	Operating or service costing.
1) Direct material cost is the major part of total cost.	1) The cost of direct material consumed is relatively small portion of total cost.
2) Output is always meant for sale to external customer	2) Service costing may be for internal consumption or for revenue earning.
3) Generally, single cost unit is adopted in output costing.	3) Multiple cost unit is adopted in service costing, for example Tonne-kilometre.
4) Costs are analysed into prime cost, factory cost, cost of production and cost of sales for collection and control of cost.	4) Costs are generally analysed into fixed and variable costs for collection and control purposes.
5) Costing procedures are similar for all output manufacturing companies.	5) The procedure for recording different costs will vary according to the nature of service.

Output costing is the method of cost ascertainment which is used in those industries where production is uniform and continuous. Such industries are engaged in manufacting tangible product. On the other hand operating or service undertaking provides services to people or customers. The difference between output costing and service costing is as under.

8. 3 Cost Sheet for Transport Costing

Transport industries include road, railway, water and air transport. Motor transport includes private cars, carriers for owners, buses, taxies, lorries etc. In transport undertaking the operating cost per ton kilometre or per passenger kilometre is ascertained.

Objectives of Transport Costing

The main objectives of transport costing are :

1) To fix the rate of carriage of passengers or goods on the basis of service costing.
2) To provide an accurate basis for quotation and fixing rate.
3) To decide the hire charges where vehicles are given on hire.
4) To compare the cost of maintaining one group of vehicle with another group.
5) To compare the cost of using own motor vehicles and that of using alternate form of transport.
6) To ensure that cost of maintenance and repairs is not excessive.
7) To ensure that all journeys have been carried out in proper time, fuel consumed is not excessive and that tyres are properly maintained.
8) To determine what should be charged against department or others using services.
9) To judge the operating efficiency of transport service by using utilisation ratio.
10) To obtain the cost of idle vehicle and loss of running time.

Collection of Cost

Cost collection or accumulation procedure is similar to that of job costing.

In transport costing, most of the details are obtained from log sheet. Each vehicle is given a distinct number and all the basic documents will contain the assigned number of respective vehicle. A Daily log sheet is maintained by the driver for each vehicle to record details of trips, running time, capacity, mileage or kilometre etc. These details enable the management to avoid idleness of vehicles, to prevent waste of capacity and to guard against unnecessary duplication of trip. The log book is generally divided into three parts as under.

The first part gives the full description of the vehicle i.e. vehicle number, date of purchase, registration number, insurance policy number, amount of premium, taxes paid, estimated life and scrap value of vehicle etc. On the basis of above information fixed charges of vehicle can be determined.

The second part contains details relating the names and address or driver, conductor, cleaner and mechanic, their salaries and wages, repairs and maintenance charges, garage rent, renewals of tyres, tubes batteries etc. On the basis of above information maintenance and repair charges of vehicle can be determined.

The third part of the log book contains the particulars related to the operating expenses of vehicle. For example, number of trips made, number of kilometres run, consumption of oil, petrol, grease, hours lost due to the vehicle remaining idle, exceptional delays such as loading delays, traffic delays and accidents etc.

The specimen of daily log sheet is as follows.

Daily Log Sheet

Vehicle No ....
Route No ....
Date of Purchase ....
Licence No ....
Registration No ....

Date ....
Name of Driver ....
Time Garage out ....
Time Garage in ....

Trip Particulars

Trip No.	From	To	Tons or Packages		Kilo-metres	Time			Remarks
			Out	Collected on Route		Out	In	Hrs taken	

Supplies
Petrol / Diesel ...
Oil ....
Grease ....

Worker's time
Driver ...
Mechanic / Cleaner ....
Conductor ....

Analysis of lost time
Loading / unloading ....
Traffic delays
Accidents ....
Others ....

Determination of Number of Cost Units

The cost unit in passenger transport is usually a passenger kilometre and in goods transport it is tonne kilometre. Such units are known as composite units. If one passenger goes one kilometre, it is taken as one passenger kilometre. If 40 passengers travel in a bus for a distance of 100 kms, it is 4000 passenger kms. (i.e. 40 × 100). Similarly if one tonne of goods are transported for a distance of one kilometre, it is known as tonne - kms. If 20 tonnes of goods are carried in a truck for 100 kilometre, it is 2000 tonnes kilometre (i.e. 20 × 100). These are called commerial tonnes kms. In short calculation of total number of cost units is as under.

Passenger kilometres = No. of buses × Distance per trip × Capacity of each bus × Capacity utilised × No. of trips × No. of days

For example : A Pune-Ahmadnagar transport company runs 4 buses between two towns which are 100 kms apart. The seating capacity of each bus is 50 passengers and actual passengers carried are 80% of the seating capacity. All the 4 buses run on 25 days in a month and each bus makes one round trip per day.

Calculate passenger kilometres for a month.

By using the above formula, passenger kilometres will be calculated as under.

$$\text{Passenger Kilometres} = 4 \times 100 \times (50 \times 80\%) \times 2 \times 25$$
$$= 4 \times 100 \times 40 \times 2 \times 25$$
$$= 8,00,000 \text{ passenger kilometres.}$$

In case of goods transport, tonnes kilometres are calculated as under.

For example - Suppose a transport company maintains fleet of vehicles for carrying goods between two places. The capacity of vehicle is :

No. of Vehicles	Capacity (in tonnes each)
10	2
5	6
20	5

Each vehicle makes 5 trips a day covering a distance of 10 kms in each trip. On average 10% of the vehicles are laid up for repairs daily and 70% of capacity of each vehicle is actually used. If the company operate 26 days in a month, the total tonne-kilometres carried by the company per month will be calculated as under.

Tonnes kilometre carried = Total capacity (i.e. Number of Vehicles used × tons carried) × average kilometres × No of trips × No of days × percentage of vehicle runs on an average × capacity used.

$$= (10 \times 2 + 5 \times 6 + 20 \times 5) \times 10 \times 5 \times 26 \times \frac{90}{100} \times \frac{70}{100}$$

$$= 150 \times 10 \times 5 \times 26 \times \frac{90}{100} \times \frac{70}{100}$$

$$= 1,22,850 \text{ tonnes kilometres}$$

Classification and Ascertainment of Cost

In operating costing, costs are classified and compiled under the following three heads. i.e. fixed costs, maintenance cost and running cost. For calculation of total cost and per unit cost, operating cost sheet is prepared. Total cost is divided by total units i.e. ton kms or passenger kms to arrive at average unit cost. Cost classification in operating costing may be as under.

1) Standing or Fixed Cost - These are fixed or constant costs and are incurred irrespective of the kilometre run. These are incurred whether the vehicle is operating or not. Such costs, therefore should not be allocated to specific journey on the basis of kilometre. But fixed cost can be suitably apportioned on each vehicle. These include garage rent, insurance, road tax, licence fees, establishment cost of work shop and head office, interest on capital, depreciation, drivers, cleaners and conductors wages if paid on monthly basis. In case of depreciation, opinion differs, whether it should be regarded as fixed or variable cost. It is sometimes regarded as variable cost and sometimes as a fixed cost, depending upon the situation given in problem.

2) Maintenance Cost - These costs are semi variable in nature. These include expenditure on repairs, maintenance, tyres, tubes, accessories and spares, overhauling, painting, hire charges of vehicles etc.

3) Operating or Running Cost or Variable Costs - These costs are those which vary in direct proportion to kilometre run and so variable cost per unit may be computed stright way. For example, petrol, diesel, lubricating oil, depreciation and wages of drivers, conductors and cleaners if payment is made according to the distance or trip. Thus, these are variable in nature and can be allocated to each vehicle.

Proforma / Specimen of Operating Cost Sheet
Jayhind Transport Company Ltd.
Operating Cost Sheet

Vehicle No. ....   No. of Trips :   Period ....
Registration No. ...   Kms. Run :   Capacity ....
Route No. ...   Total Weight Carried : No. of Cost Units ...
Cost ...   Total hours operated
Estimated Life ...

Particulars	Total (Rs.)	Per Unit (Rs.)
A) Fixed or Standing Costs Garage Rent Licence Fees Road Tax Insurance Interest on Capital		
Establishment and General Charges		
Supervision Charges Driver, Cleaner and Conductors Wages if paid on monthly basis Sub Total A		

B) Maintenance Costs		
Repairs and Maintenance		
Tyres and Tubes		
Spare Parts and Accessories		
Overhauling		
Painting		
Sub Total B		
C) Operating / Running / Variable Costs		
Petrol and Diesel		
Oil and Grease		
Depreciation		
(if per kilometre is calculated)		
Transit Insurance		
Wages of Drivers, Cleaners		
and Conductors		
Sub Total C		
Grand Total A + B + C		
D) Tonne km / Passenger km run		
E) Cost per tonne km / passenger km		

Illustrations on Transport Costing

Illustration 1

From the following data relating to two different vehicles A and B. Compute the cost per running kilometre.

	Vehicle A	Vehicle B
Kilometre run during the year	15,000	6,000
Cost of Vehicle	28,000	17,000
Residual Value of Vehicle	3,000	2,000
Road Licence (annual)	750	750
Garage rent (annual)	700	400
Insurance	600	500
Supervision and Salaries	1,200	1,200

Drivers wages per hour		3	3
Cost of fuel per litre		50	50
Kilometers run per litre		20 kms	15 kms
Estimated life of vehicles		1,00,000 kms	75,000 kms
Repairs and maintenance per kilometre		Rs. 1 = 00	Rs. 1 = 20
Tyre allocation per kilometre		Rs. 00.80	Rs. 00.60

Charge interest at 10% per annum on cost of vehicle. The vehicle runs 20 kilometers per hour on an average.

Solution :

Working Notes

1) Depreciation $= \dfrac{\text{Cost of vehicle - Residual Value of Vehicle}}{\text{Estimated life of vehicle}}$

		Vehicle A	Vehicle B
1)	Depreciation	$= \dfrac{28,000 - 3,000}{1,00,000}$ = Rs. 00 = 25	$\dfrac{17,000 - 2000}{75,000}$ = Rs. 00 = 20
2)	Driver's Wages $\dfrac{\text{wages per hour}}{\text{km. per hour}}$	$= \dfrac{3}{20}$ = Rs. 00 = 15	$= \dfrac{3}{20}$ = Rs. 00 = 15
3)	Cost of fuel $\dfrac{\text{cost per litre}}{\text{km. per litre}}$	$= \dfrac{50}{20}$ = Rs. 2 = 50	$= \dfrac{50}{15}$ = Rs. 3 = 33
4)	Interest on cost of vehicle 10%	$= \dfrac{28,000 \times 10}{100}$ = Rs. 2,800	$= \dfrac{17,000 \times 10}{100}$ = Rs. 1,700
5)	Fixed cost per kilometre	$= \dfrac{6,050}{15,000}$ = Rs. 00.433	$= \dfrac{4,550}{6,000}$ = Rs. 00.758

Operating Cost Sheet

Vehicle No... Cost unit one kilometre
Period - one year No. of cost units - A = 15,000
B = 6,000

Particulars	Vehicle A		Vehicle B	
	per year Rs.	per kilome-tre Rs.	per year Rs.	per kilome-tre Rs.
A) Fixed or Standing Cost				
Road Licence	750		750	
Insurance	600		500	
Garage Rent	700		400	
Supervision and Salaries	1,200		1,200	
Interest on Vehicle 10%	2,800		1,700	
Total Standing Cost / Charges	6,050		4,550	
Fixed Cost Per Kilometre		00.433		00.758
B) Maintenance Cost / Charges				
Repairs and Maintenance		1 = 00		1.20
Tyre allocation		00.80		00.60
C) Running / Variable Charges or Cost				
Depreciation		00.25		00.20
Driver's Wages		00.15		00.15
Cost of fuel		2.50		3.33
Cost Per Kilometre		5.133 i.e. 5.13		6.238 i.e. 6.24

Illustration 2

A transport service company is running 4 buses between two towns which are 30 kms, each way. Seating capacity of each bus is 60 passengers. The following are the particulars obtained from their books for the month of November 2008.

Wages of drivers, conductors and cleaners	4,800
Salaries of office and supervisory staff	2,000
Diesel, oil, grease etc.	8,000
Repairs and maintenance	2,800

Taxes and insurance	3,200
Depreciation	5,200
Interest and Other Charges	4,000
	30,000

Actual passengers carried were 75% of the seating capacity. All the four buses run on all days of month. Each bus makes one round trip per day.

Find out the cost per passenger kilometre.

Solution -

Calculation of Passenger Kilometres

Passenger Kilometrs = No. of buses x Distance x No. of days x Capacity x Capacity used

= 4 x 30 x 30 x 60 x $\frac{75}{100}$

= 4 x 30 x 30 x 45

= 1,62,000 kilometers

Total Passenger Kilometers

Outward journey = 1,62,000

+ Return journey = 1,62,000

3,24,000 passenger kilometers

Statement of Operating Cost

Particulars	Per month (Rs.)	Total Cost Rs.
A) Standing Charges		
Wages of drivers, conductors and cleaners	4,800	
Salaries of Office and Supervisory Staff	2,000	
Taxes and Insurance	3,200	
Interest and Other Charges	4,000	
Total fixed cost		14,000
B) Maintenance Cost		
Repairs and maintenance	2,800	2,800
C) Variable / Running / Operating charges		
Diesel, Oil, grease	8,000	
Depreciation	5,200	
Total variable charges		13,200
Total operating cost		30,000

Operating cost per passenger kilometre

$$= \frac{\text{Total operating cost}}{\text{Total passenger kilometre}}$$

$$= \frac{30,000}{3,24,000}$$

= 0.09259 or

= .093 per passenger kilometer

Illustration 3

Lucky Transport is operating a 5 ton capacity truck 25 days in a month between Pune to Manchar 50 kilometers apart. The truck makes two trips to and fro a day. Other information supplied by the company is as follows.

	Rs.
Cost of truck (with life 15 years)	4,50,000
Diesel per trip (to and fro)	150
Repairs and maintenance	2,500 p.m.
Driver's Wages	3,750 p.m.
Insurance	24,000 p.a.
Taxes	36,000 p.a.

Work out cost per tonne - kilometer

Solution :

Calculation of tonne kilometres

Tonne kms = No. of trucks x Distance x Capacity of truck x No. of trips x No. of days

= 1 x (50 x 2) x 5 x 2 x 25

= 1 x 100 x 5 x 2 x 25

Tonne kms = 25,000

In the Books of Lucky Transport Company
Operating Cost-Sheet

Tonnes-kms. 25,000

Particulars	Per month (Rs.)	Total Cost Rs.
A) Standing or Fixed Costs		
Drivers wages	3,750	
Insurance $\left(\dfrac{24,000}{12} = 2,000\right)$	2,000	
Taxes $\left(\dfrac{36,000}{12} = 3,000\right) = 3,000$	3,000	
Total fixed cost	8,750	
Fixed cost per ton km $= \dfrac{8,750}{25,000} = 0.35$		00 = 35
B) Maintenance Charges		
Repairs and maintenance	2,500	
Repairs and maintenance per ton km		00 = 10
$= \dfrac{2,500}{25,000} = 0.10$		
C) Running or Operating or Variable Cost		
Diesel		
for one month 150 x 2 x 25	7,500	
Depreciation		
For one mouth $= \left(\dfrac{4,50,000}{15} \times \dfrac{1}{12}\right)$	2,500	
Total variable cost	10,000	
Variable cost per tonne km. $\dfrac{10,000}{25,000} = 0.40$		00 = 40
Cost per tonne kilometre		00 = 85

Cost per tonne kilometre = 0.85

Illustration 4

Nita Transport - Co., Pune owns a fleet of taxies and following information is available from their records.

Number of Taxies	10
Cost of each Taxi	Rs. 2,00,000
Monthly salary to the staff	
1) Manager	Rs. 3,000
2) Accountant	Rs. 2,500
3) Cleaner	Rs. 2,000
4) Mechanic	Rs. 1,500
Garage rent - per month	Rs. 1,000
Monthly insurance premium	Rs. 200
Monthly salary to driver per taxi	Rs. 3,150
Yearly taxes per taxi	1,200
Annual repairs per taxi	2,400

Total life of a taxi is about 2,00,000 kms. A taxi runs in all 3,000 kms in a month of which 30% it runs empty. Petrol consumption is one litre for 20 km @ Rs. 40 per litre. Oil and other sundries are Rs. 5 per 100 kilometres.

Calculate the cost of running a taxi per kilometre.

Solution :

Working Notes :

1) Calculation of effective kms per month per taxi

Monthly running of a taxi	3,000
Less : 30% empty running i.e.30% of 3,000	- 900
Actual or Effective running	2,100

As effective run of each taxi is 70%, only 70% of 3,000 i.e. 2100 kms, must be taken into consideration for calculating all costs.

2) Depreciation :

$$= \frac{\text{Cost of a Taxi}}{\text{Estimated life of a Taxi}}$$

$$= \frac{2,00,000}{2,00,000} = \text{Rs. } 1 = 00$$

$$= \frac{\text{Rs.}1 \times 3,000}{2,100} = \text{Rs. } 1.43 \text{ per kilometre}$$

3) Salary of Manager

$$= \text{Rs. } \frac{3,000}{10 \text{ Taxis}}$$

= Rs. 300 per month

4) Salary of Accountant

$$= \text{Rs. } \frac{2,500}{10 \text{ Taxis}} = \text{Rs. } 250 \text{ per month}$$

5) Salary of Cleaner

$$= \frac{2,000}{10 \text{ Taxis}} = \text{Rs. } 200 \text{ per month}$$

6) Salary of Mechanic

$$= \frac{1,500}{10 \text{ Taxis}} = \text{Rs. } 150 \text{ per month}$$

7) Garage rent

$$\frac{1,000}{10 \text{ Taxis}} = \text{Rs. } 100 \text{ per month}$$

8) Taxes per taxi

$$\frac{1,200}{12 \text{ Months}} = \text{Rs. } 100 \text{ per month}$$

9) Repairs per taxi

$$= \frac{2,400}{12 \text{ Months}} = \text{Rs. } 200$$

$$= \frac{200}{2,100} = 00.095$$

10) Driver's Salary

$$= \frac{3,150}{2,100} = \text{Rs. } 1.50 \text{ per kilometre}$$

11) Petrol Consumption

$$= \frac{40}{20 \text{ kms}} = \text{Rs. } 2 = 00 \text{ per kilometre}$$

12) Oil and Other Sundries

$$= \frac{5}{100 \text{ kms}} = \text{Rs } 0.05$$

$$= \frac{.05 \times 3,000}{2,100} = \text{Rs. } 0.07$$

13) Standing Charges

$$= \frac{\text{Total fixed cost}}{\text{kms in a month}}$$

$$= \frac{1,300}{2,100} = \text{Rs. } 0.62$$

14) Drivers salary and Depreciation are considered as variable expenses.

In the Books of Nita Transport Co.
Statement Showing Cost of Running a Taxi per Kilometre

Cost unit - per kilometre

Particulars	Per month (Rs.)	Per kilo-metre Rs.
A) Standing or fixed charges		
Manager's salary	300	
Accountants salary	250	
Cleaner's salary	200	
Mechanic's salary	150	
Insurance premium	200	

Taxes	100	
Garage rent	100	
Total fixed charges	1,300	
Fixed cost per kilometre		0 = 62
B) Maintenance charges		
(semi variable cost)		
Repairs		0 = 095
C) Running or variable charges		
Depreciation		1 = 43
Driver's salary		1 = 50
Petrol consunption		2 = 00
Oil and other sundries		0 = 07
cost per kilometre		5 = 715
		or 5.72

Cost per kilometre per taxi = Rs. 5.72

Illustration 5

Amol Transport Co. Pune supplies you the following information in respect of a truck of 6 tonne capacity.

	Rs.
Cost of truck	3,00,000
Estimated life 20 years	
Diesel, oil per trip per day	75
Monthly repairs and maintenance	500
Driver's wages per month	1,875
Cleaner's wages per month	750
Yearly Insurance	7,200
Annual Road Tax	3,600
General supervision charges p.a.	7,200

The truck carries goods to and from city covering a distance to the extent of 40 kilometre each way. On outward trip freight is available to the extent of full capacity and on return trip 30% of capacity. Assuming that the truck runs on an average 25 days in a month, work out :

a) Operating cost per tonne kilometre.

b) The rate per tonne trip that the company should charge if a profit of 50% on freight is to be earned.

Solution :

Working notes :

1) Calculation of Tonne Kilometres per Month :

= Distance for outward trip + Capacity + Distance for
return trip x Capacity x No. of working days.

= (40 kms x 6 i.e. full capacity) +
(40 kms × 1.5 tonne i.e. 30% capacity) x 25 days

= 240 + 60 x 25

= 300 x 25

= 7,500 tonne kms.

2) Depreciation per Kilometre

$$= \frac{\text{Cost of Truck}}{\text{Estimated life of Truck} \times 12 \text{ month} \times \text{Total tonnes kms.}}$$

$$= \frac{3,00,000}{20 \times 12 \times 7,500}$$

= Re. 00.17 per kilometre.

3) Diesel, oil etc per Kilometre

= Rs. 75 x 2 trips = Rs. 150 per day x 25 days = Rs. 3,750

$$= \frac{3,750}{7,500} = \text{Re. } 0.50 \text{ per km.}$$

4) Repairs and Maintenance per Kilometre

$$= \frac{500}{7,500 \text{ ton kms}} = \text{Rs. } 0.07 \text{ per km.}$$

5) Drivers Wages per km.

$$\frac{1,875}{7,500 \text{ tons kms.}} = \text{Rs. } 0.25 \text{ per km.}$$

6) Cleaners Wages per Kilometre

$$\frac{750}{7,500 \text{ tons kms.}} = \text{Rs. } 0.10 \text{ per km.}$$

7) Insurance for one month

$$\frac{7,200}{12 \text{ months}} = \text{Rs. } 600 \text{ p.m.}$$

8) Road Tax per Month

$$\frac{3,600}{12 \text{ months}} = \text{Rs. } 300 \text{ p.m.}$$

9) General Supervision Charges per Month

$$\frac{7,200}{12 \text{ mouths}} = \text{Rs. } 600 \text{ p.m.}$$

10) Standing / Fixed cost per kilometer

$$\frac{1,500}{7,500 \text{ tons kms.}} = \text{Rs. } 0.20$$

11) Calculation of Profit per tonne km. at 50% of Freight

Freight = operating cost + profit

100 = 50 + 50

If   50 o.c = 50 profit

Re.   1.29 o.c = ?

$$= \frac{1.29 \times 50}{50} = 1.29$$

In the Books of Amol Transport Co., Pune.
Statement Showing Operating Cost and Freight per tonne

Particulars	Per Month (Rs.)	Per Tonne Km. Rs.
A) Fixed or standing charges		
Insurance	600	
Road Tax	300	
General supervision charges	600	
Total fixed cost / charges	1,500	
Fixed or standing charges per kilometre		0.20
B) Maintenance charges		
(semi-variable charges)		
Repairs and maintenance charges		0.07
C) Running / Variable / Operating charges		
Diesel oil etc.		0.50
Driver's wages		0.25
Cleaner's wages		0.10
Depreciation		0.17
Operating cost per ton km.		1 = 29
Add profits (50% of freight per ton)		1 = 29
Freight per tonne kilometre		2 = 58

Ans. :
1) Operating cost per ton km. = Rs. 1.29
2) Profit per ton km. = 1.29
3) Freight per ton km. = 2 = 58

Illustration 6

A person owns a bus which runs between Pune to Aurangabad and back for 10 days in a month. The distance from Pune to Aurangabad is 240 kms. The bus completes the trip from Pune to Aurangabad and back on the same day. The bus goes another 10 days in a month to Shrirampur and the distance covered being 200 kms. This trip is also completed on the same day. For the rest of 4 days it runs in the city. Daily distance covered in city is 60 kms. Calculate the rate the person should charge to passenger when he wants to earn a profit of $33\frac{1}{3}\%$ on his takings. The other particulars are given below.

Cost of bus Rs. 2,00,000

Depreciation 20% per annum.

Salary of driver Rs. 1,600 per month.

Salary of conductor Rs. 1,500 per month.

Salary of part time accountant Rs. 400 per month.

Diesel consumption 6 kms per litre costing Rs. 40 per litre.

Token tax Rs. 600 per annum.

Repairs Rs. 1,000 per month.

Normal capacity 50 passengers.

The bus is generally occupied 90% of the capacity when it goes to Aurangabad and 80% when it goes to Shrirampur. It is always full when it runs within the city.

Solution :

Calculation of Passenger Kilometers

	Passenger kilometres
a) Pune to Aurangabad and back	
Onward journey = 240 kms x 10 days	
x 50 passengers x $\dfrac{90}{100}$	= 1,08,000
Return journey = 240 kms x 10 days	
x 50 passengers x $\dfrac{90}{100}$	= 1,08,000
	2,16,000
b) Pune to Shrirampur and back	
Onward jouney = 200 kms x 10 days	
x 50 passengers x $\dfrac{80}{100}$	= 80,000

Return jouney =

$$200 \text{ kms x } 10 \text{ days x } 50 \text{ passengers x } \frac{80}{100} \qquad = 80,000$$

$$\underline{1,60,000}$$

c) Local trip (within pune)

60 kms x 4 days x 50 passengers   12,000

Total of a + b + c

(2,16,000 + 1,60,000 + 12,000) passenger kms. $= \underline{3,88,000}$

2) Distance Travelled in a Month   kms.

a) Pune to Aurangabad 240 + 240 = 480 kms x 10 days = 4,800

b) Pune to Shrirampur 200 + 200 = 400 kms x 10 days = 4,000

c) Pune to Pune local trip 60 kms x 4 days = 240

Total = $\underline{9,040}$

3) Depreciation per month

20% on 2,00,000

$$\frac{40,000}{12 \text{ months}} = \text{Rs. } 3,333$$

4) Token tax per month

$$\frac{600}{12 \text{ months}} = \text{Rs. } 50$$

5) Cost of diesel per month

Rs. 40 per litre

Consumption per litre 6 kms

$$\text{So for } 9,040 \text{ kms} = \frac{\text{Rs. } 40 \times 9,040 \text{ km}}{6 \text{ kms}} = \text{Rs. } 6,027$$

Statement of Operating Cost

Particulars	Per month (Rs.)
A) Fixed charges	
Salary of driver	1,600
Salary of conductor	1,500
Salary of accountant (part time)	400
Token tax	50
Total fixed charges	3,550
B) Maintenance charges	
Repairs	1,000
C) Running or variable charges	
Depreciation	3,333
Diesel	6,027
Total operating cost (A + B + C)	13,910

Operating cost per passenger kilometre

$$= \frac{\text{Total cost}}{\text{Total passenger kilometres}}$$

$$= \frac{13,910}{3,88,000}$$

= Rs. 0.03585 i.e.

= 0.036

Statement showing charges per kilometre

	Rs.
Operating cost per passenger kilometre	00.03585
Add profit of $33\frac{1}{3}\%$ on his taking i.e.50% on cost	00.01792
Charge per passenger kilometre =	00.05377

Calculation of profit

Sales = cost + profit

$100 = 66.66 + 33.33$

66.66 cost of production $= 33.33$ profit

for Rs. $0.03585 = ? = \dfrac{33.33 \times 0.3585}{66.66}$

$=$ Rs. $.01792$ profit

Rates to be charged per passenger

a) Pune to Aurangabad = Rs. 0.05377 x 240 kms = Rs. 12.90 or Rs. 13

b) Pune to Shrirampur = Rs. 0.05377 x 200 kms = Rs. 10.75 or Rs. 11

c) Within city = .05377 i.e. 6 paise per passenger kilometre

d) Aurangabad to Pune (Return journy) Rs. 13

e) Shrirampur to Pune (Return journy) Rs. 11

Illustration 7

A manufacturer desires to ascertain the cost of running a motor lorry for transport purposes during one week, the lorry carried a load of 30 tonnes and distance covered is 410 Kms. as given below

	Kilometers	Tonnes
Monday	85	6
Tuesday	70	5
Wednesday	80	5
Thursday	64	6
Friday	77	4
Saturday	34	4
	410	30

	Rs.
Fixed charges	600
Cleaners wages	200
Garag rent	500
Taxes and insurance	1,000
Supervision	300

Calculate the cost per tonne-kilometer.

Solution :

Statement of operating cost

Particulars	Rs.
Fixed Charges	600
Cleaners wages	200
Garag rent	500
Taxes and insurance	1,000
Supervision	300
Total expenses	2,600

$$\text{Cost per tonne - kilometre} = \frac{\text{Total Expenses}}{\text{Total tonne-kilometres}}$$

2600 / 2088 = 1.245

Say Rs. 1,25

Note : Tonne -KM : 85 x 6 = 510
                    70 x 5 = 350
                    80 x 5 = 400
                    64 x 6 = 384
                    77 x 4 = 308
                    34 x 4 = 136
                             2088 Tonne kms.

Illustration 8

Five passenger buses cost Rs. 50,000, Rs. 1,20,000 Rs. 45,000 Rs. 55,000 and Rs. 80,000 respectively. Yearly depreciation of vehicles at 20% of cost. Annual repairs, maintenance of spare parts of 80% of depreciation.

Wages of 10 drivers at Rs. 100 each per month.

Wages of 20 Cleaners at Rs. 100 each per month.

Yearly rate of interst at 4% on Capital.

Rent of five garages at Rs. 50 each per month.

Director's fee at Rs. 400 per month.

Office establishment at Rs. 1,000 per month.

Licences and taxes at Rs. 1,000 every six months.

Realisation by sale of old typres and tubes at Rs. 3,200 after every six months. 9,000 passengers were carried over 1,600 km. by each bus during the year. From the above details, extracted from the books of a transport company, find out cost per passenger kilometre.

Solution

Cost of buses =   Rs. 50,000 + Rs. 1,20,000 + Rs. 45, 000
                    + Rs. 55,000 + Rs. 80,000 = Rs. 3,50,000

Yearly depreciation (20% of Cost) = Rs. 70,000

Yearly repairs (80% fo depreciation) = Rs. 56,000

Operating Cost Sheet for the year ended.......

Particulars	Rs.	Rs.
(A) Standing Charges :		
Wages of drivers (10 x 100 x 12)	12,000	
Wages of cleaners (20 x 50 x 12)	12,000	24,000
Interest (4% on 3,50,000)		14,000
Director's fee (400 x 12)		4,800
Office establishment (1,000 x 12)		12,000
License and taxes (1,000 x 2)		2,000
Grage rent (5 x 50 x 12)		3,000
Total		59,800
(B) Maintenance Charges		
Repairs, spare parts etc.	56,000	
Less sale proceeds of old		
tyres and tubes (2 x 3,200)	6,400	49,600
(C) Operating Charges :		
Depreciation		70,000
(D) Grant Total (A+B+C)		1,79,400
(E) Passenger Kms. carried (9,000x1,600)		1,44,00,000
(F) Passenger - km for 5 Buses.		
1,44,00,000 x 5 = 720,00,000		
Cost per Passenger - Km		
= 179400 / 720,00,000		
= 0.0024916 (i.e. less than one paisa)		

Illustration 9

A transport company supplies the following details in repsect of a truck of 5 tonne capacity.

Cost of truck - Rs. 90,000

Estimated life - 10 years

Diesel, oil - as Rs. 15 per trip each way

Repairs - Rs. 500 per month

Driver's wage - Rs. 500 per month

Cleaner's wage - Rs. 250 per month

Insurance - Rs. 4,800 per year

Taxes - Rs. 2,400 per year

General supervision - Rs. 4,800 per year.

The truck carries goods to and from a city covering a distance of 50 miles each way. While going to the city, freight is available to the extent of full capacity and on return 20% of capacity.

Assuming that the truck runs on an average 25 days a month, work out : (a) Operating cost per tonne-mile

(b) Rate per tonne per trip that the company should charge if a profit of 50% on the freightage is to be earned.

B.Com. Bangalore, April 1988

Solution

Ton-Miles

Onward 5 tonnes x 50 Miles x 25 days =	6,250
Return 5 tonnes x 20% x 50 Miles x 25 days =	1,250
Total tonne-miles in a month	7,500

(a) Statement of Operating Cost per Ton-Mile

Particulars	Basis of apportionment	Amount per month (Rs.)	Cost per Ton-mile (Rs.)
A Fixed Costs :			
Depreciation	$\frac{90,000}{10 \times 12}$	750	
Repairs		500	
Driver's wages		500	
Cleaner's wages		250	
Insurance	4,800/12	400	
Taxes	2,400/12	200	
General Supervision	4,800/12	400	
Total A		3,000	
Per Ton-mile	3,000/7,500=		0.40
B Variable Cost			
Diesel	5 x 2 x 25 days=	750	0.10
Operating cost	A + B	3,750	0.50

	Rs.
(b) Operating cost per tonne-mile	0.50
Add : Profit of 50% on freightage i.e. 100% on operating cost	0.50
Freight rate per tonnes -mile	1.00
Onward 50 miles x 5 tonnes x 1.00	250
Return 50 miles x 5 tonnes x 20% x 1.00	50
Total for one trip both ways	300

Note : Total freight collected in 25 days

= 300 x 25 =	7,500
Less : Operating cost per month	3,750
Profit at 5% on freight	3,750

Illustration 10

Arun runs a tempo service at Vizag. He furnishes you the following data and wants you to compute the cost of running per km.:

	Rs.
cost of vehicle	15,000
Road licence p. a.	750
Supervisor's salary p.a.	2,650
Driver's wages per hour	4
Cost of fuel per liter	3.60
Repairs and maintenance per km.	2.00
Typre cost per km.	0.80
Garage rent p. a.	3,600
Insurance p. a.	500
Kms running per litre	5

Charge Interest @10%p.a. on cost of vehicle

The vehicle runs 20 kms. per hour on an average.

Solution

Computation of the cost of running per km.

KMS run during the year : 6,000

Particulars	Basis of apportionment	Amount per month (Rs.)	Cost per Tonne-mile (Rs.)
A Standing charges			
Road licence	per annum	750	
Supervisor's salary	"	2,650	
Garage Rent	"	3,600	
Insurance	"	500	
Interest	10% on Rs. 15,000	1,500	
Total 'A'		9,000	
Per Km.	Rs. 9,000/6,000 Km.	1.50	
B. Variable charges			
Depreciation	Rs. 15,000		0.20
Driver's wages	Rs. 4/20 km.		0.72
Cost of fuel	Rs. 3.60/km.		2.00
Repairs & Mainten.	Per km.		
Typre cost	Per km.		0.80
Total B			3.92
Cost of running per km	(A+B)	5.42	

Cost of running per tonne-Km. $= \dfrac{5.42}{5} =$ Rs.1.08

8.4 Exercises

Objective Type Questions

a) Indicate whether the following statements are True or False.

1) Service costing is applicable in canteen.
2) The unit used in service costing is simple.
3) Motor cost for passengers is ascertained with reference to per passenger per kilometre.
4) Service costing is one of the basic methods of operation costing.
5) Operating cost statement is prepared to calculate the cost in case of service costing.
6) There is no difference between service costing and process costing.

Ans. 1) True, 2) False, 3) True, 4) True, 5) True, 6) False.

b) Short Answer Type Questions.

1) State the salient features of service costing.
2) Name the four industries in which this method is used.
3) State the objectives of transport costing.
4) Give two examples in motor transport of : a) Standing Charges b) Maintenance Charges c) Running Charges.
5) What is daily log sheet?
6) What is composite cost unit.
7) What type of unit you will adopt while ascertaining cost in service costing.
8) State the features of operating costing.

Practical Problems

1) From the following data relating to the vehicle of Durga Transport Company Nashik, calculate the cost per running kilometre.

	Rs.
Cost of vehicle	1,00,000
Road licences fees (annual)	5,100
Garage rent (annual)	4,800
Insurance charges (annual)	2,100
Supervision and salary (annual)	12,000
Driver's wages per hour	2.00
Cost of diesel per litre	4.00
Repairs and maintenance per km	2.20
Tyres and batteries per km.	1.80

Kilometres run per litre 20 km.
Kilometres run annual 20,000 km.
Estimated life of vehicle 1,00,000 kms.
You are required to charge interest on cost of vehicle at 10% p.a. The vehicle runs 20 km per hour on an average.

Ans. :   Cost per km Rs. 7=00

2) Shanti Travels, a transport company, is running a fleet of 6 buses between two towns 75 km apart. Seating capacity of each bus is 40 passengers. The following particulars are available for the month of June 2008.

	Rs.
1) Wages of drivers, conductors and cleaners	3,600
2) Salaries of supervisory and office staff	1,500
3) Diesel and other oils	10,320
4) Repairs and maintenance	1,200
5) Taxation and insurance	2,400
6) Depreciation	3,900
7) Interest	3,000

Actual passengers carried were 80% of the seating capacity. All the buses run on all days of month. Each bus makes one round trip per day. Find out the cost per passenger kilometre.

Ans. : Total passenger kms 8,64,000

Cost per passenger km 3 paise.

3) Mr. Sunil furnishes you the following data and wants you to compute the cost per running km. of a vehicle "A'

	Rs.
Cost of vehicle	2,50,000
Road licence per year	800
Salaries and supervision (yearly)	2,700
Driver's wages per hour	4
Cost of fuel per litre	12
Repairs and maintenance per km	2
Tyre cost per km	1
Insurance premium (yearly)	700
Garage rent per year	1,300
Kms run per litre	20
Kms run during the year	15,000
Estimated life of vehicle (kms)	1,00,000
Tonnes per km (average)	6

Charge interest at 5% p.a. on the cost of vehicle. The vehicle runs 20 kms. per hour on an average.

Ans. : Cost per running tonne km Rs. 1 = 25

4) From the following information relating to Loyal Transport, Lonawala, calculate the cost per running kilometre.

	Rs.
Wages to Drivers per month	500
Cost of Diesel per litre	1.50
Cost of mobile oil per litre	10.00
Annual clearing and servicing	2,460
Insurance charges per year	4,000
Yearly Road Tax	6,400
Repairs and maintenance for 12 months	1,200
Cost of tyres, tubes per year	1,800
Cost of vehicle	1,30,000
Residual value of vehicle	30,000

Diesel km per litre km 4
Mobile km per litre km 10
Estimated annual run km 36,000
Estimated life of vehicle 5 years

Ans. : Cost per km Rs. 2 = 00

5) A manufacturer desires to ascertain the cost of running a motor lorry for transport purposes during one week, the lorry carries a load of 30 tonnes and distance covered is 410 kms, as given below.

	Kilometers	Tonnes
Monday	85	6
Tuesday	70	5
Wednesday	80	5
Thursday	64	6
Friday	77	4
Saturday	34	4
	410	30

Other expenses are as under.

Fixed charges	600
Cleaner charges	200
Garage rent	500
Tax and insurance	1,000
Supervision	300

Calculate the cost per tonne kilometre.

Ans. : Total expenses Rs. 2,600, Total tonne kms. 2,088 cost per tonne km and 1.245

6) Mr. S. owns a fleet of taxis and the following infromation is available from the records maintained by him.

Number of taxis 10

Cost of each taxi	Rs. 54,600
Salary of manager	Rs. 700 p.m.
Salary of accountant	Rs. 500 p.m.
Salary of cleance	Rs. 200 p.m.
Salary of mechines	Rs. 400 p.m.

Garage rent   Rs. 600 p. m.
Insurance preminum   Rs. 5% p.a.
Annual tax   Rs. 900 per taxi
Driver's salary   Rs. 350 per taxi
Annual reparing   Rs. 1000 per taxi

Total life of a taxi is about 2,00,000 kms. A taxi runs in all 3000 kms. in a mouth and 30% of the distance has to be run without any passenger. Petrol Consumption is one litre for every 10 kms. at Rs. 4.41 per litre. Oil and other sundries are Rs. 10.50 per 100 kms.

Calculate the cost of running taxi per km.

Ans. : Effective runnings 2100 Kms.

Cost per km. per taxi Rs. 1.635

7) A transport company is running a fleet of six buses between two town 75 kms. apart. Seating capacity of each bus is 40 passenger. The following particular are available for the month of June.

	Rs.
Wages of drivers, conducter and cleaners	3,600
Salary of office and supervisons staff	1,500
Diesel and other oils	10,320
Repairs and maintenence	1,200
Taxation and insurance	2,400
Depreciation	3,900
Interest on capital	3,000

Actual passenger carried were 80% of the seating capacity. All the buses run on all days of the month. Each bus made round trip per day.

Find out the cost per passenger kilometer

Ans. Cost per passenger k.m. =   3 paise

Passenger kilometers   8,64,000

8) Mr. Shinde started transport business with a fleet of 10 taxis. Expenses of operating fleet are given below.

1) Cost of each taxi   3,80,000
2) Salary of office & garage staff   38,000 p.m.

3) Rent of garage   12,000 p.m.
4) Driver's salary per taxi   4,000 p.m.
5) Insurance, tax and sundry expenses per taxi 55,200 p.a.

The life of a taxi is 3,00,000 km. at the end of which it is estimated to run are average 4000 kms per month. Petrol consumption is 12 km per litre costing Rs. 30 per litre. You are required to

i) Calculate the cost of running taxi per km by preparing a statment of operating cost and

ii) Find out the profit Mr. Shinde may expect to earn during the first month of operation, if hire charges is Rs. 10 per km.

Ans (i) Rs. 7.10 per km.

(ii) Rs., 36,000

9) A vehicle cost Rs. 15,600 and its life is estimated at 5 years, after which its residnal value is estimated at Rs. 600. Standing charges per annum are estimated at the following figures.

Insurance Rs. 850, Licence Rs. 750,

Administtative overheads Rs. 2,000

Fuel cost Rs. 2 per gallon and based on an estimated mileage of 30,000 per year; the cost of lubricant is Rs. 150. The estimated consumption of fuel is 20 miles per gallon. A set of tyres costs Rs. 1400 and their expected mileage is 16,000. The driver is paid Rs. 50 per week of 44 hours and is entitled to fortnight's paid holiday per annum. The company's contribution towards National Insurance scheme is Rs. 10 per week. For each night spent away from home, the driver is paid subsistence allowance of Rs. 10. It is estimated that the vehicle will rund 220 days per annaum and depreciation is regarded as a running cost. Repairs over the life of the vehicle are estimated at Rs. 5000.

(a) Compute figures which may be used as a basis of quoting, if company adds 10% of the total cost for profit,

(b) Prepare quotation for journey of 100 miles and return assuming no return load and a total time of two days.

Ans : Cost per mile 0.550

Quotation Price Rs. 149.93.

❖

Formulae

1. **Overheads** = Indirect Materials+Indirect Labour+ Indirect Expenses

2. **Actual Overhead Rate :**

$$= \frac{\text{Actual Overhead Expenses incurred during a certain period}}{\text{Actual Quantity or Value of the base related to the Total Production during a certain period}}$$

3. **Pre-determined Overhead Rate :**

$$= \frac{\text{Budgeted Overhead Expenses for the period}}{\text{Budgeted base for the period}}$$

4. **Blanket Overhead Rate :**

$$= \frac{\text{Overhead Cost for the entire factory}}{\text{Total Quantum of the base selected}}$$

5. **Multiple Overhead Rate :**

$$= \frac{\text{Overhead costs allocated and apportioned to each department' s cost centre or product}}{\text{Corresponding base}}$$

6. **Direct Labour Hour Rate :**

$$= \frac{\text{Factory Overheads}}{\text{Direct Labour Hours during a period}}$$

7. **Machine Hour Rate :**

$$= \frac{\text{Factory Overheads}}{\text{Machine Hours}}$$

8. Percentage of Direct Material Cost :

$$= \frac{\text{Factory Overheads}}{\text{Direct Material Cost}} \times 100$$

9. Percentage of Direct Labour Cost :

$$= \frac{\text{Factory Overheads}}{\text{Direct Labour Cost}} \times 100$$

10. Percentage of Prime Cost :

$$= \frac{\text{Factory Overheads}}{\text{Primt Cost}} \times 100$$

11. Underabsorption of Overhead :
= Overheads incurred > Overheads absorbed

12. Overabsorption of Overhead :
= Overhead Absorbed > Overheads Incurred

13. Idle Capacity Cost :
= Idle Capacity x Overhead Rate

14. Depreciation Cost :

$$= \frac{\text{Cost of Asset + Installation charges - Scrap value}}{\text{Estimated Life of Asset}}$$

15. Cost of Work Certified :
= Cost of Work to date - (Cost of Work Uncertified + Materials on hand + Plant at site)

16. Cost of Work Uncertified :
= Total Cost to date - (Cost of Work Certified + Materials on hand + Plant at site)

17. Work-in-Progress :
= Cost of Work Certified + Cost of Work Uncertified - Reserve for Unrealised Profit - Cash Received from Contractee

18. Profits on Incomplete Contracts :

* Rules regarding transfer of profits to Profit and Loss Account in case of Incomplete Contracts.

(a) Contracts which have been completed less than 25% of contract, no profit should be computed and credited to Profit and Loss Account.

(b) Contracts which have been completed by more than 25% but less than 50% of contract, the amount of profits credited to Profit and Loss Account

$$= \frac{1}{3} \times \text{National Profits} \times \frac{\text{Cash Received}}{\text{Work Certified}}$$

(c) Contracts which have been completed by more than 50% but less than 90% of contract, the amount of profits credited to Profit and Loss Account.

$$= \frac{2}{3} \times \text{National Profits} \times \frac{\text{Cash Received}}{\text{Work Certified}}$$

(d) In case of contracts completed by 90% or more than 90%, the contract is considered almost complete, the portion of estimated total profit credited to Profit and Loss Account.

$$= \text{Estimated Profit} \times \frac{\text{Work Certified}}{\text{Contract Price}}$$

19. Process Cost Per Unit :

$$= \frac{\text{Total Cost - Value of Normal Loss}}{\text{Total Input Quantity} - \text{Normal Loss Quantity}}$$

20. Value of Abnormal Loss :

$$= \frac{\text{Normal Cost of Normal Output}}{\text{Normal Output}} \times \text{Units of Abnormal Loss}$$

21. Value of Abnormal Gain :

$$= \frac{\text{Total Process Cost - Value of Normal Loss}}{\text{Normal Units Produced}} \times \text{Units of Abnormal Gain}$$

Key Words

1. **Overheads :** These are the operating costs of a business enterprise which cannot be traced directly to a particular unit of output.

2. **Classification of overheads :** It is the process of grouping of overhead costs on the basis of common characteristics and clear objectives.

3. **Factory Overheads :** These are costs which have been incurred in connection with production of a manufactured commodity before it has come out of the workshop.

4. **Administration Overheads :** These are the cost of formulating the policy, directing the organisation and controlling the operations of an undertaking which is not related directly to a research, development, production, distribution or selling activity function.

5. **Selling Overheads :** These are the cost incurred in promoting sales and retaining customers.

6. **Distribution Overheads :** These are the cost of process which begins with making the packed product available for despatch and ends with making the reconditioned returned empty package available for reuse.

7. **Indirect Materials :** These are the material costs which cannot be allocated, but which can be apportioned to or absorbed by cost centres or cost units.

8. **Indirect Labour :** These are the amount of wages paid to the workers who are not engaged directly on the production line but engaged to help the production line.

9. **Indirect Expenses :** These are the expenses which cannot be directly and conveniently allocated to specific cost units and cost centres.

10. **Fixed Overheads :** These are the overheads costs which tend to be unaffected by the variations in the volume of output.

11. Variable Overheads : These are the overheads costs which tend to increase or decrease in total amount with changes in production activity.

12. Semi -Variable Overheads : These are the overhead costs which neither remain fixed nor they vary directly with the output.

13. Controllable Overheads : These are the overhead costs which can be control by excutive action at the point of their incurrence.

14. Uncontrollable Overheads : These are the overhead costs which cannot be influenced by actions of the person in whom control of the centre is vested.

15. Allocation of Overheads : It is the process of allotment of an entire cost to a particular cost centre or cost unit.

16. Apportionment of Overheads : It is the process of distribution of overheads to cost centres on an equitable bases.

17. Re-apportionment of Overheads : It is the process of re-distribution of service department costs to production department on the basis of the benefits derived from service department.

18. Absorption of Overheads : It is the process of charging of overheads of a cost centre to different cost units in such a way that each cost unit bears an appropriate portion of its share of overheads.

19. Standing Order Number : These are the code numbers given to an item of factory overheads.

20. Cost Account Number : These are the code numbers given to an item of administration overheads or selling and distribution overheads.

21. Departmentalisation of Overheads : It is the process of allocation and apportionment of overheads to different departments or other cost centres.

22. Production Department : It is one that engages in the actual manufacture of the product by changing the shape, form or nature of material worked upon or by assembling the parts into finished product.

23. Service Department : It is one that is renderring a service which contributes in an indirect manner to the manufacture of the product but which does not itself change the shape, form or nature of material that is converted into finished product.

24. Partly Producing Department : It is one that is normally treated as service depatment, but sometime they are also required to undertake direct production work.

25. Overhead Absorption Rate : These are the rates determined for the purpose of absorption of overheads.

26. Actual Overheads Rate : It is the rate calculated by dividing the actual overhead expenses incurred by the actual quantity or value of the selected base for the corresponding period.

27. Pre-determined Overhead Rate : It is the rate calculated by dividing budgeted overheads by budgeted base for the period.

28. Blanket Overhead Rate : It is the single overheads rate computed for an entire plant to be used for all departments and all products produced in the plant. It is calculated by dividing the overhead cost for the entire factory by the total quantum of the base selected.

29. Multiple Overhead Rate : It is computed by dividing the overhead cost allocated and apportioned to each cost centre by corresponding base.

30. Direct Labour Hour Rate : It is a method of recovering overhead incurred in a department from products of the department in the ratio of direct labour hours worked for the products.

31. Machine Hour Rate : It is an actual or pre-determined rate of cost apportionment or overhead absorption, which is calculated by dividing the cost to be apportioned or absorbed by the number of hours for which a machine or machines are operated or expected to be operated.

32. Under -absorption of Overhead : It is the excess of actual overheads over absorbed overheads.

33. Over-absorption of Overhead : It is the excess of absorbed overheads over actual overheads.

34. Depreciation Costs : It is the charge made because the diminution in the value of the fixed assets due to use and lapse of time.

35. Research Cost : It is the cost of searching for a new or improved products, new applications of materials or new improved methods.

36. Development Cost : It is the cost of the process which begins with the implementation of the decision to produce a new or improved, or and imply and ends with the commencement of formal production of that product or by that method.

37. Codification of Overhead : It is the process of assignment of numbers, letters or symbols according to a systematic plan for distinguishing each type of group of overheads expenses.

38. Cost of Obsolescence : It is the sudden loss in the value of an asset due to its suppression at an earlier date than was foreseen.

39. Capacity Cost : Capacity is the ability to produce output or render service. Capacity costs are the running expenses incurred for setting up the facilities themselves and constitute largely as a function of time.

40. Idle Capacity Costs : It represents unrecovered overheads in products.

41. Cost of Training : These are costs incurred on running training departments, wages and salaries paid to trainees and production losses suffered due to training activity.

42. Methods of Costing : It indicates a systematic procedure established for ascertaining cost of product, job, process or services by using the principles of costing.

43. Specific Order Costing : It is the category of basic costing methods applicable where the work consists of separate contracts, jobs or batches each of which is authorised by a special order or contract.

44. Job Costing : It is that form of specific order costing which applies where work is undertaken to customer's special requirements.

45. Batch Costing : It is that form of specific order costing which applies where similar articles are manufactured in batches either for sale or use within the undertaking.

46. Contract Costing : It is that form of specific order costing which applies where work is undertaken to customers' special requirements and each order is of long duration.

47. Multiple Costing : It is an application of more than one method of cost ascertainment in respect of the same product.

48. Class Cost Method : It is the method of job costing where the costing of goods is done by classes instead of the unit or price.

49. Operation Costing : It is the category of basic costing methods applicable where standardized goods or services result from a sequence of repetitive and more or less continuous operations or process to which costs are charged before being averaged over the units produced during the period.

50. Process Costing : It is that form of operation costing which applies where the standardised goods are produced.

51. Operating Costing : It is that form of operation costing which applies where standardised services are provided either by an undertaking or by a service cost centre within an undertaking.

52. Output Costing : It is that form of operation costing where large number of identical products are produced.

53. Departmental Costing : It is that form of operation costing where a factory is divided into a number of departments and the cost incurred in maintaining a particular department is ascertained.

54. Operation Costing : It is that form of operation costing which refers to the determination of the cost of operations.

55. Production Order : It is nothing but a form of instructions issued to the foreman to proceed with the manufacture of the articles.

56. Job Cost Sheet : It is a cost statement prepared to analyse and ascertain the actual cost incurred with respect to the individual jobs.

57. Sub-Contract Cost : These are the costs incurred for a sub-contract where the contractor has entrusted some special work to certain expertise sub-contractor, e.g. electrification, sanitary work, painting work, plumbing work, task of digging foundations, installation of lifts, specialised, flooring, welding work, etc.

58. Escalation Clause : It is the clause which aims at safeguarding the interest of the contractor against unforeseen changes in the prices and utilisation of material and labour.

59. De-escalation or Reserve Clause : It is the clause which provides for a decrease in the contract price due to a sudden decline in the prices of inputs so that the benefits of price decreases is passed on to the contractee.

60. Architect's Certificate : It is the certificate issued by the contractee's architect specifying clearly as to the value of work so far performed.

61. Retention Money : It is a clause included in the contract agreement on the basis of which the contractee retains certain amount of the work certified which serves as a security with him and it also acts as a detergent against leaving the faulty work incomplete by the contractor.

62. Work Certified : It is the cost of that part of work-in-progress which is being completed successfully by the contractor and has been approved by the certifier.

63. Work Uncertified : It is the cost of that part of work-in-progress which is being completed by the contractor but not approved by the certifier because of the faulty work not completed according to the specifications.

64. Cost Plus Contracts : It is that modified method of contract costing in which a contractor is paid with actual cost of work done plus an agreed percentage thereof to cover overheads and profits.

65. Work-in-Progress : It is the major or minor portion of contract work done before the stage of completion of a contract, subjected to experts scrutiny based on which it may be classified as work certified and uncertified.

66. Planning Board : It is a pre-planned timetable of a particular job to be done in jobbing industries.

67. Process Loss : It is the difference between the input quantity of raw materials and the output quantity.

68. Waste : These are the discarded substances having no value.

69. Scrap : These are the discarded materials having some recovery value which is usually disposed off without further treatment or re-introduced into the production process in place of raw material.

70. Normal Loss : It is the loss of materials under normal conditions which is unavoidable, as a result normally expected quantity of output is less than the input.

71. Abnormal Loss : It is the loss caused by abnormal conditions which is excess of actual loss over normal loss, which may arise due to poor quality of raw materials, defects in machines, carelessness on the part of workers, etc.

72. Abnormal Gain : It is the result of excess of actual output over normal output due to excellent climatic conditions, for production exceptionally good material, new equipments, etc.

73. Inter-Process Profit : It is the practice of recognising profit at different processes.

74. Joint Products : It means two or more products separated in the course of processing, each having a sufficiently have value to merit recognition as a main product.

75. By-Products : It is a secondary product obtained during the course of manufacture, having relatively small importance as compared to that of the chief product or products.

76. Operating Cost : It is the cost of providing a service.

77. Cost Unit : It is a unit of quantity of product, service or time in relation to which costs may be ascertained or expressed.

78. Simple Cost Unit : It is a unit of measurement of cost with just one characteristics.

79. Composite Cost Unit : It is a unit of measurement of cost with two characteristics simultaneously.

80. Log Book : It is the book which gives performance statistics of each vehicle.

81. Transport Costing : It is the application of service costing which relates to determining cost per service unit for air, water and road traffic- both goods and passengers.

82. Power-House Costing : It is the application of service costing which relates to determining cost per unit of electricity generated and also for determining the selling prices of the power.

83. Canteen Costing : It is the application of service costing which relates to determining of operating costs and profits earned from running a canteen by industrial undertaking.

84. Hospital Costing : It is the application of service costing which relates to determining of operating costs and profits earned from providing of medical services by the hospital organisations.

85. Capative Power Plant : It is a power house generating electric power either for use within the organisation.

Bibliography

Arora M. V. - Cost Accounting - Principles & Practice
Vikas Publication, New Delhi,

Jain & Narang - Advanced Cost Accounting - Kalyani Publication

Khanna, Pande, Aahuja - Practical Costing

Kishor R. M. - Cost Accounting - Taxman, New Delhi

Mahajan Dr., Kulkarni Dr. Mahesh, Bhirud Prof. S.
Cost & Works Accounting - Nirali Prakashan

Maheshwari S. N- Cost Accounting -Theory & Problems- S. Chand

Motwani K. - Practical Costing - Pointer Publisher, Jaipur

Prasad N. K. - Principles & Practice of Cost Accounting
Syndicate Pvt. Ltd., Calcutta

Saxena V. K. & Vashista - Advanced Cost Accounting Text Book
Sultan Chand

Iyengar S. P. - Cost Accounting - Principles & Practice - S. Chand

Publication of Cost Accounting Standard Board of ICWAI

website - www.icwai.org.